Vinnie licked her lips and decided that however corrupt it might be, she could get used to drinking wine and eating cheesecake at 2 A.M. with a hot half-naked man.

Nick licked his lips, too, and she shouldn't have noticed. But she did. She froze, fork in mouth, as Nick moved to stand so close to her that she could feel his heat. Before she knew it, his hand was over hers, drawing the fork out of her mouth.

"I hear sterling is hard to digest," he said, his eyes dancing.

She relinquished the fork, a flush warming her cheeks.

"Can I take your plate?"

She thanked the Lord for her natural sarcasm, since it saved her from lunging at him. "Whatever would Mrs. Hegel say? About you waiting on the dog-sitter."

He put a finger under her chin and tilted it up. "Funny, but I couldn't give half a damn about what Mrs. Hegel would say." Then he kissed her.

Books by
Karen Kendall

SOMEONE LIKE HIM
I'VE GOT YOU, BABE
TO CATCH A KISS
SOMETHING ABOUT CECILY

KAREN KENDALL

Someone Like Him

AVON BOOKS

An Imprint of HarperCollinsPublishers

This is a work of fiction. Names, characters, places, and incidents are products of the author's imagination or are used fictitiously and are not to be construed as real. Any resemblance to actual events, locales, organizations, or persons, living or dead, is entirely coincidental.

AVON BOOKS
An Imprint of HarperCollins*Publishers*
10 East 53rd Street
New York, New York 10022-5299

Copyright © 2003 by Karen Moser
ISBN: 0-06-000723-0
www.avonromance.com

First Avon Books paperback printing: October 2003

Avon Trademark Reg. U.S. Pat. Off. and in Other Countries, Marca Registrada, Hecho en U.S.A.
HarperCollins® is a registered trademark of HarperCollins Publishers Inc.

Printed in the U.S.A.

10 9 8 7 6 5 4 3 2 1

This book is dedicated
in loving memory to Malia,
the sweetest, goofiest Doberman
ever to crack a smile.
Finishing this book without you, baby,
was nearly impossible.

Acknowledgments

A huge thank you to everyone who helped with this book: Annelise Robey, who is endlessly cheerful, patient and supportive; Lyssa Keusch, who did not burn the first draft; Stephanie Bond and Chris Hauck, who pointed me in the right direction architecturally; Larry Medefindt, AIA, who filled in the gaps in my knowledge without laughing; and Sara Schwager, who has yet to scream and run when my manuscripts come to her for copy edits.

I would also like to acknowledge Donald Martin Reynolds, author of *The Architecture of New York City: Histories and Views of Important Structures, Sites, and Symbols* (Revised Edition, John Wiley & Sons, Inc., 1994). I'm grateful to all of you!

And special thanks and love, as always, to my husband, Don, who cleans my dirty glasses and puts up with me even when the writing process is difficult, my hair stands on end, and I get psychotic with the Cheezits.

Chapter 1

The Big Apple had lost its luster, and no longer gleamed, candy-coated. After only one week in New York, Lavender "Vinnie" Hart decided that all the caramel of the Big Apple had slid right off, figuratively miring her feet and ankles in the goo.

On this gray, inauspicious late-September Monday, panic slapped Vinnie's face, and she stared aghast at her new employer.

Or rather, her new *ex*-employer. "How can you fire me when I've only been here an hour?"

The Amazon shook her fist. Was she of Latin descent? Arabic? French? Vinnie couldn't decide. All she knew was that the woman came from a fierce warrior tribe that no doubt ate the still-beating hearts of its victims.

"I fire you after wan *minute*, miss, if I don't like what I see! This is America."

"Yes," Vinnie agreed, "it is. But—"

"No but! I give you fifty-eight minutes after first one. Very generous. You go now."

It wasn't that Vinnie had gotten attached to the maniacal pace of the Manhattan real estate office in the last fifty-nine minutes. The rows upon rows of agent cubicles and hard-eyed, hard-nailed women held little appeal for her. She did feel sorry for them, each with a phone glued to both ears, fingers galloping through MLS listings on computer screens that reflected greenish light off their haggard, perfectly made-up faces. But she hadn't exactly bonded with any of them.

The brokerage was a study in hyperventilation. Every agent there took five breaths to each one of Vinnie's. They gulped down coffee—expensive designer coffee—like dehydrated marathon runners at the end of a 10k race. They barked at each other instead of speaking, and they rushed around at the pace of NASCAR drivers.

No—she wouldn't miss the place. But panic seeped through her veins like battery acid, her knees weakened, and her blood pounded with the rhythm of a two-syllable word: Adam.

How was she going to keep her little brother Adam in his expensive science academy if she couldn't hold on to a job for an hour?

Twelve-year-old Adam was the whole reason they were here, away from the sleepy prairies full of corn and wheat. Away from peace and quiet and family and friends. Around mean and bizarre people who treated her as if she were mentally challenged when she asked for directions or had trouble using the Metro-Card machines in the subway.

Well, Dorothy, she told herself, *you're not in Kansas anymore.* In Kansas, especially in Independence, Kansas, people tended to be polite. And calm. And reasonable. People in Kansas did not fire their employees after only an hour of service.

Welcome to New York.

Vinnie looked into the peculiarly vengeful face of her (ex) employer. Dislike seeped out of every pore of the woman's skin—she could sense it—but she didn't know why. "May I ask—"

An impatient snort escaped from the woman's mouth.

"—what it is that I did wrong?"

"You do everything wrong," the woman said. "You move wrong. You speak wrong. You dress wrong. You are wrong. Is all there is to it. Go." She handed Vinnie fourteen dollars and seventy-five cents in cash—having docked the twenty-five cents that the last minute in the hour would have earned her.

"I see," said Vinnie, staring from the money back to the crazy woman. "Well, thank you very much." She hitched the strap of her purse over her shoulder and shoved the money in her skirt pocket as she headed for the door. None of the busy agents even looked up, much less bothered to say good-bye.

"That—she make eleven!" announced Ms. Crazy's voice behind her. "All, all unsuitable. Why cannot find good help these days? Why!"

Eleven? I'm number eleven? That was some comfort as Vinnie headed through the heavy glass doors of the brokerage. *I think that indicates I might not be the problem here.* She crossed the lobby, looking down at the cheap pointy-toed pumps she'd bought just for this job. They were killing her feet already.

They'd worn blisters on each little toe, were pinching her big toes, and were carefully constructed to offer no padding at all between the pavement and the ball of her foot. Each step she took set her teeth on edge and served as a reminder that her finances were equally uncomfortable.

After paying the deposit and first month's rent on her new apartment, settling Adam into his new boarding school and buying the shoes, Vinnie had eighteen dollars left with which to eat for the rest of the week. But that had been workable as long as she had a job. She knew how to make do with Top Ramen and peanut butter for a few days. Anybody could. There were times when they'd had to do it in Independence.

But this—this was a serious problem. Because Adam was going to need more books, and heavier clothes for the winter very soon. And she was going to have to pay her half of the utilities on the apartment she shared in Chinatown, plus save for her little brother's next semester's tuition. She had to find another job immediately. Like in the next two days. Vinnie closed her eyes against a heavy stinging sensation, and calculated that the fourteen dollars and seventy-five cents from Ms. Crazy would pay for the subway while she searched for this new job, whatever it would be.

The biggest hitch was that without a full college degree, Vinnie didn't have many options in a city like New York. She clicked along the concrete in her cheap shoes, keeping a tight grip on her handbag while people brushed past her. She was grateful when she saw the subway entrance, because it meant she could soon get off her feet, but as usual she felt reluctant to creep underground with the rest of the urban moles. It was dank and steamy down there at the end of September, when the cool breezes of autumn hadn't gotten up the energy to circulate within the city. A cacophony of scents filled the air: a tinge of urine, some eau de b.o., and the vague looming essence of dirty concrete and metal. In the morning she could often smell a variety of baked goods, acid coffee, and stale breath. In the evening, she'd swear the smell of weariness hung in the air.

Vinnie also had a fear that the rocking and jolting of any given subway car she was on might cause the whole labyrinth of tunnels to collapse and trap her underground for all time. She told herself each time she descended a set of subway stairs that this was irrational, but when had fear ever been rational?

Fear was galvanizing, fear was sour, but it certainly wasn't reasonable. Right now it was making her feel sick to her stomach, and it had layers like an onion. She could get past the reluctance to hop on the subway, for at least that fear was concrete. But what loomed in the future was more nebulous: how to find a job—again—in a city where she knew nobody; how to keep her little brother's tuition paid; how to make a life for herself, too—even if she wasn't smart, like Adam.

Vinnie slid her Metro-Card into the slot and pushed past the turnstile, then waited with a horde of other people for the growl and rumble and hiss of the subway to arrive. She barely refrained from mooing as she and the horde clomped onto the

train like so many black Angus steer and shuffled to
find seats.

She kept a sharp eye out until she found what she
was looking for: a discarded newspaper. When you
only had . . . let's see, eighteen and fourteen
seventy-five made thirty-two dollars and seventy-
five cents . . . to live on for the next few days, you
certainly didn't want to expend even a dollar of it
for a newspaper. Vinnie pounced on it and paged
through to the classified section, unable to help seeing some of the personal ads.

> SWM seeks vivacious vixen to paddle him
> when he's been bad. Which is often!

Oh, my.

> SWF (blond, gorgeous) would like to meet
> older, very generous MM for upscale enter-
> tainment and indoor sports. Smokers need
> not apply; some hair preferred.

Well, that's blatant.

> SF seeking SF for hot, sweaty midnight mad-
> ness. Leather, rubber, oils, and toys always a
> plus. No emotional commitments, please.

Eeeuuuuuwwww.

Vinnie had a hard time believing that these ads
were for real. In Kansas, at least in the town in
which she and her mother and Adam lived, people
met each other through friends, or through church,

or at college. They didn't advertise their perversions in the local paper. They didn't walk on the wild side. In fact, she wasn't sure Kansas even possessed a wild side. If so, it was well hidden behind fields of wheat, economic depression, and strip malls—which was just fine by her.

She hurriedly paged past the disturbing ads until she found the employment section. Oh, God. What exactly was she qualified to do in this scary city full of professional this's and that's? Back home, she'd worked at the Dairy Queen all through high school and volunteered at the animal shelter. She'd taught herself to type, but couldn't honestly get much above 35 wpm without making all kinds of errors. She had virtually no computer skills. While she could file and answer the phone, every office she'd applied to in New York needed her to know how to handle a multiline system, which she didn't. And they wanted 45 wpm for typing at a bare minimum.

Even the temporary agencies to which she'd applied had treated her as if she were mentally challenged when she'd simply been polite and honest and never pushy—all characteristics that people in Kansas appreciated. These agencies had offered to train her, but she'd have to pay for the training, which she simply couldn't afford.

Vinnie didn't think she had nice enough clothes to go into, much less work in, most of the retail stores in the city. So that left . . . what?

She turned to the restaurant section and scanned several listings for *sous*-chefs, wait staff, and dishwashers. Since she wasn't even sure what a *sous*-chef was, that had to be out. Her heart sank. She didn't strictly have table-waiting experience, since most of DQ's customers had been of the drive-through variety. Which left her with the dishwashing. Ugh. She sighed.

If she had to wash dishes for Adam's sake, she would, but the job was truly at the bottom of her list. Could she be a housekeeper or nanny for some rich person? Vinnie paged through the classifieds again until she came to Domestic Help.

There were listings for chauffeurs, doormen, gardeners, handymen, housekeepers, nannies, and pet-sitters.

Pet-sitting? Now there was a job she could do. She loved animals. Vinnie scanned the columns. When she emerged from the subway in midtown, she noticed a bank of pay phones nearby. Though it would cost several precious quarters to dial these numbers, using a pay phone would be cheaper and easier than making the trek all the way back to the rathole apartment she shared in Chinatown. And she didn't particularly want to encounter her roommate, anyway.

One of the phones was miraculously free and functional. Gingerly, she picked up the receiver and wiped it with a tissue from her purse. She wasn't sure which was worse in terms of germs: New York's pay phones or its pigeons.

As she dialed the first number with the suspiciously sticky receiver at her ear, one of the nasty birds landed on top of the phone cubicle and flapped its wings at her when she shooed it away. Vinnie hoped it wasn't an omen.

Chapter 2

Nicholas Wright stared blearily at the building elevation on his computer screen, unable to concentrate. The lines vibrated and crisscrossed, mocking him.

Dead. Four-letter word meaning a profound change in his life and the end of someone else's. *Dead?* Aunt Edna, the lady who'd single-handedly defined the word "bon vivant," couldn't possibly be dead. It just didn't make sense.

Like Rosalind Russell in *Auntie Mame*, Edna St. Villiers would live forever on a silver screen in his mind. She'd been his Mame, his darling, mad-cap auntie who'd never sat still and created one adventure after another. She'd annoyed his proper parents no end, and she'd saved him from becoming just like them.

Nicholas rubbed his knuckles into his eye sockets in a useless attempt to ease his swollen sinuses. He pushed his chair back, got up, and strode to the large picture window overlooking midtown Manhattan.

He imagined Aunt Edna's soul still haggling with antiques dealers ("That's highway robbery!") and tormenting her seamstress ("Come in a quarter inch more under the arm, Henny, I want it fitted exactly.") And she'd still haunt the public library. Who would read so dramatically to the children every Saturday afternoon? Only Aunt Edna could have brought Edgar Allan Poe to life so fearsomely.

And only she could have gone out with such a bang. Upon learning that the results of a second oncology test were not what she desired, Edna St. Villiers had first had a smashing seventy-fifth birthday celebration at Le Cirque, kissed and hugged everyone dear to her, and drunk far too much. It was the last time Nick had seen her: draped over a baby grand, vodka martini in hand, belting out "New York, New York."

Then apparently Aunt Edna had gotten up next morning, donned a fresh evening gown (Givenchy) and sat in her Rolls with the garage door closed. A *Figaro* CD playing, she'd sipped at a mimosa and enjoyed the music until she simply fell asleep and never woke up.

As Nick stared out the window at nothing in particular, a sheen of moisture in his eyes caused him to blink and brought his own reflection into focus. He was a big man, with strong, angular features that gave no hint of his thoughts. He looked at that big man's outline, which radiated confidence, and wondered how he could feel so lost simply because one old lady had passed on.

He turned from the window and brushed his fingers over the leaves of the bromeliad on the credenza. It lived a peaceable life, happy with light and a little water now and then. It grew slowly, not at a manic pace, and it didn't get attached to anything. The plant lived for itself.

Smart plant. Low-maintenance. Unlike a woman.

And with that thought, his telephone rang. Nick sighed inwardly as he punched the speakerphone button. "Nicholas Wright."

"Nickie, it's me."

He really, really hated it when she called him Nickie. "Hey, Dana."

"You're picking me up at seven for the Polaski reception, right? Just wanted to remind you."

"Dana . . . I just had some bad news. I'm not sure I'm up for—"

"Nickiiieeee. I'm counting on you to be there. Please? I want to close the Beckworth deal, and you can help me do that. They just bought that place in the Hamptons, and it needs everything redone."

"Dana—"

"Just for a little while. A martini, a few canapés, a little charm turned on Sondra Beckworth . . . painless, really, I promise. She'll melt like butter in your big handsome hands."

"Fine," said Nick abruptly. "Look, I've got a meeting."

"Okay. So what's your bad news?"

"My great-aunt died."

"Oh. I'm sorry. Well, she was old anyway, right?"

Nick gritted his teeth and stared at the phone for

a long moment. "She was in her seventies. I'll see you this evening, Dana. Good-bye."

Dana Dvorak had been born with all parts assembled, soul not included. She was stunningly beautiful, had a talent for interior design, and—provided they didn't contain too many calories—would have been willing to eat her young, limb by limb, for business contacts. Since she currently had no young, she slept with men like Nicholas for those contacts instead, while Nick enjoyed her on a purely aesthetic level.

Nicholas had no romantic illusions about Dana or anyone else, and he never would. Love was for Disney and children, saps and novelists. Relationships between men and women were companionable business deals, like the one his parents had.

Nick found Dana convenient, even if he didn't always like her. The faint dislike allowed him to keep a very satisfactory emotional distance from her. He didn't have to worry about crushing her feelings, they could send each other business, and she looked good on his arm. The only difference in their perspectives about the relationship was that she wanted to make it legal, and he didn't.

Aunt Edna would have despised her, Nick thought, with a wry twist of his lips. His parents would like her, even if they found her style a bit flashy.

But John and Bitsy Wright would find her coachable: within six months, his mother would have her hair toned down two shades, from blond to ash. She'd downgrade her two-carat diamond studs to a small pearl on each ear. And she'd have Dana in white, gray, and khaki instead of the black she favored.

Nick shook his head. He preferred Dana blatant and rapacious, true to her nature, and not disguised by an ancient prep school standard of good taste. She was a vulture, not a dove. And he had no problem maintaining emotional distance from a vulture.

He glanced at his watch, shut down his computer, and shrugged into his jacket. He was due at Aunt Edna's attorney's office in twenty minutes.

Nick blinked his eyes to get rid of more of the annoying moisture gathering in them. He reminded himself that despite his great-aunt's passing, he was on top of the world. He'd brought home yet another prestigious design award, the office building he'd just completed in Rome was being featured in next month's *World Architecture* magazine, and last week he'd won a bid over ten other top architectural firms to create the new headquarters for Yeah! Cola, a carbonated soft drink that was taking the nation by storm.

Nick loved to win. It had become, over the years, a pattern for him—a pattern which, curiously enough, Aunt Edna had warned him against.

"What, you want me to lose?" he'd laughed.

"I don't want you to think in terms so black-and-white," she'd said. "I don't want your life to be about chasing trophies."

To this day, the comment bothered him. But what the hell: He really was on top of the world. He just hadn't expected it to be quite so lonely.

* * *

George Hutchins, Esquire, officed in an old brown-
stone that had seen better days. He had opened a
creaky door that led to creaky floorboards, and he
greeted Nick with a creaky handshake.

Nick shifted in the cracked leather club chair the
man had shown him to, and listened uneasily to the
words enunciated by the old guy. They comprised
the last will and testament of Edna St. Villiers.

He'd been upset to hear of her death, and hadn't
paid much attention on the phone to the attorney's
hint that her will and estate were a tad bizarre.
Aunt Edna had been a woman of extensive means
and five ex-husbands whom she claimed she'd
never been able to properly house-train. Knowing
her well, Nick had understood that her terminology did not apply to the husbands' methods of re-
lieving themselves but to their willingness to do her
bidding.

Apparently in the last year before her death, all
five ex-husbands had shown up again to profess
their undying love for Aunt Edna. This, Hutchins
explained, had given her the "willies," and she'd
sent them all away. Then she'd promptly sold off
most of her possessions and deposited a gargan-
tuan lump sum of cash into a single bank account.
The day before she'd died, she had withdrawn it
all, and the cash had disappeared into thin air.

When Nick told him this was preposterous,
Hutchins agreed. He had an investigator on the
case. He'd damn well better, Nick had expostu-
lated. It occurred to him that perhaps Hutchins
himself had taken the money. But the old relic had a

sterling reputation, and Aunt Edna had been no fool . . .

At any rate, it was in a less than peaceful frame of mind that Nick listened to the rest of what the lawyer had to say.

Hutchins's voice rumbled from deep within his bony chest, producing a certain vibration that to Nick's ears was like nails on a blackboard. He read from an official document attached to blue background paper.

"*My dear Nicholas, you know how I despise a cliché, but this one is unavoidable, darling. If that humorless old prig Hutchins—*" the lawyer paused, clearing his throat.

"*—is reading this to you, then I am dead. Deader than a doornail—though what a doornail is, I can't imagine, or why it should be more dead than any other sort of nail. Come to think of it, a nail cannot really be dead, can it, for it was never alive to begin with . . . but I digress.*"

Hutchins's sparse eyelashes fluttered in irritation, and Nick swallowed an unseemly urge to laugh.

"*Yes, Nicholas, I am dead, though I truly do regret it. What a bother! Having to write dreary epistles such as this one, and paying Hutchins (have YOU ever seen the man smile?) ghastly sums of money just to administer and organize, which he enjoys doing anyhow. Oh, dear, am I digressing again? Perhaps so.*" Hutchins sighed.

"*Back to the topic at hand . . . I've passed on, as they say, and you may now refer to me as the (fashionably) late Edna St. Villiers. It follows, then, that*

I can no longer baby or bathe or walk my sweet dog Daffodil, and I hereby bequeath her to you. I know I can trust you to give her a good home and maintain her in the lifestyle to which she has become accustomed . . ."

"Now, wait just a minute!" said Nick.

Hutchins peered at him from over his spectacles. "Yes?"

"*Dog?*"

"Dog," affirmed the old guy.

People left houses, cars, stocks, and bonds in wills—not canines. Not that he gave a damn about Edna's money, but he had no room for a dog in his life. He was never home, for one thing. "Aunt Edna is leaving me a *dog* in her will?"

"Correct."

"That's not possible."

"I'm afraid it is," the older man said, with a harried sigh.

"When did she even acquire this animal? It must have been during the past eight months, when I was in Italy."

Hutchins shrugged.

Nicholas tried to digest it. He imagined a nasty little pug waddling around his apartment, emitting asthmatic snuffles. Or worse, a fluffy poodle with pink bows on its ears and a shrill yap that would shatter his eardrums on a Sunday morning.

"Mrs. St. Villiers has left you the bulk of her estate, which in the absence of her money, comprises her Doberman pinscher Daffodil—and explicit instructions for her daily care."

"*Doberman?*" Nicholas noticed in a moment of

shocked irrelevance that the man *didn't* smile. Hutchins's thin dry lips hadn't even twitched once while he'd read to the end of Aunt Edna's outrageous letter. *Doberman? Holy Jesus.*

"But . . . I live in a *penthouse*."

Hutchins's skinny brows rose a fraction of an inch. "Congratulations."

"What I mean is—I can't descend twenty-five floors every two hours just to let this . . . this . . . *dog* out."

The lawyer placed his elbows on top of his mahogany desk and steepled his fingers together under his chin, as though he were praying for Nick to vanish from his office, along with the last traces of Edna St. Villiers and her eccentricities. He said nothing.

Nick continued to argue with him anyway, because the finality of his silence echoed with doom. "The board of my building doesn't even allow animals!"

Something twitched within the withered bag under Hutchins's left eye. A nerve, long left for dead. The man had a nerve . . .

"Not to mention an animal with the legs of a thoroughbred and the teeth of a crocodile and the attitude of a Tasmanian devil!"

Hutchins stood up with a slight creak. "I believe we've concluded our business. Let me buzz my assistant, Carol, and she'll bring Daffodil in for you."

"Wh—uck!" Nick's throat constricted in outrage, and he leaped from his chair. "You can't mean—for God's sake—I can't take her *now*."

"Carol? Yes. The Creature."

"Wait just a minute—"

A chain rattled ominously somewhere behind the closed door of Hutchins's office.

"You don't understand!" Nick felt like a turkey around mid-November. "I have two back-to-back client meetings. This isn't possible . . ." But apparently it was.

"Wooof."

Nick braced himself as the knob of Hutchins's door turned. If the dog was vicious, he'd lunge at it: take its legs out first, flip it on its back, and clamp the snout shut just as he'd seen the Crocodile Hunter do with dangerous reptiles. The key was to bowl it over immediately with a right shoulder to the chest.

The door swung wide, and Nick closed his eyes as a blinding flash assaulted them. Lightning? A gunshot? He opened them a tiny slit and registered the horror of interlocking rhinestones that made up the Creature's collar, blazing under the fluorescent lights of the office.

He looked down at the floor for relief, only to spy eighteen crimson canine toenails under the body of the beast.

Once his eyes adjusted, Nick stared. Just stared.

The Creature sat daintily on her haunches, ears tuned straight ahead, with a bubble-gum pink tongue poking disconcertingly through her incisors. She had large liquid eyes that gazed beseechingly from him to Carol, the woman on the other end of her leash. And she wore a red velvet jacket with a ruffled collar and sleeves.

This is a nightmare, Nicholas told himself. *No, a night*bitch. *I will get that spinning sensation in just* *a moment and claw my way to the surface of the dream, never to imbibe again.*

The problem was that he hadn't ingested anything mind-altering last night. Unless Manhattan's tap water had fermented in the last twenty-four hours. Or the filet mignon from that restaurant on Madison had been extracted from a particularly Mad Cow . . .

He brought himself back to the present, where he was facing neither mares nor cows but an over-dressed, manicured carnivore. "Nice doggie," he said.

Daffodil grinned at him. Really. It was a bona fide Fido smile, goofy in its extremity: She pulled her lips all the way back from her pink gums and tilted her head.

Goofy? Are you kidding yourself, Wright, you crazy bastard? The bitch is preparing to gnaw through your knees! And under his horrified, fascinated gaze, Daffodil's snout grew like Pinocchio's nose until it was inches away from his *huevos,* his balls, his precious family jewels.

"Holy sh—!" exclaimed Nick, wrapping both hands around the proboscis. After all, *his* were not rhinestones, but the real thing.

Somehow, though his hands were clamped around her snout, Daffodil's pink tongue escaped the cage of her own teeth and emerged to lick his skin. She emitted an almost human and very feminine whine.

"Hungry, are we?" Nick asked with an uneasy laugh.

"She's trying to greet you," said the woman

named Carol. "She's really a very nice dog."

"Right."

"You can let go of her nose," Carol said with asperity. "She's not going to bite."

Nick uncurled one finger at a time. After all, this was Big Jim and the Twins who were on the line. A man couldn't be too careful.

Once free, Daffodil slurped every inch of his hands and sighed gratefully when he scratched her behind the ears. Well, look at that! She was just like a normal dog.

He moved farther down her neck until he found the area just between her shoulder blades (did dogs have shoulders?) and scratched there. Daffodil lifted one hind foot, red toenails and all, and moved it around in a forward circle until he stopped. He'd found her sweet spot.

Nick raised his eyes to human level again only to find that rat Hutchins had disappeared. Carol handed him her end of the leash, two sterling silver dog bowls, and a thick brown envelope labeled, "Dogma of Daffodil." The woman had to be kidding.

She was not. "Let me show you to the elevators."

Nick thought about clanging the dog bowls together and bellowing until Hutchins came out of hiding. Then he thought about Aunt Edna, and the fact that she'd entrusted him with the care of her beloved pet. To be fair, Hutchins was only doing his job.

But Nick didn't feel good about this whole situation. And none of it added up. What had Aunt Edna done with her money? And why had she done

whatever it was the day before she died? Had one
of her five ex-husbands bumped her off in hopes of
inheriting? His mouth tightened. He didn't know
what to think. The bottom line: He was stuck with
a mystery and a dog.

"Oh, hell," Nick said aloud to Daffodil. "Let's go.
I guess we can stop by a morgue and nab you a . . . a
femur bone or something on the way home."

Chapter 3

Nothing in life made Vinnie more uncomfortable than a job interview. She'd always gotten her jobs in Independence from people she'd known since before she could walk. They knew her and didn't need to hear some speech about how dedicated and proactive and brilliant she was.

Therefore, she'd never understood quite how much her palms could sweat, or her knees could tremble, or her throat could close up until she'd gone on a big-city interview. So far she'd blown every single one of them, with the exception of Ms. Crazy, who'd hired her on the phone, sight unseen, to come in for a probationary period.

She could blow an interview in a hundred different ways, it seemed. She could blank out entirely and not be able to recall any of her accomplishments. She could be overly friendly, which seemed to be viewed with extra suspicion here in New York.

She could stutter, catch her heel in the carpeting,

or show up late after having to replace her panty hose en route. (That had been a particularly bad experience, since the only shade available in the corner drugstore was Deep Cocoa.)

She discovered two different Interview Personas: Vinnie the Clam and Vinnie of the Verbal Diarrhea, and she never knew which would take over until she'd parked her behind in the hot seat. In short, interviewing for jobs really sucked.

For this pet-sitting interview in Central Park, she'd donned a pair of jeans and running shoes. They were the only footwear she owned comfortable enough to walk in, and she figured the dog wouldn't be evaluating her clothes.

As she approached the agreed-upon meeting point, Vinnie couldn't mistake Nicholas Wright. He was the only man standing in the middle of the pond. Moreover, he was trying to retrieve an overdressed Doberman from the quaint little island in the middle of the pond, where the dog was clearly having the time of her life harassing New York's geese.

Wright had sounded on the telephone like a man who needed help. She'd just had no idea how badly.

Under normal circumstances, Vinnie thought, Nicholas Wright would be one gorgeous man. Even in his current situation—wet to the knees with some duckweed trailing from his left elbow—he wasn't hard to look at. If a girl were to ignore the furious stream of vile language spewing from between his chiseled lips.

And a girl could easily do that while looking on with interest at the breadth of his shoulders, the poetic way the hair blew off his forehead in the morning breeze, and the fine set of buns under his expensive-looking cordovan belt.

"Daffodil!" Wright shouted, putting his hands on his hips and leaning forward aggressively. This caused the fine gabardine cloth of his trousers to stretch more tightly across his backside.

Vinnie bit her lip before forcing herself to look away. She dug into her leatherette handbag.

"Come, you insane animal! *Come!*" Wright took another step into the water. "God damn it, Daffodil!"

"Hold it right there," Vinnie ordered, completely forgetting to be nervous. She dug a Milk-Bone from under her hairbrush and keys.

Wright turned and stared at her.

"Hello," she said with a smile. Then she whistled and waved the Milk-Bone at the dog, who was now backing slowly away from an enraged, hissing bird. *Oh, beware Bad Mutha Goose.*

Daffodil was no fool. She might have a brain the size of a walnut, but all its neurons were firing. She could be bitten on the butt by a pissed off goose that was clearly voting her off the island, or she could be scratched behind the ears and enjoy a Scooby Snack.

With a splash, she careened back into the water. Giving Nicholas Wright a wide berth, she did a canine version of the butterfly until she'd reached the shore and scrambled out, making a beeline for Vinnie's unsuspecting crotch.

Vinnie blinked, sidestepped, and distracted her with the Milk-Bone, which the dog snatched and devoured. Then she shook water all over Vinnie, who accepted the impromptu shower with grace.

She watched the dog gobble down the snack, taking in the crimson toenails, rhinestones, and velvet with raised brows. In the meantime, Wright sloshed to shore and poured water out of first one, then the other of his tasseled cordovan loafers.

"I'm Vinnie Hart," she said to him, as he picked the duckweed off his elbow. "I believe we spoke on the phone?"

He dried his right hand on his pants, then extended it to her. "Yeah. Nicholas Wright." He appeared to be at a loss for further words.

Her lips twitched. "Bacon. You definitely need some bacon."

He looked nonplussed. "Pardon?"

"Carry some bacon in your pocket in a Ziploc baggie."

Wright looked revolted.

"It's got to be better than the duckweed," she said.

He pursed his lips. "I'm thinking more along the lines of a bullet."

"I don't believe that for a second," Vinnie told him.

"Why not?"

"Because any man capable of shooting a dog wouldn't wade after her into nasty water up to the knees."

"If he were stupid, he might," he said.

"Don't be so hard on yourself. You're just ignorant, not stupid." Vinnie turned to the side and raised her knee to avoid Daffodil's crotch-seeking nose, before she realized how her words had come across. "Ooops." Her face flamed. "I didn't mean for that to sound—" She looked away. Great, she was blowing *another* interview.

"Do you always insult your prospective employers, Ms. Hart?"

"I just meant you might not be used to dogs—"

"Or is it just strangers in general?"

"I really didn't mean—" Vinnie began again. She glanced up again to find he was laughing at her. "Oh."

His face was transformed by the humor. If he'd been gorgeous before, now he was—good Lord. Her mouth went dry. And so did her brain. There were no adjectives. He resembled a younger, hipper Cary Grant—or maybe a lighter-haired JFK, Jr. In short, he was . . . yummy.

"Of course," he said, "I always go out of my way to lose all dignity in the presence of women, myself." He began wringing out his pant legs. "I make it a daily habit to chase four-legged demons into duck ponds." He picked up Daffodil's choke chain and leash, which had evidently slipped right off her rhinestone-clad neck, and shook it at her.

Daffodil ducked behind Vinnie, but couldn't get away again since Vinnie had a firm grip on her collar.

Nicholas said in pleasant tones, "Unless you'd like to be sold for pennies to the nearest Chinese restaurant, come here."

Daffodil shook again, spraying them both with fetid green water. Then she panted at him.

Vinnie sympathized. Under any other circumstances, she'd probably pant at Wright, too. He was a pantable kind of guy. The kind of guy for whom you'd be absolutely willing to paint your toenails blood red. If you were human.

She looked from Daffodil to Wright and back again. She couldn't really be his dog. What kind of guy painted his dog's toenails and dressed her? Vinnie would swear he wasn't gay. He'd appraised her in a single very male glance—not rudely, but with a definite glint of appreciation in his hazel eyes.

"She was my great-aunt's dog until two days ago," Wright said, by way of explanation. "I wasn't expecting to inherit."

"I'm so sorry," Vinnie said. "Is your aunt . . ."

"She went out with a bang."

Vinnie looked down at her feet, not sure how to respond to that.

"Anyway," Wright continued, "this hound from hell is now mine. I made the mistake of going to work for the past day and a half. Let's just say she had no problem entertaining herself."

Uh-oh. "Separation anxiety?" Vinnie inquired.

"Is that what it's called?" Wright stuck his feet—which she couldn't help noticing were very large—back into his sodden loafers. "Gee, it's not just a taste for crown molding? An idea that window screens are chewy? A curiosity about the roots of exotic plants?"

"You left her alone in a strange place."

Wright's jaw worked. "I had this charming idea of the animal snoozing by my fireplace until I got home. A fantasy, I now realize."

"Your aunt was with her all the time? Was she retired?"

"My aunt was never, ah . . . working-class."

"Working-class." *Is that a real term?* Vinnie couldn't even imagine that there was an entire class of people who *didn't* work. She looked down at her cheap running shoes with their worn treads, at her faded jeans. She hugged her leather-look purse tighter under her arm. "Oh."

"I don't think Daffodil is very old—what do you estimate?"

Vinnie watched the dog root in some weeds at the base of an oak tree. "Still a puppy, really—she's maybe nine or ten months."

"That would explain why I've never encountered her before. I was in Italy working on a project until recently."

Italy. People like Nicholas Wright really jetted off to Italy for projects? Wow. Vinnie tried surreptitiously to tuck in her T-shirt.

"Aunt Edna probably took her everywhere."

Yars, darling, absolutely everywhar. Vinnie mustered a smile. "Is she housebroken?" Without even thinking about it, she'd taken control of the interview, and was speaking as if she already had the job.

"She knows how to break up a house, yes."

Vinnie laughed. "I meant does she, um, pee inside?"

"I know what you meant. Yes, she does appear to be housebroken, thank God. It seems to be her only virtue."

Wright's eyes sparkled with annoyance. In a moment of irrelevance, she noticed that they contained the same shades as his marbled silk tie: gray, blue, brown, and green.

"Are you sure that, um, you should keep this dog?" Vinnie hesitated. "You don't seem to like her much." *What are you doing, idiot? Don't talk yourself out of a job!*

He sighed. "It's not that I don't like her. Or that I don't like dogs. I guess I'm just not used to animals in general and had no idea what to expect." He began to roll up his sleeves. "I have an obligation to keep her. The problem is that I'm never home, and that's not fair to her."

That's where you come in. Go ahead. Say it. "Well, that's where I come in," Vinnie chirped in her best sales voice. *Congratulations, Doofus, you haven't blown it yet. Think about Adam!*

Nicholas Wright seemed to notice the difference between her normal voice and her sales voice, for he narrowed his eyes.

She smiled her most winning smile.

His eyes narrowed even farther. "So tell me about your background and qualifications," he said.

Uh-oh. Just the words "background" and "qualifications" had her shivering. *Well,* she could say, *I have none, other than being qualified to serve up your dog ground in a bun at Dairy Queen.*

No! Think. AdamAdamAdamAdamAdamAdam-Adam. I'm a really nice person, and I like animals? Just give me a chance? I do okay at taking care of an agoraphobic mother and bringing up a teenage boy? Vinnie opened her mouth, and, to her horror said, "I used to be with a traveling circus and work with lions and elephants. So I have extensive knowledge of animal training." Oh, *great*. It was Vinnie of the Verbal Diarrhea who'd taken over this time—and morphed into a total liar, to boot.

"Lions and elephants?"

She gulped and barely refrained from smacking herself in the forehead. "Yes, and I grew up on a farm. So I'm used to goats, chickens, horses, you name it. Lizards and deer, too, courtesy of my little brother Adam."

"But what about dogs?"

"Oh, dogs! Yeah, those too. We *always* had dogs around."

Wright was looking at her strangely, not that she could blame him. She'd always been a horrible liar. She did worse at lying than she did at standardized tests—or interviews.

"I worked at the county animal shelter during high school," she mustered on. That was true. She was on steadier ground now. And the part about the goats, lizards, and deer was also true. Adam had brought home all kinds of creatures.

"How old are you?"

"Twenty-six."

He waited for her to detail what she'd been doing since high school, to elaborate on what made her qualified to do this job. The awkward pause stretched on and on. Finally, Vinnie blurted, "I'm horrible at interviews."

To her surprise—and maybe his own, judging by his expression—he said, "That's okay."

They were back to the pause thing again. Vinnie thought about drowning herself in the duck pond, but that wouldn't help Adam at all. Maybe she should have dyed her hair black and pretended not to speak English. Maybe she could convince a third interview persona to emerge: Vinnie the Sexpot, who would squeeze her boobs between her upper arms, thrusting them up into Nicholas Wright's face. *Very bad idea*, she scolded herself. But she was getting desperate.

"Since you helped me get the demon out of the pond," Wright said, "I'm going to pretend you never mentioned the circus, and you can start over." He smiled at her. Actually smiled at her.

Relief didn't wash over her in a gentle ripple: it body-slammed her with the force of a four-foot wave. "Okay," she said. "Now that you think I'm a complete liar, I've never been in the circus. Sometimes my life just feels like one."

He laughed.

"I've blown five interviews in the last two days, and I was trying not to ruin this one, too. But I get nervous and say the first thing that pops into my head."

"That's actually very normal," said Wright. "So just tell me about yourself."

She swallowed. "I'm from a tiny, economically depressed town in Kansas. My mother is agoraphobic and has . . . problems. I've basically raised my little brother. There aren't many career options in our town, so I've had a lot of jobs that . . . that you probably won't think are any big deal. What I told you about the animal shelter is true, and so I do have experience with dogs, cats, and rabbits. Oh, and lizards and deer."

"But not lions and elephants," Nicholas said gravely.

She could feel her face hot-flashing neon like a caution light. "No."

"I'm actually relieved to hear that. So what brings you to New York?"

"My little brother Adam got into the Gotham-Young Science Academy. He's really, really smart. But he's never been away from home before, so I'm here, too. And I need a job to pay for the rest of his tuition and books and all."

"You're paying for your little brother's school?"

Vinnie nodded, and left it at that. She didn't need to go into details about her mother and the pathetic amount of money she earned as a church organist, or her struggles and panic attacks about even leaving their home to walk down the road to First Presbyterian.

"Gotham-Young's expensive. Is anyone helping you? What about your father?" Wright asked.

Vinnie rubbed at a nonexistent spot on her jeans. "My father died in a military training accident when I was fourteen."

"I'm so sorry."

"It was a long time ago." Vinnie raised her chin and avoided Wright's gaze. Her mouth didn't tremble, and she was proud of that. Years—it had taken years—before she could think of her father without tears threatening. "Anyway, Adam got a partial scholarship. He was light-years beyond his classmates at his public junior high, so he smoked the entrance exams. Adam's brilliant." She couldn't keep the pride out of her voice. "He'll be a famous scientist one day, mark my words."

Wright seemed to look at her with new respect, and Vinnie told herself to stand tall and not squirm. It was easier to talk about Adam than about herself.

"He's twelve years old, and he's creative but methodical at the same time . . . he's at that awkward stage between being a child and being a teen, full of intelligence and yet full of insecurities. This move is rough on him. He's got only two friends, and—" She stopped herself. What did highbrow Nicholas Wright care about an unknown teenager's turmoil? "I'm babbling."

"No you're not," he said. "I can actually relate well to what he's going through. I went to boarding school in first grade." His mouth twisted.

"*First grade?*"

He nodded.

Vinnie stared at him, trying to imagine what it was like to be away from your parents for months on end, at age six. "When—when did you see your parents?"

"On holidays," he said in matter-of-fact tones. "And summers, when I wasn't at camp."

Camp, too? She said nothing.

He returned her gaze with a quizzical expression. "I had lots of buddies," he told her reassuringly. "It was no big deal. Character-building, and all that."

"Character-building"? The term made Vinnie unexpectedly furious, though all she said was a polite "Uh-huh." Character-building. Yeah, that was a great way to describe what happened when colossal burdens were laid upon the shoulders of young children. She simmered.

Wright was looking down at his wet pants. "Listen, I'm going to have to change for a meeting. Would you mind continuing this discussion, or interview, at my place?"

She looked at him warily. Perhaps she was from Kansas, but she hadn't just fallen off a turnip truck. Was it safe?

Probably. A man who was taking care of a dog he didn't want, who had waded into a duck pond after said dog, a man who wanted some sort of nanny for the critter—well, he wasn't likely to be one of those guys who carved women into small pieces. "Okay," she said.

"Giddy-up, Daffodil," Wright told the dog. "Say good-bye to the geese."

Bemused, Vinnie followed them out of the park. Did this mean that she probably had the job?

Chapter 4

Nicholas had no idea why he was still talking to this woman, after she'd tried to tell him she'd been in the circus. But she'd had the foresight to bring that heaven-sent Milk-Bone, and there was a vulnerability about her that indicated, irrationally, she might be honest underneath the colossal lie.

Not to mention that so far he'd interviewed several unprepossessing candidates for Dober-sitter. They included an albino woman who weighed perhaps ninety pounds soaking wet, a lanky student who reeked of marijuana and evidently didn't believe in showers, and an arrogant chain-smoking Frenchman who'd demanded a salary of eighty thousand a year plus medical benefits. Why hadn't Nick thought to just call a pet-sitting service?

So it was not with optimism that he had set off for Central Park a fourth time, only to encounter the Budweiser Babe with the Milk-Bone.

Vinnie Hart really did look as if she'd stepped out of a beer poster. She had the body, she had the cheekbones, she had a honeyed blue-jeaned walk. She exuded wholesome, heartland sex.

The Budweiser Babe was long, she was cool, she was effervescent—-and damned if he didn't have the instant urge to pop her top.

Nick considered himself a Manly Man, with many of the average Manly Man's behavioral patterns and characteristics, but he wasn't normally such a pig.

Maybe it was the enticing swell of a pair of spectacular breasts against said top, or the chestnut gold tangle of her abundant hair, or the delicious way her jeans molded to the curves below her waist.

Maybe it was the generous sweetness of her mouth. Or maybe it was the flash of those all-American baby browns, fringed by thick, sooty lashes, but Nicholas had immediately, primitively wanted to—*ahem*.

Nicholas had wanted to have his wicked way with her, in every wicked position he could, as wickedly as possible, right there on the muddy, squishy shore of the pond with God and all the geese watching.

Good Lord! He'd never had such an explosive reaction to a woman before. But there it was, in all its rude glory. Something about her had his personal cigar just begging for a light. Not to mention a long, slow drag.

Oink, oink. His Inner Pig had gotten off to a fast trot. Nick firmly put it back into its sty, and led the way to his building on Fifth Avenue. Over the past couple of days he'd palmed a key to the service entrance off of Pete, the doorman. This had cost him fifty bucks, but it enabled him to smuggle Daffodil in and out without running into other residents. So far, so good.

He unlocked the shabby back entrance and led Vinnie and the Beast down the narrow dingy corridor to the service elevator. "I, uh, bring her in and out this way so she doesn't uh, track mud in."

The Bud Babe seemed to accept this without question, and soon they were all headed skyward in the massive lift. Daffodil hated the elevator, but since he'd started hefting her bodily into it, she didn't have much choice. She quivered and braced her legs when the floor started to rise, and Vinnie bent down to soothe her.

Nick tried very hard not to stare at the girl's heart-shaped denimed butt as she murmured to the dog.

"I know, baby—floors aren't supposed to move, are they? It's a very uncomfortable feeling. But it's okay."

Daffodil licked Vinnie's hands and tried to dig all eighteen toenails into the bottom panel of the elevator. She quivered again as they reached the twenty-fifth floor with a slight mechanical thud.

Vinnie had bent down to scratch Daffodil behind the ears. When she looked up again, Nick had his door open and saw her face change. He tried to see his familiar surroundings through her eyes. Was his place really that intimidating? He supposed it might be, to a girl from rural Kansas.

Floor-to-ceiling windows looked out over Fifth Avenue and Central Park. Black leather and steel

Philippe Starck chairs flanked a massive white marble fireplace. Over it hung his favorite painting: an original museum-worthy Pollock.

A built-in teak bar on one wall gleamed with sterling accessories and stemware.

The kitchen featured burled walnut cabinetry, artistic brushed nickel fixtures, and stainless-steel Viking appliances.

The Bud Babe surreptitiously tried to rub some mud off the toe of her sneaker with the tread of the other one. She tucked her hair behind her ears and straightened her spine. More than her clothes, more than her expression, these small gestures indicated that the surroundings were indeed far grander than she was used to. Nick felt suddenly self-conscious about the luxury that surrounded him and focused on trying to make her more comfortable.

"So . . . Vinnie." Why was this incredible, edible, beddable Bud Babe's name Vinnie? He repeated it, feeling one eyebrow quirk into a question mark.

"I know, I know—most of the people you meet named Vinnie are probably beefy and Italian and maybe even have hairy backs. They wear gold chains and black leather jackets and talk like Tony Soprano," the Bud Babe said. "But that's not me," she added unnecessarily.

Nicholas nodded, finding himself fascinated by her mouth.

"In my case Vinnie is short for Lavender."

"Lavender?" That was worse than Vinnie. In the space of a few sentences she'd gone from Bud Babe to Italian thug to Regency Miss.

"It's because right before I was born, my father won a Purple Heart, and since our last name was H-a-r-t, people in town started calling Daddy 'Purple.' So when I was born, he and Mama thought it'd be really cute to call me Lavender." She shrugged apologetically.

"I see."

Vinnie pushed her mass of flyaway hair behind her left shoulder. "I'm babbling. Sorry."

"No, not at all," Nick assured her, even though it was true. "Ah, would you like a drink?" He hadn't offered the other candidates so much as a spritz with his plant mister. Then again, he hadn't felt like taking any of them back to his apartment.

Vinnie shook her head. "No, thank you, I don't drink. I don't like the taste of alcohol."

Excellent. So if he hired her, he wouldn't come home to find her passed out on the floor. "Fruit juice? Soda?"

She looked as if she showered regularly—*no, Nick, don't think of her naked*—and she had enough body weight to hang on to an eighty-pound dog. This was promising, the circus comment notwithstanding.

Daffodil alternated between slobbering over Vinnie's hands and dancing in maniacal circles around her, grinning like a loon.

"Oooohhhh," Vinnie crooned to Daffodil, who finally flopped by her side. "You're nothing but a big overdressed teddy bear, are you?"

Teddy bear with fangs, thought Nick. *And less-than-aromatic by-products*. Aloud he said, "She's a little high-maintenance."

Vinnie nodded. "Her breed generally is, but it also might have something to do with diet and exercise. What does she eat?"

Welcome rage filled Nicholas's mind now, instead of uncomfortable lust. "Allen Edmonds, Cole Haan, and Bally," he said bitterly. "Medium rare. Only one of each."

Vinnie blinked. "Pardon?"

"Shoes," he elaborated. "Expensive leather ones. And Italian belts à la carte."

Daffodil yawned, completely unconcerned, and got up again to nudge Vinnie's knee.

"And where does she exercise? Or play?"

"Preferably in traffic," Nick muttered.

"Excuse me?"

"I've only had her for three days. And I should probably explain that I've never owned a pet."

"Not even when you were younger?"

He shook his head. "No. My parents would never have tolerated an animal in the house—and besides, I was away at school most of the time."

Vinnie looked at him now as if she felt sorry for him.

"So tell me more about your experience," he said, trying to put things back onto an interview basis. "Your non-circus experience."

Vinnie blushed fire, and he immediately felt sorry for making her uncomfortable again. She twisted her purse strap around her finger.

"Our family's always had animals—my little brother used to bring critters home on a regular basis, and since our cabin was on a couple of acres, we kept them. The ones that Mama couldn't toler-

ate in the house would hang out in the shed." She
smiled and clasped her hands around one knee.
"Like the miniature goats and the baby deer."

"Goats? Deer?"

She nodded.

"I suppose you are qualified to take care of a
dog, then."

"Oh, yes." She flashed him a perfect, pearly
white smile from behind those kissable lips. "Did
you know that deer like bubble gum?"

"No," said Nicholas. "I didn't know that."

"My little brother Adam left several packs of
Hubba Bubba out on his desk one day, and darn if
Scooter—that was the deer's name—didn't eat
them, wrappers and all. She got really sick later,
and left deer plop in the house. Mama wasn't too
happy about that, and so after Adam had scientifi-
cally determined that Scooter wasn't going to blow
bubbles out of her you-know-what, she insisted
that anything with hooves had to live in the shed."

"That seems a reasonable request."

"Well, yes, but Adam had spent six weeks' al-
lowance on a plush dog bed for Scooter, so he
didn't think it was reasonable at all."

"Did er—Scooter—actually use the dog bed?"
Nicholas asked, fascinated. The idea of having a
wild animal loose in one's house was beyond him.

"You bet. Scooter slept every night on the floor
of Adam's room. Well, for all seven nights she was
allowed in the house."

"And what happened to Scooter? Do you still
have her?"

Vinnie shook her head, sending tendrils of her

rich golden brown hair flying. "No, Billy Amos, a local farmer, took her after the miniature goats came along."

Nick rubbed at his eyes. "How do goats just . . . come along?"

Vinnie grinned. "Goats come along when a fellow church member's wife throws a hissy fit and bans them from *her* yard. They jumped up on the hood of her new Maxima and left scratches and dents."

"Bummer."

"She threatened to make goat stew if we didn't take them."

Holy Jesus. Did people in Kansas really make goat stew? Surely not. It was the heartland, not the hinterland.

Daffodil suddenly rolled to expose her belly for scratching. "That's not at all ladylike," Vinnie told her, but placed her sneakered foot square in the dog's midriff and began to rub.

Evidently the treads of a running shoe were dog belly heaven, for Daffodil squinched her eyes shut and sighed with satisfaction.

Nick stared at the beast and shook his head. "She just ate my German dictionary."

Vinnie laughed. "Then I'm sure she's fluent."

"Up to the Q's, anyway. Right before we left to meet you, I found her trying to get the little black P tab off her tongue."

"You know, I don't see any toys around here. If she had some toys, she might leave your stuff alone. And once she has regular exercise and playtime, she'll probably sleep more during the day."

"So when could you start?" asked Nick, valiantly keeping the desperation out of his voice. For better or for worse, he was about to hire a brunette Elly May Clampett.

"Today, if you'd like."

"You don't have another job?"

Vinnie stuck out her chin. "I had a great job, I thought, but the crazy woman fired me after fifty-nine minutes."

Alarm bells rang in Nick's head. Was this Vinnie Hart a psycho? An arsonist? A terrorist? Perhaps a psycho arsonist with an advanced degree in terrorism? Terry Nichols had been from Kansas, hadn't he?

"Why?" he asked, not revealing his sudden misgivings.

She adopted a bad generic foreign accent. "Because I luke wrongk, I dress wrongk, I yam wrongk. I do ayvrythingk wronk. Ees all there ees to eet."

His lips twitched. "Sounds like a winner of a boss."

"Yeah, well. I know I'm supposed to say something harmless and bland like 'We didn't see eye to eye' or 'the situation didn't work out,' but this woman was just plain nuts."

"Did you, ah, go to her office in running shoes and jeans?"

"No, I did not. But I didn't think that an interview for dog-sitting would be formal. Should I have worn a skirt to meet Daffodil?"

Heaven forbid, given the Beast's way of greeting people nose to crotch. Nick choked and dropped his gaze, feeling a flush start behind his ears. "You

look fine. Don't worry about it. I was just curious."
She looked more than fine. She looked . . . *Nick,
my boy, don't go down that path again. When you
raise your eyes to her this time, you will think of
Jeanne Kirkpatrick in a grass hula skirt, or Janet
Reno in a thong.*

"I have references," said Vinnie, defying all his
efforts to visually replace her. "You can call my junior college instructors. You can call the Dairy
Queen where I worked for six years. You can call
the Pet Parade shelter. They're all in Kansas,
though, so you'll have to pay long-distance
charges. But I have the numbers right here." She
dug in her backpack and produced a neatly typed
sheet of paper, which she handed to him.

"Unfortunately I don't have anyone you can talk
to in New York, because Adam and I just got here
last week. I've got to get a job right away, though,
to pay for his school, so you'll need to let me know
as soon as possible."

That's right—she was paying for her little
brother's school. Nick had to respect that. He
hadn't met many girls her age who were willing to
give up their own goals to put their little brothers
through an expensive private academy. Most of the
girls he knew had rich parents, or trust funds, or
both.

He found himself wondering if this little guy
Adam knew just how lucky he was. And he decided
that if they could come to a salary agreement, he was
going to hire Vinnie Hart—regardless of whether he
had to think daily of Janet Reno in a thong.

Chapter 5

Vinnie restrained herself from leading the elevator attendant into a jubilant square dance, but couldn't wipe the astonished grin off her face. Nicholas Wright, though gorgeous, had obviously fallen on his head recently, because he was going to pay her the mind-boggling sum of twenty-five thousand a year just to take care of his dog!

As they descended the twenty-odd floors from the swank penthouse apartment (the likes of which she'd only seen in movies), she glanced again at the elevator attendant. Surely he wouldn't mind if she just hooked her arm through his and danced them around in a small jig?

Hmmmm. Probably a bad idea, since his face was greenish and beaded with little drops of perspiration. "Are you feeling okay?" Vinnie inquired. "Because you don't look so good."

He blinked in surprise. "Oh. Uh. I'm okay. Just a stomach virus, I think. Thanks for asking."

"Can't you go home and lie down?"

"Not necessary, miss. Besides, I've gotta keep my check regular."

"I know *exactly* what you mean." Vinnie frowned. Then she dug into her backpack. "Listen, I have just the thing for you. It's chamomile tea . . . here you go. Take these." She handed him three individually wrapped tea bags. "Add very little sugar, or none at all. You'll feel much better."

"That's very kind of you, miss. Thank you."

"Go make yourself a cup as soon as we get downstairs, okay? You look really ill. And I'm not some weirdo—they're perfectly safe."

"No, ma'am, you don't look like a weirdo." He smiled.

"Well, that's a relief."

They stood in silence for a moment before she asked, "So how long have you worked here?"

"Three years, miss."

"May I ask you a question?"

"Shoot."

"The man who lives in the penthouse—"

"Mr. Wright?"

"Yes. He's not a weirdo either, is he?"

The attendant laughed. "No. I don't think he has time to be a weirdo. That's got to be the busiest man in New York, if not on the planet."

"I see. Just curious, because I've taken a job with him, and though I gave him *my* references, it's not like I have any on *him*."

"He's all right. He's lived here for five years, pays his bills on time, never has any wild parties that I know of. Which is probably a damn shame, since that place of his is beautiful, isn't it?"

"Yes," Vinnie agreed. "It is. Like something out of a magazine."

"Funny you should say that—he's an architect, and his work is in magazines all the time."

"Really? Wow."

"Yep. *Architectural Digest*, that type of thing."

"Well, thanks for the info," she said, and stuck out her hand. "My name's Vinnie. I'll probably be seeing you a lot."

"I'm Richie. And thanks for the tea. You need a cab or anything? Pete'll get you one."

Vinnie shuddered at the thought of what a cab would cost from Fifth Avenue, where they were, to the seedy tenement in Chinatown where she was living. "No, thanks."

"Okay. Catch you later, miss. Have a nice day."

"Bye. You too!"

Her feet were hot and sore by the time she got "home." Unfortunately, her roommate Sorrel hadn't left yet. Vinnie tried to be open-minded, but Sorrel's habits, choice of food, and personal hygiene were beginning to alarm her. She'd found Sorrel through a newspaper, too, and kind of wished she hadn't.

Vinnie opened the door of the fifth-floor walk-up to a cacophony of wailing that her roommate considered music. In the background it sounded as if a fire were burning, and punctuating the wails every so often was a shimmy with a tambourine.

Sorrel stood barefoot on an overturned crate in a ripped black T-shirt and gypsy rag skirt. Her toenails were neon green, and her hair . . . Sorrel's hair was short and platinum blond, with chunky green highlights. Her head resembled nothing so much as a type of winter squash, the name of which Vinnie couldn't remember.

As if her personal appearance weren't startling enough, Sorrel seemed to be inflamed today with some sort of Goth Martha Stewart disease. She had stapled black plastic garbage bags over every square inch of wall space in the living area, and was now painting strange shapes upon them.

"Decorating?" Vinnie asked, over the din.

"Yessssss," said Sorrel.

Ooooohhhhhhwhaaaaaaahhhhhh, wailed her music. *Clang clang, crackle pop. Hissssss. Ooooooohhhhwhaaaaaahhhhhhhh.*

Sorrel swayed to it, and Vinnie wondered if she'd been smoking something funny. Vinnie also wondered what exactly Sorrel studied. She'd mentioned being a grad student. Please God her subject wasn't interior design.

Vinnie thought about mentioning that half the living space was technically hers, and that she didn't care for the Hefty Look, but decided against it when she saw her roommate's eyes, the pupils as wide and black as old vinyl LPs. Dear God, New York was full of some strange people . . .

She bypassed Sorrel and squeezed into the tiny galley that served as their kitchen, wanting a cold Cherry Coke and a moment of privacy in her tiny, dingy bedroom. She opened the funky seventies era refrigerator, recoiled, and slammed it shut.

OhGodohGodohGodohGodohGod what was it in that baking pan? It was deep red and glistening and . . . and . . . and made her want to vomit. Something from inside an animal. Vinnie lurched to the sink and dry-retched.

Once she'd composed herself, she ran out of the kitchen, grabbed her backpack, and headed for the door. "Late for an appointment!" she yelled in Sorrel's direction.

"Yeah, whatever," her roommate mumbled.

Oooooohhhhhhwhaaaaaaaahhhhhh, wailed her music. *Clang clang, crackle pop. Hisssssss. Oooooohhhhhwhaaaaaahhhhhhhh.*

Vinnie slammed the door and began taking the stairs two at a time. *I think I'm living with a Satanic serial killer. And there's not much I can do about it . . . besides sleep with a chair under my doorknob and a baseball bat in my bed.*

Vinnie concentrated on putting all thoughts of shiny dead meat and creepy music and Hefty Bag Décor out of her mind. She knew she was going to have to go back to the apartment in Chinatown to sleep, but for now she took the subway back uptown, where she could walk in Central Park and see some nice, normal people jogging or feeding the ducks or reading books under trees. The sky had cleared, and it was a beautiful afternoon.

She looked wistfully at a couple of young mothers playing with their little boys in the park, and wondered for the twentieth time that day how Adam was doing. Was he settling in okay? Had he made friends with his roommate or any other boys? Was he homesick? Was the food there decent?

Since she had the afternoon off while Nick

checked her references, she decided that she'd go try to have lunch with Adam.

The Gotham-Young Science Academy was located in a weathered Romanesque building. Vinnie made her way there at a brisk walk, barely noticing the shop fronts and restaurants lining the busy streets.

Yesterday on Madison Avenue, she'd made the mistake of checking the price on a jacket she'd liked. The saleswoman who'd approached her had an expensive nose job and, Vinnie concluded, an eighteen-karat stick up her butt. She'd behaved as if Vinnie were infected with some disease, when all she'd done was pull the price tag out of the jacket pocket. Granted, after reading it, she'd staggered against the window and left a handprint on the glass. But that was because the price was, well, staggering. What kind of person paid $970 for a jacket?

Vinnie wondered if Nicholas Wright bought jackets like that. Probably so, if he could afford to pay a dog-sitter 25K a year.

The thought of Nick made her heart beat a little faster. He was, for lack of a better word, hot.

Her first impression—from the front—had been of a wide, solid chest blocking the doorway. Then she'd noticed beautiful hazel eyes with deeply etched laugh lines at the outer corners. Burnished coppery gold hair, a little mussed as if he'd been running his fingers through it. Tanned skin. A chiseled mouth with a heavier bottom lip. And a jaw so rock-solid that you could found an insurance company upon it.

Nick looked like he'd stepped straight out of a Calvin Klein ad: the kind of guy who flashed before you in fantasies of white sand and unbuttoned shirts and azure blue water. He made you think of endless skinny-dipping, perhaps with dolphins and bottomless flutes of champagne.

And he'd held on to her hand far longer than necessary. He'd seemed to be gazing into her soul, though Vinnie knew it was far more likely that he'd been checking out her breasts. Men couldn't help themselves, even though God had very kindly shortened their snouts over the years, lowered their ears, and removed their curly tails. Oh—and replaced their cloven hooves with toes. Yep, Vinnie knew all about evolution.

Soul-gazing or breast-goggling, though, Nicholas Wright was one gorgeous man. She blinked and reminded herself that it wasn't Nick she'd be spending time with, but his spastic, overdressed dog. And that was a good thing, since he was undoubtedly just another rich jerk underneath his nice manners.

She shook her head. She wouldn't have to learn that lesson twice, since her ex-boyfriend had taught it to her well. She'd been so idiotically thrilled when William had first asked her out . . . not processing for a while that he wanted to spend most of his time *in*. And that while she was good enough to take to bed, she certainly wasn't marriage material. He was country club. She was wholesale club.

Her dad would have summed William up in an instant, long before she'd dreamed of having babies with him. But Daddy hadn't been around to protect her . . .

This train of thought brought her to the door of Adam's school. Vinnie shook off thoughts of William the Wanker and went in to sign the visitor's book and track her little brother down.

Adam sat by himself at a small table in the school's dining hall. He looked small, bony, and dejected, his curly red hair tousled and his glasses sliding down his freckled nose.

"Hi, Adam!" Vinnie called cheerfully. "I thought maybe I'd join you for lunch."

"Hi," he said, brightening for a moment.

She walked over, set down her backpack, and hugged him. He responded wholeheartedly for a moment before hunching his shoulders and pulling away. He glanced around the room nervously, at other loud tables full of boys talking, laughing, making faces.

She understood immediately that he was afraid hugging his sister wasn't "cool." Vinnie smiled at him, burying the silly kernel of hurt, and sat down in the chair opposite Adam.

He began picking at his sandwich.

She noticed that boys at other tables had hot meals—it looked like meat loaf with mashed potatoes and peas, or a pasta dish in a pink creamy sauce. "Why aren't you having a hot lunch?" she asked Adam.

"The meat loaf's different from how you and Mama make it. And there are dried roaches in the other stuff, and the noodles are *green*."

"Oh, Adam, honey, I don't think they'd put bugs in the food here."

"They do! Go look at it."

Vinnie knew, from long experience, that arguing without information would get her nowhere. She got up, saying she'd be right back, and went over to the kitchen area behind the stainless-steel counter.

"Excuse me," she said to a man in a white uniform. "Can you tell me what's in the noodle dish?"

He jabbed a finger at the blackboard hanging over the counter, and repeated what was written there. "Spinach pasta with grilled chicken and sundried tomatoes."

"Thank you." Mystery solved, Vinnie went back to the table to explain it to Adam. She didn't know how to get around the fact that sun-dried tomatoes could easily look like dried bugs to the average twelve-year-old.

"Adam, those are sun-dried tomatoes, not roaches. And the noodles are green because they're made with spinach."

"I don't believe it. They just pulled the legs off a bunch of big old New York roaches. And spinach macaroni—Yuck! Why don't they make anything normal here?"

She knew he wanted a grilled cheese sandwich on white bread with a sliced apple and some potato chips, but she was fresh out. "Listen, honey, normal is different in different places. Up here spinach pasta may be pretty normal."

Adam jabbed a fork at the neon green pickle on his plate. "I hate it here."

Vinnie's heart sank. "It'll get better. You'll make some friends soon, and you'll enjoy your classes, and little by little you'll get used to it."

"I don't think so."

"Mama is so proud you got in, and so are all your teachers back home. Remember how excited Mr. Gorman was? And what a great letter he wrote for you? Let's give it a little longer than two days before you give up on it. Okay?"

"These kids all know each other already. I don't know anyone."

Makes two of us, she thought. "Well, you've got to give it a little time, like I said."

"And they're mean. They act like they know everything in the world."

She put her hand on his. "Adam, remember when we talked about how it would be different here? You're used to being the smartest kid in school. But here all the kids are smart, and it's going to take a little getting used to. You're not going to feel as unique as you did back home, but you'll probably learn a lot more."

Her little brother continued to desiccate the pickle, and her heart went out to him. She wanted to protect him from these feelings of loneliness and alienation more than she wanted to breathe. But she couldn't make friends for him, or do his adapting and growing up, as painful as it was. She couldn't protect him from everything.

It had all been much simpler when he was a baby, then a toddler. She could change a diaper, she could feed him, or burp him, or rock him. She could solve his problems then, even when it took a bit of trial and error. She'd been a good mother to him—and to Mama.

Mama hadn't left her bedroom for a year after Daddy's funeral. A whole year. And for a year after that, she hadn't left the house. Though she still suffered some symptoms of agoraphobia, she could now manage the garden and go into town, only because Vinnie had finally dragged her, hysterical, to therapy.

At fourteen, Vinnie'd become nursemaid, yardman, cook, and parent. She'd muddled through insurance paperwork and learned how to fix leaky faucets. She'd called her mother twice a day from the high school pay phone, to make sure she was changing Adam's pull-up pants and giving him lunch. It wasn't that Mama was wholly incompetent—she just needed to be instructed and checked upon. When Daddy had died, her adult drive seemed to die with him. Mama was *there*, just not all there, not even after a year, when Vinnie sat her down and told her the insurance money was mostly gone, the military benefits were limited and she'd have to get a job—both of them would, for Adam's sake. Even then, Mama had asked Vinnie what she should do. And it was Vinnie who went and talked to the church board and reminded them of how beautifully Mama played the organ.

As Vinnie sat across from Adam, all these thoughts running through her mind, her resolve strengthened. If she had survived those miserable years, Adam could survive at least a semester at the Gotham-Young Science Academy.

Much as she might want to give in to her instincts to coddle him and swaddle him and never make him suffer any discomfort, it wouldn't be doing him any favor in the long run. Adam needed to stand on his own for a bit. And after all, she was only a phone call and a subway ride away. She was here with him in New York to provide moral support, but not to let him be a weakling like Mama. She could not, would not, allow that to happen.

"How were your classes this morning? What did you have?"

He shrugged. "English, chemistry, math."

"Chemistry? Weren't you looking forward to that?"

"Yeah. The math teacher's mean, though."

Vinnie folded her arms. "Well, a lot of teachers are stern on the first day so you kids don't get any ideas about pushing them around." She grinned. "You know that, right?"

"I guess."

"Well, it's almost one, so I should get going. You've still got my phone number at the apartment, right?"

Adam nodded.

"And here's a new work number. I, um, switched jobs today."

"Why?"

"Long story. But I think I'll like this new job. Call me if you need to, okay? I love you."

Adam looked around again, clearly agonized by her use of the weenie, sissy "L" word. Oops.

"Yeah," he said in a low voice, "me too. Bye."

Chapter 6

Nicholas awoke after a miserable night of cozying up to a bed buddy who had six nipples instead of two. While he was a big fan of hot, sweaty restless nights with a baby-oiled, buck-naked woman, this was entirely different.

He found himself squished into six inches of ever-shrinking bed space, courtesy of the eighteen scarlet-painted Dober-nails digging into various parts of his anatomy. The dog was stiff-arming him out of his own bed.

"That's it!" he snarled at 6 A.M., leaping from under the two inches of covers she hadn't wrestled from him.

Daffodil immediately jumped out of bed, too. Then she tried to lick his hand, and when he pulled that away, his most private part.

Nick flew back as if burned. "No!"

She looked injured, and followed him to the bathroom. Nick put his other hand over his backside to guard against her inquisitive nose, only to have that licked, too.

"Do you mind? I'd like a moment of privacy, here." He shut the door in her face, only to hear a mournful, pathetic whistle.

He emerged again and patted her head. "Nice doggie." She gratefully assaulted him again with licking, and followed hard on his heels to the kitchen. Nick got her some food before making coffee, but she ignored it to abase herself at his feet.

"Why are you so needy?" Nick was used to peace, coffee, and the *Times* in the morning, in that order. He liked his solitary mornings. And he did *not* like having his toes licked by a slimy oversize tongue. He curled them around the bottom rung of his Italian barstool and glared down at Daffodil. She gazed piteously up at him, as if to say that being needy was her job.

What was it about the neediness that bothered him? It made the back of his neck prickle. It gave him chills.

Nick sighed. He took a sip of orange juice (the cappuccino was still brewing) and climbed from the stool. Awkwardly, he patted Daffodil's head and scratched down her spine until he found that magical sweet spot again, and her leg began rotating. She assumed a blissful expression.

"Yeah, well," said Nick, "I'd like somebody to find my sweet spot, too."

On her first day of work, Vinnie gave a sigh of relief to emerge from the mole hole, and actually enjoyed the walk from the subway station to the elegant burgundy awning of Nicholas's building. It was her first day of Dober Duty. She smiled and nodded at the doorman when he greeted her, and walked inside to the elevator, where Richie waited, his complexion normal and healthy today.

"Feeling better?" she asked him.

"Like a new man, miss. That tea really did the trick. Thanks again."

"You're welcome. My mama used to give that to me when I felt bad."

"Wise woman, your mama."

Vinnie felt her smile wobble a bit. "Sometimes."

She had to fight the urge to call and check on Mama every day. *Mama is a grown-up*, she silently repeated to herself. *Mama's never balanced her own checkbook*, her conscience snapped back. *Mama forgets to get the mail for days. Mama doesn't know what to do without you.*

Well, right now Adam needed her more than Mama did, and her mother was going to have to learn to stand on her own two feet. But Vinnie still felt guilty, and she still missed her and worried about her. Would she remember to take her calcium pills every day? Would she eat enough? Would she—

Vinnie gratefully let Richie interrupt her thoughts.

"So, you start your new job today?"

"Yes."

"What exactly are you going to be doing for Mr. Wright?"

"Oh, just taking care of his dog. She's pretty high-maintenance . . ." Too late, she caught the look on Richie's face.

"His *dog*?"

"Yeah . . . why is that so strange?"

"Er. Well, it's just that dogs aren't allowed in the building."

"What? You're kidding."

He shook his head.

"Listen, I might not have been supposed to say anything. Will you do me a favor and forget I mentioned it? Just until we get this straightened out."

Reluctantly he nodded. "Yeah. I owe you one."

And that was a good thing. She couldn't have another job fall through. How could she be a dogsitter for Nick if dogs weren't allowed in his building? And would he be angry with her for spilling the beans? But honestly, how had he expected to pull this off? The dog had to do her doggie business, after all. Suddenly she remembered how he'd made a point of entering the building through the back.

Heart thumping, she exited the elevator at Nick's floor and knocked on his door.

He opened it looking edible, smelling of a wonderful citrusy aftershave, sporting still-damp hair. *Oh, yum . . .*

She wanted to touch that insurance-company solid jaw of his, and was grateful when Daffodil bounded over to distract her, stub wagging madly. "Good morning," Vinnie said, scratching the dog instead of her own strange itch.

"Good morning," he said, in his deep, easy voice.

She wouldn't mind having a cassette tape of that voice, even if it were only reading the telephone book, or a Chinese takeout menu, or even *Webster's New Collegiate Dictionary* . . . "Er," she articulated. "We need to talk about something sorta *urgently*."

"Yes, we do. There were a couple of things I forgot to mention to you yesterday—"

"One of them being that dogs aren't allowed in your building?"

He looked nonplussed. "As a matter of fact, yes."

She folded her arms. "Then how is this situation possibly going to work out for either of us?"

"I'm working on an angle to pitch to the board."

"There's a board? For a residential building?"

"Yes."

"We don't have those in Kansas, I don't think."

Nick smiled a devastating *Gentleman's Quarterly* smile, which worked like a bellows to force all the breath out of her lungs and ignite a weird electricity in the air.

Oh, my. He should smile like that more often. Or maybe not. It did funny things to the backs of her knees.

"I'm betting a lot of things in New York are different than what you're used to," he said.

Starting with the men. She nodded.

"How did you know about the pet ban?"

Darn. "I sorta mentioned to the elevator guy that I'd be working for you as a dog sitter. I'm sorry."

Nick frowned. "This is going to get expensive."

"Huh?"

"Paying all the building employees to look the other way."

Vinnie put her hands on her hips. "That's *bribery*," she admonished.

"So it is." Nick looked amused. "Do you not have *that* in Kansas?"

His gentle sarcasm made her feel like a rube, and she didn't appreciate it.

"Why don't you come on in and sit down." He moved to one side, and Vinnie went past him, chewing on her lip.

Delighted, Daffodil nudged her backside briefly before rocking forward on her extended front paws, leaving her own Dober-butt in the air. Then she *woofed* playfully.

Vinnie opened her backpack and removed a cheap stuffed monkey she'd bought for the dog at her corner drugstore. It was hairy and blue, with long skinny dangling arms and legs. Daffodil accepted the monkey graciously and took it over to the hearth to inspect it.

Nick sat down on a leather ottoman, and Vinnie sat some distance away on the couch.

"So, you have a problem with my paying off the doorman and the elevator guy?" Nick asked.

"It's not exactly . . . moral," Vinnie said.

"Moral," he repeated. Then he grinned. "How is it really any different from giving Daffodil that monkey?"

"Pardon? The monkey isn't a *bribe*. It's a gift."

"You gave it to her just now so she'd go off into a corner and not distract us. Correct?"

"Pretty much," Vinnie admitted.

"So it's a bribe for good behavior."

She opened and closed her mouth. "I don't think it's the same thing at all! And you don't have a rule against blue monkeys posted anywhere in your apartment."

He nodded. "But it's my apartment, right?"

"Yeah . . . ?"

"Therefore, I should be able to decide if animals are allowed in it."

She thought about this. "Well . . . only if you own it."

"Oh," said Nicholas in a wry voice, "I do own it. I make a hefty mortgage payment each and every month to own it. So you see, the pet rule is a stupid rule."

"But it's still a rule," Vinnie insisted.

"A rule I intend to get changed."

"Well, fine, but what if we get caught before you do that?"

"We will. Even with the payoffs, it's only a matter of time."

Oh, great. "Will I still have a job when we get caught? I don't mean to be pushy, here, but my little brother's future depends upon me keeping a job."

"I understand," said Nick. "We'll work it out somehow."

He sounded blithe, just like William when there were rules to bend. Confident that they didn't apply to *him*, but only to common folk. It enraged Vinnie, but she tamped down her anger. She didn't have that many options.

"Really, it'll be okay."

She nodded curtly.

"Now, let me give you what I believe must be Daffodil's daily planner, courtesy of Aunt Edna." He fished a packet out of his briefcase and handed it to her.

Vinnie looked from the packet to him and back. "*Dogma of Daffodil*? You're kidding, right?"

"Nope. Apparently Aunt Edna had some very particular ideas about how to care for Daffodil. I'd like to try to honor her last wishes. She was . . . very kind to me when I was younger, or there's no way I'd become a doggie dad."

"Are you any other kind of dad?"

The blood drained from his face. "Jayzus, no!"

"Sorry. I didn't mean to offend you."

"I'm not offended," Nick assured her. "It's just a damned scary thought."

Funny, he didn't look like much would scare him. Vinnie let the subject drop but studied him covertly while she opened the packet concerning Daffodil. Why would a guy who was obviously successful be that afraid of having a family? She decided it was something to do with his background. He'd been a little too vehement about the subject; not just casually dismissive like your average swinging bachelor.

She slid a flowery notebook out of the packet and opened it to find that every page was covered with spidery, old-fashioned, almost illegible handwriting.

Though it was handwritten, the little book contained a table of contents full of odd subject matter. The headings included Wardrobe, Jewelry, Grooming, Toys, Exercise, Deportment, Recipes, Health/Medical History, Favorite Music/Television Programs, and General Likes/Dislikes.

Bemused, Vinnie looked from the book to Nick. "Have you looked at this? Because—no disrespect intended toward your great-aunt—it's borderline insane."

"Aunt Edna had her eccentricities," Nicholas said. "No, I haven't had time to look at it. I didn't think caring for a dog would be too complicated."

"Well, let me give you a hint." She flipped through a few pages. "Daffodil's favorite television program is *Masterpiece Theatre*. And she gets a shampoo, blow-dry, and manicure once a week at a place called Poochie Bliss."

Nick's jaw slackened, and his brows rose.

"She enjoys an eclectic taste in music, but whale sounds and birdcalls are of special interest . . . Twice weekly, she's to eat chicken liver mousse, made with white pepper only, because the black makes her sneeze."

Slowly, Nick let his head fall into his hands, and his shoulders began to shake. He ran his long fingers through that damp coppery hair of his, until it stood up in funny little tufts. When he looked up, he gasped, "I don't believe this."

"Would you like to know where Daffodil's winter coats are tailored? The ones that aren't mink, silver fox, or cheetah, that is?"

"No, no, no! Please stop."

"Perhaps you'd like to go by the canine bakery after work, to procure her preferred pork-flavored sticky buns with mint jelly in the center?"

He groaned.

Vinnie flipped through a few more pages. "Oh, and she gets a weekly massage at—"

"Enough!" shouted Nick.

"You don't want to hear about the doggie play groups?"

"No." He stood up and headed toward the kitchen, which was open to the room they sat in, and bigger than Mama's living room, possibly as big as their whole cabin. "I need more coffee. Would you like some?"

"Sure." Vinnie put the notebook aside and followed him, looking around in awe at the rich wood that covered even the refrigerator, and the gorgeous marble countertops. The man even had *art* in the kitchen! It wasn't anything she could recognize, but since it was cool and curvy and multicolored, had no discernible use, and stood on a lighted pedestal, it must be art. She wondered if he had art in his bathrooms. Or was it disrespectful to pee in front of art?

Nick approached a vast, black, complicated machine that seemed to be the mother of all coffeemakers. Wow, look at that thing. She hoped it came with an instruction manual, because otherwise she'd never master its complexities.

"Café au lait? Cappuccino?" he asked.

She'd heard of Oil of Olay, but not Café Olay. "Cappuccino," she told him, trying to sound as if she'd had it before.

He nodded, and did something incomprehensible to the big machine. Whatever it was, the aroma was like heaven. This stuff didn't smell *at all* like Mama's coffee at home.

While they waited for the hissing, steaming, gurgling monster to churn out their beverages, Vinnie asked Nick, "So . . . the notebook talks about all these clothes of Daffodil's. Where do you suppose they are?"

"I don't have the slightest idea." Nick ran a hand over his jaw. "I'll have to call old Hutchins, Aunt Edna's attorney, and ask him."

They went over a few more details, then Nick gave her his work number and a key to the apartment, along with a security code for the alarm system.

Her virgin sip of cappuccino was like a rainbow in her mouth. The longer she stayed in New York— and it was already nine days—the more Vinnie was convinced the city was on an entirely different planet than rural Kansas.

Nick told her to have a nice day and started for the door, his own cappuccino in a travel mug.

"Um, Nick?" she said tentatively.

"Yeah?"

She put down her cup and walked over to him. "You kind of . . . let me—" She stood on tiptoe and smoothed her hand over his hair, erasing the wild tufts he'd created.

His hair was soft, yet had an energy of its own. He stood absolutely still, his eyes wide and his breathing shallow. She could smell the traces of soap on his skin, a tinge of deodorant, and a deep and almost drinkable essence that was unique to him. He smelled wonderful, and she knew an urge to bury her face in his neck. She stepped back immediately.

"Sorry," she said. The gesture now seemed far too intimate—like something a lover or wife would do. And lord knew, she would never be either to someone like him.

"Don't be," he said, his voice a little thick. "It was very . . . sweet." And then he was gone, and her only companions in his fabulous penthouse were Daffodil and the by-then-soggy blue monkey.

Chapter 7

Nick took the main elevator down to the lobby when he left for work. He straightened his tie and tried not to remember the way Vinnie's fingers had felt, moving through his hair. He'd gotten one of those deep spine shivers, and his scalp still tingled.

How was it that a virtual hillbilly of a dog-sitter could affect him more by touching his scalp than Dana did when she touched far more personal areas?

He shook off the thought and groaned as the elevator stopped on the next floor down. A premonition told him Mrs. Blount was about to invade the car from her apartment on the twenty-fourth floor.

"Nicholas," she boomed, in her Tudor tones. She always pronounced each syllable of his name, with a curious emphasis on the last. It sounded as if the queen of England were calling him Nickel Ass.

Since she and Aunt Edna had loathed each other, her pronunciation of his name was probably no accident.

A martial light gleamed in Mrs. Blount's eye as she thumped with her cane into the elevator. "Nickel Ass," she repeated, "what sort of depravity are you indulging in upstairs?" She looked him up and down, shaking her head.

Nick recalled that she'd once told a mutual acquaintance that he was too handsome for his own good. *Gigoloesque*, was how she'd uncharitably put it. Of course, the acquaintance had lost no time in gleefully repeating this juicy tidbit.

But depravity? She'd never accused him of that. He raised his brows. "Beg pardon?"

"As you very well should!"

"Mrs. Blount, have I offended you in some way?"

"Someone or something, Nickel Ass, is howling in your apartment during the day. Howling. I can't hear myself think! I can't read, and I certainly can't nap."

How could he be so unmoved at the thought of Mrs. Blount not getting her beauty rest? "I don't know what the noise could be," he lied smoothly. "But I doubt it's in *my* apartment."

"I'd wager my mink that it's coming from upstairs, and you're the only person upstairs."

"Are you sure it isn't from below? Or from one of your neighbors on the twenty-fourth floor?"

"Pffft. And are *you* sure you're not playing hooky from work, pleasuring some young lady beyond the breaking point?"

"*Mrs. Blount!*"

"Well, the noise sounds almost human. But I suppose it could be a dog. You aren't harboring a canine on your premises, are you, Nickel Ass?"

"Of course not."

"Because you know that's against the rules."

"Absolutely."

"And you know that I'm president of the board."

"How could I forget?"

"Hhmmmpppff."

"I really think you should be investigating your other neighbors, Mrs. Blount, and not trying to embarrass me."

"Do you." The elevator reached the foyer, and she thumped out, the old three-legged witch. "Good day, Nickel Ass."

Nick bared his teeth at her. "And to you." Great. If Mrs. Blount was on the warpath, he'd have to warn Vinnie to be extra careful with Daffodil. It wouldn't do for them to run into each other, especially not before he'd prepared an appeal of the animal ban to the board.

Vinnie and Daffodil had managed to rip the left arm off the blue monkey within an hour of Nick's departure. The monkey hadn't been manufactured to withstand incisors roughly the size of tusks, and blue fuzz adorned assorted rugs in the apartment.

Vinnie had chased Daff away from both a wooden sculpture and a plant, and was looking around for some sort of sewing kit when the buzzer rang. Unsure of how to use the thing, she simply walked over and pressed down on it. "Hello?"

"Ya, this is Pete at desk. You are Miss Hart?"

"Yes."

"We haf a delifery for a Miss Daffodil St. Villiers-Wright?"

The *dog* was getting deliveries? "Um, okay."

"Shall we bring it up to you?"

"Yes, please." Vinnie went to the jar that Nick had told her contained "petty cash" for any expenses that came up. When she lifted the lid, her eyes widened. Slowly she counted five tens, five twenties, and five one-hundred-dollar bills. Nick thought $650 was petty?

She knew she needed to tip the man who brought up the package, but she didn't know how much. In Independence it was normal to tip a pizza guy about two dollars. What did you tip a bellman for bringing a package up twenty-five floors? Surely ten dollars was too much, but there was no smaller change.

Her dilemma was solved within five minutes. She sternly told Daffodil to get away from one of Nick's elaborate architectural models, and put her in one of the guest bedrooms to hide her. Then she opened the door to a cart stacked with five trunks.

"Ya, you will sign here, please, Miss?" The bellman extended a clipboard.

"These are all for the d—all for, uh, Miss Daffodil?"

"Ya. They arrive from attorney a few blocks west."

Bemused, Vinnie signed for them, and gave him the ten-dollar bill. For five trunks, it wasn't unreasonable. Five trunks! What could be in them?

"Thank you, Miss Hart."

She dialed Nick's number at work.

"They came from Hutchins?" he asked.

She checked the name on the return label. "Yes."
"Go ahead and open them."

Vinnie hung up with the husky tones of Nick's
voice still tickling her ears. She let Daffodil out of
the bedroom, scolding her gently when she found
the dog snoozing in the middle of the guest bed, her
head on the raw silk pillows. Unfazed, Daffodil followed her out to the living room, sniffing at the
trunks.

Vinnie opened the first one to discover a plethora
of designer doggie sweaters and coats. Shaking her
head, she went through them: a purple angora
sweater with matching leg warmers, a turquoise
blue cashmere with coordinating scarf, and a
cherry red Shetland with a plaid-trimmed hat.

Vinnie examined the hat, which had obviously
been custom-made for a Doberman, with little
cutouts for the ears on top. This . . . confection . . .
tied under the chin using cords trimmed with pom-
poms.

Daffodil eyed it with suspicion and barked.

"It's pretty bad, isn't it, girl?"

Next Vinnie pulled out sweaters in magenta,
peridot green and ice blue trimmed with a darker
shade of rabbit fur. They all had some sort of acces-
sory as well. Quite frightening.

Underneath them lay the doggie Burberry, the
doggie silver fox, the doggie snowsuit with matching booties; the mink, the gold-mesh opera shawl,
and the sequined canine cape. Was there no end?

Vinnie glanced at Daffodil, busy chewing on her
toes. "You obviously have a better social life than

I've ever dreamed of having. And you shop at expensive boutiques. Most of *my* clothes come from Walmart."

Daffodil yawned.

"What's worse, all this stuff has to be *dry-cleaned*. Whoever heard of dry-cleaning clothes for a dog? I'm starting to understand just how spoiled rotten you are."

Vinnie opened the next trunk, which was Vuitton. Inside this one was a pink-satin-covered mattress and disassembled brass frame for a dog-sized canopy bed. Unbelievable.

There were also three sets of custom-made satin doggie sheets with trim that coordinated with three different canopies to stretch over the top of the bed. The throw pillows matched all the sets, and were shaped like a bone, a cat, a moon, and a star.

Vinnie's own sheets came from Kmart, and they were a cotton-poly blend.

Trunk number three held a carefully wrapped Irish leaded-crystal punch bowl, a water filter, and oversize linen dinner napkins to tie around Daffodil's neck during meals. Dinner napkins, for Pete's sake.

Vinnie couldn't imagine what was in trunks four and five. Four proved to contain gourmet food and toys. And five contained—oh, the spring/summer wardrobe, of course. Little silk T-shirts, a windbreaker, a white linen jacket that buttoned up the back. *Skirts*, for the love of God, in floral prints with ruffles. Nick's Aunt Edna had been certifiably insane. She wondered what the rest of his family was like.

Vinnie sat back on her haunches and shook her head. "You're going to need an entire closet of your own, Daffodil. And you know what's conspicuously absent from your wardrobe?"

The dog just looked at her.

"Play clothes, sweetie. What on earth did you do in all these ruffles and furs? And rhinestones, for crying out loud."

Vinnie bent forward and grasped the collar, turning it to find the clasp. It was difficult to work, but she got it off with some muttering. She gazed at the blazing collar for a moment before tossing it into the food/toy trunk, where it landed in a bag of gourmet dog food she'd opened to inspect.

Daffodil rolled onto her back, all paws in the air, and rubbed her now-bare neck back and forth on Nick's thick, hand-loomed living room rug, which looked wickedly expensive, like everything else in the place.

"Glad to have that off, are we? I'm not surprised." Vinnie closed the lids of the trunks that contained clothing and dragged them one by one to the guest bedroom she'd stuck Daffodil in before. There were three to choose from. What did the man do with three extra bedrooms?

Nick's "apartment" was more like a modern palace, and working in it made her feel like Cinderella—with no hope of a fairy godmother. She opened the mahogany wardrobe that served as the room's closet and began hanging up Daffodil's ridiculous coats and jackets on the beautiful polished wooden hangers inside.

The sweaters she folded and placed in the drawers, side by side with their matching accessories. She stacked the trunks along the far wall, feeling very small. She'd just taken a job as a maid—to a *dog*. A dog that obviously had a pedigree worth more than twenty of her own.

Vinnie shook her head and went out to get the parts to the canopy bed. In order to put it together, she would have to call Nick again and ask where his toolbox was. She dialed his direct line.

"Nicholas Wright," he answered the phone in harried tones. In the background, a man was shouting.

She had obviously called at a rotten time. "Uh, wrong number!" she squeaked, and hung up the phone.

Moments later it rang beside her. "Vinnie?" said Nick's voice.

"Yuh?"

"It's past the millennium. I have caller ID."

She felt like crawling into one of the dog trunks. "Um. Right. Sorry. You just sounded really busy, and I hated to distract you."

"Don't worry about it," he said in clipped tones. "Oh, for God's sake, Ty! So apply for a zoning variance."

"Excuse me?" Vinnie asked.

"What? Never mind. I was talking to an intern."

She felt beyond silly and insignificant. Hereafter, she certainly wouldn't call Sir Architect at work. But she was stuck for the moment. "Um, Nick? Do you have a toolbox somewhere?"

"Yes. Why am I afraid that this has to do with the contents of those mysterious trunks?"

"Because you have good instincts. One of the trunks contains Daffodil's canopy bed, and I—"

"Her *what*?"

"—figured I'd put it together."

"She has a canopy bed?"

"Yes. With a pink satin mattress and three sets of sheets and little doggie throw pillows."

"I'm going to be sick."

Vinnie laughed. "Well, to be honest, that was my own reaction. But I thought I'd put it together, since that's where she's probably used to sleeping."

"I have *got*," said Nick, "to see this." Then he yelled, "City Hall, of course! File it with Lorna."

"Huh?"

"Listen," Nick told her. "I've got to get out of here and run by a job site to inspect something. Give me thirty to forty minutes. Then I'll swing by and help you assemble it."

"You don't have to—"

The line went dead.

Vinnie felt like a complete moron. She had interrupted a mover and shaker's day in order to put together a dog bed. She was sure he had better things to build—like banks and churches and soaring skyscrapers. And *she* needed basic help with a screwdriver. Nice.

While she waited for Nick, she wandered around the palace and tried to take it all in. Her new boss had some strange taste in art and furniture. The apartment was all about modernity, and somehow made her feel backward. The rooms were chic and bleak. And so clean that they squeaked. His furniture was interesting, but darned uncomfortable. One chair was shaped kind of like a boomerang, and a couple of others looked like they'd been fashioned from giant paper clips: cold steel, with leather strips on which to perch. The cushions of the couch might as well have been made of concrete.

Angry squiggles leaped from the painting over Nick's fireplace, which contained architectural books and looked as if it had never been lit. He had lots of beautiful, stark, black-and-white photographs on the walls, but none of them contained people.

Vinnie decided he didn't spend much time there at all—at least, not in his living room. She wandered into his office, arrested by the floor-to-ceiling shelves of books. She'd never seen so many books outside a public library, and the walls of words thoroughly intimidated her. Novels competed with philosophy texts, which jostled tomes on art and architecture, which gave way to the Harvard Classics. Geez. She wondered if there were Yale Classics, too. A scary thought.

Famous names jumped out at her: Tolstoy and Chekov and Conrad and Wolfe; Hardy and London and Rand and Camus. Dante and Molière and Faulkner and Whitman. They went on and on, in no particular order. And with each name, she felt smaller and smaller. Less educated. Had Nick actually read all these books? When had he found the time? Did the guy not watch TV?

Vinnie herself wasn't sure she could live without her episodes of *Friends* and *Buffy*, even if she was down to reruns. She liked to read, but working all the time and taking care of Mama and Adam hadn't left all that much time for it.

It occurred to her that this job was different, though. Taking care of a dog wasn't nearly as intense as taking care of an active little boy. She'd actually have some free time! Free time that she was paid for.

Vinnie continued taking stock of the office, which seemed to have the one comfortable chair in the whole apartment—the one at Nick's desk. That indicated to her that he spent most of his domestic time in his office, working.

Impossible to miss were the six architectural models mounted on high white shelves that blended seamlessly with the walls. What she saw surprised her. Far from being models of blocky commercial structures, they were dynamic, rhythmic, asymmetrical buildings. *Were* they buildings? Or modern art? Vinnie found herself climbing onto Nick's office chair to look more closely, while Daffodil eyed her curiously.

Yes—there were tiny little people and trees around them. But these were like no other structures she'd ever seen. They were absolutely wild! The models, particularly one, had . . . petals for walls. Or were they wings? The whole tiny building seemed poised to take flight, to float among the clouds instead of being anchored to the earth. She marveled at it.

She bent forward, wobbling a little on the rolling chair, and peered over the unusual roof to see an open courtyard in the center, containing a futuristic, sculptural fountain. Wow! How cool! And there were tiny flagstone paths meandering around it.

"Different, no?" said Nick's voice behind her, and Daffodil barked.

Vinnie jumped in surprise, lost her balance on the edge of the chair, and grabbed for the shelf in reflex. Bad idea. The white painted board was set elegantly—not bolted—on two modern supports. It came free in her hands, and toppled with her, architectural model and all.

"Jesus Christ!" Nick moved astonishingly fast for a big guy, since he managed to catch her before she hit the floor or his desk. However, she still clutched the darn shelf, and the model . . . oh, no. Was that the model crushed between them, lodged behind her right shoulder and what must be his chest?

She tried to ignore the sickening crinkle of the delicate foam-core, just as she tried not to feel how strong her employer's arms felt, locked around her. And boy did she not want to think about what her tush pressed against, because that would be just plain *wrong*. How could she notice something like that, at a time like this? She'd just destroyed his property and would now probably be fired.

He put her down, the mangled model hit the floor, and they both spoke at the same time, while Daff ran to investigate the strange object.

"Are you okay?"

"I'm so sorry! Oh, God, I'm sorry . . ." Vinnie bent down and picked it up, sending an anguished glance his way.

A muscle worked in his jaw, and he swallowed as he gazed down at the twisted heap. "It's okay. I can rework it. Really, are you all right?"

"I'm fine. I'm just . . . *stupid*," Vinnie blurted. She waited for him to start yelling.

He didn't. He just picked the model up and set it on his desk, then averted his eyes from the thing. "No you're not. It was an accident."

"Yeah, but I know you're mad. You can go ahead and yell. It's okay, really." She braced herself.

"I don't want to yell."

"Yes you do. Come on." In Vinnie's experience, men who were mad hollered.

"Why do you assume that I want to yell?"

She shrugged. Her dad would be cussing a blue streak in this situation, if he were still alive, though he would've apologized later. William would yell, too—as he had the time she'd blown his speakers— but she didn't want to think about him, or his creative uses for those rolling dollies that slid under his fancy sports cars.

He'd yelled at her for not ignoring the skanky naked girl with the toe ring whom he'd hidden under the Porsche in his garage. The one that had meant "nothing," kind of like Vinnie herself.

Nick was eyeing her, expecting some kind of answer, which she was darned if she was going to give him. She cast about for a subject change.

"Who yells at you, Vinnie?"

"Huh? Nobody. So can I see that building"—she pointed at the model—"in real life? It's beautiful! Where is it?"

His brows snapped together, and he set the shelf

back into place, then shoved the rumpled miniature onto it. "Where is it?" He laughed without much humor and tapped his temple with an index finger. "Right here."

"So it's not built yet?"

"It'll probably never be built, Vinnie. So don't worry that you messed up the model."

"Why do you say that? It's absolutely gorgeous. There should be buildings that cool everywhere."

He shot her a wry smile. "Thanks. But reality dictates otherwise. Your average commercial client wants a nice cost-effective box."

"Oh."

"So my firm does lots of those, and we get paid very well to do them."

He walked out of his office and into the cavernous designer kitchen, where he reached into the refrigerator and retrieved a beer. Icehouse.

Hmmmm. Icehouse was fitting, somehow.

Then he checked his watch and put it back. "Boxes are easy to design, easy to construct. What can I say?"

If they're so easy for you, then why do you have to reach for a beer before you talk about them? But Vinnie didn't say it aloud. "So why did you do those models in your office? None of those are boxes. Not remotely."

He waved a dismissive hand. "I did those in grad school, and for a couple of years after I graduated. They won competitions, they won me a spot at the top architectural firm in New York. But when push comes to shove, nobody really wants to build them. They're just little foam-core dreams." He hunched his shoulders, audibly cracking his neck in several places.

She winced at the sound, and at his words. *Little foam-core dreams*. So she'd only smashed a little piece of the man's imagination, his hope, his passion. That was all. And he was making light of it.

"So where's this ridiculous dog bed?" Nick asked. "I can give you half an hour. Then I've got to run downtown for a consultation. Then back here again to change. Then out for the evening."

"I really didn't mean to bother you with this." Vinnie got embarrassed all over again. "I know how busy you are."

Nick waved a hand again, trying to be casual, but even his version of casual was intense. "If we don't get her bed put together, she'll keep trying to sleep in mine." He opened a closet and dug a yellow toolbox out from under a bunch of sporting equipment.

"So is the rest of your family as . . . um, interesting . . . as your great aunt Edna?"

"Nope, not at all." Nick threw the lid open. "My parents are very conventional—they do everything by the book. Aunt Ed wrote her own book, as you can see."

Vinnie laughed. "She certainly did."

"I probably get my wild ideas from her side of the family." Nick secured two pieces of the little bed frame with a nut and bolt. "She was always an advocate of thinking outside the box."

"Were you close to her?"

Nick dropped the next bolt, and it bounced on the hardwood floor before skidding into a pile of blue monkey fuzz from Daffodil's toy. He picked it out gingerly. "I adored her. I used to wish when I was younger that I could go live with her, just because she made everything so much fun. But she couldn't keep up full-time with a little boy, and my parents would never have stood for it—wouldn't look right, you know? However accidental my birth was, I was their responsibility."

She caught her breath. *Ouch.* What kind of parents would ever tell their son he was an accident? And a responsibility? For goodness sake! Had they referred to his doctor's visits as scheduled maintenance?

For all their own parents' flaws, Vinnie and Adam had known they were planned and wanted.

Nick's revelation was probably unintentional, but it made him seem more human, less Untouchable Rich Guy.

As she helped him put together the insane little canopy bed, she noticed that he worked competently with his tools just like any average guy she knew in Kansas, and he even cussed a little when he had difficulty with another one of the bolts. While Vinnie couldn't say she approved of cussing exactly, it made him seem normal. But that was a dangerous path to go down. Vinnie didn't need to think of her boss as normal or human. A boss was a boss was a boss. A person who wrote her checks, no more, no less.

While Nick finished assembling the little bed frame, Vinnie made up the mattress part of it, complete with silly bed skirt, ruffled pillowcases, and all. Nick helped her set it in place on the frame, and

Daffodil immediately climbed onto it, turned a couple of circles, and flopped with her nose at the foot and her stubby tail at the head. She heaved a great sigh, as if to comment that finally, she was comfortable.

Vinnie tucked the little bone-shaped pillow under the dog's chin, and covered her with the little satin comforter that matched the current set of sheets. Nick snorted. "Why," he asked, "do I have this awful feeling that my life as I've known it is over?"

He checked his watch and headed for the door after grabbing a cardboard tube of blueprints.

"Thanks for your help," she called after him.

"No problem. Back in an hour or so."

Vinnie looked up once again at the mangled model and winced. She still couldn't believe he hadn't yelled. And he'd made the time to stop by and put the dog bed together. Maybe Nick wasn't just another rich jerk.

Chapter 8

Later that night, Nick stood with a martini in hand, watching Dana operate like a well-oiled machine at the Polaski reception. She was a female trophy, and he'd won her by being the best—he was cynical enough to admit it. She was the commercial proto-type of a woman, the long-limbed glossy equivalent of the architectural box.

He always marveled at her sheer package power: Her smooth honey blond hair was pulled straight back from her serene forehead into a tight, elegant chignon. Turquoise blue eyes owed some of their intensity to contact lenses, but they riveted the un-suspecting at first glance. She had full, lush An-gelina Jolie lips, and she could turn on warmth and charm with a switch hidden in her breastbone.

At least Nick's theory surmised that it was lo-cated there, since no other area of her body had room. Dana didn't sport any spare flesh.

What she did sport included a pair of Manolo Blahniks, a form-fitting cocktail dress, and a diamond tennis bracelet. Unless Nick had guessed wrong, she wasn't wearing anything else.

Now, this would be a stupid move if Dana weren't such a mistress of manipulation. For Sondra Beckworth, her ultimate quarry, was a good thirty pounds heavier and had *not* gone to the top man in New York for her eye tuck and nose job.

But Dana, being Dana, had brought Nick along to introduce to Sondra as her "very good friend and architectural consultant." It was Nick's job to make Mrs. Beckworth feel like the most fascinating woman in the world while Dana made Gavin Beckworth drool onto his long-cold potsticker.

Nick calculated that Gavin had been twirling that same potsticker on that same toothpick for a good twenty minutes.

If this reception had been a cartoon, Gavin's eyeballs would be extended on stalks, one hovering just over Dana's cleavage, and one swooping around her waist to stare down at her smooth, tight ass.

It was pathetically clear to see that Gavin would like to be the toothpick in Dana's hot potsticker, which meant that Nick needed to keep Sondra's back to them. He executed a step-ball-change, and Sondra unconsciously followed suit.

She looked up at Nick meltingly and asked for the eleventh time, "Oh, do you really think so?"

He smiled and nodded and reiterated that Dana would be fabulous at mixing Sondra's Hummel figurines with Gavin's African mask collection.

Inside he winced at the sheer ghastliness of the whole evening, not to mention its setting at the Trump Palace.

He repressed a grin at the thought of Aunt Edna, who'd made a big point of not setting a toe of her well-heeled shoes inside the "monstrous vulgarity."

Nicholas hated it himself, loathed the overstated glitz and shininess of the place, but the price of getting big commercial business was schmoozing, and while he'd done it initially to help the firm and old Mr. D'Orsay, the owner, he'd somehow become good at it. If only it didn't make him so sick inside.

He continued to smile and nod at Mrs. Beckworth, while out of the corner of his eye he looked around at the roomful of people Aunt Edna would have described as "the wicked, the pretentious, and the foolish." He took a rather large mouthful of his martini and held it, pickling his tongue so it would behave and not say what he actually thought.

"Good design," he heard himself say, "is all about what makes you comfortable. You're the ones who will live in the house, and it should reflect you and Gavin and your personal style." Heaven help Dana while she tried to mix the Hummels and the African masks. Perhaps she could position the Hummels so that they peered out from the mouth- and eyeholes of the tribal pieces, just like Keebler elves.

But Dana would somehow pull it off, and then, knowing her, she'd con a bunch of Hamptonites into attending a party or two at the bodacious new Beckworth Bungalow, so that Sondra and Gavin would feel they had friends there, and not just people whispering behind their backs. Ugh.

Nick felt sicker to his stomach with every passing

quarter hour. He reached the end of his martini and gnashed down ferociously on the olive.

Mrs. Beckworth's eyes widened, she gave a delicate shiver, then licked her lips.

Nick choked. *Please God, don't let Sondra be imagining that I'm the plastic sword in her olive?*

Well, get real, Nick—of course she is. That's why Dana towed you along, and you know it.

The problem was that he thought Mrs. Beckworth would be a really nice person, if she weren't married to such a jerk and surrounded by people who played on her insecurities.

"So tell me about your children," he prompted, and watched her face change completely. She positively glowed as she described them, and Nick steered her a few feet to the left, where the lighting was kinder to the skin graft around her nose.

As she described her two daughters, he noticed that Gavin had finally traded his potsticker for a succulent Swedish meatball, but that too, remained snug on its toothpick while he watched Dana's tongue snake out to lick some condensation from the edge of her cosmopolitan glass.

"Would you like another drink?" he asked Mrs. Beckworth, when he could get a word in. He now knew that Sally and Rose were seven and nine respectively, were teaching their dolls elementary Spanish, and loved to ice-skate. Nick had to admit they sounded really cute, and wondered if they had a playhouse.

Mrs. Beckworth said she'd love another drink, and while Nick fetched her another glass of

Chardonnay, he contemplated exactly what little girls would require in a playhouse.

He wasn't sure why, but it was more fun than thinking about the structural supports for Mr. Southwick's Soda Dome, future home of Yeah! Cola—a project that took up all too much of his time.

It seemed to him that if the Beckworths were spending huge sums of money to redo their home, the girls should benefit, too—and have a place to retreat from the specter of the Hummels dancing around the African masks. To witness such horror could damage young minds.

Another quarter hour went by, and Nick had now had enough of the reception. He caught Dana's eye and tugged on his earlobe, their pre-arranged signal for "get me outta here."

She shook her blond head.

He stared at her fixedly and tugged on his other earlobe.

Dana frowned at him.

He firmly inclined his head toward the door, then quirked an eyebrow, looking down at Sondra, then over to Gavin, then back. His message was clear: I'm leaving, and you will, too, if you don't want to blow your deal, because if Mrs. B gets a load of the look on Mr. B's face (not to mention the tent in his trousers), you're history.

Dana put her hand on Gavin's shoulder and laughed, but began to extricate herself while Nick did the same.

"I've so enjoyed meeting you, Sondra. Will you

be at the opening for the Tanzey Gallery next week? Dana did the whole interior space, and you might enjoy seeing it."

"Are you the architect?"

He nodded. He knew she'd be there, if for nothing else then to see him again. He felt even more nauseated. He was not going to do this for Dana anymore.

"Take care of your little girls," he said. "They sound wonderful."

"Oh, I will, thank you. You're such a sweet man."

Right. Sweet? He felt like Chester the Cheetah. *It ain't easy being cheesy.* He forced himself to kiss Mrs. Beckworth's cheek and clasp her hand. Dana would expect no less.

Mrs. B actually blushed.

Oh, honey. Get away from this crowd and go home to Sally and Rose. Enjoy their innocence, and stay away from men like me.

Dana was furious when they got outside. "I wasn't ready to leave yet!"

That was his girl—all the warmth of a snapping turtle. "And I was. Dana, I don't feel good, and I've had a rotten day."

"Oh, get over it," she snapped. "I had another good prospect there and didn't get to her."

"So lift a finger, call her, and invite her to something else."

"Thanks, Nick. Ever heard of killing two birds with one stone?"

"Yeah, except I'm tired of being the stone."

Dana must have heard a real edge in his voice, because she abruptly switched tactics. She knew when not to push him.

Instead her hand landed on his knee and slid up to his thigh as they sat in her chauffered car. The glass was up, so she didn't worry about the driver hearing. "You're a great stone, though, Nickie. You always hit 'em right between the eyes."

Usually he knew what to do when Dana's hand landed on his thigh. But that night he felt like knocking it right off. He shot her a look, unmoved by her stunning profile.

Oh so casually, she slid those expensively manicured fingers back down toward his knee and let them drop to the leather seat.

The car soon pulled up to his building, and she waited for him to invite her inside.

He didn't. "Good night, Dana," he said. "It's been a real pleasure."

Nick wearily stepped into the elevator and nodded a hello to Mike, the nighttime attendant. He almost always started his day with a nod at Richie, and ended it with Mike.

The car shot upward smoothly, with a barely perceptible lurch, and soon Nick was unlocking his front door, anticipating a solitary Icehouse and an hour of Letterman. He would relax for the first time that day. Just the thought of it made him unwind a couple of notches, and he raised his shoulders, leaned his head back, and cracked his neck for the second time that night.

As he entered and tossed his keys on the polished hall table, he heard claws scrambling on hardwood. Then the apartment became suspiciously silent. A sense of foreboding crept over him as he called, "Daffodil?"

No answer.

He knew by now that if she didn't come bounding to greet him with her peculiar doggie smile, she had destroyed something.

Great. She'd probably eaten another plant. He knew for a fact that he'd closed his closet door, so she couldn't have gotten hold of any more shoes or belts. So it was a plant, he concluded, or maybe another corner of the kitchen rug, for which she'd developed a taste.

He sighed, walked into the kitchen, and flipped on the lights.

He illuminated disaster. Nick's jaw worked for a moment. "Daffodil!" he roared. Then he erupted into loud curses that would have Mrs. Blount lecturing him for a week.

Two of the doors on his custom burled walnut cabinets—which were handmade, no less—two of them hung mangled and chewed at the bottom.

"Daffodil!" he yelled again. "Get in here!"

He saw only a red-toed paw first, then two inches of nose. "Come," he ordered.

She hung her head and gazed piteously at him.

"Come," he said again.

She inched forward. If she'd had much of a tail, it would have been between her legs.

"What is this?"

She hung her head down even farther. Then she crept forward, her little stump wagging uncertainly.

"Bad girl!"

She whistled mournfully out of her nose.

"Yeah, well you damned well should be sorry. You've only been alone for two and a half hours." Nick rubbed a hand over his eyes and thought about just how long the little old Italian craftsman would stall him before coming over to replace the doors. He would doubtless insist upon ordering the materials from his homeland, too, and they'd take months to come in.

"*Bad!*" he repeated.

She abased herself at his feet and snuffled under his cuffs to lick his ankles.

Despite his rage, he couldn't help but chuckle. "You little manipulator. And I suppose now you need to go out, too, just when I wanted to flop on my bed and watch *Late Show*."

Daffodil's ears tuned straight forward at his mention of "out," and that was the end of her apology. She danced toward the door, and when he didn't follow immediately and just glared at her with his hands on his hips, she snorted her disgust.

"Plants," he said severely, while locating her leash. "Shoes, belts, window trim, rugs, and now my Italian cabinets! Aunt Edna must have had a score to settle with me, because I'm being punished for something."

He slipped the choke chain over her head, noticing that the ghastly rhinestone collar was gone, though she did sport a little terry bathrobe. She hauled him to the door.

"What am I going to do with you? Do I have to hire a dog-sitter twenty-four/seven?"

Only a few hours earlier, Vinnie put the key in the lock to her own apartment door, and was immediately sorry.

In the tiny living area, lined wall-to-wall-to-ceiling with black garbage bags, was a sight she did not want to behold.

There, cross-legged, sat four naked women around a bank of candles. Sorrel was one of them, and she was chanting over something raw and shiny in a dish.

Vinnie knew it was the animal heart she'd run from yesterday, and she closed her eyes, feeling bile rise in her throat. Where did people as sick and bizarre as Sorrel come from?

Hugging the wall, she inched past the women and hurtled into her room, where she threw her toothbrush, a couple of pairs of socks and panties, plus a clean T-shirt into her backpack.

Behind the door, she could hear Sorrel and her pack of naked crazies intone something about female empowerment.

Vinnie was all for Woman Power, but didn't think it necessary to seek it butt-naked in the dark, surrounded by candles and Hefty bags, over some poor animal's no-longer-beating heart.

Riffs of bizarre music accompanied Sorrel's voice, and Vinnie looked down to find that her knees were shaking. In fact, her whole body was trembling in disgust. She slung her backpack over her shoulders and reluctantly opened the door.

The three other naked crazies had their right hands piled on top of each other, over Sorrel's, which was placed directly on the heart in the dish.

Vinnie made a mad dash past them and out the apartment door, which she slammed with force. *Now what?*

Her stomach lurching violently, she ran down the smelly, urine-tinged hallway and pressed the button for the elevator.

At this hellhole in Chinatown, there was no polished wood in the elevator and definitely no Richie. The car stank of urine and metal and grease and body odor. It stank of more things that she couldn't define and didn't want to know about.

The elevator scared her silly, and she had to take deep breaths before forcing herself to enter. She was terrified of getting stuck in it, and she thought longingly of the golden open prairies of home, where the sky was visible and the air was fresh and people didn't decorate with Hefty bags or room with naked witches.

When the car came, she covered her mouth and nose, trying to hold her breath until street level, but the darn thing was so slow that twice she had to gasp for putrid air.

She felt perspiration pricking at her scalp and under her arms, and her stomach roiled in preparation for a bad episode. *No,* Vinnie told it almost hysterically. *I am not going to puke in this elevator. I'll die if one more smell is added to the others.*

It was her only conscious thought before the car lurched and thudded to a halt, the doors blessedly opened, and she ran for the street, where her body got the better of her and she retched violently into the gutter.

Gasping, she dug into her backpack for something to wipe her mouth on and came up with a pair of socks. Though she hated to do it, she tossed them into a nearby trash can after use and debated where to go.

She wasn't going to show up at Nick's, that was for sure. She couldn't go to Adam's school. That left her with only one option: an expensive hotel room for which she didn't have the money.

She thought longingly of Nick's "petty" cash jar, but put the idea out of her mind. She was no thief.

Vinnie had been walking for three or four blocks when she saw the flashing sign for an all-night diner—the solution to her problem.

The solution was shabby but clean, and the food smelled good. She figured if she kept ordering cups of coffee and the occasional side item all night, they'd let her stay.

A bored waitress led her to a booth, and Vinnie slid in, dumping her pack on the other seat to discourage anyone from joining her. It was seven-thirty when she ordered her first cup of coffee.

She managed to put off the second one for an hour, but at that rate she was still going to run a tab of twenty to thirty dollars by morning, which she didn't feel she could afford.

However, she had one emergency credit card in her pocket, and her situation certainly qualified as an emergency. Bedding down with the exhibitionist witches back there was out of the question. Vinnie had acquired a new vocabulary word since arriving in the Big Apple: *Fuhgeddaboudit.*

She decided to splurge on a thick wedge of chocolate cream pie, since she'd been so unlucky as to lose the contents of her stomach. The coffee was the worst thing in the world to pour into it, but the pudding in the pie would probably go down nice and easy. Besides, it made her think cozy thoughts of Bill Cosby and warm family life.

When the pie arrived, however, she thought not about Bill but about Nick. He was kind of like a human slice of chocolate cream pie . . .

Oh, stop it, you fool.

Richie, the elevator guy, had told her about Nick's girlfriend, the fancy designer. She wore five-hundred-dollar shoes and had one of those quilted Chanel handbags that Vinnie had read about in a magazine—they cost around two thousand dollars.

She wondered how anybody could just casually plunk down two grand for a purse. It seemed insane . . . Richie had said it *might* be a knockoff, you never knew, but he doubted it.

Miz Designer never said a word to him, and he didn't speak much to her, either, except to extend the courtesy that was his job.

Vinnie munched on the crust of her pie and wondered why guys as nice as Nick gravitated toward snotty women.

She'd seen it before in Independence, too: Lots of men seemed to put up with being treated badly by beautiful women. And if they were lucky enough to find a girl who was beautiful *and* nice, they got bored. Why was that?

Vinnie wondered if she should practice being snotty so she'd have packs of men barking at her heels. But she didn't *like* snotty people. And you at least had to like yourself in this bizarre world, or you just wouldn't survive.

So she ate another forkful of chocolate cream pie and decided she'd have to forgo the packs of men.

Naturally, that called forth Murphy's Law in the form of a middle-aged gentleman who asked if she was eating alone.

Uh-oh. "I'm uh, waiting for a friend," Vinnie told him.

"Can I keep you company until she gets here?" He jingled the change in his pockets and leered at her.

"Um . . . no." It was a bald answer, but she knew she'd never get rid of him if she let him sit down. And while she hated being mean to people, you couldn't encourage random men when they annoyed you. ". . . I'm um, sick," she added, by way of apology. "Very contagious. Walking pneumonia."

He backed away with a two-fingered salute. "Feel better soon."

"Yeah." She hoped this wasn't going to happen all night.

Chapter 9

"So you see, the dog's evil!" said Nick to Vinnie the next morning over cups of cappuccino. He seemed to have forgotten the debacle with his architectural model.

Vinnie tried not to laugh just as hard as she tried not to yawn in his face. She failed at both endeavors. Her mouth twisted of its own accord into a giant shoulder-shaking yawn.

"She's not evil. She's just probably never been left alone, and she needs to be crate-trained."

Nick looked puzzled, then hopeful. "You mean I can have her boarded up in a plywood box and shipped to Timbuktu?"

"No. But you can send me out to buy a dog cage—a crate—and when you leave, you just put her inside. That way she doesn't have access to plants, shoes, dictionaries"—Vinnie glanced at the cabinet doors and winced—"or anything else. You give her a toy or a bone while she's in there, and she learns to chew on it instead."

"A doggie jail," Nick murmured. "Now why didn't I think of that?"

Vinnie laughed, and Daffodil wagged her stub and rubbed her nose on Vinnie's jeans.

Nick glared down at the dog. "Yes, sweetheart. Enjoy your day of freedom, because tonight you're going directly to jail. You're not passing 'Go' and you're certainly not collecting two hundred dollars."

Daffodil stopped wagging her tail and assumed a dubious expression.

Vinnie told herself to focus on Daffodil, and not on how good he looked or how good he smelled. He was wearing a different aftershave, which reminded her of open water and sunshine and expensive yachts.

The two ends of his tie dangled down his chest, and his shirt collar was open two buttons, where some curly golden ginger hairs peeked out. *Unnnh!*

She really needed to get a grip on herself. To hide a sudden blush, she bent down and scratched Daffodil's head, then kissed her nose.

When the heat in her cheeks had faded a bit, she straightened—just in time to see Nick look quickly away from her chest.

That doesn't mean anything, silly. Men have magnets behind their eyeballs, causing them to swivel toward anything that features two bumps. They can't help it—they're programmed that way from birth.

She pretended not to notice, which was easy since another yawn overwhelmed her. And she told herself that his sexy new aftershave was almost certainly a gift from his showpiece girlfriend, who almost certainly stayed over quite often.

"You feeling okay?" Nick asked, pretending not to notice *her* pretending not to notice.

"Yeah, why?"

"You just look tired."

Oh, gee, maybe that's because sitting upright on a hard plastic bench in a diner all night isn't restful. "Nah," she said. "I'm fine."

She wondered what on earth she was going to do that night. No telling what plans Sorrel had. Maybe she'd be having a naked séance and trying to contact the poor animal whose heart she had in the fridge.

Vinnie shuddered. She really didn't want to go back there to find out. And she didn't want to say anything to Sorrel, either, since the creepy chick would probably decide to raise tarantulas in Vinnie's underwear drawer for vengeance.

"You look like you're going to be sick," Nick told her.

She smiled wanly. *The concept of tarantulas in your underwear could do that to you.* "No, really. I'm fine. Just didn't sleep well last night."

Nick gave her a searching look. "Everything okay?"

When she nodded, he set down his cup, grabbed the two ends of his tie, and knotted it using the door of the microwave as a mirror.

His hands were long-fingered and deft—beautiful, with just a sprinkle of the same golden ginger hair behind the knuckles. How could a man's *hands* be so sexy? Geez, she hadn't even seen the parts of him that a woman would normally look at.

But one thing was for sure: Even if Nick possessed a well-disguised peg leg, she'd sure rather see *him* naked than Sorrel and her buddies.

Nick buttoned up his top button—a shame—and pulled the tie snug around his collar. Then he pulled out his wallet and removed a hundred-dollar bill.

"Will this cover the cost of a doggie jail?"

"I think so. And probably a little black-and-white-striped convict suit for her, too."

He grinned. "From what I saw, the damned beast doesn't need any more clothes. Throw her in jail in her birthday fur."

Vinnie put a hand to her heart. "Oh, the cruelty!"

"Uh-huh. That's me, Head Mean Guy What's in Charge. I must have had a rare attack of mercy last night, since I didn't throw her live into the oven."

"Oh, I hear dog is overrated as a dish," Vinnie told him.

He pretended surprise. "Even with chipotle sauce?"

Vinnie had no idea what a chipotle was, but she nodded. "Yeah. Gets tough and chewy. Stick to steak—you'll be happier."

"All right, if you insist." Nick swept up his briefcase and a roll of blueprints. "My housekeeper, Mrs. Hegel, will be coming today. She'll do some cooking and cleaning. I should warn you that she's not at all excited about the dog."

Vinnie watched regretfully as Nick's all-too-fine buns retreated and disappeared beyond his front door. Then she drank another cappuccino and looked at Daffodil, who was eyeing the homemade sticky bun left untouched on Vinnie's plate.

"Oh, no. You're definitely not getting my sticky bun. You can have a rawhide chew, though." Vinnie dug one out of her backpack and yawned again. "Can you imagine that Nick has a cook? Well, a housekeeper who cooks. I hear she's not going to like you much."

That turned out to be an understatement, and all Vinnie's hopes of being able to take it easy and watch soaps and HGTV were dashed. Mrs. Hegel marched into Nick's apartment at precisely 8:59 A.M., unfolded a full apron from her squat black leather purse, and flapped it at Daffodil before the dog got close.

"Please to remove ze canine from ze kitchen," she said in crisp, Teutonic tones. When Daffodil just blinked and crept forward, she extended a long bony index finger, and screeched, "OUT!"

Vinnie said mildly, "I'll get her leash," and the Frau nodded and headed for the refrigerator with a pen and a notepad.

As Vinnie returned with the extend-a-leash, she heard another high-pitched screech, and then sputtering in what must have been German.

Daffodil gave a yelp and her back legs gave way on the slippery parquet floor as she tried to scramble out of the kitchen.

The Frau brandished a wooden cooking spoon, a martial light in her eye.

"Did she, um, sniff you?"

"Yah, the nasty beast!"

"It's just her way of sorta shaking hands," said Vinnie.

"It was not in mein *hand* zat she vas interested," the Frau said, in outraged tones.

"Yes, well, I'm trying to get her to read Amy Vanderbilt, but she has a short attention span."

The Frau simply shot her a black stare.

"Right. We were just going for a walk. Nice to meet you." Vinnie returned her glare with a perfunctory smile and clipped the leash onto Daffodil's choke chain.

It didn't look as if they were going to get a nap, seeing as how Frau Hegel had commandeered the penthouse. Vinnie wondered if she'd get picked up on vagrancy charges for napping on a park bench under a newspaper. It sure was tempting to risk it; but first, they'd locate a crate for Daffodil.

Nick returned at 9:30 P.M. to a dark apartment. This was unusual: Vinnie usually left on some lights. He flipped the hallway switches, took a couple of steps inside, and stopped dead.

There in the center of his living room was a large doggy cage, complete with snoozing canine inside. And in front of the open door was a motionless Vinnie, curled into a fetal position.

His first panicked thought was that she'd fainted or was hurt, and he ran over to her, dropping to his knees.

But she was breathing normally, if heavily, and he realized that she was asleep. By the looks of it, she'd been out for at least a couple of hours.

Next to her, Daffodil blinked, yawned, and swiped a paw over one eye, as if to complain about the sudden onslaught of light.

"Pardon me, Your Highness," he said, "but I was worried about your friend, here."

Vinnie continued to sleep, and he took the opportunity to study her. Her lashes brushed dark circles under her eyes, but other than that her skin was lovely and creamy, with a natural healthy pink around her cheeks.

He wanted badly to touch her, which was irrational. One didn't fondle one's employees, even if they happened to be passed out on one's rug.

It wasn't professional, and it wasn't gentlemanly. He just knew that, even though he'd never actually found an employee passed out on his rug. Not once.

Aunt Edna had—but the passing out had been due to a bottle, and she hadn't wanted to fondle the employee at all. She'd rather have kicked him. Nick wasn't entirely sure she hadn't.

He stared at the sleeping girl on his rug and found himself without the heart or the desire to wake her up, even if she *was* sleeping on the job. Or was she? Her hours had ended at six.

She looked so peaceful, and he didn't like the thought of her taking the subway home by herself at that hour. Of course, he could always put her in a cab, but why not let her sleep? She looked exhausted.

Nick slid one arm under her knees and eased the other under her shoulders. He lifted her easily and carried her to his bedroom, where he laid her on the mattress, removed her shoes, and tucked her under his summerweight down quilt.

Vinnie stirred slightly, rubbed her nose, and rolled onto her side. He brushed a strand of hair off her forehead, resisting the crazy urge to kiss her, and left the room, closing the door behind him.

Vinnie felt warm and cozy. She was lying on a heavenly mattress under a soft quilt, and everything smelled deliciously of Nick . . . the best smell in the world. Better than the air after a spring rain. Better than cinnamon buns hot out of the oven. Better than . . . hmmmm . . . she opened her eyes. Where was she?

She jolted upright, hands clutching the covers. She'd fallen asleep out there in the living room. And now she was in Nicholas Wright's *bed*. Aaaaack!

She began to breathe normally again as she realized she was fully clothed, and there was no sign of him. Nick wasn't reclining next to her, leering and smoking a cigarette.

Darn.

What? I did not mean that. I absolutely did not. Vinnie looked around, but couldn't see much because it was pitch-black outside, and the only illumination in the room crept in from the hallway, through the inch of space under the door. She slid out of bed and felt along the wall for a light switch. Bingo.

Nick's bedroom was spare and elegant like the rest of the apartment. It contained a simple blond wood platform bed, two nightstands, and a dresser. The wall opposite the bed featured a framed blueprint of a building site, a big boxy design on a square corner lot.

The design looked nothing like the models in his office. It seemed professional and competent and . . . and . . . average. She found herself wondering why Nick wanted to see this blueprint every night before falling asleep, and not his more interesting concepts.

She brought herself back to more immediate concerns. Like the fact that she had fallen asleep on the job, in Nick's house. Some employee she was! First she destroyed the man's property, and now she'd proven herself irresponsible. Vinnie smacked herself in the forehead. Please God Daffodil hadn't destroyed anything while she'd been snoring on her boss's rug.

Shame swept over her—Nick must have picked her up and stuck her in his bed! He had carried her—all 135 pounds of her—oh, how embarrassing. And he'd slid off her yucky gym shoes. She wondered if her feet smelled, and wanted to die. She sat on the end of his bed, wondering what to say to the man. Did she really have to walk past him to get out of here? Couldn't she just climb out a window? Where was Spider-Man when you needed him?

She tiptoed to the door, holding her shoes, and opened it a crack. Lights were on in the front of the apartment, meaning Nick was still awake, even though her watch told her it was two o'clock in the morning. The man had insomnia as bad as her own. Darn. It stood to reason that the one thing they'd have in common would be inconvenient.

She'd have to speak to him. Apologize. Convince him that she wasn't as bad a hire as she seemed, honest.

Vinnie slipped her running shoes onto her feet and tied the laces. Then she padded down the hallway. Nick was in his office, frowning at his computer. He'd pulled Daffodil's canopy bed next to the desk, and the dog lay on it in a canine stupor. She had to giggle at the contrast between the prissy pink satin bed and Nick's no-nonsense work space.

She bit the giggle in half when he looked up at her. "Sleep well?"

"I can explain."

He folded his arms and waited.

"I know it looks like I was sleeping on the job. But I actually didn't fall asleep until after I was supposed to be gone."

He raised an eyebrow.

"I was trying to get her used to the new crate. And she was making a ruckus every time I left and shut the door. I was worried that all your neighbors would figure out you had a dog in here."

He nodded.

"So I got her to lie down in there, and I lay down with her, outside the crate."

"And you fell asleep."

"Well, I never went home the night before . . ." His eyebrows went up again, and she realized how that sounded. *Oh, please, someone just shoot me.* "I know what you're thinking, and it's not like that at all. I'm not a big partier. I just have a really strange roommate, and I didn't want to be around her. So I sat up all night in a café."

"That sounds miserable."

"Yeah. It was." She paused, and when he didn't say anything, she asked, "So, you're not going to um, fire me?"

"Why would I do that?"

"You believe me?"

"Yes."

"Oh, thank God." She felt weak with relief.

"Vinnie, you seem to think I'm some kind of ogre. Why do you expect me to raise my voice to you or fire you for something ridiculous?"

She opened and closed her mouth. "I—uh. My dad was career military. He ran a pretty tight ship." She said nothing about William, who'd just liked to throw his weight around.

Nick looked at her for a long moment, during which he seemed to see a lot of things she wasn't telling him. He shut down his computer, got up, and stretched. "Well, you're not fired. But even if I did fire you, it's not like this job is any big deal. You'd find something else."

She stiffened. "This job IS a big deal. To me. I don't have a full college degree, and you've heard it said: It's a jungle out there."

"It's a jungle with a lot of jobs in it."

"Not jobs I'm smart enough to do . . ." She let her voice trail off. What was wrong with her? She was standing here telling her own employer she was stupid. *Good one, Vin.* To switch the focus from herself, she said, "Adam's the smart one."

Nick's brows knit. "You're plenty smart, Vinnie."

"Yeah, well." She gestured at the diplomas

framed in one corner of his office. "It's not like I have some fancy Ivy League education."

"And you think that means you're not bright?"

She shrugged.

"Well, it doesn't. Education has nothing to do with intelligence. It has to do with knowledge." Nick touched her arm, and she did her best to ignore the jolt of feminine electricity that shot through her at the gesture. "In fact, some of the most obtuse people I know are highly educated. They've memorized so much that they can no longer think straight."

Vinnie laughed and changed the subject. "So what are you doing up so late? Do you always work at 2 A.M.?"

"I'm often up at odd hours. In this case, I'm contributing a design for an auditorium to an open competition. And since I intend to win, it takes a lot of hours that I don't have during the day."

"What do you get if you win?"

"Recognition. Acclaim. Champagne. Probably a raise . . . and the chance to build the structure."

Those were all good things. So why did his eyes look so empty?

Chapter 10

Vinnie stared out the kitchen windows at Manhattan, while Nick poured her a Cherry Coke, eyeing the can dubiously. The city glittered against the night sky like a trove of urban treasure. "There are so many thousands of buildings out there," she said to him. "Do you have a favorite?"

"I have many favorites," he said. "I have favorites for each period of New York's architecture. It's evolved and changed so much over the centuries . . . Can you even imagine that at one time there were only a few teepees at the Southern tip of Manhattan?"

Vinnie shook her head. "No way."

"Yeah." Nick's eyes had lit up, and he gestured widely with his right hand, sweeping it across the window to encompass her view. "Believe it or not. Manhattan was known as Manna Hata to the Indians, or Island of the Hills."

"Hills?" Vinnie asked. "What hills?"

Nick laughed. "Well, there are a few. But the only original ones remain in Central Park," he explained. "The Dutch and English settlers eventually leveled most of the rest and used the dirt as landfill to extend Manhattan's shoreline."

"Really?"

Nick nodded. "Broadway used to be an Indian path, before Verrazano came. Bowling Green literally used to be used for bowling. The first city hall was actually a Dutch tavern!"

"No way." Vinnie laughed.

"Would I lie to you?"

Oh, probably.

"And Wall Street got its name because the Dutch erected a huge wall from the East River to the North River, thinking to fortify and protect their city of New Amsterdam from the British."

Nick had become even more animated as he spoke to her about the history of his city. He extended his hand to her. "Want to take a midnight architectural tour?"

"You're crazy, Nick."

But his expression was like a little boy's. "So? There's no law against being a little nuts. Come on."

"But—it's dark out there!"

"Manhattan's never truly dark. You'll be able to see clearly. And at this hour, there won't be much traffic." He tugged at her hand.

She couldn't resist his infectious enthusiasm. "Okay . . ."

"We'll grab a cab. First stop, the Dyckman House

at 204th and Broadway. The only eighteenth-century farmhouse still standing in all of Manhattan . . ."

Once they'd crated Daffodil and gotten outside, Nick got them a cab within seconds, and was soon regaling her with more anecdotes.

Vinnie tried to imagine New York teeming with cattle and goats and chickens, instead of stockbrokers, lawyers, and retailers, but found it almost inconceivable—just as inconceivable as being out on a sort of date with Nicholas Wright, a breeze blowing through her hair and her knee touching his in the cab. She thought about moving it away, but didn't. While the cab smelled of musty vinyl and grease and falafels, Nick's subtle aftershave overrode it, tantalizing her and making it extremely difficult not to bury her nose in his neck. Darn the man! Couldn't he smell of mothballs, or menthol or stale cigarette smoke? No—he had to expel crazy-making pheromones.

She tried to ignore them and focus on his explanation of what a gambrel roof was, and how the one on the Dyckman House was high-shouldered. Shoulders? Yes, his were spectacular . . .

Flared eaves? Right. She could feel her own eaves flaring, reaching out to this man whom she couldn't have. Fieldstone and gables . . . whatever those were. Aw, man. She could gable at this guy all night long. Or was that goggle? Nick knew an entire vocabulary of architecture terms that she didn't come close to understanding . . . but it was still a pleasure to hear him talk about the city that was his home.

They went to St. Paul's Chapel next, which Nick

said was a great example of Wren-Gibbs architecture, built in the style of Christopher Wren, some guy in England who had built tons of churches.

"St. Paul's is the only pre-Revolutionary building still in regular use today," Nick told Vinnie, as she stared up at its temple-front portico and massive Ionic columns. Though she figured that the little mostly naked guy up in the pediment's sculpture niche was made of stone, she shivered as she thought of him weathering New York's winters with no clothes on.

"Are you cold?" Nick asked.

She shook her head and pointed upward. "No, but he must be."

Nick laughed and slung an arm around her, to her surprise. "Vinnie, your point of view is always refreshing."

She grinned. "Thanks—I think."

"That's St. Paul, with his sword, book, and beard."

Nick next directed the cabbie to some tavern on Pearl Street that he told her was an example of Georgian architecture, also called the Colonial style. It looked very normal to Vinnie, who couldn't help but notice the low balustrade around the roof, surrounding a perfect spot for kissing hot men in the moonlight.

Nick did not seem to be following her train of thought, which was a pity. He was already moving on in history to the Stamp Act, the Townshend Acts, and the American Revolution.

Vinnie listened as he detailed how the Georgian style gave way to the more severe American Federal style, which rejected all things English and extended from the 1760s to the 1830s.

A great example of the Federal style, Nick explained, was City Hall. "George Washington was inaugurated at the original building (now destroyed) in 1789 as the first president of the United States."

Having forgotten all of her high school history, Vinnie was surprised to hear this. "I would have thought Washington was inaugurated in, well, Washington," she said.

"Nope. The capital was moved there much later. Anyway, our current City Hall was conceived and built by the architects Mangin and McComb, and completed in 1811. But it suffered lots of damage over the years and had to be encased in new stone in the 1950s—a huge, painstaking project."

Nick directed them down Vandam Street, where they looked at the Federal row houses, and then over to the countinghouses on Schermerhorn Row, along the south side of Fulton Street. These were four-story brick buildings built for commercial purposes, now part of the South Street Seaport Historic District.

From there they headed in the cab to the Federal Hall National Memorial, and to the row houses at Washington Square North. Nick told her about the Greek Revival style, and Americans' fascination with all things Greek. "We considered ourselves the New Athens, with our democratic states . . ."

"How do you remember all this?" Vinnie asked him, amazed.

"Am I being a geek?" Nick laughed.

"No, not at all—I'm just impressed. You obviously love what you do."

He nodded.

"But your own models—they don't seem to reference history at all," she said. "They're like nothing I've ever seen . . . so modern."

Nick fell silent. "Yeah." He said the word abruptly. "But there aren't too many clients out there with a taste for the cutting edge of modern."

He leaned forward and asked the cabbie to take them to Eleventh and Broadway, where he pointed out a building, now apartments, which was one of New York's first "cast-iron palazzos."

When Vinnie blinked, Nick explained that with the new cast-iron technology of the mid-1800s, the weight of the architecture could be supported by the metal frame of the building, rather than load-bearing walls.

"The roots of the modern skyscraper are here," he said. "But at this point in time, architects still hid the armature of the building with decorative masonry. Soon they'd develop the passenger elevator, another characteristic of the modern skyscraper."

He paused, searching her face. "I'm just hitting the highlights for you, Vinnie—there are all kinds of buildings in this city we could look at."

She nodded.

"Am I boring you?" he asked.

"No, not at all." And it was true—though she didn't understand all of his terminology, she responded to his enthusiasm and the entertaining anecdotes he told interspersed with the wealth of information.

"For the first skyscrapers, you've got to look to Chicago, but there is one early example here in New York by Louis Sullivan—on Bleeker Street.

"Sullivan was Frank Lloyd Wright's teacher . . . look how he's opening up the building, revealing its structure, even though the metal is still surrounded by Art Nouveau terra-cotta . . . but Lever House, designed by the firm of Skidmore, Owings, and Merrill, is the first modern skyscraper in New York, a monumental glass box. Recently it was renovated by Philip Johnson, a huge name in architecture."

Vinnie smothered an escaped yawn as they pulled up to Lever House, which rose eerily into the black sky, a monumental, fenestrated glass "L."

"Last one for tonight, I promise," Nick murmured beside her. "You're finally getting sleepy."

"I'm sorry," Vinnie said. "It's not the tour, I promise."

"Then it must be the company," he teased.

"No—"

He looked at his watch. "It's only 4:15 A.M.—I can't imagine why you're fading on me. So I'll make this brief: This was designed as the one skyscraper in Manhattan that you could actually walk *under*. And it would never be approved today, because the architect only utilized 25 percent of the commercial airspace where the tower is. It's remarkable: that clean empty space. A lot of wicked-expensive air."

Vinnie had to laugh at the concept of even air being expensive in Manhattan, but it was true. Everything was expensive on a tiny island packed with eight million people. She still couldn't get over what a simple cup of coffee cost there.

Nick gazed down at her, an unreadable expression in his eyes. "You've got lamplight dancing on your nose," he said.

Her nose was shiny, and that was his polite way of telling her. Vinnie wished she had a compact with her, and hid the offending schnoz with her hand.

Nick covered it with his own, wrapping his warm fingers around hers and pulling down. "Don't hide it," he murmured. "It's very cute. And the light bounces from there into your eyelashes."

"Um," said Vinnie.

"And that," he continued, "illuminates your eyes to the color of warm cognac by a fire . . ."

If anyone else had said these things to her, she would have laughed.

". . . and that's intoxicating," Nick finished, his mouth very close to her own.

How could she have yawned only minutes ago? Her blood hummed with awareness, her skin prickled, and every nerve ending in her body clamored for the brush of Nick's lips against hers.

Sleep? Oh, no, she didn't think so.

She drank in the smell of him—the leather of his jacket, the naughty nautical essence of his aftershave, the musky nuances of his skin. His lips touched hers at last, and he lost no hesitation in claiming her mouth.

Nick's kiss spoke volumes about him: suave on the surface, practiced, even a little facile—but underneath dwelled strong, wild currents that caught her fast in a violent undertow and swept her out into the deep.

The man who kissed her, that night in the yellow cab, was not a man who built boxes or coldly designed for money and acclaim. The Nick who kissed her exulted in the organic, embraced the amorphic, worshipped curves. She knew that from his touch alone.

Chapter 11

Though the most primitive urges had Nick dying to take her right there in the cab, somehow the squeaking of the brakes, the blue turban of their driver, and the unwavering glare of the lighted fare box brought him to reality. He raised his head from Vinnie's, and she fell back against the seat, looking shell-shocked.

Damn, did he ever want her naked and willing and under him, but not in a taxi at Sixty-third and Lexington.

They both stared out opposite windows of the cab until they arrived at Nick's building, where Vinnie murmured something weak about going home.

"Sweetheart, it's almost five o'clock in the morning. You'd be turning around to come back here in a couple of hours."

She admitted the truth of this, but obviously had reservations.

And so, come to think of it, did he. He couldn't

be climbing on the dog-sitter, for Pete's sake. She was a simple country girl who'd never been exposed to a lifestyle like his. They had nothing in common, and a sexual liaison between them could only end in disaster and misunderstanding.

Besides, he'd break her big heart, once she found out he didn't have one; that he specialized in emotional distance. For Christ's sake, he couldn't even tolerate affection from a *dog*. What did he have to give a normal woman?

Dana Dvorak was perfect for him.

Yet he held out a hand to Vinnie. "Come on. I promise we won't finish what we just started. It was a bad idea . . . a product of moonlight over Manhattan. We'll make coffee. Read the paper. I'll go to work. You'll walk the dog. Deal?"

After a moment's hesitation, she put her hand in his. "Deal."

Vinnie marveled at the instant personality change she witnessed in Nick. Geez, even superheroes needed a phone booth to pull it off. But he just became someone else the moment he stepped out of a yellow cab. The box-man was back, his feet planted on concrete, standing in the shadow of the huge vertical cube behind him. She followed him into it, not knowing quite what to think—except that she was crazy for kissing her boss.

Another careless rich guy. What was she, stupid? Did she have to learn this lesson twice? Hadn't the first time been painful enough? William had actually laughed when she'd dreamily murmured something about getting married one day. *Laughed.*

Cinderella only married Prince Charming in the fairy tale. And he'd seen her all dressed up, first. Guys like the prince didn't run all over the country with a glass slipper after some country chick in faded denim.

While she lectured herself, Nick started the monster caffeine machine and disappeared quickly into his bedroom.

Vinnie stared for a long moment at his walls of books. Then, shaking herself out of her thoughts, she released Daffodil from her crate, clipped the leash onto her collar, and led the dog out the door and down the hall to the service elevator.

Rubbing her eyes, she yawned and scratched Miss D behind the ears when the car lurched and caused the dog's legs to tremble. They exited the elevator and trekked down the narrow hallway to the service door. They were almost there when a voice like Queen Elizabeth's called out, "Miss! Miss, whose dog is that?"

Oh, no. Vinnie froze, which meant that she now couldn't pretend she hadn't heard the lady. She turned reluctantly to find the woman thumping toward her with the aid of an ornamental cane. Her iron gray curls quivered in disapproval, and her lips cowered under harsh vertical lines.

"I am Agnes Blount, the president of the board of this building. I demand to know whose dog that is."

Vinnie never lied. But she had to protect her job for Adam's sake, and that meant protecting Nicholas so he could keep Daffodil. "Why, she's my dog. Sit, sweetie. Sit." It would never do for Daffodil to sniff Agnes Blount's privates. The thought made her shudder. If a mere dog was illegal, then one that displayed crude tendencies would send her right over the edge.

"Your dog." Agnes looked down her nose at Vinnie, taking in her no doubt wildly mussed hair, her rumpled, slept-in clothing, and her shabby running shoes. "And just who might you be?"

Vinnie thought fast before extending her hand and introducing herself. She chose a name she'd seen on a list outside the main door. "I'm Talley Hunter's cousin. Just visiting for a couple of days."

"I thought I knew all of Talley's cousins." Mrs. Blount frowned.

Vinnie met her gaze as evenly as possible. "Well, I'm a second cousin once removed. I'm visiting from Kansas."

"I see. Well, young lady, I hope you'll enjoy your stay in New York. But for future reference, we do not allow animals in the building, so you'll have to leave your dog at home."

"Oh, please don't blame Talley," said Vinnie quickly. "She didn't know I was bringing her."

Daffodil whined and strained toward the door. "It was great meeting you, Mrs. Blount. Have a nice day." Vinnie escaped thankfully out the door and headed across the street to Central Park, where Daffodil tried to pee and chase some ducks simultaneously. It didn't work well.

"I believe those ducks are laughing at you," Vinnie said to the dog. They stayed out a good ten minutes, just to make sure Agnes Blount wasn't lurking in the hallway when they went in again.

Upstairs, Nick hunched over a soup-bowl-sized

cup of cappuccino, wrapped in a white terry robe. She tried very hard not to look at the damp triangle of male chest inevitably exposed.

"Hey," she said to him, hiding her face in the cupboard that held his mugs. She chose one as big as his, needing fortification.

While she poured, she told him about the encounter with Mrs. Blount.

"Great," he said, rubbing his eyes. "Now she'll be questioning Talley about her cousin. And if she sees you again, the game is up."

"I could dye my hair and wear dark glasses," Vinnie kidded.

"Absolutely not. Your hair is beautiful." Nick stared at her, and the stare led to an uncomfortable silence. She knew they were both thinking about the kiss.

"Er," he started. "About what happened out there—I just want you to know that I didn't mean to make you uncomfortable."

"Oh. It's okay. And . . . thank you for letting me sleep, and for the tour. I learned a lot."

"It was fun to share some of the city with you."

"Yeah. And it's not like I wanted to go home, like I said."

"You didn't want to go home?" he prompted gently. "Oh, right. The strange roommate. Where is home, Vinnie?"

"Chinatown."

"What is it that causes you not to like your roommate?"

Vinnie took a gulp of cappuccino. "She's all right." She met his quizzical gaze. "Okay, so she's not all right. She's bizarre. And freakish. And when I walked in the other night she was sitting around nude with a bunch of other women, chanting over a dead animal heart in a dish."

Nick looked repulsed.

"So I kind of freaked, and that's why I spent the whole night before last sitting in a café. Which is why I was so tired yesterday and fell asleep on your rug."

"How did you find this roommate of yours?"

"Through a local paper."

Nick pushed a pad and a pen toward her. "Give me her full name and address. I'd like to get her checked out for you."

"Oh, that's not necessary." In the face of his unwavering stare, though, she wrote it down.

"Vinnie, I know you're not from around here, and I don't want to scare you, but there are some strange people in this city."

She nodded. "Yeah, I've noticed."

"In the future," Nick said, "if this weirdo makes you feel at all uncomfortable, you can come here. I don't want to think about you sitting up all night in a coffee shop."

Vinnie looked down into her cup. Ridiculous to feel the sudden sting of tears, but she'd felt panicky and on edge ever since she'd arrived in this city. His unexpected kindness disarmed her.

"Okay?"

She nodded.

"And I won't . . . bother you, if you know what I mean."

A small laugh escaped her. *You won't? That's too bad.* "I know what you mean."

Nick shrugged. "I'm a red-blooded guy. I'm sharing a cab in the moonlight with a hot woman—well, what can I say? Instinct kicks in, and my body goes on autopilot. Sorry."

Nick thought she was hot? Her nerves hummed at the idea. Her libido's tail wagged frantically, until she gave a sharp tug on its choke chain and told it not only to lie down, but to play dead.

Nick yawned. "I've got to get dressed. Help yourself to more coffee."

"Thanks." Vinnie dug the toothbrush out of her backpack and tried not to think about Nick naked as she walked to the powder room. What was wrong with her? Had her wholesome prairie roots sprouted leaves of perversion after less than two weeks in the city? She scrubbed furiously at her teeth. Maybe if she got them squeaky clean, her mind would follow suit.

A few hours later, Nick blinked in shock as he read the report faxed over from a local investigator. Vinnie was living with Single White Whacko, and SWW had a rap sheet as long as his arm. She'd been a ward of the state for several years before dropping out of high school. She'd been picked up on numerous charges, ranging from prostitution to shoplifting to possession of illegal substances. Even more disturbing were charges of animal cruelty to first a parakeet and then a cat.

Nick was by no means Vinnie's keeper, and he

hadn't known her very long, but he wanted her *outta there*, so to speak. This Sorrel woman was a criminal and a creep.

He drummed his fingers on his desk and thought about things. He had three guest bedrooms and a dog who got lonely and destructive at night. He had a business and social calendar that often kept him away from home eighteen hours out of the twenty-four.

Why not give Vinnie a break and a room until she found a normal person with whom to share an apartment? Someone who wasn't unpredictable, scary, and potentially dangerous?

He wasn't really under the illusion that he was being kind. The bottom line: It was no skin off his back—he'd hardly see her, and the damned dog would be kept under control.

Chapter 12

Adam Hart hunched his shoulders and tried his best to become invisible as he walked down the east hall of Gotham-Young Science Academy. He wished that, like Harry Potter, he had a cloak to help him in his quest for invisibility, and perhaps even a Nimbus 2000 so he could get away from the likes of Joey Balthus and his band of butt-heads.

Balthus and the Butt-Heads had been badgering him since day two of the semester, the first day he'd been on his own and not flanked by Vinnie or a smiling school official.

Balthus was a muscle-bound kid whose voice had already deepened, just like his adolescent mean streak. Because he was so big, he naturally commanded respect. Unfortunately he also commanded other boys' pocket money, CDs, care packages, and anything else he felt he should have.

Balthus's Band of Butt-Heads consisted of boys who had let him take their belongings and harass them until he'd decided they'd been wormy enough to be his friends. Then, having paid their dues, they in turn could help him torture other boys.

As the new kid, Adam pretty much wore a "Kick-Me" sign on his back. As the new kid with glasses, a squeaky voice, and none of the right clothes or cool gadgets, he was an especially entertaining target.

Adam breathed a sigh of relief as he got to his locker unmolested and dialed the correct sequence on his combination lock. He popped it off and opened the door—jumping back with an unmanly screech as a huge toad leaped out at him.

Shouts of laughter erupted behind him as Balthus and the Butt-Heads enjoyed their joke.

Adam swallowed his heart, which had raced into his throat, and fought the twin demons of helpless rage and humiliation.

He picked up the toad, which was obviously as startled and frightened as he'd been, and stroked its cold, clammy head with a skinny forefinger.

He looked with disgust at the weekend's worth of by-products it had left on his social studies book. "Well, you couldn't help it, could you, if some jerk stuck you in there on Friday?"

The toad's throat swelled in indignation, and his eyes bugged out.

"I feel the same way," Adam told it.

"Look at Hart-the-Fart!" Balthus yelled to the rest of the Butt-Heads. "He's making friends with the ugly-ass toad!"

"Well, nobody else'll talk to him," said a kid Adam thought of as Balthus's head sidekick. "He's too lame."

"Go back to Oz, Hart-the-Fart," said Balthus.

"Maybe Dorothy'll let you wear her ruby red slippers. And her panties, too." He guffawed at his own wittiness.

Adam unzipped a pocket of his backpack and carefully put the toad inside, leaving a two-inch gap in the zipper so the creature could breathe.

Then he turned to Balthus. "You know what you are?"

"No, Hart-the-Fart, what am I?"

Adam swallowed. "You're nothing but a big, ugly, smelly a-a-anus." He almost didn't have the guts to say the last word, and he knew he was going to pay for it with a few teeth and who knew what else, but he was too angry to care. He was mad for himself, but he was even madder that the jerks had tortured the toad all weekend just to get at him.

"*What* did you call me, Hart?" Balthus advanced upon him, while the Butt-Heads whistled and shook their heads.

Adam's knees shook, and his glasses slid down his nose from the sweat of sheer terror, but he stuck his chin up. "You heard me."

Then Balthus's fist connected with his right eye, knocking off his glasses—and then his nauseous stomach. He doubled over in pain. His only satisfaction was puking on the bully's brand-new Air Jordans when Joey kicked him in the ribs. He continued to be sick in the principal's office.

Vinnie put Daffodil in her crate with a brief apology and rushed to Gotham-Young as soon as she finished speaking with the principal.

She ran the ten blocks from Nick's to the school,

hardly able to bear the thought of Adam hurt, with a black eye and a broken rib—or of Adam humiliated, because he'd thrown up in front of a bunch of people—or of Adam being in any way psychologically injured because of some bully.

She wasn't a violent person, and she couldn't form even a blurry visual picture of the bully in question, but she wanted to smack him, scream at him, shake him until his teeth rattled.

At present, she didn't feel rational; just ran on full maternal instinct. She was an angry female bear rushing to protect her cub.

"I'm here for Adam Hart," she said curtly to the administrative assistant at the school's front office.

"Oh, yes, Mrs. Hart," the woman said, her tone sympathetic. "Will you have a seat while I buzz Mr. Anglin?"

Vinnie didn't care about the woman's assumption that she was Adam's mother, and she didn't care about Mr. Anglin, either. "I just want to see Adam, right away."

"One moment." The woman buzzed the principal. "Mrs. Hart to see you. Yes, I'll do that." She stood up. "Right this way, Mrs. Hart."

She showed Vinnie into an office full of people, whom she completely ignored until she'd hugged Adam and inspected his bruised rib, his swollen lip, and his black eye. He seemed glad to see her at first, then embarrassed.

"I'm okay," he said in gruff tones. But his voice cracked on the second syllable of "okay," and it broke her heart.

She turned to the other people in the room: the

principal, whom she'd met when she brought
Adam the first day, a square, heavyset boy with
blond hair, a snub nose, and an expensive blue
blazer, and, finally, a man who looked just like the
boy and a woman who kept looking at her watch.

The bully's parents were impeccably turned out,
and Vinnie regretted not taking the time to change.
She could see that her jeans and running shoes impressed neither Mr. and Mrs. Bully nor Principal
Anglin.

Instead of embarrassing her, however, their rude
once-over made her angry. How dare they, when
their son had physically attacked Adam?

So instead of sitting down and folding her hands
demurely and waiting for an explanation, she
spoke first. "I left Adam here confident that he was
in good hands. I was obviously mistaken."

"Miss Hart—" began Anglin.

"Madam," said the snotty woman, "your son in-
sulted mine, and he responded in a manner common to boys of this age."

Vinnie gasped. "Excuse me? Are you saying that
you find it acceptable that he assaulted Adam?"

"Ladies—" Anglin began.

"I'm merely saying that Joey was provoked."

"Martha, quiet," instructed the father.

The mother glared at him.

"He put a toad in my locker!" Adam said. "The
poor thing was in there all weekend. He did it to
scare me, and then they made fun of me—"

"The little maggot called me an anus!" said the
square boy named Joey. "*Nobody* calls me an anus."

Vinnie would have laughed at his outraged

expression—under any other circumstances.

Finally, Anglin raised his voice enough to break in. "All right, that's enough. The long and the short of this situation is that both boys exhibited hostile behavior toward each other."

Anglin turned to the boys. "Now is your chance to tell us why, and to promise that it won't happen again. Adam, you begin."

"Why does *he* get to talk first?" Joey complained. "*His* grandfather didn't donate a wing of the school."

Oh, boy. This is not a good sign. Vinnie's nostrils flared, but she kept her mouth clamped shut.

Adam folded his skinny arms across his narrow chest. "Joey is mean. He and his buddies—"

"Never mind the others," said Anglin. "We're only here to talk about you and Joey."

"Okay. Joey is mean, and he hates me because I'm the new kid. He took my jar of quarters from my room—"

"Do you have any proof of that, young man?" The father—old block—spoke up for his chip.

"Well, it's *gone*, sir, and I heard him laughing about it later, and he and all his friends had candy bars."

"My son has plenty of money. He doesn't need to steal."

"Please let him finish!" said Vinnie.

Adam tried. "He plays mean jokes on me, like the toad in my locker, and he crushed my Intergalactic Eiffel Tower—"

"Speaking of the toad," interrupted Anglin, with a severe look at Adam.

He assumed an even more miserable expression, but slid out of his chair and got his backpack, which he unzipped. Out of it he brought a monstrous toad that it took him both hands to hold. He brought it over to Vinnie.

"I know you'll take care of him," he said. "He's gotta be hungry and thirsty. Look him up in the *World Book Encyclopedia* and find out what he eats, okay? Probably flies and slugs and stuff."

Vinnie swallowed. She looked at the toad.

It looked back at her.

She looked at Adam.

He looked back at her.

She looked at the rest of the room, and they looked back at her, too—the smug adults who were collectively letting down her little brother. She was darned if she'd join them. "I'll keep him for you, Adam," she promised.

He beamed. "Thanks."

There was nothing for it but to take the cold, clammy, nasty critter—and it weighed a ton!— from Adam and . . . and do *something* with it. Vinnie reached down for her own backpack, which was just like Adam's blue one, only hers was dark green. She unzipped the large side pocket and gently stuck the toad in it, keeping her hand over him until she had the zipper mostly closed.

"Make sure you leave him an air hole," Adam reminded her.

She nodded. Her backpack hopped a couple of times, then quivered before it went still.

Snooty Mrs. Balthus had drawn her feet up *very* close to her chair, and Vinnie could see the underside of her nose reflected in the little gold plates that held the leather bows on her shoes. The nostrils were pinched in horror.

Mr. Balthus was staring at Vinnie's chest.

She pulled her jean jacket closed and glared at him.

Anglin twiddled his thumbs and looked bland.

"Adam, go ahead and finish," she told him. "Why did you and Joey get into the fight?"

"I never even hit him!"

"You *puked* on me, Loser." Joey's face twisted in disgust.

"Joey, stop calling Adam names," instructed Anglin.

"He's the one who called me an—"

"Quiet, please."

The kid returned to sulking.

"Adam?"

"He put the toad in my locker, and it jumped out at me when I opened it. I could tell it was scared, so I tried to calm it down. Then they made fun of me for talking to it, and I called Joey an anus."

"A big, ugly, smelly one."

"Yeah, that. And so he punched me in the stomach, and in the eye, and kicked me in the ribs. I did puke on him, but it's not like I meant to."

Anglin shot Joey a severe look. "Do you know that violence is unacceptable and against the rules here at Gotham-Young?"

"I didn't even hit him that hard," Joey muttered.

"Did you hear me?"

"Yes, sir."

"Then repeat it."

Joey sighed heavily. "Violence is unacceptable and is against the rules here at Gotham-Young."

"Normally I would be forced to suspend you, young man. But since . . ."

Vinnie's eyes narrowed. *Since your grandfather donated a whole wing of the school . . .*

". . . this is a first-time offense . . ."

Adam's eyes widened at the whopper.

". . . both of you boys will be put on probation and given a task to perform. Adam"—he turned to the boy—"do you understand that it is never appropriate to call a classmate names?"

"But—"

"Do you understand that?"

"Yes, sir."

"Then repeat it."

"It is never appropriate to call a classmate names."

"Both of you: Remember the statements you have just made, for you will each be writing them a hundred times on your homeroom blackboards."

The boys groaned.

"That will be all. Please apologize to one another, shake hands, then you are excused to go back to class."

Adam and Joey looked as if they would rather eat live cockroaches than apologize or shake hands, but they did so anyway.

Vinnie said, "Adam, I'll call you later to check on you."

Her little brother hunched a shoulder at her.

Her heart squeezed again at the sight of him so

alone, in such a hostile environment. Was she doing the best thing for him by leaving him there?

Back in Chinatown, Vinnie walked past the corner Dumpster and the dry cleaners and the Chinese grocery store. She went past all the little stalls hawking Oriental merchandise, from slippers to scarves to mugs to embroidered handbags and colorful paper dragons. She went past the restaurant that kept all of its menu items swimming in aquariums for passersby to lock eyeballs with.

She'd never get over her first encounter with live shrimp. They were horrid, beady-eyed, multilegged critters, pale as death—and there were hundreds upon hundreds of them in a single tank.

They were like something out of a Far Side cartoon, except they had none of Gary Larson's appeal. Vinnie came to the conclusion fast that she wouldn't be eating shrimp for a while. Eeeuuuuww.

Finally, she arrived at the pet supply store on the fringes of Chinatown. The toad was heavy in her backpack, and she marveled again how it could weigh quite as much as it did.

She went in and approached the counter. "Excuse me," she said to the man behind it, "but I need to know what a large toad enjoys for meals."

She unzipped the pocket of her backpack enough to show him the toad's head. It, of course, tried to make a leap for freedom, but she blocked its escape route. Why, she didn't know. She'd be all too glad to have the thing vamoose. But she couldn't do that to Adam.

"Huh." The man scratched at his scraggly beard.

"That guy'll eat slugs, or mealworms, or blood-worms."

Vinnie probably looked as thrilled as she felt. "I see. Well. Do they come in a box, like cereal, or what?"

The guy shook his head at her and went to a large nasty aquarium. He stuck in a beefy hand and retracted it full of slimy gray insects, which he dropped into a plastic bag.

Vinnie felt faint.

"Here's your slugs," he said, tying a knot in the bag and plunking it down on the counter. "And I'll getcha some mealworms."

"Th-thanks." She swallowed and tried not to look at the bag. *The things one would do for family . . .*

He came back with the worms tied in another bag.

"Um. I guess I also need some kind of . . . house . . . for this toad. A house he can't get out of."

"Aquarium," he said succinctly. "Small. Screen top. Nice bowla water in there for 'im. Be happy as a clam."

Great. All she needed was to spend more of her money on this animal. But thirty-eight dollars later, she was equipped to be a toad-owner.

She took the toad back to Nick's until it was time to leave for the day. She popped him in the aquarium with a piece she'd broken off a bush, and used one of Nick's sterling silver spoons to drop a few slugs and worms in with him. Then she sterilized the spoon with boiling water and had a good laugh as Toad and Daffodil got acquainted.

"What should we call him, girl?" she asked the dog, who snorted and watched in fascination as the creature's neck expanded to an impossible diameter.

"He's showing off for you, isn't he?" She shook her head. "Typical male. We'll call him . . . Prince Charming." He'd remind her of what "dream" guys really were.

Adam wasn't crazy about the name when she talked to him a few hours later. "That's so *girly*."

"Well, what would you prefer? Robo-Toad? Teenage Mutant Ninja Toad?"

"Nah. I'll think of something. So did he eat?"

"Yes. I really didn't want to watch, but the bugs I gave him are gone."

"Aww, man. I woulda watched. I think it's cool."

Yeah, she thought, *but you think bodily functions are cool, too. It's an age and gender thing.*

"So how are you doing?"

"Fine. I have a lot of math homework. And a report to write. There's a ton of reading for English, too."

"Has that Joey kid said or done anything else?"

Silence.

"Adam?"

"No. Not really."

"What does 'not really' mean?"

"He said he was gonna get me."

Great. "Should I talk to Principal Anglin again?"

"No. It's just talk. I think."

His voice sounded small, tinny. Alone and afraid. Vinnie's stomach twisted. "Well, you know I'm here. Keep me updated, okay?"

"Yep. Well, I should go now. Like I said, I have a lot of work."

"All right. I love you."

"Yeah. Bye."

She thought about him for a long time that night, and what it must be like to be in his twelve-year-old shoes. She thought about him until Sorrel freaked her out again, and she slept again—or tried to—with a chair wedged under her doorknob. She just couldn't face another night in the café, and despite Nick's kindness, she didn't want to go knocking on his door.

Chapter 13

Nick looked serious when Vinnie came in for work the next morning. She was exhausted, having hardly slept at all. When she'd gone near the kitchen, Sorrel had sent her a mocking glance and continued to cook something foul on the tiny stove in their apartment kitchen.

When she went out to change one bizarre CD for another equally demented one, Vinnie dashed in to get one of her Cherry Cokes out of the fridge.

Whatever was in that pot sure smelled horrible. Fearful but yet fascinated, she swung her gaze to the pot. A wooden spoon handle stuck out of it, and it seemed to beckon her closer. She shrank back when she saw the contents: large insect shells.

Sorrel was simmering dead bugs on their stove.

Vinnie clutched her Cherry Coke and backed up step by step until she bumped into Sorrel, returning from the living room.

She recoiled. Then mutely, Vinnie pointed at the stove.

Sorrel shrugged. "Cicada shells. It's an old Chinese medical remedy."

Vinnie didn't ask for what. She'd met plenty of very nice, polite, and downright wonderful Chinese, and none of them had roasted dogs or boiled insect shells in their kitchens.

She flashed Sorrel a strained smile, and fled to her bedroom, trying not to wonder if her roommate had collected or purchased the cricket-things alive. Maybe she'd visited the same pet store Vinnie had. Maybe . . .

Just to reassure herself, she walked to her poor excuse for a dresser and opened the top drawer. Nope. No tarantulas or crickets in there, thank God.

But she didn't want to think about what mysterious illness or disease Sorrel might be trying to cure.

Vinnie sterilized her toothbrush in rubbing alcohol before using it that night, and made sure no part of her touched the toilet. She wore rubber thongs into the shower in the morning, and didn't touch Sorrel's grainy green soap or her weird homemade shampoo.

It was a relief to see Nick's nice, normal face—none of it pierced—that next morning. But he certainly did look serious.

"Vinnie, we need to talk."

Oh, Geez, no. He's going to fire me. What did I do? "Talk?" she said brightly. "About what?"

Somebody heard Daffodil. Or Mrs. Blount talked to Talley Hunter and discovered she doesn't have any second cousins visiting from Kansas.

"Yes." Nick slid a fax across the black granite kitchen island. "About your roommate."

"Why? You found something out?"

Vinnie decided not to tell him about the crickets. It made her sick to even think about it, really.

"Yeah, you could say I found something out. Read that. Sorrel Slater's got a criminal history, and it indicates that she's not a good person."

Vinnie read the fax in silence. Then she got up and poured herself some cappuccino.

"Nice, huh?"

She nodded. "And I apparently owe you three hundred dollars for that information."

"What? No you don't."

"Yes, Nick, I do. This invoice is marked 'paid,' and I sure didn't pay it." Vinnie closed her eyes. And she had to find someplace else to live. That was clear.

"Look, Vinnie, I did this as a favor to you. Don't worry about the money."

Where she came from, three hundred dollars wasn't a favor. It was a debt.

But Nick went on. "I actually have a proposition to make."

Oh, great. Now he was going to proposition her?

"I have a lot of room here," he said. "I'm never home. And I have a dog that obviously needs attention around the clock. I also have a nosy downstairs neighbor who will most definitely notice if Daffodil turns cartwheels in that cage every night, or howls the blues at the moon. We know she's capable of both."

Huh-uh, Vinnie thought. *He is not about to say what I think he's about to say.*

"You have an unacceptable living situation. You also have a need to save as much as possible for your brother's tuition. So why don't you take one of my guest rooms for a while, at least until you find a decent roommate?"

Wow. He said it. Vinnie stared at him. "Me, move in here?"

"Exactly."

She shook her head. On the one hand, it was the answer to her prayers. It was a beautiful place, she loved the dog, and she loathed Sorrel.

But on the other hand . . . it was an incredibly bad idea. Nick was her employer. She was on shaky ground already, being attracted to him. And she had to think about Adam. She couldn't jeopardize the job, and she also couldn't see how to explain to him that she was living with some guy.

She shook her head again. "Thank you, but I couldn't do that."

"Why not?" Nick's voice held a note of persistence, a note, truth be told, of *in*sistence.

What would Mama say? Even she wasn't that sheltered. She would know that Vinnie couldn't afford an address on Fifth Avenue in New York. She'd probably assume the worst.

Vinnie could just see them, home at Christmastime, talking to Al at the hardware store or Letty at the diner.

"Yeah, I'm living with this gorgeous guy on Fifth Avenue, but we're not involved. I'm just there to take care of his dog." Right. Al would fiddle with his watch, and Letty would snap her gum, and within two minutes it'd be all over town that Vinnie had set up as a floozie in New York. That she was earning Adam's tuition the old-fashioned way—on her back.

"Nick, it's very sweet of you to make the offer, but I just couldn't."

"Sweet? This has nothing to do with sweet. This has to do with bald, utilitarian reasons: my convenience and your need to be safe and save money. We don't have to make it any more complicated than that."

She sighed. "It's very tempting, Nick. But what happens when you want privacy? Or when I have to explain the situation to Adam, or my mother? Or anyone else?" *And what's your snotty girlfriend going to say?*

"If I want privacy, I shut my door. Or I warn you ahead of time. No biggie. As for Adam or your mother—tell them the truth."

Vinnie said nothing, just stirred her cappuccino.

"Promise me you'll at least think about it, okay?" Nick got off the barstool and began the ritual of knotting his tie in front of the microwave.

"I'll think about it," Vinnie promised.

She didn't have to think all that hard.

"You can't break the lease," Sorrel hissed the next day, as Vinnie packed her things into cardboard cartons.

If they'd been in Kansas, Vinnie would have gone

out of her way to be polite and try not to hurt Sorrel's feelings. However, they were not, and Sorrel gave her the creeps like no other human being ever had. So all Vinnie said was, "Watch me."

"You'll forfeit your deposit, and I'll hold you to the remaining five months."

"We'll see about that." Vinnie grabbed a handful of T-shirts and panties and shook them, just in case. She still wondered where the bodies of the crickets had gone.

Nick shouldered past her hissing roommate with an icy "excuse me," and Vinnie sighed with relief that he was there, even if she did have a wad of panties in her hand. She stuffed them deep into the box.

She'd tried to tell Nick that it wasn't necessary for him to come, but he completely ignored her to whistle for a cab.

How did he do that, anyway? The two-fingered New York whistle mystified Vinnie. She'd tried it a couple of times to get Daffodil's attention, but just ended up with spit on her fingers.

Nick did it easily, with earsplitting results. And regardless of the fact that he was fitting her move in between two meetings, he was fitting it in.

He was being a gentleman, defying all the stories she'd heard about how rude New York men were. She'd been warned that they'd let doors slam in her face, and expect her to pick up dinner tabs, and that they said the "f" word in just about every sentence, as if it were punctuation.

Nick had done none of those things, although of course she'd never been out for a meal with him.

Somehow she knew, though, that he'd never lean back, rub a full belly, belch, and let her pick up the tab.

Anyhow—it was very comforting to have Nick giving Sorrel the evil eye while Sorrel gave *her* the evil eye. It sort of balanced things out. And this way, Sorrel wouldn't beat her with a bloody headless chicken or pull anything else out of her sick, twisted bag of tricks. She'd become genuinely scared of her since reading the fax, and Nick had known without asking that she didn't want to be alone with her.

Nick packed a few books and her radio and (with raised brows) her Eeyore bedroom slippers. She tossed him her pillow and a blanket, and he threw those into his box, too. Then he picked up the toad. The expression on his face was priceless.

"That's Prince Charming," Vinnie told him, and he choked. "Adam gave him to me."

Nick and Prince Charming checked each other out. Neither seemed delighted to meet the other. Prince Charming puffed out his throat, then ate half a bug.

She'd done the toiletries in the bathroom first, and all that remained was an unhealthy pot of purple mums on her windowsill. They made her think of her own unhealthy mum—and Vinnie made a mental promise to call her that evening, though she still didn't know how to explain the sudden address change.

Nick grabbed the pot in his free hand, having already slung the strap of her duffel over his shoulder, wedged the toad under his arm, and picked up her big suitcase in his other hand.

He shot Sorrel a warning glance as he headed for the door. "I'll be right back up. I'm just taking these down to the cab."

Sorrel sneered at her. "Well, Dorothy, you must be a really good lay." Except she didn't use the word "lay," but its filthier alternative.

It wasn't worth arguing with her. "I guess so," Vinnie agreed, stacking two boxes on top of one another.

Sorrel looked disappointed that she hadn't shocked her or angered her. So she tried scaring her instead. "You know, that guy could be a real psycho."

The irony was too much. Vinnie laughed.

"You've known him, what, a week?" Sorrel continued. "You don't know anything about him, do you?"

Vinnie sat on the boxes and folded her arms. "I know that he doesn't decorate with Hefty bags, chant over animal hearts, or cook crickets on the stove. And right now, Sorrel, that's good enough for me."

Nick came back through the door, and Vinnie grabbed the two boxes she'd been sitting on. He took three others, the last ones.

As they exited the apartment, Vinnie shot her roommate one last look. "Get some help, okay?"

Nick cast a sidelong glance at Vinnie as they lurched and bumped along in the cab, headed back uptown. He knew she had misgivings about the move, and hell, to be honest, so did he.

He wondered what had gotten into him—he wasn't normally such a Good Samaritan. He liked his life uncomplicated, and he really didn't need an extra woman cluttering it up. But Vinnie needed help. And so did that little brother of hers.

He shied away from the idea of a lonely little boy stuck in a prep school by himself. It hit too close to home. Adam Hart was none of his concern, but he could at least help his sister to help him.

When they pulled up at his building, Nick waved Pete over and shelled out a twenty. "Do me a favor, okay? Take these up the service elevator. And make sure Old Biddy Blount isn't around when you do it."

Pete nodded. If he found anything odd about the situation, he didn't let it show on his bland face. The twenty disappeared like magic, and he extended a gloved hand to help Vinnie out of the cab.

Nick got in it again, since he was taking it back to the office. He waved good-bye, and she followed the loaded cart to the service entrance.

Vinnie let Daffodil out of her crate, which was upside down, kissed her on the nose, then unloaded six cans of Cherry Coke into Nick's fridge.

The boxes and suitcases could wait to be unpacked—she was still getting used to this whole idea and needed the comfort that her favorite beverage brought her. Although she had to admit that Nick's cappuccino was giving Cherry Coke a good run for the money. Before long, she'd be so sophisticated that she wouldn't know what to do with herself.

She popped the top on one of the cokes, and used her calling card to reach Mama, who answered on the fourth ring. "Hel-llooo?"

"Hi, Mama. It's me. How are you?"

"Lavender, dear. It's so nice to hear your voice. I miss you and Adam something fierce."

The wistfulness in her voice had Vinnie wincing, just as her use of her full name did. Lavender. Geez—why had her parents saddled her with that name? She guessed it was better than Polyester, or Moon, or something like that—but not much.

"I miss you, too, Mama. And I know Adam does."

"How is he? Is he making lots of friends? Is he happy?"

Vinnie thought about square, obnoxious Joey and tried to squash her anger. "He's fine. He's . . . getting to know the other boys. And he's learning a lot."

"But is he happy, Lavender?"

Vinnie hesitated. "Um, I think it'll take him a little longer than a week to get settled, Mama. He's homesick, just as you'd expect."

"Poor thing. I don't want him miserable, you hear? If he's not happy in a couple months, you promise me you'll pack him up and bring him home."

A couple of months? Her mother had to be kidding. But Vinnie knew she wasn't. Part of Adam's social problems stemmed from the fact that Mama had kept him inside with her so much; coddled him and never encouraged him to play with boys his own age.

Vinnie had done her best to drag him to parks and throw a ball with him, but this wasn't very effective. She worked too much, and baseball, soccer, and football weren't exactly her top skills.

"Promise me, Lavender. You hear?"

"Yes, Mama. I hear." But she didn't promise. How was her little brother ever going to learn and grow to his full potential if he wasn't forced to deal with challenges?

While she'd wanted to kill Joey Balthus and knock his parents' heads together, that wouldn't help Adam deal with a future situation.

"How's church, Mama? What are you playing this Sunday?"

She listened to the description of last Sunday's flowers, donated by the Pauleys. Offerings were down, and Pastor Brownlow was a little frustrated since they were trying to add on to the Sunday school. She was learning two new hymns for the coming weekend and practicing five others that she knew from way back when. That darling Smathers girl would sing solo to one of the new ones. Didn't she just have a voice like an angel?

Vinnie agreed that yes, she did. "Um, Mama? When you send me the tape, you'll need to send it to a different address than the one I gave you before."

Her mother had plans to send her weekly tapes of the church services, so she and Adam could listen to their mother play and also receive the benefits of Pastor Brownlow's sermons, even as far away as New York.

"A different address? Already? You've moved?"

"Mama, my roommate here was not a nice girl." Vinnie left it at that.

"Oh, I think I know what you mean."

Vinnie strongly doubted that she did. "So I've moved to another place."

"Good for you, dear. I don't want my daughter living with some brazen hussy."

"Yeah." Vinnie cleared her throat. "So, do you have a pen?"

"Just a moment . . . okay. Got one. Shoot."

"The new phone number is . . ." She gave it to her mother, stalling for just a little more time. "And send any letters or packages to me care of"— gulp—"Nicholas Wright, at—"

"Excuse me?"

"Wright. W-R-I-G-H-T, at—"

"I said, *excuse me*? Lavender, *who is this man*?"

"It's not like it sounds. I work for him."

"*What?*"

Vinnie closed her eyes and rubbed the cold Cherry Coke can across her forehead.

"What happened to the real estate office? What exactly do you do for this man, Lavender?" Mama's voice held a hint—or two or three—of hysteria.

"I'm his dog-sitter." It sounded ridiculous even to her own ears. And lame. "The real estate office didn't work out."

"Lavender Hart, I brought you up better than this. I *knew* no good would come of you two going to New York—"

"Mama, listen! It's *not* what you think."

"I may live in a small town, Lavender, but I didn't just fall off the apple cart!" Her mother was hyperventilating by then. "You come home right now, and we won't tell a soul about this. You'll spend some time with Pastor, and he'll set you right again. You get out of that nasty, nasty city! And you bring my boy home to me. You hear?"

Vinnie decided it was time to talk turkey. "Ma, you're overreacting. I AM NOT SLEEPING WITH THIS MAN!"

Of course, she'd no sooner said that than the front door slammed. Mrs. Hegel gave a loud Teutonic sniff, and Vinnie could have sworn she heard her mutter, "Yah, right."

"What was that?" Mama asked. "That noise?"

"That's Mrs. Hegel."

"Who is she, the madam?"

Vinnie swallowed a giggle at the idea of the dour, cadaver-faced Mrs. Hegel as New York's Heidi Fleiss.

"I wasn't born yesterday, Lavender, I know how these things work."

"Mama, I told you. It's not like that. My roommate had a criminal record, okay? I needed to get out of there. I'm only staying with Nick until I find another place."

Why did everyone assume that she was sleeping with Nick? Even her own mother?

If only. Vinnie froze on that thought, and smacked herself in the forehead.

"Mama—"

Mrs. Hegel screamed from one of the guest rooms, and Vinnie remembered the toad.

"Mama, I've got to go. I promise there's no . . . um, *hanky-panky* going on here. I promise. Okay? I'll talk to you soon. Bye."

"*Nein, nein!* Enough! First there is dog, then there is *Schlampe*, and now revolting *uber*-toad. *Nein!* I quit, I QUIT."

"Mrs. Hegel, I—"

The woman shook a blue-feathered duster at Vinnie. "You, you should go back where you came from. Herr Wright does not need the likes of you around, nor your dogs, nor your frogs! Zis was decent household before you show up, *Fraulein*. Now is filthy zoo!"

Why was everyone so hostile toward her? It was really starting to piss her off.

"Look, Mrs. Hegel, I'm sorry you don't like me. I'm sorry you don't like the dog. But *I* had nothing to do with the dog coming here, okay? I'm just here to keep her under control. And she's very clean, since she's bathed, massaged, groomed, and manicured every single week. So you're imagining the filth.

"Now, I apologize for the toad, but I can't do much about that either. I tell you what: I'll keep out of your way, and you keep out of mine. How does that sound?"

The Frau shook the duster at her again, and Daffodil barked at it, whereupon the Frau lost some of her bluster and shrank against the wall. "Take ze beast away, yah? While I am here. We make deal, yah?"

Vinnie nodded. So the old battle-ax was afraid of Daffodil. "Fine. We'll go out for a long walk." She got Daffodil's leash and her backpack, and they left the building to go to the park. As they crossed Fifth, Mrs. Hegel's words echoed in Vinnie's head.

You should go back where you came from. Was this some kind of conspiracy? Unfortunately, Vinnie was tempted to be swept away by it. Going back to Kansas sounded good, except for the weekly lectures from Pastor about wholesomeness and purity.

Except for dragging Adam back into a situation where he wouldn't grow or learn to his full potential.

Except for working once again for Dairy Queen, or the telephone company, or the Appletree Inn. They were all fine businesses to work for, but something had been gnawing at Vinnie's insides for a long time. A longing of sorts, a nameless call to do something else.

And she wasn't going to go back to Kansas and let her mother backslide into dependence on her again. So no matter how the sunflowers and the barns and the wheatfields called to her, no matter how much she missed the breathing room and vast blue sky, she was staying right there in New York. And for the time being, at least, she was staying with Nick.

Chapter 14

Nick knew Vinnie was in his apartment because he could smell her scent. He knew intellectually that she was there, too, but that knowledge was different. He stood in the kitchen and inhaled the traces of green apple shampoo and a floral soap with hints of . . . jasmine, was it?

Nick had had a lot of experience with women's perfumes, but this essence of Vinnie's was simple, uncomplicated, fresh. Completely different from Dana's wickedly expensive custom-blended perfume. Dana's was sexy, but cloying somehow. Vinnie's was so soft, tantalizing, that he found himself sniffing the air like a hound just trying to find more of it.

He looked around at his kitchen, which still held hints of her presence in it that day. The ceramic cookie jar with Scooby-Doo on it was new. He picked up the lid to find gourmet dog treats inside.

She'd left a receipt for canine vitamins and heartworm tablets on the black granite countertop. And

the multipage instruction booklet for his cappuccino machine was upside down and folded awkwardly, as if she'd tossed it there in frustration.

Other than that, the only sign of her was the
muted volume of *Friends* seeping out from under a
guest room door.

He was oddly disappointed that she didn't come
out to greet him, but then why would she? And the
dog wouldn't bother. He was sure Daffodil snored
by her side. Some guard dog she was.

Nick opened the refrigerator to see what Mrs.
Hegel had left him to eat. Hmmm. Looked like a
nice sauerbraten and some sort of green bean salad,
with a freshly made cheesecake for dessert. He got
a beer instead. After a day like today, he was simply
too wound up to eat.

If he had to look at another half-baked, worse-
than-amateur drawing on a cocktail napkin by
some smug executive who didn't know Gaudi from
Mies, but knew "what he liked," he was going to
eat every building model in his office. With a side of
fries.

He was beginning to have fantasies of living
alone in a lighthouse on the coast of Maine. He'd
grow a mangy beard down to his ankles and wear
monk robes and never have to schmooze with a
client again. He'd design weird tree houses for disturbed urban youth. He'd—he glugged down half
the beer. He just needed to turn off his brain. What
a day.

He'd rushed from an eight o'clock meeting at the
Wiedner site to a nine-thirty at the Blevins site.
Then there'd been the ten-thirty breakfast at the

Waldorf, and after that the lunch session with Keegan and Fineman.

There'd been a problem with the scheduled delivery date of the steel for the Jankowski project, which wasn't really his, but Nadelman was on vacation, so . . .

And the new intern had screwed up some specs on the Soda Dome site, so those had to be ironed out.

His in-box was overflowing with paperwork, and there'd been too many e-mails to count.

Nick took a deep breath, just glad to be home and not have the phone ringing next to his ear on top of it all. If they didn't make him a full partner after this year from hell, he'd—

He'd what? Quit? Start designing dog houses for a living? Yeah, right. Nick gulped down another quarter of the beer and loosened his tie. His cell phone vibrated in his pocket, and he took it out and set it on the marble counter without looking at the incoming number. He knew it was Dana, and he had no desire to talk to her.

No, the person he wanted to talk to was Vinnie, but she was obviously occupied with Chandler, Monica, Joey, Rachel, et al.

Morose, Nick made his way to the sofa with the dregs of the beer and turned on the late news for a daily update on the city's body count, the state of the union, and the latest stock market plunge.

The body count was low for the evening, the president still knew how to pontificate, and the market was down another ninety-three points. Nick checked out the football scores, got lectured by an unnaturally perky woman about which dryer sheets beat static cling the best, and saw all over again that Chevy was like a rock. He raised his feet and lowered his lids simultaneously, and before long he was asleep.

Vinnie let out a satisfied sigh as the *Friends* rerun ended. Then, somewhat reluctantly, she slid out from under the covers of Nick's guest bed and asked Daffodil, "Out? Do you need to go out?"

Daffodil only yawned.

"I guess not, then." Vinnie hitched up her flannel pajama bottoms, and stuck her hair, which was flying every which way, into a scrunchie. "Okay, sweetie, let's brush our teeth."

Daffodil followed her to the small bathroom, and Vinnie put a big dollop of Crest on the dog's Scooby-Doo toothbrush. This process, out of all Aunt Edna's instructions, gave her the most giggles.

Daffodil sat down, and Vinnie knelt beside her, pulling back one of the dog's lip flaps, or jowls, or whatever they were called. She scrubbed at the dog's teeth until Daff got squirmy and pulled back to lick at the mint flavor. Then they repeated the process on the other side.

While Vinnie wasn't entirely sure that the dog's teeth benefited greatly from the nightly ritual, she liked to follow the old lady's instructions as best she could. Daffodil ate a lot of toothpaste, but it didn't seem to harm her.

Vinnie rinsed off Scooby and put that brush away in the medicine cabinet before washing her hands and brushing her own teeth. Then they went to the armoire that held the dog's wardrobe. Although she'd been revolted initially by the concept of dressing a dog, Vinnie was starting to get a kick out of it. She picked out a pink flannel nightshirt studded with little fluffy lambs for Daffodil. They climbed into their respective beds (she'd been working on getting the dog to use her own) and turned out the light.

Daffodil began snoring almost immediately, but Vinnie couldn't sleep. She knew Nick was home. She'd heard him come in, but didn't want to intrude on his space. It was odd living with someone you didn't know, and not being entirely sure what his habits were—his likes and dislikes. Her instinct was just to keep out of his way for a while.

She must have finally fallen asleep for an hour or so, because a noise next to her head awoke her. Vinnie sat bolt upright in bed, heart pounding, before she realized that the strange noise was Prince Charming, Adam's toad.

She shuddered. The last thing she wanted was a multipound toad in her bed. Vinnie got up and put a couple more books on top of Prince Charming's aquarium, to ensure that it didn't happen.

Then she climbed back into bed and stared at the ceiling. Her stomach growled, and she remembered that she hadn't eaten any dinner, partly because she hadn't gone out and gotten anything, and she knew better than to touch the dinner Mrs. Hegel had left for Nick.

If she and Mrs. Hegel got along better, she could ask the woman to teach her how to make some of those dishes. They sure looked good. Vinnie had never made anything that didn't come from Mama's orange 1970s Betty Crocker binder book.

Alone in the dark, she pondered why Mrs. Hegel and the people at Adam's school and women like Mrs. Blount treated her as they did. It must have something to do with the way she looked. She knew her clothes weren't stylish, and she supposed her hair wasn't either—it was just a lot of hair, cut in no particular style, hanging down her back.

Lots of the women she saw in New York were very sleek. Sleek and expensive-looking. She knew she didn't look expensive. She looked like a country girl, which is what she was. Why was that bad? Why should she pretend to be something she was not?

Vinnie's stomach growled again. It felt like it was trying to digest her internal organs. She was starving.

She peered at the clock. 1:49 A.M. Surely Nick had some crackers or something in his pantry that she could eat? She could always replace them tomorrow.

Vinnie slid out of bed again and wiggled into her Eeyore slippers. She circled around the sleeping dog and shuffled to the door.

The penthouse was dark and silent, but moonlight mingled with the light of the streetlamps, dancing in the big picture windows. While the noise of traffic was omnipresent, none of the shouts or whistles or buzz of machines marred the post-midnight hours on Fifth.

Vinnie padded silently through the hall, out into

the vast living space, and into the open kitchen. Mrs. Hegel's domain, the pantry, existed in another little hall beyond the cavernous wood-paneled refrigerator.

Mrs. Hegel must have all kinds of goodies stashed in that pantry. Vinnie's mouth began to water as she wondered if perhaps, just maybe, the Teuton had any chocolate hidden away in there.

For sure there would be no Captain Crunch or other sugary cereal. Mrs. H wouldn't believe in such products. But the possibility of chocolate, for baking, was strong. And maybe dried fruit or homemade cookies, or . . . Vinnie stopped dead.

The figure of a man loomed large in the little hallway. A half-naked man in only a pair of gray sweatpants. Nick was in the pantry.

She would have retreated and crept back to bed, growling stomach notwithstanding, but he turned and saw her before she could scram.

"Hey," he said.

She swallowed, hard. His chest and shoulders in the dim moonlight were . . . oh, Lord, what would Pastor Brownlow say if he could've read her mind at that moment?

"Hi," she managed to squeak back. "I was . . ." She couldn't tear her eyes away from that flat, muscular belly and the way the sweats hung low on his hips. ". . . hungry." The red-gold hair on his chest called to her fingers. What would it feel like to run them through it?

She remembered Nick's lips on hers the other night, and worse, the way his skin had felt—hot and smooth—and worst of all, the way he'd smelled, that man-smell that she'd wanted to bury her face in.

Vinnie no longer cared about finding chocolate. She'd found something better in the pantry. Something she'd love to put inside, something that would sate her hunger.

Aaaack. What was she thinking? Maybe her mama was right, and the city had ways of corrupting people. Maybe she'd moved into the Devil's Den, and Nick was smooth, smiling, sexy Satan himself.

His eyes were smoky in the dimness, and his mouth played a silky curve like a sonata. The melody of it shot straight into her veins and had her knees weakening. How did he do that with just a smile? Just a smile in the darkness . . .

Nick was a demon. Nick was a dish. Nick was dangerous. She should back away now and retreat to her bedroom.

"Hungry?" he repeated. "Yeah." His eyes went to her hair, falling out of its scrunchie again. Then they moved lower, and she took a deep breath. Finally, Nick's eyes rested on her Eeyore slippers, and a corner of his mouth turned up in a little quirk.

It was a quirk she wanted to eat with a spoon. Dear God, the man's mouth was going to undo her right on the spot—and he hadn't come close to touching her.

It wasn't that she imagined his mouth on any part of her body—though her skin tingled and her nipples tightened in response. It was the curve—

that sonata curve—of his lips that played havoc with her nerves.

Nick's bottom lip held a faint sullenness, a sexy tinge of indulgence, the bravado of the bon vivant. And his upper lip slid into it with an edge of wickedness that produced two illegitimate dimples on either side of the whole package.

Bastard dimples, that's what Nick has, she thought in a fog of insane, unexplained desire. The little love children of his mouth.

Vinnie shifted from one foot to the other, all too aware that she didn't look her best. She couldn't be exactly appealing in her faded, worn blue plaid flannel pajamas. But then, who expected to run into a hot man in the pantry at close to 2 A.M.?

Besides, it was a darn good thing she looked bad, because Nick was Forbidden Fruit. If she went anywhere near tasting his apple, not to mention his serpent, she'd be kicked out of this Garden of Eden for sure.

"Lavender," Nick murmured.

When he said her name, it didn't sound quite so stupid.

"Lavender, would you like a glass of wine?"

"I—"

"Oh, that's right. You don't drink. Tell me, why is that? Does your decision stem from religion, philosophy, or just plain flavor?"

Vinnie pushed Pastor Brownlow to a far corner of her mind, and shrugged. "Flavor, pretty much. I've just never liked the taste of alcohol."

"Hmmm. Have you ever had good alcohol?"

She looked at him blankly. "If you mean expensive, then no."

"I'm going to give you the gift of a good Gewurtztraminer," said Nick.

"A what?" It sounded like something Mrs. Hegel would use to clean a toilet.

"It's a German dessert wine, Lavender. Sweet, light, and joyous."

Vinnie eyed him suspiciously. How could a wine be joyous? If anyone but Nick had said it, it would've sounded pretentious, and flowery, and kind of . . . gooberish. But it *was* Nick who'd said it, and the adjective rolled off his tongue quite naturally.

Don't think about Nick's tongue, stupid.

She shrank back against the wall as he turned from the pantry. After all, it wouldn't do for them to touch in any way. She followed him into the palace's kitchen, where he took a bottle of pale golden wine from a separate refrigerator. It had glass doors that displayed at least fifty bottles of both red and white.

Wow. Vinnie didn't want to think about how much money was sitting right there in that fridge. Even if each bottle only cost around five dollars (she tried to give him the benefit of the doubt on not squandering dough) if there were fifty bottles, then he had two hundred fifty dollars in there. *Sheesh.* Back home, she and Mama had a budget of seventy-five dollars a week at the Super-K for groceries.

Nick had over three weeks of their grocery money in there, just on nonessential items. It must be nice.

As Nick cut the foil off the bottle and opened it with a fancy vacuum gadget, Vinnie tried to imagine how anyone could drink fifty bottles of wine. She didn't think she could do it even in a year.

But that was before she tasted the Gewurtztraminer.

Nick handed it to her in a beautiful crystal goblet with a long stem. He raised his own in a toast, holding it by its stem.

She held hers the same way, raising the glass aloft uncertainly.

"To my new roommate," he said, and drank.

"Um, yeah." Vinnie drank, too. The wine was delicious, like nothing she'd ever tasted. Fruity and sweet and a little tart all at the same time.

"Can you taste the hint of blackberry?"

Nope. What kind of insane question was that? He was talking like a textbook again. But she nodded, just so she wouldn't feel like a doofus.

Nick gazed at her over his glass and laughed, his bastard dimples appearing to tease her.

"What?"

He shook his head. "You're a darling, Lavender Hart. You really are."

A darling? She'd never met a man with the word in his vocabulary. William had certainly never called her a darling. He'd called her babe, which irritated her.

Vinnie frowned at Nick, unable to figure him out. She swallowed more of the wine, because it was so good.

And she thought of what Mama and Pastor Brownlow would think of her slurping wine in her pajamas with this guy at 2 A.M. Even at communion, Pastor only served grape juice.

I'm a grown woman. And I'm not in Kansas anymore. Vinnie took another sip of the wine and felt a lightness down to her toes in the Eeyore slippers.

Nick's chest hair glinted against the background of the undercabinet lighting he'd turned on, and she tried not to think about what it would feel like against her cheek. Springy, and soft, and oh-so-warm . . . she looked away. If she were going to live with this man, she should get to know him better, but *not* in the carnal sense. *Boss*, she said to herself. *Bad*. Then she said *rich* and *jerk*. Except Nick wasn't a jerk. Darn it. Why couldn't he be more of a jerk? She reminded herself that he'd only asked her to move in so Daffodil wouldn't eat all the furniture.

Oh, he's a jerk. The jerk is hiding in there somewhere, just waiting to pop out. Jerk-in-a-box. Just make conversation with him . . .

"So, Nick. How did you get interested in architecture?"

He swirled the wine in his glass, seeming fascinated with it. "When I was a kid, my parents spent years designing and building their 'dream house' in Greenwich, where they still live. I saw a lot of design magazines, and blueprints, and cross sections of spaces. I even tried to help." He laughed, but it wasn't a happy sound.

"I sent them drawings from school, on notebook paper. And when I was home on breaks, I'd do models for them out of Legos. Hey, those are still around, right?"

She nodded. "Yeah. My brother had them. So . . . did your parents like your designs?"

"Oh, get real." He tossed back the contents of his glass. "I was six, seven, eight. What did I know?"

"They must have encouraged you, or you wouldn't have gone into the field."

"Oh, sure they did." His voice was dry as bone, even though he'd just saturated it with wine. Then it changed, and he suddenly mimicked a patronizing female voice. "Very good, Nickie. Go work on it some more now—run along and don't bother Mummy until it's perfect." He laughed again.

Vinnie shivered at the sound: it reverberated with masculine strength and denial. The boy who'd been in the way had been sent off to school and educated to perfection. But his walls of books hadn't taught him how to pet a dog, or to relax, or to do anything but win. No wonder he had a bad-tempered housekeeper and a snotty girlfriend. He wouldn't know what to do with warmth or affection.

She wanted to know more about Nick, jerk or not—at least the Nick who wasn't the box-man. She thought again of the unusual models in his office. She'd fix the one she'd crushed, even if it took her a year. "So who's your favorite architect of all time?"

"Frank Gehry," he said without a moment's hesitation.

Vinnie had never heard of the guy, and Nick must have read that in her expression.

"He's what they call a postmodern architect," he explained, "and that's something that's very hard to define . . . I guess you could say that the postmodern concept questions all of our assumptions about logic and order. Turns everything on its ear, you know?"

She didn't, but she listened anyway.

"In simple terms—"

The only kind he thought she'd understand? She told herself not to be defensive.

"—Frank Lloyd Wright broke open the box, and Frank Gehry continues to build on the extreme edges, using all kinds of unusual materials and twisting those edges into forms that have nothing to do with the box anymore."

"Oh." It was all she could think of to say.

"He's part artist, part architect, part poet with a new vocabulary."

The passion was back in his eyes, his voice, his gestures. She could see the life force in the man, pulsing at his neck, cording the muscles on his forearms . . . Nick the robot was gone, and she was glad. She liked the hidden Nick better, the boyish side of him that got excited.

"This Gehry guy . . ." she said. "Will you show me something he's built?"

"I wish. We'd need to fly to California. Various problems are holding up the new Guggenheim Museum he's designed for lower Manhattan."

"Oh." She tried not to be so disappointed. The boy in him wouldn't come out to play, now. Unless . . . "Will you show me something *you've* built?"

His eyes went flat again, and he swallowed some more wine. "I'm . . . not really working on anything that interesting right now. Boxes, like I said."

She could sense his frustration, wished he would talk about it. But he sidestepped the subject.

"So, do you like the wine?" Nick moved closer to her.

She nodded.

"I thought you might." He was staring at her mouth.

Why, she didn't know. She probably had a big fat glob of toothpaste stuck in the corner, or she'd drooled in his presence, like the idiot she was.

Lord knew *she* didn't have any dimples, but Nick's index finger was reaching out to touch *something* about her mouth—and then it stopped, in midair. Which was a good thing, because, for example, if he'd changed flight plans and sent the finger to her nose, instead, she'd have been cross-eyed.

Oh, geez. Just being in the presence of the man was making her brain babble. Vinnie took another sip of wine, and Nick walked to the fridge.

She tried hard not to stare at his backside, but wasn't entirely successful. So she let her gaze wander to his naked shoulders instead, and the fascinating indentations of his spine, and the way smooth, taut muscle fanned out from it on either side.

Then there were the shoulder blades—again, smooth with satin skin and muscled—and she denied categorically that she wanted to—darn, she didn't know—*gnaw* on them or something.

Vinnie had yet another sip of wine as Nick leaned into the fridge, and those sweatpants molded like a cupcake wrapper to his buns.

She was a sick and perverted woman. When he came out with a cheesecake, she was glad to be able to fixate on it, instead. Her stomach gave a mighty, audible growl.

Nick turned and laughed. Then his face sobered. "Did you have any dinner?"

She shook her head. "Neither did you, by the looks of it, since Mrs. H's tray in there is untouched. You'd better be careful, or she'll beat you with one of her wooden cooking spoons."

He laughed. "Ah, the dreaded *Kochlöffel*."

The what? It must be the German word for cooking spoon—unless it was an unflattering adjective to describe Mrs. Hegel herself. Vinnie kind of hoped it was.

"She hasn't beaten me up yet," Nick said. "Though I'm always careful to make it look like I've cleaned my plate—whether it's true or not." He took a knife to the cheesecake and cut it into four giant pieces. "So has Mrs. H threatened *you* with a cooking spoon?"

Vinnie shook her head. "Just the feather duster. So far the cooking spoon's been reserved for Daffodil. She doesn't like either of us much, though."

"Don't take it personally. Mrs. H doesn't like anybody. We're all going to hell in a handbasket, like the rest of society." Nick put a slab of cheesecake on a plate and handed it to her.

Vinnie blinked at the size of the portion, but was honestly too hungry to turn it down.

Nick hefted one onto a plate for himself, then ladled caramelized blueberries over both pieces.

"Why doesn't Mrs. Hegel like anyone?"

"Who knows? I tease her and call her Mrs. Sunshine."

Vinnie grinned around a mouthful of the most insanely delicious cheesecake she'd ever had. She couldn't help a little moan of pleasure.

"See why I put up with her moods?"

She nodded. Then she grinned again at the thought of what Mrs. H would say if she knew the fruit of her labors was being snarfed by the likes of the *dog-sitter*. What a crime. It made the cheesecake taste even better.

The wine was amazing with it, too, cutting through the sweet creaminess of the cake and surrounding it with a golden glow in her mouth. Vinnie gave a sigh of pure pleasure, and even the twin Eeyores on her feet began to look cheerful.

She licked her lips and decided that however corrupt it might be, she could get used to drinking wine and eating cheesecake at 2 A.M. with a hot half-naked man.

Nick licked his lips, too, and she shouldn't have noticed. But she did. She looked down at her plate again and scraped the last of the caramelized blueberry sauce off the plate. She froze, fork in mouth, as Nick moved to stand so close to her that she could feel his heat.

He did that lip-quirk thing again, and before she knew it, his hand was over hers, drawing the fork out of her mouth.

"I hear sterling is hard to digest," he said, his eyes dancing.

She relinquished the fork, a flush warming her cheeks.

"Can I take your plate?"

She thanked the Lord for her natural sarcasm,

since it saved her from lunging at him. "Whatever would Mrs. Hegel say? About you waiting on the dog-sitter."

Nick put their plates into the sink, then walked back to her. He put a finger under her chin and tilted it up. "Funny, but I couldn't give half a damn about what Mrs. Hegel would say." Then he kissed her.

Chapter 15

The lyrics of every sappy love song to pollute the planet converged into one spark in Vinnie's head. Or maybe it was an entire galaxy of pudgy cherubs singing, "Hallelujah!"

Or maybe it was just that thousands of her hormones were flown instantly to the moon. Whatever it was, that kiss of Nick's created a Big Bang.

She could get drunk off a kiss like this one, for it didn't just affect her lips. No, Nick kissed all five senses, and kissed them well. She could taste him (dense, hot, sweet, faintly musky) smell him (starch, wine, soap, lime) touch him (heat, satin, stubble) hear him (a gruff sigh, a rumble of pleasure) and see him (those hazel eyes, caressing her, devouring her—and the sensual mouth, coming to possess her).

Vinnie leaned into Nick, her shoulders fitting snugly under his. She felt his hands twine through her hair, massage her scalp, pull her even closer to him. Her breasts pressed through the flannel of her pajama top and found his heat, begged for his touch.

Her belly pressed against his—

"*Aaaaarrruuufff!*"

Vinnie leaped back at the bark from Daffodil. The dog had crept up on them in the kitchen, and all the little blue sheep on her nightshirt seemed to frown in disapproval.

She barked again, and shoved her nose at Vinnie's thigh, as if to move her back even farther from Nick.

"Out, Daffodil?" Vinnie said the words unsteadily, "Do you need to go out?"

"You're not taking her out at this hour," Nick said. "I'll go."

"Thanks."

Daffodil and her little sheep danced toward the door.

"Aw, man. I have to take her out wearing that?"

"She does have a bathrobe, believe it or not," Vinnie told him wryly.

"Yeah, I know—forget it. Come on and embarrass me, Lambsy-Daisies." Nick got the leash, and slipped the choke chain over her head.

Daffodil looked up at him dubiously, then back at Vinnie.

"Yeah, I know she's better than I am, but if you want to go out, you've got to come with me."

They exited, and Vinnie, still reeling from the kiss and remorse, fled to her bedroom.

She turned on a little bedside lamp and sat, knees drawn up to her chin, on the bed. "I knew it was a bad idea to move in here," she said to Prince Charming.

He blinked at her and hopped to the other side of his cage to avoid the light.

"I just knew it! Too good to be true, and all that."

Prince Charming just radiated toadity at her.

"Remind me"—she shook her finger at him—"that if I kiss Nick again, he'll turn into one of you."

P.C. manufactured all of his charm into gas and puffed out his throat with it.

"Hey, don't act offended, dude. You'd be proud to have him as one of your people."

How could she have kissed Nick again? Of all the stupid, bone-headed maneuvers . . . How could she *not* have kissed Nick? That wicked mouth, those dimples, they'd positively *called to her*, hadn't they? They had.

And besides, *Nick* had kissed *her*. He'd pulled the fork out of her country-fried mouth and kissed *her*. Really, all she'd done was stand there. Where was the guilt in that?

Pastor Brownlow flew through her mind like some kind of Halloween ghoul. "Intent," he reminded her. *Intent*.

Okay, so he had her there. If Daffodil hadn't interrupted things, her intent would have been naked as a jaybird right there on the kitchen floor, along with her and Nick.

The thought of Nick slipping out of those sweats in a single, fluid movement had her biting her own kneecap, which hurt.

She was losing all semblance of sanity since mov-

ing to New York. She'd escaped from the psycho
roommate only to find herself indulging in gluttony
and, and, sluttony. So what if that wasn't a word. It
seemed to fit. Plus she was having predawn conversations with a toad.

She was nuts, plain and simple. Nuts. And being
nuts was a luxury she couldn't afford. She had to
be composed, and sane and well behaved for
Adam's sake. Adam did not need a sister who was a
lunatic.

What Adam needed was a role model, and a
caretaker, and an older, wiser voice of reason.

Role models, caretakers, and voices of reason did
not get naked on kitchen floors with their employers. They did not suck face with their employers
until angels sang. And they did not covet their employers' buns.

"Is that clear, Lavender Hart?" She said it sternly,
out loud.

Prince Charming ate a slug to punctuate her
statement, and Vinnie ditched the Eeyores, shoved
her feet under the covers, and turned out the light.

Half an hour later, she was still awake, and she
knew Nick was, too, because she could hear the
low sound of the television in the living room.

Nick winced as Daffodil's tongue slid between a
couple of his toes. "You know, that's disgusting,"
he said to her in conversational tones. "Why do
you feel the urge to do that?"

She cocked her head at him, crept forward, and
buried her head in his lap. When he didn't respond,

she poked him with her nose until he scratched her. "You're pathetic and needy," he told her. "Like a little kid begging for affection." His hand froze on her knobby black head. *Jesus*. Did the dog's constant need for touch remind him of his own unmet needs as a child?

Horrifying thought.

He swallowed. He looked down at her big brown eyes and saw rejection there. Dejection. Something inside him twisted. Impossible to maintain emotional distance from a determined dog.

"Okay, look," he said to her. "You've got to quit licking my toes. Sand between them is okay. Dog spit is not. And there's something about toe-licking that is just *too* pathetic. We have to find a compromise here."

No response.

Nick gritted his teeth. "Look, if I let you lick my face, will you stop with the toes?"

She appeared to consider it, and so Nick steeled himself for the experience. He bent his head forward, until his face was in front of the dog's nose.

Slurp. Daffodil's tongue was huge, wet, and smelly. Nick preferred Vinnie's, he really did. But he let the dog lick his face, and her simple love unknotted something inside him. Instead of feeling incredibly stupid, he felt somehow peaceful.

Until he heard the low laughter from the doorway. He shot to his feet and glared at Vinnie, mortified. "It was either that or my toes. I *hate* having my toes licked."

She'd clapped a hand over her mouth, and her

eyes danced. "I've never seen anything so sweet in my life."

"I'm *not* sweet," Nick muttered, mopping at his face with his sleeve.

"Of course not."

"Why aren't you asleep?" he growled.

"Why aren't you?"

He shrugged. "Can't."

"Me either. We seem to have a mutual insomnia problem. So I was thinking . . . will you show me some more of your favorite buildings? I really like the city at night."

He blinked at her. Was she seducing him? "Okay."

"Just *no kissing* this time. Got it?"

Irrational disappointment. "No kissing. None at all."

Nick got them another cab and closed his eyes against the sight of Vinnie's delicious jean-covered rear climbing in ahead of him, and sliding across the seat.

He quickly conjured Janet Reno, shakin' it in a tiny red G-string.

While he knew that he should have more respect for Justice and his elders, it was the only way he could function without embarrassing himself. And it didn't help that all the buildings they were going to see were tall and narrow and hard, jutting proudly up into the skyline like so many—*aw, hell.* What was wrong with him?

It was just that Vinnie had really nice, uh, *dorm-*

ers. And he'd like to peel back her cladding and expose her great structure beneath. Span her spandrels, so to speak. Explore her atrium. Rock her to her foundations.

You're losing it, man. Losing it. Nick told the cabbie to run them down Fifth to the Guggenheim first, which was the most unphallic place he could think of, and a great place to start their second Manhattan-after-midnight tour. He helped Vinnie out of the cab and watched her expression.

"It looks like a giant spaceship." She giggled. "It's really cool, though."

"Funny, that's exactly what people said about it in 1956, when Frank Lloyd Wright completed the building. Lots of people hated it. I think it's beautiful, with all those inward-tilting curves."

"Was Frank Lloyd Wright any relation to you?"

Nick shook his head. "No. The name's always been a challenge to live with, though. And it makes it especially ironic that most of what I do is boxy commercial space—since his whole oeuvre attempted to destroy the box."

Vinnie gazed frankly at him. "So why do you do it?"

"I told you," Nick said, his voice curt to his own ears. "That's what people want."

She didn't say the words, but they echoed around them anyway. *But it's not what you want.*

He found himself annoyed by her insight. How had someone as simple as this uneducated country girl managed to see what he hid from *himself* most of the time? Nick's defenses sprang up. He made great money, was never short of work, and would soon make partner, unless he missed his mark. Which he never did.

He turned the topic back to the Guggenheim Museum in front of them. "You should go see the interior one of these days—it's spectacular. Inside the original space, you walk down the huge spiral from the top, and daylight pours in from the glass dome overhead. Wright created an architecture here that's essentially art . . . art that you can walk into." He laughed. "Problem with the building was that it gave all the curators fits, trying to hang work on those slanted, curving walls. So finally in 1992 Gwathmey, Siegel and Associates did an addition behind the original structure—one that has nice, flat walls for paintings."

After a few more moments, Nick helped Vinnie back into the cab.

"Where to next?" She smiled up at him, her hair lifting slightly in the night breeze. The chestnut strands glimmered gold under the city lights, streaming over her shoulders to her breasts.

Anywhere—with you, Nick caught himself thinking. *I'd like to show you the world . . . because you're so open to it. Not hard and cynical, like me.* Vinnie possessed a quality he hadn't seen in a long, long time: wonder. A simple gratitude for what the world had to offer . . .

What he wouldn't give to wrap wonder around himself again, like a shimmering quilt. "Where to?" he repeated. *Straight to hell, if I give in to desire for this girl, if I ruin the best part of her, break her heart.*

He cleared his throat. "We'll go to some of the city's most famous landmarks, okay? Enough with the architectural history lessons." He slid in beside her and said to the cabbie, "The Chrysler Building on Lexington, please."

Vinnie clapped her hands as they approached it. "Oh, I love this building! I didn't know what it was called."

"It's fun, isn't it? Built in 1930, by William van Alen. Art Deco at its finest, with all those zigzagged arches . . . it's great at night, huh?"

She nodded.

"For a short time, it was the tallest building in the world, until the Empire State beat it out the very next year in 1931. All the architects of the time were trying to outdo each other in height."

"Like guys in a locker room," Vinnie murmured.

Nick burst out laughing, especially when she clapped a hand over her mouth.

"I can't believe I said that!"

He shrugged. "It's true, though. Anyway, do you see those things at the corners of the building, way up high? Mounted like gargoyles? Those are huge replicas of the hood ornaments from the 1929 Chrysler. And there are actual hubcaps mounted up there in the mosaic wheels of automobiles . . ."

They went to Grand Central Station, at Forty-second and Park, next. And then the famous Empire State Building, and last to Rockefeller Center, where Nick promised to take Vinnie ice-skating when it got colder.

Yeah, that was it. He'd put these weird feelings he had for his dog-sitter on ice, so to speak. Because the more time he spent around Vinnie, the more he wanted to—*oh, for God's sake, Wright! For the last time, NO.*

Nick got her home to the apartment without kissing her, but he didn't get any sleep at all that night.

Chapter 16

Vinnie came inside after smuggling Daffodil up the service elevator—a roughly four-times-daily routine. They'd gone for a long walk on this beautiful November day.

Daffodil had received mixed reviews on the day's outfit. Older ladies and young girls adored her pumpkin-colored crushed velvet jacket and little French beret. Businessmen had stared, guffawed, or pretended to cough to hide their smirks. A boutique owner had rushed out to find out how the beret stayed on Daff's head (an ingenious combination of black elastic and Velcro). Another dog had objected vocally to the dyed-to-match feather. And Vinnie, in her ancient track suit, had just felt underdressed. She had to face facts: It was a little mortifying when a dog was more fashion-forward than she was. Vinnie looked like the hired help, and tried to shrug it off, since that's exactly what she was.

She drew the line, though, when a local doorman

touched his hat to Daffodil, murmuring "Madam," as they walked by.

"Have you had enough homage for the day, beastie?" she asked the dog as she unlocked Nick's front door.

She was met by a grim-faced Mrs. Hegel, wiping her wet hands on her apron. "You," Mrs. Hegel said.

"Vinnie," Vinnie reminded her pleasantly.

"Fraulein Hart," said Mrs. Hegel.

She sighed.

"Schmall boy call for you."

"Oh my God. Is he all right? What did he say?"

For the first time ever, she discerned an emotion other than sourness on Mrs. H's face. "Yah. He says will you please come and get him at school. He is crying."

Vinnie's heart palpitated. Without thinking, she handed Daffodil's leash to Mrs. Hegel, whirled, and ran out the door.

Oh, Adam, sweetheart, what's wrong? Is it that Joey kid again, or something else? Are you just homesick?

She thought about splurging on a cab, but one glance at traffic told her she'd get there faster on foot.

Adam was in Principal Anglin's office again, but not because he was in trouble. He'd tucked his skinny body into one corner of the office couch, and he was all knees, elbows, ears, and misery.

She felt an active pain in her chest at the sight of

him. His eyes behind the glasses were red-rimmed, though his mouth and chin were stubborn. He didn't run to hug her—just stayed where he was.

"I want to go home," he said. "I just want to go home."

Vinnie walked over, kissed his forehead, and gathered him into a hug. "I know you do, sweetie. I know you do."

Principal Anglin just shook his head. "It's normal for boys Adam's age to feel unsettled during their first experiences away from family."

Vinnie nodded. "I'm sure it is."

"This will pass. I told him there was no need to call you."

She folded her arms. "I disagree. I'm very glad that Adam called me. He needs to know that I'm available for him when he needs me. And he needs to know that help is available when he asks for it."

Anglin nodded.

"It seems to me," she said pointedly, "that once a part of a building has been donated—something along the lines of oh, say, a wing, for example— that it's not possible to take it back. It's now part of the structure, is it not?"

Anglin shot her a dirty look and shifted his weight from one foot to the other.

"Am I right?" Vinnie pressed him.

He folded his arms and glared at her. Finally, he nodded.

"I don't think I need to say any more, then."

He shook his head.

"Surely there have been other complaints against

this boy Joey. And if there haven't been, may I suggest that intimidation is a factor? You could talk to some other boys individually."

Anglin looked at his feet, then started to speak.

Vinnie rode right over him. The good thing about being a country girl was that she knew all about plain speaking. "Adam and I are going to leave for a while, to discuss this situation and his ideas for dealing with it. I'll let you know when he'll be back."

She and her little brother walked out into the crisp, golden red November day and blinked in the sunshine.

"I don't like him," said Adam. "He pretends to be kind and helpful and all, but he doesn't do anything."

Vinnie put an arm around his shoulders. "You know what, buddy? There are a lot of people like him in this world. So it's good that you're getting to see one in action. That way you'll learn what to do about people like him."

"What do you mean? Can we tell *him* to go home?"

She laughed. "No, not exactly. But we can either make him do his job, or we can work around him."

"How?"

"Well, I gave him a little hint in there. A little push. If he ignores it, then I'll think of something else. How about some ice cream?"

"Double scoop? On a cone?"

She nodded.

"First person who drips is a rotten egg."

"You bet."

Vinnie knew she'd lose, and the irony lay in the fact that she was trying to be the best egg possible.

Adam got one scoop of double-chocolate-cherry-fudge, and one scoop of vanilla-peanut-caramel-fudge. The nice older man at the ice-cream parlor made them so big that Vinnie didn't know how her little brother could carry the cone, much less keep the scoops balanced.

She herself got one scoop of chocolate-mint, and grinned as Adam perfected what he called his "twirl-a-lick."

Once he'd ensured that no drips were imminent, he asked, "So why did your phone number change? You didn't explain in your message."

Vinnie narrowly avoided slicking her nose with her ice cream at the question. She should have been expecting it.

"Well, the number changed because my address changed. My roommate turned out to be not so nice a person, so at the moment I'm living where I work. Just until I find another place," she added hastily.

"Oh. Kind of like me."

"Exactly."

Adam didn't ask her any more about it, and she sighed in relief. "Have you talked to Mama lately?"

He nodded. "Yup. It was a quick call, because she didn't want to run up the bill."

"Did you say anything to her about Joey, or . . ." Vinnie let her voice trail off. She didn't feel right asking her brother to omit things or lie to their mama.

"No. I remembered what you said about how she worries. I told her I was fine. She couldn't do anything about it anyway."

"No, she couldn't."

"It's good that she'll go around town, now. I remember when she wouldn't leave the house."

Vinnie herself remembered a time when Mama wouldn't leave her bedroom. She nodded. "Yes, the counselor and the medication are helping. I don't think she'll ever enjoy traveling, though, Adam."

"Prob'ly not. She'd never get on an airplane, or go very far on a bus."

"She's driving her little car, now, though. We should be very proud of her for that."

He nodded.

Vinnie decided it was time to "go there" with Adam about the subject of independence. "Hey, kiddo?"

"Huh." He licked a big drip of vanilla off the chocolate scoop.

"You know how I explained to you about Mama—that if we did too much for her, she'd never get any better?"

"Yeah."

"Well, it's really tricky. Because we want her to know how much we love her, but we also want her to be healthy."

He twirled his cone.

"She knows she can call us if she needs to, but since we're pretty far away she has to do all the things for herself that we used to do. She can't be a . . ." Vinnie hesitated. "A baby anymore. She's got to go to work, and go to the bank, and go to the grocery store. She's got to do her laundry and her dishes."

"I know." Adam took an actual bite, sloppy though it was, of the vanilla ice cream. Then he asked her a grown-up question. "So what's your point?"

She had to chuckle. He was a smart kid. "My point, sweetie, is that I'm trying to do the same thing with you. I won't always be around to make the Joey Balthuses of the world go away. Do you know what I mean?"

Adam stopped dead in his tracks. "Vinnie, I'm *not* going back there. Please let me come home with you. *Please.*"

Take him home? As in, to Nick's? There was no way. Her face must have reflected her unconscious answer, for Adam went, in an instant, from being wise and grown-up to pathetic and twelve again.

"I won't go back there," he said again. And his eyes filled with tears. One of them fell directly on his ice cream, and another rolled down his nose.

In his agitation, Adam let his cone drip onto the pavement. While she refused to call him a rotten egg, the situation sure did stink.

Vinnie put her ice-cream-free arm around Adam and hugged him, but he pulled away.

She tried to think of something to say to make him feel better; something that would lend him the strength to deal with the situation. Her brain failed her, and Adam dashed violently at his cheeks.

She remembered that for a twelve-year-old boy, crying in public was probably worse than being burned at the stake.

Vinnie guided him into Central Park, where they sat together on a bench. "Adam, tell me more about what's going on at school. It's not just Joey Balthus, is it?"

He shook his head. "It's—it's—everything. The food sucks, I can't sleep at night, there's sooooo much homework, and there's no TV except in the common room, and Balthus and the Butt-Heads control whatever's on, and you can't watch anything cool. The teachers are mean, and the only kid who's nice to me is a dork, just like me. I don't wanna be the school dork anymore. I wanted to be different here, start over. Be cool."

"Adam," she said helplessly, "you *are* cool. I think you're the coolest."

"You have to say that—you're my sister. And it's not true."

"Well, let's see. What is it that makes a dork a dork, exactly?"

He shrugged. "I dunno."

"They're smart, right?"

"I guess."

"And they're interested in things that a lot of other boys aren't interested in."

"Yeah."

"And maybe they don't have Incredible Hulk muscles."

"Nope."

"Well, I can think of a lot of people who must've been dorks at your age, then. Alan Greenspan, for example. And he runs the whole economy. And how about the president? Do you think he was a big meaty kid like Joey?"

Adam shrugged.

"How about Mother Teresa, or half the CEOs on the Fortune 500 list, or the world's great poets and scientists and artists? I bet lots of them were skinny, unpopular kids. And look who they are today."

Adam said nothing.

"I can't improve the food, sweetie, but I could bring you a sandwich a couple times a week. How would that be?"

"Grilled cheese?"

"Yes. Grilled cheese. With a pickle on the side and some potato chips."

He thought about it.

"Now, why can't you sleep?" Vinnie asked him.

" 'Cause I just can't. It's noisy, and Balthus and them said they were gonna get me one night."

"Get you how?"

"Said they're going to super-glue my lips closed and put my hand in warm water so I pee in my bed."

"I think that's just a lot of talk," Vinnie told him. "Now what else? The TV you can live without, can't you? If we maybe go see a movie on the weekends?"

" 'Kay."

"And the homework? Is it too much, or is it too hard?"

"Both."

"Do you need help with it?"

He didn't answer.

Aha, she thought. Now we're really getting somewhere.

"Adam?"

"I've *never* needed help before," he muttered. "Never."

"But you do now?"

"I feel *stupid* at this school. Nobody else seems to think it's that hard."

"Yeah, but Adam, they've been in these tough schools a lot longer than you have, so they're probably used to it. Remember Mrs. Gruber told you your brain is like a muscle? And it grows stronger the more you exercise it?"

"I guess."

"Well, just like you wouldn't be able to lift a fifty-pound weight until you can lift a—"

"I can too."

"Fine." Vinnie amended her example. "A hundred-pound weight, then. You have to work up to it by lifting a fifty-pound one first, and then sixty and so on for weeks and weeks and even months before you can do the hundred-pound one."

Adam kicked at the leg of the bench.

"Know what I mean?"

Finally, he nodded. "How's Prince Charming?" he asked.

"Fine. He eats a lot of bugs."

"Can I see him?"

Vinnie hesitated. Should she take him to Nick's and let him see the toad?

"Sure." Mrs. Hegel would scare the daylights out of him and put an end to this business of his wanting to go home with her. "Sure, we'll go over there now."

Chapter 17

Body snatchers had obviously come and taken Mrs. Hegel away, leaving a look-alike fairy godmother in her place.

Bemused, Vinnie checked in the coffin-sized refrigerator, the pantry, and inside a couple of large cabinets to see where the real Mrs. Hegel had been stashed. The imposter had on a smile as bright as Christmas lights, and took Adam into the kitchen for homemade chocolate-chip cookies and milk.

While Adam asked her where she was from, and why she talked funny, and whether they had Nintendo and Playstation 2 and Xbox in Germany, Vinnie waited for the droid Mrs. Hegel to morph into some kind of aproned Teutonic Chucky doll and slay them both. Would she use the side of a metal spatula? Her rolling pin? Or her teeth?

Vinnie decided the sharp edge of a spatula was her best bet, even though Mrs. H tried to fake her out by putting it in the dishwasher.

"Yah, *Liebchen*, ve have Nintendo. Now Playstation 2? *Was ist das?*"

Liebchen? Oh, please. Adam was a *Liebchen* and she was a *Schlampe*? Vinnie folded her arms over her chest. Mrs. H had yet to offer *her* a cookie.

Vinnie listened as the two chatted, and Mrs. H's face positively glowed when Adam told her that her cookies were much better than Mama's.

Sheesh. Mama would pull him out of New York in a heartbeat if she'd heard that little bit of sacrilege.

Adam asked Mrs. Hegel if she made grilled cheese sandwiches, too. Mrs. H looked blank for a moment but said she was sure she could. Adam told her he was pretty sure the secret lay in the cheese. You had to use the good kind, the skinny square kind that came flattened between plastic wrappers.

Mrs. H looked horrified, but nodded with the culinary wisdom of the ages.

Vinnie swallowed a good giggle, since she hadn't swallowed a cookie.

"So," Adam asked the housekeeper, "have you met my toad?"

Mrs. H's nostrils tightened and she blinked rapidly. "Yah," she said. "I have." She exchanged a glance with Vinnie. "And a very fine specimen of toad he is, too."

"His name is Prince Charming," Adam told her. "I came over to see him. Thanks for the cookies and milk."

"Yah, you're velcome, *Liebchen*."

Vinnie took her little brother to the room she

was staying in, only looking back once to see if the spatula was flying toward her neck.

"This place is waaaay cool," said Adam, looking around. "Check out that squiggly painting over the fireplace. Oooh, and this chair is like some kind of leather hammock or something." He stopped, fascinated by one of Nick's models, which took up an entire console table. "Wow. A whole miniature building, with miniature people and cars and trees and everything. That *rocks*."

"My . . . er, roommate . . . is an architect," Vinnie told him. "He builds real buildings, like the ones all around us."

"He does?"

Vinnie nodded.

"That's awesome!" Adam's eyes shone.

They went into her bedroom and she showed him Prince Charming, who was sitting rather glumly in his mini-aquarium.

"He's getting fatter."

Vinnie had to agree. The little guy could put away some worms and slugs. "Well, I don't think he gets much exercise."

"That box is pretty small. Couldn't we get him a bigger one?"

"Adam, the bigger ones cost a lot of money. I can't afford one right now."

"But he's not happy."

"Well, maybe when I can save some more money we can figure something out."

Adam shoved his hands in his pockets and sat on her bed. He gave a mighty yawn, and she remembered that he hadn't been sleeping well lately. While she knew he'd object instantly to the suggestion of a nap, there were other ways to accomplish it.

"Why don't you get out your reading for English, and I'll get my book, and we'll just lie here and read for a little while? Then we can take Daffodil for a walk. Sound good?"

He shrugged. "Sure, okay."

Within twenty minutes, he was asleep.

Vinnie didn't expect him to nap for more than an hour or so, but he must have been exhausted. When Daffodil began to squirm and pace, Vinnie didn't have the heart to wake him up. She scribbled a note to him and left it in his English book, then quietly got herself and the dog ready to go.

Mrs. Hegel was still puttering around the kitchen, and the body snatchers seemed to have replaced her, because none of her former warmth toward Adam appeared. She pointedly ignored Vinnie and the dog and kept on chopping onions.

Vinnie waited until she turned her back, then made a face and snatched one of the cookies she hadn't been offered.

She slid it deep into her coat pocket and got the requisite plastic baggie from the kitchen drawer. New York code required that one pick up after one's dogs.

"Adam is sleeping, Mrs. Hegel. I left him a note that I'm taking Daffodil for a walk, but I just wanted to let you know."

"Yah," Mrs. H muttered. Thwack, thwack, thwack.

"Okay, then. Have a nice evening."

Thwack, thwack.

Vinnie gave up. She should have taken *two* of the darn cookies.

Nick came in after a long day to find Vinnie in his kitchen, peering at one of Mrs. Hegel's German cookbooks.

She looked delectable at the island, with her wild hair held on top of her head, her chin on her elbows, and her truly spectacular derriere in the air.

If Nick weren't such a gentleman, he could've definitely seen possibilities in her position. Oh, yes. Great possibilities. Okay, so he wasn't a gentleman.

"Hello," he said to her, hoping that she wouldn't move.

"Hi," she replied. She did. She tucked some stray tendrils of hair behind her ears, and they framed her face, more lovely than a pair of two-carat studs could ever be. "Um, Nick, I have to—"

"No, you don't." He threw resolve and logic and good behavior out the window. Thoughts of her had been driving him crazy. "All you have to do is"—he rounded the island and took her in his arms—"kiss me again."

"Ah, Nick, there really is—"

He sealed her lips with his own, and God it felt good. She was stiff at first, and then she melted into him. He delved into her mouth, wanting to taste every inch of her, and his body hummed with heat. Damn, did he want Elly May naked. And really there was no reason why they couldn't—

"*Hey! Get off my sister!*"

Vinnie shot out of his arms, and Nick whirled at the high-pitched, cracking adolescent voice. It was an angry voice, and it belonged to a skinny red-headed twerp with glasses. Worse, the twerp was wielding a heavy silver candlestick that had once belonged to the great architect Louis Sullivan.

Nick had bought the pair at auction, and had not intended for them to be used this way.

"Adam! Put that down *now*." Vinnie's voice shook.

"Are you okay?" He ignored her order.

"I'm fine. He wasn't hurting me, Adam. He was . . ." Her voice failed. "He was kissing me."

"Why?"

"Because sometimes grown-ups . . . do."

"Did you want him to kiss you?" Adam asked, lowering the candlestick. He glared at Nick.

"I, um. Oh, God." Vinnie's face had turned the shade of Adam's Chief's jersey. "Yes. Yes, I did. Now go and put that candlestick back where you found it, and don't ever do that again."

Nick watched all this in absolute silence. What was Vinnie's little brother doing in his apartment?

Adam came back into the kitchen and folded his arms across his skinny chest.

"Nick, this is my brother Adam. Adam, this is my employ—uh, roommate, Nick."

"Roommate," Adam repeated scornfully.

"Yes, roommate." Vinnie's voice was firm again.

"I'm not stupid, Vinnie. Men and women aren't supposed to live together unless they're married. Mama and Pastor have both told me that."

Poor Vinnie. Nick couldn't imagine how she was going to explain this to her brother's satisfaction.

"Mama and Pastor don't live in New York, Adam, and—"

"So the Bible doesn't apply in New York?"

"That's not what I'm saying. Adam, my former roommate was a dangerous crazy person. I didn't feel safe staying there. So I'm staying here until I find another place."

"Did you kiss your other roommate?"

Vinnie shuddered. "*No.*"

"Is kissing this one part of your job? You said he's your employer."

"*No!* Oh, my God. No, that's *not* part of my job. And I won't be kissing him anymore." She shot Nick a look pregnant with meaning.

"We were just trying an experiment," Nick added.

"Yes," Vinnie agreed brightly. "A new kind of kiss that Nick wants to show his girlfriend."

Nick blinked. Girlfriend? How did Vinnie know about Dana? And it wasn't as if Dana were really his girlfriend. More like a bed-buddy.

"What kind of kiss?" asked Adam. "Aren't there only three? The reg'lar, the butterfly, and the icky French one? Sure looked like you were doing the icky French one."

"No, actually. We were trying the new . . ." Nick's eyes lit on the cookbook. ". . . *German* kiss."

"German?"

Nick nodded.

"What's different about it?"

Nick looked down at his dimunitive would-be

murderer. "Well, when you get to the middle of it, both people have to jump and click their heels together."

"You guys didn't do that."

"We hadn't," said Nick in the voice of reason, "gotten to the middle of it yet. You interrupted us." It would serve the kid right if he tried the new German kiss on one of his first dates. Too bad Nick would never get to witness it.

"So what other kinds of kisses are there?" Adam was clearly fascinated in spite of himself.

Nick thought fast. "Well, the Russian one."

"And how's *that* work?"

"Both parties have a tongue-of-war with a vodka-soaked beet."

"Huh-uh."

"Yes. I promise you." Nick assumed his most serious expression. Behind Adam, Vinnie coughed into a paper towel.

"And then there's the Italian one, where the two people involved suck red wine through either end of a Crazy Straw."

"I think you're a big liar."

"Who, me?"

"Well, whether you're lying or not, don't practice this stuff on my sister anymore, okay? I wouldn't want to have to hurt you." Adam stood in what he probably thought of as a mean Clint Eastwood stance.

Nick bit his lip, since the kid resembled nothing so much as a carrot-topped preying mantis. Damn, but he was skinny.

"Adam," said Vinnie, "it's not nice to threaten

Mr. Wright, and especially not in his own home, where you are a guest. I'd like you to apologize."

"I didn't threaten him, exactly—"

"Adam!"

"Fine. Sorry, *Mister* Wright. But you can practice those lip-locks with Daffodil or someone else, can't you?"

"I, ah, suppose that I could, yes. Apology accepted."

Adam was still looking at him sideways. The kid wasn't stupid, and knew a noncommittal answer when he heard one.

Vinnie said, "Adam, I'd like you to go to my room, please, and close the door. Mr. Wright and I need to talk."

"Are you gonna kiss him again?" the boy demanded.

"No. Now, scoot."

He sighed heavily but did as he was asked.

A long silence ensued, until they heard the door to Vinnie's room slam.

"So," Nick nudged her.

She rubbed her arms as if cold. "So," she repeated. "Here's the situation. Adam is having a rotten time of it at school. He's the target of a group of bullies, and he's homesick and lonely and feeling a little out of his depth."

"I see," said Nick, and he did—all too well. He remembered his own days at Choate. But as an only child he hadn't had a sister like Vinnie to intervene.

Suddenly he knew what she was about to ask, and it started an unexpected war inside him. He was also amazed that she had the wherewithal, the sheer chutzpah, the set of big brass balls needed to ask him such a thing.

But she did. "Nick, I'm afraid that if I force him to go back to school tonight, it's going to be all over for him. That he'll dig in his heels and decide he hates it so much that he'll stop trying at all, and ruin his chances for a great future. He's so bright, he's so fragile, he's such a combination of child and adult right now!"

Nick saw the passion on her face, the frustrated love, the desperation. His gut churned. It roiled with a horrid, gaseous response, and he realized with a shock that it was jealousy.

Oh, that is pathetic, Wright. You're jealous of a skinny, prepubescent Annie-kid? But he was. Where had *his* Vinnie been, when he was six and seven and scared shitless in the hallowed halls of Choate? Where? Aunt Edna had come to visit, of course, but never had he had the option of leaving school and going home with her. Not except during the summers, occasionally.

"Adam needs me," Vinnie was saying. "He needs support right now. Needs a haven."

Yeah, or maybe he just needed to grow up fast, as Nick had. It sucked, it really did, but after you lost a few teeth and a whole lot of dignity, you picked yourself back up and went on with your scrawny schoolboy life. You set goals and you achieved them. You did your work.

"So I'm asking you, even though I know this is *soooo* out of line, if he can stay here with me for just a week. Just until I can boost his confidence again and make sure the school is taking steps to protect him."

The nasty kernel of jealousy blossomed again in Nick's stomach, and he swallowed. It was hideously embarrassing to be jealous of a twelve-year-old boy. It made him angry. How could he?

Wouldn't he have killed for a sister, a champion, like Vinnie? Someone who loved him enough to fight his battles? And the kid deserved a break. Just as he had.

"Of course," Nick said. "He can stay for a week. Can't do any harm."

Vinnie's eyes pooled, and her face glowed with gratitude. She launched herself at him. "Oh, thank you, Nick. Thank you, thank you, thank you."

He accepted her hug awkwardly, feeling completely undeserving of it. If she only knew what was going through his mind. God, he was a selfish bastard.

Nick tossed restlessly in his bed, trying not to think of the snug little family unit ensconced next door. Vinnie, Adam, Daffodil, and Prince Charming all shared a room while he himself lay alone.

Not that he wanted to bed down with a kid, a dog, or a toad. But they were holding Vinnie hostage in there, and there was no way he could get to her.

If he even tried to spirit her off and have his way with her, Daffodil would whine, Prince Charming would swell and look even uglier, and Adam would hit him with whatever came to hand.

Hell. His hip bachelor pad was becoming a cross between a zoo and a day-care center, and he couldn't say it was a welcome transformation.

Nick was wide-awake, hungry, and horny. He threw the covers back and left his bedroom for the pantry, in search of he didn't know what.

Funny, but the light in the back hall was already on, and there he found Vinnie, sitting cross-legged on the parquet floor with her back against the wall, eating handfuls of dry Captain Crunch cereal.

Since he was barefoot, and a mouthful of Captain Crunch is, to the muncher, generally louder than a twenty-one-gun salute, she didn't hear him. So when he said, "You're up awfully late," she first blew half her mouthful of Captain Crunch crumbs all over the floor, then choked on the remainder.

Nick tried not to laugh and knelt on the floor to pound her on the back, though he wasn't at all sure it helped. Vinnie's hair was wilder than ever, and as she leaned forward to cough, it seemed to get in her mouth. So Nick gently took it in his hands and held it back before giving her another healthy whack between the shoulder blades. A final, whole Crunch nugget flew out of her throat and hit the opposite wall, and Vinnie heaved for breath.

"Are you okay?" Nick asked.

"Water," she rasped. "Please."

Nick let go of her hair, not without regret, and brought her a glass of water. He settled down beside her again as she sipped at it, and shook his head at her.

"Well, geez, you scared the living daylights out of me! You can't sneak up on people like that." Her voice was hoarse, and she quivered with outrage and probably mortification.

"I didn't mean to sneak," he said mildly. "What's with the dry cereal? Is there no milk?"

Vinnie stuck her chin out. "I have a thing for dry Crunch."

"It's a delicacy, eh?"

"No. More of a comfort food."

"I see." Nick touched her shoulder lightly, through a white terry-cloth robe that could be described charitably as old, and by most people as mangy. "And why do you need comfort, Vinnie? Hmmm?"

She sighed, and retrieved the runaway Crunch cube with her toe. Slowly, she drew her knee up, pulling it towards them. "I just don't know what to do about Adam." She leaned back and deliberately bonked her head against the wall. Then she did it again.

"Hey," said Nick. "Stop that. You're going to hurt yourself."

Vinnie just looked at him, frustration written all over her face. "I don't know what to do," she repeated.

"Seems to me that you're doing the best you can."

"Am I doing the right things, though?"

Nick shifted uncomfortably. "That's hard for me to say. I've never had a brother, since I'm an only child. And I certainly don't have any parenting skills—nor will I ever." He punctuated the sentence with a short laugh.

"You don't want kids? A family?"

He sighed. "I'm not . . . emotionally equipped . . . for kids and a family."

"Why not? What do you mean?"

He ran a hand through his hair. "I—Oh, hell. You learn your parenting skills from your parents. Mine had none, okay? They're not bad people, but they were rotten parents. And I'll *never* expose a kid to that. Not ever."

"Expose a kid to what, Nick?" Vinnie's voice was only a little over a whisper.

"To not being wanted! To being a burden. To being sent off to various places, *like a goddamned package.*"

An odd, strangled sound came from Vinnie's throat. It was the echo of something he couldn't handle, and with which he didn't want to come face-to-face.

He refused to look at her, refused to see it in her eyes. He would throw up. "Don't say a word, okay? Not one. I don't want your pity."

"O-Okay."

"We were talking about Adam. Not me. *Adam.*"

"Right," said Vinnie, after a deep breath. "I just want what's best for him. I want him to be happy. I want—"

Gently, Nick took her chin in his hand and turned her face to his. "That's a good question, Vinnie. What do *you* want?"

She froze, and her expression went from anguished and worried to blank. She said nothing.

"Hmmmm?"

"I want for Adam to have opportunities, and for my mother to recover fully."

She was all worry and aching responsibility. "Tell me about your mother, Vin. What's wrong with her, exactly?"

Vinnie sighed. "She struggles with depression and agoraphobia—meaning she has a terrible time even leaving the house. Her bedroom became a co-coon for her after my dad died, and she was afraid to come out of it and face the world. It was like she turned into a little girl again, and I became the mom. I had to. She couldn't, or wouldn't, do any-thing." Tears filled her eyes, and they undid Nick.

He put an arm around her shoulders and gave her an awkward squeeze. He wasn't much good at giving comfort, but she made him want to try. "But she's well enough now for you to leave her on her own?"

Vinnie sighed again, and dashed at her eyes with her knuckles. "I don't think she'll ever be a hun-dred percent 'normal,' you know? But I dragged her into counseling, and she's on some medication, and she now plays the organ for the Presbyterian church. These are huge steps forward. Huge. You can't imagine what a battle it's been. And I finally had to make a choice, for Adam's sake. I had to get him out of there . . ." She began to cry in earnest.

Nick wrapped both arms around her. He still felt weird, but it was necessary. "Oh, Vin. Oh, sweet-heart. You've been through so much. You're amaz-ing . . ." He dropped a kiss on her hair, stroked her back, rocked with her.

"No I'm not," she choked, and sobbed harder.

"You are, you are."

"No." She pulled away from him and gave him

an anguished glance. "No." More tears streamed down her face. "Because the truth is that I wanted to leave. I was dying to leave. Just walk away from her. I didn't do this just for Adam. I did it partly for me—because I couldn't take any more . . ." She put her head down on her knees and shook.

"And you're beating yourself up now? That's crazy." Nick put a finger under her chin and tilted her face up. Even tear-streaked and swollen, she was beautiful. "Vinnie, you've given one hundred percent for years. Even a saint would have to take a break. You're only human."

"I feel so selfish." She mopped at her face with her pajama sleeve.

"You've got to be kidding me. *Selfish*? No, honey. You're not selfish." He gave a short bark of unamused laughter. "*I'm* selfish. I could give you lessons."

She smiled slightly at that and wiped her other pajama sleeve over her face. He pulled her arm down gently and used the pads of his thumbs, wiping under her eyes, which widened at his gesture. "Now, I want you to tell me about *you*. What you want, not what you think you need to give other people."

She said nothing, just bit her lip.

"You know what I'm asking, Vinnie. You've got to have goals of your own."

"I can't think about that right now."

"Talk to me. What do you dream about doing with your life?"

She stabbed at the floor with her big toe. "One day, I'd like to have a degree in social work. I'd like to help people . . . individuals and families who are disadvantaged, or maybe end up in situations like we did, where I was too embarrassed to admit to anybody that Mama wouldn't get out of bed for days on end. For a long time I didn't know there were names for the problems she had, much less ways to treat them. I had to figure all that out. In a small town, especially, you don't go asking for help if you don't want everybody to know your business—even isolated and outside of the town center like we were, in the cabin."

Nick looked at her sweet, earnest face and thought about all the opportunities she'd been denied. Opportunities to be a child, to be carefree, to read and explore what interested her. How had she managed? And not become bitter? She had a generosity he would never have. She was remarkable.

Vinnie squirmed under his gaze, clearly uncomfortable talking about herself. "Geez, Nick, why so serious? I mean, what do *you* want? Let's turn the tables."

He gazed at her for a long moment. "You," he said. "I want you, Vinnie."

Chapter 18

Her breath caught in her throat, and the final piece of Captain Crunch disintegrated under her big toe. Nicholas Wright wanted her.

He demonstrated how much he wanted her with his lips against hers—hot, seeking, unwilling to take no for an answer. Vinnie gave in, and he used the advantage to haul her onto his lap so that her threadbare robe fell open and her breasts pushed wantonly against his chest, held back by nothing but a thin T-shirt.

Worse, but even more forbidden and delicious, was the way Nick's hardness pushed against her through her cotton pajama bottoms.

He shifted her as the kiss continued, so that her legs straddled his and the contact increased.

The stubble on his cheeks and chin scraped her every time he took a breath, and she wondered how it would feel on her bare breasts. Shamelessly, she wanted nothing more than for Nick to pull up her shirt and take her nipples into his mouth, her breasts into his big hands. The thought alone had her breathless, beyond excited, and even on the edge of wild.

Nick seemed to sense it, and traced the outer slopes gently with his fingers, but didn't move inward.

Her thighs trembled, dropping her lower against him, and teasing them both.

Oh, God, why wouldn't he touch her breasts? She was going to go crazy if he didn't . . . Nick pulled his mouth from hers, and she gasped. He was breathing hard, too, observing her from under lazy lids, a sexy smile playing over his mouth. His dimples flashed, and just as she thought she'd die if he didn't touch her *now*, heat and moisture encircled a nipple. Still, he didn't take it into his mouth, just warmed it through the T-shirt, circling the other with a feather-light index finger.

It wasn't until she whimpered that he actually bit her lightly through the thin cotton and drew one breast into his mouth while his palm cupped the other.

Madness, pure madness, and spiraling heat, and a trembling longing with hot, hot pulse points enveloped her. Her whole body shook, and dear God, Nick had only touched her breasts. Through clothing.

Her thoughts suspended completely as Nick nuzzled her other nipple, captured it, teased it, suckled it. The former one, now abandoned, felt wet and cold and wanting. Couldn't the man have two mouths?

Nick kicked the hall door closed and tumbled

her onto her back, lifting the T-shirt and shoving it up under her arms. Then his hands were on her bare flesh, worshiping, kneading, fondling. Vinnie's eyes flew open, then closed again as he squeezed her breasts together and took both nipples into his mouth at one time.

With his hardness at her core, touching her in just the right place, she came on the spot, rocketing and thrashing against him, his mouth still pleasuring her nipples.

He pinned her with his body as she thrashed, and didn't stop. With wonder, with cloudy astonishment, Vinnie felt herself climbing again, even higher this time. Every muscle in her body clenched with tension, she barely noticed when Nick yanked her pajama bottoms down. She wouldn't have noticed at all without the sensation of prickly wool rug under her. Then Nick's mouth on her breasts was replaced by simple fingers, while he himself went south.

Her entire body trembling, she shot over the edge into spectacular vibrance as Nick's tongue made a single, long hot foray.

She felt drunk, insensible with sensation when she opened her eyes. Nick lay between her legs, grinning at her and tracing her navel.

"My blood is boiling," he said. "May I have you now?"

She didn't trust herself to speak. She just nodded dumbly.

"Perhaps you'd like to cool down, though," he said. Then his dimples flashed, and he winked at her.

Vinnie lay spent on the rug while Nick opened the hallway door and peered around.

Oh, my God! She thought. *Adam! Adam could be awake. He could have walked right in here. What kind of slut am I?* But she couldn't force herself to move.

She heard the refrigerator open, and a certain amount of rustling. Still she lay, unable to move. And presently Nick came back, loaded down with a full tray. He dumped it on the floor, then turned the old-fashioned key in the lock.

Vinnie managed to get her elbows under her and semi–sat up to look at the tray. "Are we having a picnic?" she asked.

Nick's answer was a wolfish grin. "Exactly." He knelt down and yanked off her pajama bottoms entirely, along with her panties.

"Hey!"

"Are you having a bad time?" he asked.

She shook her head.

He stripped off her robe and T-shirt. Then he shucked his own pants.

For the first time, Vinnie got to see him entirely naked, and the sight was worth the wait. Nick had a taut, disciplined body, with beautiful, athletic legs. His large hands and feet had not been false advertising, either.

Vinnie liked the looks of everything about him, but she didn't have long to look, it seemed. Nick made a pillow out of her robe and tucked it under her head. Then he knelt between her legs and pulled the tray toward them.

"What—" Vinnie began.

"Ssshhh. You can have your way with me next time, okay?"

"Uh—yeow! That's cold!"

Nick had placed an orange slice (convenient hole in the center) around her left nipple, and now he evened things out with another. Goose bumps erupted all over her torso, and sticky juice ran down the slopes of her breasts.

Nick grinned, and added a lime slice over her belly button. Then he put two maraschino cherries on her nipples. "A bit cliché," he conceded, "a bit Tom Wesselman, but I like them."

Vinnie said nothing, having no clue who Tom What's-It was. She was torn between a desire to laugh and just plain desire. She couldn't believe she was letting Nick deck her out with fruit!

But he wasn't even close to finished. He added raspberry sauce to his feast, trickling it in delicate chef's dribbles over her breasts and belly.

Over those he trickled chocolate syrup, creating a duo-tone Pollock effect on her skin. Next came the blueberries, not to be outdone by the honey-slicked banana.

Vinnie watched him peel it, denying until the last possible moment that he was going to do with it what he did. She watched as he squeezed golden honey upon it in fat driblets. And then, finally, she shook off her denial and felt it slide between her legs, the honey immediately losing the battle with gravity and traveling toward her.

She'd gone from hot to cold to hot all over again, and her body was humming with the ridiculous, the sublime, and the erotic all at once. It wasn't a tune she was familiar with. But then again, she'd certainly never used a hallway in quite such a fashion, or held a banana between her thighs.

Nick added the final touch when he dusted her with multicolored baking sprinkles, and she began to laugh. He did, too, until he knelt before her, finally ready to begin his feast.

"This beats a whipped-cream bikini all to hell," he murmured.

Vinnie tried not to think of how many he'd encountered as his mouth covered hers again in a slow, deep kiss. Her arms went around his neck and her fingers twined through his hair, massaging his scalp, until he took her wrists and pinned them ever-so-gently above her head. "This is all for you," he said. "Next time, we can do whatever you want, okay?"

She nodded, afraid suddenly that there would be no next time. That this was an aberration, a mistake, a—

Nick's mouth closed over a breast again, suckling through the delicate flesh of the orange slice, his tongue circling her cherry-capped nipple. And that was the end of thought. The orange and cherry disappeared, leaving nothing but juices running down her skin. Nick took care of those quickly, his tongue a magical instrument—hot, soft, wet and thorough. He bit the soft flesh and kissed it, bit again, torturing her with exquisite, urgent sensation. Tension in her built, ebbed, built, ebbed as he moved between exciting and tender, tips and then dips.

218 ‧ Karen Kendall

Nick followed the rivulets of raspberry and chocolate all over her body, descending as low as the tops of her knees.

And then, finally, he approached the banana, wicked intentions all too clear. His dimples were out in force, flashing naked against the stubble of his face.

Nick bent over her and nudged the banana, which slid in the honey against her. Vinnie moaned helplessly as he slid it up a couple of inches, and then down again, into the pool of honey between her legs.

It wasn't nearly hard enough for her, and he knew it. He teased her a little longer before nipping the top right off of it, waggling his eyebrows at her, and swallowing.

She shifted her hips restlessly, and he seemed to take the hint. Nick bit the banana all the way down to the juncture of her thighs, and brought this piece up to her own mouth. After a slight hesitation, she took it from him. When had she turned into such a kinky chick?

She didn't know, but Vinnie savored the banana, honey and all, until it was gone, and Nick spread her legs to get the last piece.

By the time Nick had gotten all the honey, Vinnie's tension was climbing frantically again, and he pulled her back down with a hand on her belly.

"Pill?" he asked thickly.

She shook her head. "Condom," she managed, and he nodded.

A few seconds later, the dim memory of the banana was gone and Nick entered her with a slick, hot surety.

His whole body shook against hers, and Vinnie realized that he was holding back an enormous tension of his own. Every muscle of his buttocks was taut with restraint, likewise his abdomen, his chest, even his arms.

She spread her knees wide and ran her hands along his hard thighs as she rocked against him.

He was so strong he moved her along the carpet, though she clung with every thrust and tried to meet him. A thick, liquid pleasure built within her, unlike the quicksilver of her other climaxes.

As Nick rocked harder, and took her breasts again into his mouth, she came apart in slow, thick liquid motion. She threw her head back and arched into it as she shook, and Nick gave a last mighty thrust, groaning her name into her hair.

Chapter 19

The return to consciousness was slow and most unwelcome for Nick. He'd gone and gotten on the dog-sitter. Was still on her. And he didn't feel like getting off. Though he was probably crushing the life out of her ... Nick rolled to the side, nuzzled her hair, and pillowed his head against one of those marvelous breasts. He wanted her again ...

Suddenly his head was rudely knocked to the floor, as Vinnie sat upright.

"Adam!" she exclaimed, in horrified tones.

"Adam?" Nick asked, rubbing his head.

"He's in the apartment!"

"Asleep, and separated by many walls, several rooms, and a locked door."

"I can't believe I let this happen, and with him *here*."

He kissed her breast, traced the swell of it in the darkness, drawing his fingers across her skin and up to the hollow of her neck, where her pulse beat erratically. "It's okay, Vinnie. No harm done."

"No, it's not okay! What kind of person am I?"
She scrambled around for her pajamas.

Nick sighed. "You're human. And why don't you
focus on yourself sometimes, instead of always on
your brother? You're not his mother, Vinnie. Why
don't you finally let *her* do some of the worrying?"

She released her breath in a hiss, dropping the
flannel pajamas to the floor. "I told you! My
mother can barely take care of herself, Nick! Much
less her son. I have to do the worrying."

"Shhhh," he said. "I'm sorry. Relax."

"I can't."

"Yes you can, honey."

"You're a fine person to tell me that, Guy Who
Never Sleeps."

"Did I or did I not relax you very recently?"

"Now you're playing dirty."

"Oh, sweetheart, I can get much dirtier than
that . . ." He kissed her again, and ran his hands up
and down her still-nude body, caressing her warm,
creamy skin. Her rigidity melted under his touch,
though his own increased.

"Hey!" she said, feeling the nudge against her
belly.

"Let's just ignore that, okay?"

"Um. If you say so."

"Come on, honey. Stay with me a while. Stay
naked . . ."

She pulled away. "No." She picked up her pajama bottoms again and climbed into them. "I
don't know how I let this happen. This was an incredibly bad idea . . ."

"Why?"

She all but glared at him. "Come on, Nick. You know why."

He avoided her eyes.

"Yeah," she said, "that's what I thought."

"What?"

"I work for you. That's the only relationship we should have, and we're putting this mistake behind us, okay?"

"Vinnie—"

He was now talking to the hand.

"Nope. I don't want to hear it. No speeches, nothing about how it was comfort sex, *nada*."

"Comfort sex! Is that what you think it was?"

She threw on her T-shirt top and twisted her hair into a knot. She blew out a breath. "I don't know what it was. All I know is that it's not happening again. We are total opposites in every way. I want a husband one day, and kids of my own. You're never getting married, and you freak at the mere mention of children. That's a pretty good indication that we shouldn't be doing what we just did."

Nick opened his mouth to refute her words, but she was right. So what could he say? He yanked on his sweats and unlocked the door.

Vinnie all but sprinted to the back hallway to check on Adam.

Nick wished he could change places with Daffodil and howl at the moon.

Vinnie felt wicked as she made her way to the bathroom. She prayed with all her strength that Adam was asleep and she wouldn't encounter him.

How could she possibly justify what she had just done?

Hours earlier, she'd promised both herself and her little brother that she wouldn't even kiss Nick again, and then she'd gone and gotten beyond dirty with the man. Worse, she'd done it with Adam in the same house.

What was she thinking? She supposed the problem lay in the fact that she *hadn't* been thinking. She'd only been feeling, and acting on sheer animal instinct.

Honestly, how could she have said no to a man like Nick? He chased such an answer right out of a woman's vocabulary.

He didn't even make love like a normal man. No, with Nick the sex had been unreal, an orchestrated picnic of sight, smell, texture, and sensation. The man had played her, a lowly fiddle, like a concert violinist, bringing her to pitches and heights she'd never dreamed existed. Three orgasms in one night? She'd had that many with William over the course of a *year*. And he'd thought he was a gift to women. Hah. She hoped he didn't yell too much at that girl with the toe ring. Then again, the chick *had* let herself be rolled naked under a car. That didn't speak well for her self-esteem.

Vinnie locked the bathroom door and threw off her robe. Then she got into the shower and turned the taps on full blast. Another miraculous thing about Nick's palatial apartment was that the hot water appeared instantly, with no wait.

As it drilled into her neck and back muscles,

more of her reasoning power returned, and with it doubts, fear, and self-recrimination. She had just slept with her employer. She had jeopardized her job.

Worse, that employer had a girlfriend. A girlfriend that she—and he—had conveniently just forgotten back there. Vinnie was appalled at herself and him. He had cheated, and she had been an instrument of hurt to another person.

How could she have done that? And how could she expect to compete with a gorgeous model-type interior designer who was part of Nick's world?

She belonged in Nick's world about as much as a pygmy belonged on a basketball court. She also had Adam to think about—she wasn't just a carefree single girl.

Vinnie scrubbed every inch of her body while the hot water also made her ruefully aware that she had rug burn on her butt. Well, what did she expect? The man had moved her about six feet along the darn carpet.

Vinnie rescrubbed herself, and thought, mortified, of how she'd told her mother she wasn't sleeping with Nick. She clearly remembered the sense of outrage the assumption had engendered in her. Outrage and righteousness, too.

Deciding that she probably had raspberry sauce and pulverized Crunch nuggets in her hair, she washed that, too. Then she conditioned it. And she shaved her legs. Still she felt dirty, and still Nick's hot water continued to flow, with no sign that it would ever cool.

That made her angry. The man had endless wealth,

it seemed, and every luxury that wealth could buy. He even had another, expensive woman. And yet Vinnie had just given him herself, too.

Why did some people get everything, while others got nothing? Vinnie shut off the hot water abruptly and grabbed for one of Nick's thick towels. She thought of Mama's little cabin, where if you wanted a shower, you had to take it first thing, and quick, before running any other appliances. And it had to be a short one, too, or you'd find yourself shivering as you shaved the goose bumps right off your legs.

Nick took his hot water for granted, just as he took Mrs. Hegel for granted, and probably her. *He's used to getting what he wants*, Vinnie told herself. *But don't get any silly ideas that he'll want you for more than sex. He'll be just like William, in the end. Except that he hasn't lied about wanting to get married.*

Vinnie stood wrapped in the plush towel and glared at herself through the steam fogging the mirror. *Hey, Stupid. You're an uneducated, country-fried dog-sitter, and he's a hot-shot Yale architect, a slick city guy. You have nothing in common.*

She pulled her pajamas on and towel-dried her hair before creeping back into her room. Daffodil opened one eye and grumbled at her, but Adam slept like the dead as she slipped in next to him and gave herself to sleep.

This situation was intolerable, it really was. Nick lay alone in his bedroom, listening to Vinnie shower down the hall. What he'd wanted to do was get into the shower with her. What he'd wanted was to make love to her again. What he'd wanted was to sleep with her in his own bed, with her bottom snug against him and his arms around her and his nose buried in her hair.

Apparently it didn't matter what he wanted, and it didn't matter that they were in his home. A skinny redheaded little twerp was ruling his roost. A little twerp that he hadn't invited, and for whom he didn't feel any particular affection.

It wasn't like he hated the kid. He could even find it in his heart to feel sorry for him. But he was most inconvenient, and his sister was obsessed with him, and he had that disturbing tendency toward violence with candlesticks.

Nick wondered why Adam didn't employ some of that pluck to fight back against the bullies. And suddenly he realized that sister and brother were alike in one respect: They found courage on each other's behalf, but perhaps not for themselves. Vinnie would never in a million years have asked him if *she* could move in. But she hadn't blinked an eye before asking if her brother could.

He wondered when she would get on with her own life. She couldn't be a dog-sitter forever. What would happen to Vinnie once Adam grew up and didn't need her anymore?

Nick knew she'd find another job, get married, or both. Have kids of her own. The thought disturbed him more than it should have. After tonight, the thought of Vinnie with some other guy was completely unacceptable.

Nick rolled to his stomach and slapped the pillow over his head. He felt . . . guilty. As if he'd sullied her purity or something. He'd gone a little overboard with the banana, though she'd been too stunned to protest much.

And she'd enjoyed it, he thought in his defense. So why did he feel like he'd just taught a nun to sunbathe nude and slurp mai-tais?

He should be pounding on his swelled chest, full of smug satisfaction that he'd given the girl three orgasms in a row.

The thought of her open to him, helpless and whimpering for release, made him so hard again that he could no longer lie on his stomach. He rolled over and fantasized briefly about throwing kid, dog, and toad all in the crate in the living room, and covering it like a canary cage. Then he could have Vinnie all to himself.

Unfortunately Child Protective Services, not to mention the SPCA, might have something to say about that. Nick beat his head on the pillow and tried counting sheep, but they kept morphing into bananas as they leaped over the fence in his mind.

Vinnie dreamed that she was back in Kansas, somersaulting through the clouds in a blue sky. She swooped down Main Street in Independence, past Sayer's Hardware and Hille Music, and DeFever-Osborn Drugstore and Great China Restaurant.

People stared and pointed at her as she flew, and she realized suddenly that the annual Neewollah parade for Halloween was coming right behind her.

Floats and baton twirlers and costumed kids and all. Every single last person in it pointed at her, and she realized she was naked.

Next thing she knew, she was sitting, still naked, in a pew of her church with a banana between her legs while Pastor Brownlow, in his Sunday robes, tried to remove it with a pair of long-handled barbecue tongs.

Vinnie woke up in a cold sweat, feeling like the biggest slut on the planet.

"Ow!" said Adam, next to her.

"Huh?"

"You just kicked me."

"Sorry." Vinnie rolled out of bed, found some socks, and pulled on her robe. "Come on, lazybones. Time to get ready for school."

Adam pulled the covers up to his chin and said nothing.

"Adam?"

Still, he was silent.

"Come on. You don't have to sleep there, at least for the next week. But you do have to go to classes. Okay?"

"What, Mr. Big-Shot said I can stay?"

"For a week. And don't call him that. He's being very nice about this."

Adam yawned.

"Do you want some breakfast?"

He nodded.

"Then go take your shower and meet me in the kitchen."

Vinnie approached the huge kitchen with trepidation, knowing that Nick would probably be sitting at the bar, sipping his cappuccino and reading the *Times*.

Sure enough, he was.

"Hi," said Vinnie, gruff with embarrassment.

"Good morning. Did you sleep well?" A smile danced in his eyes over the modern white coffee cup.

She shook her head, her eyes darting to the pantry.

"Neither did I. I wanted you in my bed."

"Sshhhhh!" Vinnie hissed, jerking her head toward the back bedrooms. "We've gotta talk, but not now."

She helped herself to a cup of coffee and gave Daffodil, who'd followed her, a morning cookie. While the dog snarfed it inelegantly, she gulped down half her cappuccino without realizing that she'd forgotten the sugar. Finally, the bitter taste reminded her, and she blinked. *Sugar. Sugar on the side. That's what she was to Nick, a little sugar on the side.*

"Don't you have a girlfriend?" she blurted. *Aaack. I can't believe I asked him that.* But after what they'd done last night, she was entitled.

Nick eyed her over his cup. "Nooooo," he answered slowly. "Not really."

"What does that mean?"

Adam chose this moment to enter the kitchen, his red hair slicked down and his glasses a little steamed. One shirttail hung out of his pants, and he hadn't tied his sneakers. "What's for breakfast?"

"What would you like? Do you want me to make you bacon and eggs, with toast? Or do you want cereal?"

"Cereal," said Adam. "With banana."

Nick spit his coffee onto the financial section's front page.

Vinnie's ears burned as she nodded, and she retrieved the Captain Crunch from the pantry, averting her gaze from the long, fringed wool rug.

She poured some into a bowl for Adam, and forced herself not even to look Nick's way as she got a banana from the bunch in the fruit bowl.

Nick rustled another section of the paper and held it up to his face. But when she pulled back the first section of peel, and stole a glance at him, he was watching her.

He cleared his throat and looked away. Vinnie took a knife and, nostrils flaring, cut the banana into about twenty skinny discs that landed with little grainy plops in Adam's bowl. She drenched the mass in cold milk and set it in front of her brother, who gave them both an odd glance, then climbed onto a stool and dug in.

Vinnie took her coffee and fled. "I'm going to get dressed now! Then we'll take Daffodil and walk you to school, Adam."

Nick and Adam were left to eye each other uneasily.

"So," said Nick, trying to remember what it felt like to be twelve years old. "You're not too crazy about the new school, huh?"

Adam hunched his shoulders over the cereal

bowl. He looked incongruous perched on Nick's expensive Italian barstool, his grungy gym shoes resting on the rung. His sharp elbows, knees, and ears poked out at funny angles.

"Nope." He shoved a big spoonful into his mouth and munched somberly.

"Do you like New York? The city?"

The kid wouldn't even look at him. "Nope." Munch, munch.

Nick took a sip of coffee and tried to think of something else to ask him. What were twelve-year-old boys into? What did they get excited about? Girls? It was a good possibility.

"I bet a good-looking kid like you already has a girlfriend."

Adam let the spoon drop against the side of his bowl and turned his head to give Nick a scathing glance. Then he refocused his attention on his cereal. "There aren't any girls at Gotham-Young."

Nick cleared his throat. *This conversation's going well.* He couldn't wait to get the hell out of his own apartment and go to work.

Chapter 20

Two hours later, he was deeply regretting that he hadn't just stayed in bed this morning. Hmmmmm . . . with a soft, pliant, willing Vinnie. Kissing her all over, burying his face in her gorgeous hair, falling into her impossibly warm, beautiful, understanding eyes.

"Wright? Wright, are you listening to me?" Jerry Southwick's voice interrupted these pleasant thoughts. "I said you're half a million over our proposed budget."

Nick took a deep breath and steepled his hands on the table between them. "Jer, as I've tried to explain to you, contractors don't work for free. Especially the ones who can actually read a damned blueprint and won't build the whole project upside down."

"I understand, but that one bid came in significantly lower!"

"And it was from a company I won't use ever again. The guy does shoddy work."

"So keep an eye on him."

"I can't be there every minute, and I'm telling you I don't trust him."

"How bad can he be? Every phase of the building has to pass inspection."

"Jerry, this is true. It is also true that he's got a bunch of illegals working for him who can't read and screw countless things up. And I'm telling you, if we have to stop and redo everything at each inspection stage, it's going to cost you a lot more than half a million in time, materials, and general frustration. Don't try to cut corners here."

"Then let's shave some more off the materials end."

"Jer, it's not like concrete and steel go on sale in January and July, okay? You want your North American headquarters built out of plastic?"

"Very funny, Wright."

Nick eventually got the grumbling Southwick somewhat placated and out of his office, and took off running to another job site, where the construction foreman had exceptionally bad news.

"Colonial artifacts? Here?" Nick swore.

"Yep." Silas, the foreman, hocked up a loogie and spit it on the now-hallowed ground. Charming.

"But we took borings of the site! How could we have missed this?"

Silas shrugged. "Dunno. They found an ole musket, though, an' some other such things, when they went digging for the foundation."

Nick cursed. This meant delays of weeks, possibly months, while excavations took place and various historical societies got hysterical . . . the client was going to kill him, even though they had gone through all the proper procedures.

He hopped into a cab and went back uptown, headed for a zoning board appeal. It really wasn't the time to think about Vinnie sitting beside him, wearing nothing but her beautiful shy smile. But there she was, and he couldn't do a damned thing about it except spring a woody that felt bigger than his blueprint tube. Jayzus! Didn't he have enough to worry about, without careening through midtown looking like he was attracted to a hairy cabdriver?

He *knew* he shouldn't have gotten on the dog-sitter. Nick paid the guy, who squinted at him suspiciously as he crab-walked into the building, disguising his unfortunate state as best he could. He dodged into the men's room and stood in a stall, conjuring Janet Reno one more time. He needed emergency deflation.

Damn it, Janet! Okay, today you're wearing a red see-through baby-doll nightie, and you have the claws of Freddy Krueger . . . thank you, God, for giving me this incredibly warped imagination. Nick's woody was gone in seconds flat, with a few more apologies to Justice.

He rode the elevator to the sixteenth floor, made his case in front of the zoning board, and had it promptly rejected. Could the day get any better?

Yes, it could. Nick walked into his apartment on this chilly late-November evening to find all the windows open and the fire alarm going off, while plumes of black smoke billowed from his Viking oven. Vinnie was waving a damp towel between a god-awful charred mess and the open kitchen window. Daffodil was attempting to bark, though Adam's hands were clamped around her snout to keep her quiet. The television blared in the background.

It was all Nick could do not to turn around and run. What had happened to his once-peaceful apartment? Jayzus, he needed a hard hat to walk through his own door at night. "What is going on here?"

Nick grabbed a couple of kitchen towels and hoisted the charred mess into the sink, instructing Vinnie to close the oven door and turn it off. He ran cold water over the disgusting, smoking mass.

Then he methodically eliminated the sources of noise: First he turned off the television. Then he popped the cover off the alarm and tweaked the wire loose. And then he turned to Daffodil and silenced her with an authoritative, "No!"

Finally, there was blessed silence.

"Hi!" Vinnie said, with false, flip cheer.

"Hi," Nick growled.

The kid just squinted at him.

Nick ran a hand over the back of his neck and stared at what used to be his pristine apartment. Cartoons with torn edges adorned his wood-paneled refrigerator. Schoolbooks spilled over his dining room table. Dog toys peeked out from under coffee tables and other furniture. A *flowered pillow* adorned his Phillipe Starck chair—design sacrilege!

He felt sure he had stumbled into the wrong

apartment. And yet, under all the clutter, it was his. He just wasn't used to sharing it. Not with a dog, or a woman, and especially not with a kid.

"I tried to make a pie," Vinnie said, by way of explanation. "Sorry."

"Is that what it was?" Nick asked. "I thought it was a biological weapon."

Adam cracked up, and it was good to see the kid smile. Nick quirked an eyebrow at him, and they exchanged a moment of male solidarity.

"It would have been a perfectly good pie, if I hadn't forgotten about it," said Vinnie defensively.

"I'm sure. What kind was it?"

"Apple."

"It's really cold in here, Vin."

"Yeah, I know. Sorry."

They all looked at the black smoke still hovering in the air.

"Tell you what—Adam and I were about to watch *Lord of the Rings* on video. Let's get a bunch of blankets and huddle up with hot cocoa together until the smoke clears. Sound good?"

"Er—" said Nick. But shortly thereafter he found himself sharing the couch with them under a goose-down quilt, wincing at the dental hygiene of Orcs. At first he felt awkward, and wouldn't have minded losing the kid. But Adam's rapt fascination with Tolkien's adventure was infectious. Against his will, Nick found himself enjoying this odd family experience. What in the hell was wrong with him?

Once the movie was over, he watched the ritual of bedtime between Vinnie and Adam. Observed her loving but firm handling of the boy. Yes, he needed to go to bed, even though he wasn't tired. Yes, he needed to brush and floss his teeth. Why? So he wouldn't look like an Orc when he grew up.

Nick hid a grin at this, as well as a disconcerting wave of tenderness for Vinnie, who looked tired herself. While she dealt with Adam, he called Daffodil, and made his way into the dog's bedroom. She wagged her little stump of a tail while he pulled pajamas out of her armoire—these adorned by little yellow ducks. "Okay, you. Work with me here. I have no idea how to get these on you."

She grinned up at him. He got down on his knees and dropped the top over her head. Of course she took the opportunity to lick his face. Nick shut his eyes and folded his lips inward, since he *had* made a deal with her: face for toes. When she was done, he opened his eyes. She looked back expectantly, huge brown eyes mournful under their little ginger Dobie-dot markings. What did she want? A kiss?

Nick balked. Kiss a dog?

"Go ahead," Vinnie said behind him. "It won't kill you."

He cleared his throat, feeling incredibly stupid to be: a) on his knees; b) trying to dress a dog in pajamas; c) having a witness to his first canine kiss.

Daffodil licked his cheek, and both females waited. *Oh, hell.* Nick dropped a quick smooch onto the head of the pooch.

Vinnie clapped and looked delighted.

Nick felt like a kindergartner who had successfully glued macaroni to a piece of construction paper. "Damn it," he growled, "how do you get her paws into the sleeves?"

"One at a time," said the annoying person he'd invited into his home.

He picked up a paw, winced at the red toenails, and maneuvered it gracelessly through the sleeve. "Remind me again why the dog has to wear pajamas?"

"Because you wanted to honor your great-aunt's wishes."

"Right." Nick got the other paw into the opposite sleeve. "You know she's up there laughing at me."

"No doubt about it."

"You could help."

Vinnie looked at her watch. "Nope. I'm off the clock. And this is too entertaining."

"Off the clock," Nick muttered, shoving a dog leg into the little duck printed pants. "How's that? You're staying here for free."

"What are you saying, Nick?" Her voice had gotten ominously calm. "That my off-hours belong to you, too?"

"Uh . . . no. No, that's not what I meant. I was kidding."

She folded her arms and glared at him. "No, I don't think you were. And this," she lowered her voice, "is why last night was a really bad idea."

Nick pulled Daff's pajama pants up with a snap. "Are you saying I took advantage of you last night, Vinnie? Because that's absolutely not true! You said it was comfort sex then, and now you're saying you were obligated because you work for me? You can't have it both ways!"

"We can't talk about this with Adam next door," she whispered, her face flushed.

"Fine. But we *will* talk about it. Now." He gestured for her to follow him, and closed the door on Daffodil. He grabbed two coats from the hall closet and led Vinnie out the French doors to the rooftop terrace.

"Okay, now what's this all about?"

Vinnie shrugged. "I guess it's obvious that I feel really weird about what happened."

"That makes two of us."

"It can *never* happen again."

"Why?" Nick tried to keep his voice light, even though her words killed him.

"Because of several things, all of which are obvious. One, I work for you, and it's too awkward. Two, I have to set an example for Adam. And three, loyalty is very important to me, and you have a girlfriend, Nick! *You have a girlfriend.* I don't know what you meant by that 'not really' business, but I don't buy it. 'Not really' is a cop-out that men use when the woman in question isn't convenient."

"I disagree. Sometimes 'not really' is the truth: That off and on there's been a woman whom I've slept with. But I no longer want to sleep with her. Unfortunately, I still have to see her for business."

"Oh," said Vinnie in a small voice. "Well, regardless of all that, I do work for you, and I have a little brother who doesn't need to be getting ideas into his head. And I belong to a church that truly

frowns on the type of behavior that . . . that . . .
we, um, engaged in last night. So it can't happen
again."

Nick doubted strongly that Vinnie's church published any rules against Forbidden Fruit—well, he
took that back. Ahem. He doubted that her church
had ever interpreted Forbidden Fruit to mean the
sorts of things they had actually done with fruit last
night. Forbidden Fruit was a metaphor, generally
speaking, not a literal thing.

"Let's take the fruit right out of the equation.
Surely your church doesn't frown on, say, the mis-
sionary position?"

"Nick! My point is about sex between two people who aren't married."

"But—and I'm not saying this to be a jerk, really—
obviously you've had unmarried sex before."

Vinnie turned her face away. "Well, I wasn't a
virgin. Virgins my age are really difficult to find
these days—even in Kansas. But that doesn't mean
my um, nonvirgin status is good."

"Are you under the impression it's bad?"

"At least I did think I was going to marry the
other two guys."

Her unspoken statement was that she was in no
danger of marrying *him*. While Nick should have
been relieved that Elly May had no romantic illusions about him, he was instead offended. Chopped
liver, was he? No—just a City Slick Dick, in her
eyes.

He said quietly, "I'm glad you didn't marry those
guys, Vinnie. I would never have met you."

"Well, I'm glad I didn't marry them either, especially the last one, who turned out to be an incredible jerk. But that doesn't change the fact that I feel guilty about having sex with someone outside a relationship that's going to lead to marriage."

"Why? Why can't you just enjoy yourself?"

"Oh, that is such a *guy* thing to say! Because, for the last time, *I have responsibilities. I have an example to set for Adam.* You just don't seem to get that."

"Vinnie, you need to have your own life, and Adam needs to go back to school. He's got to toughen up. Crying and running away doesn't solve anything."

Her eyes flashed. "You are soooo out of line here, Nick! What do you know about it?"

"I know because I've been there."

"And that makes you an expert? You know what? Just because you were ignored as a kid, just because your needs weren't met, doesn't mean it's right."

"I never said it was right, Vinnie. But is it necessary for Adam's needs to be met in *my* apartment? And get in the way of whatever this is between us?" Nick felt ashamed the minute the words were out of his mouth, but there was no taking them back.

Her normally serene face went livid. "There is nothing between us, Nick. We're from two different worlds, and there's no bridge between them. You obviously don't understand family ties—and if my little brother bothers you that much, then Adam and I will both leave tomorrow."

Chapter 21

"No." Nick said it forcefully, and Vinnie turned to stare at him.

"What do you mean, 'no'?" This guy was worse than William. He was selfish beyond anything.

Nick took her hand. "I mean that I'm sorry. And I don't want you to go. I . . . enjoyed spending time with you and Adam tonight. I guess I'm just not used to being ruled by a kid's priorities. And I see you taking care of everyone but yourself."

"I don't need to be taken care of, Nick. But thanks."

"Apology accepted, then? You'll stay?"

She gazed at him levelly for a long moment. "Apology accepted. Just don't interfere with my decisions regarding my brother, okay?"

Nick nodded.

"We're a family unit."

"Yeah."

His one-word reply said it all: Nick didn't really

understand what that meant. She felt sad for him.
Maybe they could teach him. Maybe that was the
reason they'd all met. "I'm going to bed myself,
now, Nick."

His eyes said he wanted to come with her. His
mouth—the mouth that, God help her, she could still
feel on her skin—said only, "Good night, then."

"Good night."

Nick regretfully watched Vinnie disappear into her
bedroom. He supposed he'd spend another hour
with Letterman and a drink before turning in. He
flipped on the tube and wandered around, picking
up clutter. He stacked Adam's schoolbooks neatly
on a chair. He corraled all the dog toys into a corner. He removed the offensive flowered pillow.

Now the apartment looked neat again. Neat and
sterile. Like a TV stage of where an architect would
live. Nick cursed and threw the flowered pillow
back into the Starck chair. He wandered into the
kitchen to pour his drink, where a clear plastic bag
full of something dark gray caught his attention.

He walked over to check it out, only to find that
it was a bag full of live slugs. Nick held it up, inspected it, and grimaced. Without a doubt, he found
Mrs. Hegel's menu more appealing than Prince
Charming's.

Nick shook his head. Life had gotten interesting
since Vinnie'd arrived. He seemed to be acquiring
quite the penthouse zoo: dog, girl, toad, and now
homesick munchkin. Why should he be surprised
to find bags of bugs on the kitchen counter?

* * *

It was several days later that Nick noticed his left-overs were disappearing. He figured that either Vinnie or Adam was eating them, and that was a good thing. It was when he returned home early one evening to change for a dinner that he discovered what was really happening.

As he got out of the elevator on his floor, Vinnie backed out of his front door with a foil-covered plate, obviously piled high. Balancing it in one hand, she locked the door with the other.

"Don't bother," Nick said, startling her. "Where are you off to with the food?"

"Oh, uh. Um." Vinnie stared at him. "Well, I didn't think you'd mind. And I figured that what Mrs. Hegel doesn't know won't hurt her. It's just that I hate to see food go to waste, and I've seen you put stuff down the disposal before, or feed it to Daffodil—"

"Vinnie, it's fine. Just a simple question."

"Oh." She fidgeted. "Well, there's this old guy who hangs out under the scaffolding a few blocks away. He's there most days, until the cops chase him off. He comes back, though, and I bring him food."

He said nothing. He was silent because, again, she'd stunned him.

"The first time I met him, he was dead drunk, and he'd sort of curled up into a ball. When I asked him if he was okay, he wanted to know if I'd get him a bottle of something. So I said no, but I got him a cup of soup instead."

"You got him a cup of soup."

She nodded. "And I stood there until he drank it.

He said that I seemed like a nice young lady, and that I reminded him of his daughter." Her voice caught on the word.

"So I asked where his daughter was, and he told me that she didn't speak to him anymore. Because of this and that, but mostly the booze."

"Oh, Vinnie. You can't help this man. This is a guy who's let his life get so bad that he lives on the street. He's a lost cause."

"*Nobody* is a lost cause." She said it quietly, but fiercely.

"Sweetheart, do you know how many people like him there are all over the city?" Nick put his hand on her shoulder, wanting to hug her for her goodness, but protect her from it as well. Her generosity was going to get her hurt one day—if the damage hadn't occurred already, insidiously. Nick's instincts told him that it had. Where was the woman herself, underneath this compulsion to help others?

Vinnie pulled away from him and gripped the plate as though it held the answers to the mysteries of the universe. "How can you just turn your back, Nick? How can you pass these people every day and not try to do something to help?"

"Vinnie, I guess we're looking at the problem differently. Is this guy handicapped in any way? Is he nuts?"

She shook her head.

"So he chooses to drink and sit on the sidewalk instead of doing something else."

"Nick, he's drinking to block some kind of pain."

"That's probably how it started. Now it's most likely a disease that he has no control over. Vinnie, honey, how's your food going to get to the root of his pain and make it go away, along with the alcoholism?"

"Stop it!" Vinnie swiped at her eyes. "At least he won't starve if I bring him food."

"And he won't seek help, either. Have you tried to get him to a shelter? Maybe they have some kind of treatment program there."

"He won't go."

"Then he doesn't want help."

"Nick, it's not as simple as that! Imagine being in his position, having nothing, nobody who cares . . ."

"What he needs is a job."

"And how exactly is he supposed to get one, if he has no address and no hope?"

Nick sighed. "I don't know how to solve that problem. Look, I'm not going to stop you from taking him food. I just want you to be careful. Don't let yourself become a victim, here, Vinnie. Remember that you've only got one heart, and you can only share it with so many people."

She stared at him. "What's that supposed to mean?"

"Take it at face value, no more, no less." Nick pushed the elevator button for her and went inside.

He stared at the building diagram on his bedroom wall while he inserted cuff links and adjusted them. It was a depiction of his first completed project. He'd designed and oversaw its construction. Every inch of it had been under his control, unlike any aspect of his emotional life growing up.

Vinnie was putting her heart out on a paper plate with leftover food for some homeless old man, who would just wish it were booze.

Nick had put his heart out there for his parents, growing up. He'd twisted and turned every which way to elicit their approval and their love. It hadn't done any good. He no longer took the risk of rejection.

They weren't hateful, exactly. Just removed. He'd been a birth-control slip-up, someone who would not exist if not for a forgotten pill.

They'd done their duty by Nick. He had excellent table manners, some skill with a tennis racket, and a good education. He'd even had a trust fund to get him started in life. He couldn't complain. He really couldn't. So what was it about Vinnie and her heart and that paper plate that drove him crazy? What was it about the kid, and the toad and the vagrant that got under his skin?

Was it that they had her love and he didn't? Ridiculous. He was a grown man.

Nick walked into the kitchen and adjusted his tie in the microwave's reflection. He had no desire to go to this dinner. And he certainly wouldn't tell Vinnie how much rubber chicken and parsleyed potatoes went to waste at such things. Enough to feed an entire platoon of old homeless men. Sickening. The thought of Vinnie with her one paper plate, taking off with Mrs. Hegel's leftovers, was going to haunt him all night.

She made Nick feel . . . selfish and spoiled. Insu-

lated from the world's problems. This girl from rural Kansas, for God's sake, showed him up, made
him take stock of who he was and how he was lacking. Nick couldn't say he appreciated it, exactly . . .
but perhaps in a way, he did.

Miss Elly May from Kansas, who all but sported
a rope belt and pigtails, showed him up in a hundred different ways, for all his education and
prominence.

Her ability to care for a single old man on the
streets of Manhattan humbled him. Shameful as it
was, he no longer truly saw the homeless as individuals. They were simply members of a vast, disturbing mass labeled by his brain as "problem: sad." He
passed them as he might pass a stone bench, or a
garbage receptacle, or a city bus—they'd become a
part of the landscape of New York.

Nick grabbed his overcoat out of the hall closet
and wished he were spending the evening in, with
his ramshackle roommates, instead of out, with a
hundred acquaintances who bored him stiff. Daffodil followed him to the door and wagged her
stump at him. Since nobody was around to see,
Nick dropped another kiss on top of her head and
told her he'd be back soon.

Chapter 22

Of course the first person Nick saw at the dinner was Dana. Dana and the twins were beautifully packaged. They were hitched up high, and they sure were mighty: the high beams on and riveting the gaze of every man for yards.

Nick knew every one of those men was wishing that by some freak accident, some stroke of unbelievable luck, the little knot at the nape of Dana's neck would come untied and the twins would spring forth, free, wild, and hungry.

He nodded at her instead of shaking his head. She stood quite deliberately in a draft from the door, sipping some sort of trendy martini. Even he had trouble looking away from her breasts, but he did, if only to have a private chuckle at her expense. The high beams were costing her dearly: goose bumps had sprung up all over her ass, and were plainly visible through the thin fabric of her dress. She'd likely have pneumonia by the end of the evening.

"You haven't returned my calls, Nickie."

"Calls?"

"Don't tell me: phone trouble."

He shrugged.

"I'm not used to this kind of treatment."

He needed to tell her they were history. But not in public—that wasn't fair.

"Tell me, Dana," he said conversationally, "what do you think about the homeless problem?"

She stared at him. "What?"

"You know, the poor unfortunate souls in Manhattan who don't have anyplace to live."

"Nick, what the hell are you talking about, and why? Giuliani cleaned all that up, anyway, thank God."

He tried to imagine her taking a paper plate of leftovers to an old man on the street, and failed miserably.

Then he wondered why he was holding Dana accountable for something he'd never done himself. Had he ever once volunteered in a soup kitchen?

Nick felt self-loathing rise in his throat, like bile. He fought it down, completely missing whatever it was that Dana was saying to him. He'd done something kind very recently: He'd taken in Vinnie. Not to mention the toad. And the brother.

"So why don't we?" Dana asked.

"Huh?"

Her ice-blue eyes flashed, and her nostrils flared in anger.

Hell. What had he missed?

Dana apparently didn't feel like telling him a second time. She threw her martini in his face.

Nick supposed that on some level he deserved to have a drink thrown on him. Dana might be a bitch, but even she deserved some sort of explanation. The problem was what exactly he was going to say to her. He hailed a cab and thought about it.

Dana, I have the hots for my dog-sitter.

Dana, you're exquisitely beautiful and beyond desirable, but I find your personality repellent.

Dana, babes, it's been fun, but get lost. Find another schmuck to schmooze with your clients.

He couldn't say any of these things. But what he could say, he supposed, was that he'd met someone else. That covered things, didn't it? And it was true. He'd met Vinnie, who, compared to Dana, was a being from another planet.

The cab finally stopped in front of his building, and he paid the driver and got out.

It was unfortunate that he had to check the mail, for otherwise he could have avoided Mrs. Blount, who was departing the building with an escort approximately one third of her girth.

Mrs. Blount was a whole lot of woman in the daytime, garbed in dove gray or camel or plum. But Mrs. Blount upholstered in sequins and surmounted by mink was monumental.

He wouldn't have spoken to her by choice, but when she surged out of the elevator, humming a bar from *La Traviata*, her eyes narrowed and focused on him, taking in his wet suit with disapproval. She opened her mouth to speak and he cut her off, ever so pleasantly.

"Attending the opera this evening, Mrs. Blount?"

"Yes, Nickel Ass, we are. I've been meaning to—"

Nick stuck his hand out to her escort. "Nicholas Wright," he said in genial tones.

"Alfred Knorr," the gentleman replied, and shook.

"Knorr. Are you any relation to—"

"Nickel Ass!" Mrs. Blount interrupted. "I've received your written motion to allow pets in the building. However, since I got it a day after the deadline, I won't be able to put it on this month's meeting agenda."

"How curious," Nick said, with a fixed smile. "Since I put it into your mailbox myself, on the very day of the deadline."

She shrugged and tried to wipe all traces of malice from her face. "Isn't it a pity that I must have checked my mail already that day."

"Isn't it."

"Nickel Ass, I continue to hear disturbing noises from your apartment."

"You must mean from someone else's apartment."

"No, they're from *your* apartment. I borrowed a stethoscope from a doctor friend, and we put it up to the ceiling." She said this with actual pride in her voice.

Nick's voice shook as he got out a "really?" and tried to imagine Mrs. Blount on a ladder with the instrument to the ceiling. "You should be careful at your age. Don't fall."

"I'm still quite spry, not being a day over fifty."

Being a gentleman, Nick did not snort.

"Anyhow, Nickel Ass, I quite clearly heard the jingle of a chain."

He put his hand over his mouth. "Busted. You didn't hear the crack of the whip, though, did you? Or me begging for another spanking? Now *that* would be embarrassing."

"Listen here, young Wright. You think you're very clever, don't you? You make a sport out of mocking little old ladies—"

"Oh, no, never. Never would I mock any little lady over fifty."

She reddened, and the twiggy gentleman next to her coughed into his handkerchief.

"My point, Nickel Ass, is that I believe you are harboring a canine in your apartment, and that's not all. I spoke with Talley Hunter, and she has not a single cousin from Kansas, neither once nor twice removed. Yet I continue to see that disreputable-looking girl with that ridiculous fashionista dog. The girl could use some style lessons from the dog, by the way—"

Nick pulled himself up to his full height of six-foot-three and looked down his nose at her. "Some people have different priorities, you know." Like putting their little brothers through private school, then probably college.

Mrs. Blount sniffed, and the hairs of the mink around her shoulders seemed to rise in hostility. "So you know this girl."

"Mrs. Blount, are you questioning me about my acquaintances or my supposed dog?"

"If you have a dog, you're under obligation to get rid of it immediately."

"I've admitted to having no such thing. And it seems to me, Mrs. Blount, that if you're an officer of the board, you yourself have an obligation to perform the duties of your office in a timely manner. My motion was turned in on time, and you know it."

"How dare you?"

He simply gave her a bland stare.

"If a dog is discovered on your premises, the board can legally ask you to leave."

Yeah, and if I discover you on my premises, snooping for a dog, nobody will blame me for throwing you out a window. He didn't say it aloud, but it was very tempting. "Good night, Mrs. Blount, Mr. Knorr. Have a lovely time at the opera." Was that a growl he heard out of the woman, or was her mink still alive?

Chapter 23

Dana Dvorak checked her red lipstick in the mirror of the cab, baring her teeth to make sure none of the scarlet shade had touched them.

She noticed the reflection of the driver's wide eyes, and stared him down while she pulled her long silver fox closer around her chest. She'd allowed it to fall open, and he'd seen the Twins fall out.

Big deal. So the guy had gotten an eyeful that he'd never see in his own country, where the women were repressed under veils.

By the end of the night, Dana planned to have Nick back firmly under her thumb. While she'd thrown the drink out of sheer temper, it actually gave her an advantage. One, she knew he'd be home, because he could hardly spend the night out in a wet suit. And two, it gave her a reason to apologize.

Dana normally didn't *do* apologies, but the circumstances demanded this one, if she were ever to angle a ring out of the damned man. And no red-blooded American male could turn down an apology delivered naked, with only a fur coat and spike heels to accompany it.

Nick would be groveling to *her* before long, and she'd have him flat on his back under one of these heels, while he begged for mercy.

The cab arrived at his address, and Dana slithered out, not bothering with a thank-you. She still had the key from when she'd had Nick's living room faux-finished—back when he'd been in Italy.

She rode up the elevator without saying a word to the attendant, other than, "I'm expected." Since he'd seen her often enough before, he didn't question her.

Dana got out, clicked in her Manolos to Nick's door, and didn't even bother knocking. She just inserted the key, let her coat fall open, and walked in.

"Hi, Nickie," she called.

Adam Hart had never seen a naked woman before. Not as naked as this, anyway. He'd seen his sister and his mama in bras and underwear, but never a six-foot slut in nothing but a fur coat. Wow. From his position on the floor, she made him think of that old song by the Tubes, "Attack of the Fifty Foot Woman."

Adam, hidden by the half wall that separated the formal living room from the foyer, had been prodding Prince Charming over a series of hurdles in an attempt to give the toad some exercise. As he watched, wide-eyed, the fur-draped slut adjusted her hair so that it flowed over her shoulders, which she rolled back so that other parts of her jutted out like dangerous weapons.

Holy Cow, thought Adam, *she's a real live Fem-Bot!* From that Austin Powers movie Vinnie didn't know he'd seen.

He couldn't help it—he was curious. So he stood up to get a better look, and she saw him, and screamed. It was the scream that made Prince Charming leap, and then the toad sat in front of her, his throat swelling to mind-boggling proportions.

The slutty naked woman screamed again, and clutched her coat around her. Then Daffodil came galloping out to see what all the noise was about, and the slut screamed a third time.

Daff ran right up to her and started sniffing, and Miz Naked backed up against the door and shrieked some more. By that time, Vinnie and Nick had come running, and everybody stared at each other.

Vinnie was the first to get her wits about her, and she grabbed Daff by the collar and hauled her away from Miz Naked, who was sobbing with fear.

Nick said, "Dana, it's all right. She doesn't bite," and Miz Naked pointed at the toad, still shaking. Then she pointed at Adam. And finally at Vinnie and Daffodil.

"Who *are* these . . . *creatures*?" the slut asked, her voice trembling.

"What in the *hell* are you doing here?" Nick asked her.

"I'm not a creature, I'm a *person*," said Adam. "And so is my sister."

Nick acted as if they were all at a cocktail party or something. "Dana, this is Lavender Hart, my dog-sitter. And her brother Adam Hart. Vinnie and Adam, meet Dana Dvorak, an interior designer I work with."

The really tall chick stared at them all some more.

"Shall I introduce the dog and the toad, too?" Nick asked her.

"Have you gone *crazy*?" she spit at him.

Adam didn't know, but he thought it was pretty crazy to be walking around in a coat and shoes with no other clothes on. He had a feeling he might get in trouble if he pointed that out, though.

Happily, Nick seemed to agree. As Adam picked up Prince Charming, who'd left a terrified puddle on the floor, Nick stopped being quite so polite to Dana.

"Have *I* gone crazy?" he asked her. "I'm not the one barging naked into someone's home."

"I am NOT naked."

"Yes, she is," Adam said.

Dana shot him a dirty look.

Apparently Daffodil decided to find out the truth. Vinnie had let go of her after making her sit, but she could still smell the silver fox. And she'd decided that something was wrong: Why was this human wearing a fox costume?

She lurched forward again and took the hem of Dana's fur between her teeth.

Dana objected vocally, and tried to pull it away.

Nick told Daffodil to let go.

Daff just dug her doggie heels in and pulled harder.

Adam got a premonition, but not in time to stop what happened next: Miz Naked's skinny heels slid in the toad piddle as she pulled back.

At the same moment, Nick pried Daffodil's jaws apart and the dog released the coat. Dana lurched, wobbled, screeched, and went down hard, legs splayed in front of everybody.

Vinnie leaped to cover Adam's eyes, and hustled him to his room. *OhmyGodohmyGodohmyGod*, she kept repeating, while he tried not to giggle.

Nick convulsed into helpless laughter, but extended a hand to help Dana.

Dana used language Adam had never heard before, really bad words. Her mama needed to wash her mouth out with soap, then go buy her some panties.

He heard her screaming some more, and then the front door slammed hard enough to shake the windows. Adam resolved, from that day forward, to stay away from tall, naked chicks.

Chapter 24

Vinnie was absolutely horrified. How could it be that under her supervision, her twelve-year-old brother had seen, to put it in extremely vulgar parlance, his first beaver shot?

This was all her fault. She was the one who had brought an impressionable young boy into a bachelor pad. She shouldn't be living at Nick's herself, much less exposing Adam to this kind of environment.

What on earth would Mama say if she could have witnessed the scene? It didn't bear thinking about.

"Adam," she said severely, "you will forget you ever saw that awful woman. Do you understand me?"

He nodded. "Why would she come to somebody's house with nothing on?"

"I have no idea," Vinnie said in strangled tones.

"Do you think maybe we should do a clothing

drive for her, like we did in Independence for those really poor kids? Maybe she can't afford—"

"Sweetie, any woman who can afford a full-length silver fox coat and those expensive shoes can certainly afford other items."

"So—"

"Adam, I don't want to talk about this right now, okay?"

"But—"

"I know I've taught you to think the best of people and give them the benefit of the doubt, but sometimes you just can't, okay? Now open your math book and do your homework."

Vinnie could hear their host still gasping between guffaws out there. She made sure Adam had his attention on the math homework before going out to confront Nick.

" 'Not really,' huh?" she whispered fiercely at him. "Somehow I get the feeling that woman doesn't know how 'not really' she isn't your girlfriend!"

Nick looked up, his eyes streaming. "Wait," he said, putting up a hand. "You have no idea how much she deserved what just happened. Honest to God."

"Do you have buck-naked women drop in on you often?"

"First time in my life," Nick said. "I promise you."

"I don't know whether to believe you or not. And are there more women out there who also aren't 'really' your girlfriends?"

Nick shook his head and got hold of himself. "No. Vinnie, I'm not like that."

"I don't know what you're like," she said, folding her arms. "I just have a feeling I'm waaaay out of my league here. I'm going to do my best to find another apartment tomorrow."

"Vinnie—"

"I think this is an uncomfortable, unnatural situation for both of us"—she lowered her voice to a whisper—"and we've only complicated it by having sex."

Nick now looked utterly serious. "I don't know why you think it complicates things. For me, it's clarified them."

She was mystified. "How?"

His lips quirked up in a smile, and those dastardly dimples flashed her. "Well, I'm very clear on the fact that I want more sex with you."

"SSSHHHHHHH!" Vinnie hissed, gesturing over her shoulder toward Adam. "Well, you can't have it."

"Please?"

"No! We've been over this. Listen—where can we talk freely?"

He stood up and put a hand on her shoulder. "In my office. Come on."

She followed him into the room, where she was intimidated all over again by the floor-to-ceiling bookcases. Each book seemed to mock her. Each one of those volumes stiffened its spine at her and reminded her of how poorly educated she was.

Vinnie sank into a leather club chair and stared

at them hopelessly. God, where would a person start? Even if she read fast, and took only a week to read each one, that would be thousands of weeks . . . years and years and years. And in the meantime, thousands more would be published. Good grief.

So how many books did a person have to read in order to be considered educated, much less "well-read"?

To Vinnie, that was an even greater gap between her and Nick than his money.

"So, have you read all these?" she asked in a small voice.

"A good number of them. Why?"

She shrugged. "Just curious."

"Quite a few of them are reference books—not the kind that you open up at chapter one and devour."

She nodded.

"Now, what's all this talk of moving again? I kind of like having you around. And Daffodil adores you—she hasn't destroyed anything at all lately."

Well, geez. What a compliment—he kind of liked having her around. Like he was getting used to new wallpaper or something.

She knew she was overreacting, but the comment infuriated her, especially since they'd had sex in the pantry the other night. A lot of it.

"Well, I'm glad you kind of, sort of, somewhat like having me around. That makes me feel warm and fuzzy all over, Nick, but—"

"Hey, I didn't mean it like—"

"It's still not a good idea for me to stay here, given what happened between us."

"You enjoyed it, too, Vinnie."

Darn it. Now why did he have to bring that up? She bit her lip. "Yes, I did. But like I said, it can't happen again. Where would it lead, Nick? Be honest."

He threw up his hands. "Lead? It leads to enjoyment between two people. What's wrong with that?"

"I can't do casual, Nick. It's not in me. I don't believe in it—I wasn't raised that way."

He gazed at her for a long moment, obviously frustrated, then nodded silently. "I guess I have to respect that."

"Thank you."

"But I don't want you to feel you have to leave. Let's be friends, Vinnie. And I promise you that we won't have any more scantily clad visitors." He shifted his weight off the desk, where he'd propped his long body, and stood up. "Deal?" He held out his hand.

She took it, trying not to tingle at his touch. Trying not to remember what that hand had felt like on her bare skin. "Deal," she said firmly. She ignored the little devils in her brain that urged her to rip off her clothes and throw herself naked on his desk. Was whatever exhibitionist disease Dana had contagious? Or was she just experiencing a base competitive instinct? Vinnie wasn't sure, but she needed to let go of Nick's hand right away, walk out of that office, and close the door on him.

* * *

Nick sat down on his desk again once Vinnie had retreated. He'd won a round and lost a round. She would stay—and for reasons beyond the dog, that had become vitally important to Nick—but she'd be untouchable. •

It was for the best, Nick told himself. The last thing she needed was for him to dim the light in her eyes; turn her basic goodness to cynicism. Vinnie was pure—unselfish in a way that was completely foreign to him. Everyone, in his experience, had an ax to grind or an apple to polish or a back to stab. Everyone but Vinnie, who seemed to be fresh out of axes, apples, or knives. He still couldn't quite credit the fact that she lived for everyone but herself.

Nick felt colossally selfish in comparison. He supposed his self-absorption stemmed partially from being an only child. But another reason for it was that he'd always had to look out for himself. In the absence of nurturing from his parents, he'd had not only to find approval from within, but seek it from outside. And that had meant setting goals, achieving them, and either receiving recognition or patting himself on the back.

He supposed he'd never quit trying to impress his mother and father, either. Surely if he got straight A's, or was chosen captain of the lacrosse team, or won the state championship for public speaking, they'd see how worthy he was of their love.

Nick snorted. How stupid he'd been. He'd have

been better off rebelling in the classic sense—screwing up, experimenting with drugs, getting kicked out of school. Then at least he'd have earned their disgust, or their hatred, or some stronger emotion than the blasted neutrality they'd always shown.

And still, he'd thought he could compete and win, and thus be handed their love like a trophy.

Nick had competed for grades, sports positions, class rankings, graduate school acceptances, merit scholarships, and design awards. He'd then competed for internships and jobs at the best architectural firms in New York. And even now, he and the other architects competed for recognition, for projects, for reknown—and ultimately for partnership, the step Nick was ready to take. He never backed down, and he never stopped. Nick was sure he even competed in his sleep.

But if there was one goddamned thing for which Nick refused to compete, it was love. Somewhere deep inside him, it was too painful, too much of a lost cause.

He still remembered the exact day upon which he'd realized that he was attractive to women—that they, in fact, would compete over him. It was one of the sweetest days of his life: when both Susan Whitfield and Blaire Childress had asked him to the school dance. He'd been just a little older than Adam, and though he hadn't wanted to hurt either girl's feelings, the double invitation had been a source of wonder and pride to him.

Years later, Nick didn't acknowledge it often, but he still rather enjoyed being chased by women. And it happened a lot.

So it was very ironic that the one woman he currently wanted to chase him refused to do so. Even if it was for eminently sensible reasons, it irked Nick by putting him back into that age-old position: wanting something he couldn't have.

Chapter 25

Nick groaned inwardly as old D'Orsay popped the cork on a second bottle of champagne. The old man loved the stuff. It bubbled and foamed, trying madly to escape the confines of the Tiffany flutes into which D'Orsay poured it. Nick knew just how it felt, which was odd, since his back still tingled with the warmth and slight sting of satisfying, congratulatory slaps.

He should be dancing a jig on top of the old man's desk, since the celebration was twofold: Nick had just won a prestigious design award for a theater in Providence, and he'd landed them a huge condominium project on the Upper West Side. That had sealed his status as the firm's golden boy.

He should be strutting like a rooster, doing backflips in the end zone, or beating on his chest like a big gorilla. Old man D'Orsay and McDonough hadn't actually said it yet, but the word "partner" hovered in the air. And Nick had earned it, by God.

So why didn't he feel more jubilant? Why, when

D'Orsay overfilled his glass and the foam spilled over the side, did he want to applaud it? At least some of the champagne's natural effervescence wouldn't be lost inside a smug gullet.

Nick's collar felt half an inch too small. It was strangling him, and the cross-stitching of his Bally loafers cut across the tops of his feet with unprecedented viciousness. He felt filled with helium—as if his suit would explode at any moment. It stretched tight across all the hot air and ego inside him. He felt absolutely hollow inside: a man of no substance, sipping a wine of no substance, to celebrate two victories of no substance.

What the hell was wrong with him? He'd be written up in the *New York Times*. He'd make partner, a goal of such long standing that he couldn't even remember a time when it hadn't driven him. He'd attract hundreds more new clients for the firm and probably receive a huge bonus in return.

So why did his thoughts keep straying to his dog-sitter and a needy twelve-year-old? Nick wondered how much a bottle of self-esteem cost, or a year of judo lessons. Most of all, he wondered how much it would cost to have Vinnie look at him with wonder and honest affection all the time, instead of skepticism and a slow, deliberate detachment.

He tried to shake off the strange mood.

He laughed and joked with D'Orsay and McDonough, wondering if they needed another condo development quite as badly as a young boy needed support.

The atmosphere in the room stifled him, made him itchy. Weren't they all a little too self-satisfied?

"Gentlemen," he said, draining his glass and pretending to savor the bubbly, "thank you for the impromptu celebration, but I'm drowning in paperwork for the Southwick project. Another variation on the zoning ordinance, to accommodate yet another design change. The man is going to drive me to an early grave."

D'Orsay stood up and told him in jovial tones not to worry: They'd create a hero's mausoleum for him.

"Thanks," Nick said dryly and turned to leave.

"Just a reminder: It's your turn to host the holiday party, Wright."

"So it is," Nick nodded. "We can have it at my place. I'll get right on it."

"I'm sure Miss Dvorak will be happy to help you with the arrangements." McDonough winked. "But you can commandeer a couple of interns, too, if you need them."

"Thanks. I'd prefer the interns, if it's all the same to you."

McDonough raised a brow and looked discreetly delighted. He'd always had a thing for Dana. A lot of men did. They were welcome to her, the poor bastards.

Nick decided that in spite of his excuse, he was leaving early, and he was walking home instead of cabbing it. He needed to clear his head.

He was no longer surprised to find extra people—or animals—in his home, and Vinnie certainly didn't disappoint him that afternoon.

Nick found a Goth teenager with black lipstick

and blue highlights playing twenty-one with Adam at the kitchen bar, while an old lady perched in his favorite leather chair and listened to Vinnie argue with a bureaucrat on the telephone.

So much for relaxing. He immediately felt guilty at the thought, however, since Adam needed friends, and it sounded like the old lady needed help. It was just a little disconcerting that the friends and help had to be achieved in *his* apartment. Nick sighed. He was being selfish again.

"What do you mean, you can't find her in the system?" Vinnie asked. "She's had the same social security number since 1940."

Daffodil came running as soon as she heard the door open and close, and a pathetic, one-and-a-half-eared kitten skittered after her. Vinnie'd rescued it a few days earlier, and he hadn't had the heart to make her take it to a shelter.

Nick scratched them both on the head, waved at Vinnie, and introduced himself to the black-lipped young tramp in his kitchen.

"Oh, sorry," said Adam. "This is Darla. We met in the park."

"Nice to meet you, Darla," Nick murmured, still trying to figure out why anyone would wish to paint her lips black.

"Yuh-huh," said the girl.

She was just as skinny as Adam and clad all in denim and black leather. But she also had a series of disturbing tattoos on her neck, a pierced nose, and a pierced eyebrow. He hoped for her sake that the tattoos weren't permanent.

"I'm smokin' Darla at Starcraft," Adam said proudly. "I'm awesome!"

"Congratulations," Nick told him.

Darla grunted.

Charming.

"I wish I had my own computer," Adam mourned. "Vinnie says 'one day.' But who knows when that'll be . . ."

"Hmmm," said Nick. He stored that little bit of information and turned his attention back to Vinnie, who was telling the bureaucrat, "That's ridiculous. Social security has been sending Mrs. Hoskins a monthly check for eighteen years, now. She can't just have disappeared from the system." Vinnie sighed.

"Yes, she's at the same address. No, she has *not* expired. She's sitting right next to me. Who am I? I'm just her friend. She's exhausted and tired of trying to deal with you people. The local office told her they couldn't help her, and she didn't have the energy to walk to another office. She has terrible arthritis at her age."

Nick wondered where Vinnie had collected this latest beneficiary of her sympathies. He supposed it didn't really matter. The main thing was that she was indefatigable.

He'd won an award and a contract that day. She'd won another heart. Vinnie loved to slay needy people's dragons, didn't she?

Nick walked over to Mrs. Hoskins and introduced himself there, too.

"What a lucky young man you are," she said, beaming at him. "Your wife is a real treasure."

Nick froze for an infinitesimal moment, then de-

cided it wasn't worth going into explanations.
"Yes, I am." *Wife? Yeah, right.*

A wife was something he'd never have. He liked
Vinnie. He lusted after her—these days to the point
of torment—but that was it. And even if he ever considered marriage, there was no way he'd go into it
with someone who loved the entire rest of the planet,
pushing him firmly to the back burner. Nope. He'd
been there before, and he'd never be in that position
again. What a laugh that he had to be intrigued by
this woman, out of the four million in Manhattan.
God certainly enjoyed His little ironies.

An eternity went by before Vinnie got Mrs.
Hoskins's social security mess straightened out,
and Nick put the old lady in a cab back to her
home. He ordered a pizza for the two youngsters,
fed Daffodil and put Mrs. Hegel's dinner in the
oven for himself and Vinnie. He was becoming a
regular family man. Nick shuddered at the thought
and lunged toward his office.

Vinnie was lost in a fog as she took Daffodil for
their midmorning walk the next day. Her thoughts
kept turning to live mannequins who tumbled into
men's apartments wearing nothing but monstrous
breasts and thousands of dollars of fur skinned off
several poor unsuspecting animals.

But she had to admit, even without the breasts
and the fur, Dana Dvorak would be intimidating.
She was beautiful in a way that Vinnie could never
be beautiful: polished, sophisticated, well traveled,
well-read. Dana was expensively beautiful the way
Nick was expensively handsome.

Both of them made her feel smaller, lesser in comparison. She had untidy hair and wore cheap clothes and had little education.

Vinnie thought about Dana's soft, elegant, lovely hands, and looked at her own—the one gripping Daffodil's extend-a-leash. Her hand was dry and chapped and ringless, with uneven nails that seemed to crack and split no matter what she did.

Even though she knew Dana's secret: a top-of-the-line manicurist who probably did special silk wraps and warm paraffin dips, Vinnie could never afford it.

She sighed and looked down at Daffodil, prancing down the sidewalk next to her. Even the darn *dog* got a manicure each week, in keeping with peculiar Aunt Edna's instructions.

Vinnie noticed that through a series of turns she and Daff had ended up on Madison Avenue, and they trotted past one expensive boutique after another.

Suddenly Vinnie had had enough of feeling like a lower life-form. Daffodil's clothes were ridiculous, and she was tired of taking them to the dry cleaner after the dog rolled in the grass or splashed mud on them.

"Dog," she said, and Daff looked up at her curiously, "it's time we took you to the Gap and got you some kids' T-shirts. Aunt Edna wasted an astonishing amount of money on you."

Unaware that her wardrobe was about to change drastically, Daffodil wiggled her stub of a tail.

"And you know what else?" Vinnie made another impromptu decision. "Next time we go to

Poochie Bliss, you're getting your nails done in blue, not red. You're entirely too uptown, and it doesn't really suit your personality."

Vinnie felt better. She was no longer going to be shown up by a dog, and she had actually been in New York long enough to use the term "uptown." Why, it made her feel more sophisticated already.

She took the next right, leaving Madison Avenue and its tendency to give her an inferiority complex. They walked and walked, Daffodil showing no signs of tiring. Vinnie didn't really want to go back to the penthouse, since Mrs. Hegel was there today, muttering and chopping at things with a cleaver. So they continued to walk and people-watch and gaze at all the different buildings.

She and Daffodil walked until they began to see lots of students with backpacks, which told her they must be near some sort of university. Vinnie eyed them wistfully, wondering what it would be like to be able to study full-time at a college in New York.

She shook off the thought. Maybe someday she could go to school, but for now it was Adam's turn. He had a far more promising future than she did, with his talent for science and math. He was the one who should go to the fancy private institutions. Her grades and test scores had always been okay, but nothing to get excited about—or provide a good scholarship.

She thought about Nick, asking her what it was that she wanted before they'd made love.

What Vinnie wanted had everything to do with the practical, with what she could achieve realistically. What she *dreamed* of—now, that was entirely different.

Life was full of ironies. Could she make the time to study with this dog-sitting job? Of course. But she couldn't afford to pay two tuitions, nor could she save for Adam's college while blowing money on her own.

Vinnie had always been sensible, always found the solutions to the family's problems. She'd had to. There hadn't been time for her to dream on her own behalf.

She sighed again, and Daffodil shoved her doggie nose against her thigh. She scratched the funny little knobby bone on top of the dog's head.

What did she dream of? Changing the world—that was all. Vinnie dreamed of such impossibilities as social justice. Food for the starving, shelter for the homeless, an end to animal cruelty. Peace and love for all.

She was a sap, and she knew it—but the knowledge didn't change her feelings.

Vinnie resolutely turned her eyes from the bulging backpacks full of books. She was a dog-sitter, not a student, and that wasn't likely to change anytime soon.

Vinnie sat at the kitchen bar that evening, writing a letter to Mama, while covertly watching Adam and Nick, who had gone from truce to establishing some sort of friendship.

"Remember: pressure points," said Nick to Adam.

Her brother nodded obediently.

"Someone's hassling you in, say, a bar." He met Vinnie's glare apologetically, and cleared his throat. "When you're older, I mean. Anyway, some guy's harassing you. You take the neck of your beer bottle and jam it up into the pressure point under his jaw, hard. Don't give him any time to back away from it. Then you'll be surprised at how easy it is to walk that guy right outside and get rid of him. You can also do this with two fingers, see—"

"Ow!" Adam said, as Nick demonstrated to him.

"—sorry, but it's important to show you. And remember, I did that very lightly. You'd do it hard, right from the get-go, to make sure the guy knows you're not messing around."

"Cool."

"Now, you can do the same thing on the wrist. See? Get him right there—"

"Ouch!"

"Yep, it hurts, doesn't it?"

Adam nodded.

"The point is, you don't have to be bigger than him, you just have to know exactly what you're doing. Now I'm going to show you a few more tricks . . ."

Nick demonstrated to him how to press at the hollow of an attacker's throat, above the clavicles. He showed him how to bend the first joint of the pinky finger double to cause excruciating pain. And he taught him how to stomp with his heel between the fourth and fifth metacarpals of a bad guy's foot.

Vinnie wasn't so sure it was a good idea to teach Adam how to hurt people. But if someone was trying to hurt him first . . . hmmmm. It was a difficult dilemma. She supposed Adam *did* need to know how to defend himself, and if it gave her little brother more confidence, then maybe she should keep quiet.

There was something about the way Nick and Adam interacted that squeezed her heart. Both looked so earnest, and Nick radiated an intensity that told her he'd once been a scrawny preadolescent, too—hard as it was for her to believe. She thought again of how hard it must have been to be sent off to boarding school at age six, knowing nobody and not even being able to go home to Mom and Dad.

Nick's life might be filled with all the luxuries money could buy, but it sure sounded like his boyhood had been tough and solitary—perhaps even lonely.

She was drawn out of her thoughts by her brother's next question. "So, um, Nick?"

"Yes?"

"You being a famous architect and all—"

"I'm not famous," Nick broke in. "I'm just well-known."

"Whatever. Anyway, since you're good at making buildings for people, do you think you could show me how to build a bigger house for my toad?"

Nick blinked.

Vinnie said, "Adam!"

Adam said, "What?"

Nick pursed his lips. "A house for a toad, huh?"

"Yup. See, his aquarium is too small, and he's getting fat, and he's not happy."

Nick walked to the fridge, got a beer, and popped the cap off. "What does a toad need to be happy?"

"I was thinking about it. He'd need a little pool, and a kind of mud pit, and maybe like a garden room with plants."

"The toad Florida room," murmured Nick, and swigged from the bottle of lager. "Hmmmm."

"Adam," Vinnie said, "don't bother Nick about your toad, honey."

"No, it's okay. I've worked with a lot of different clients, but I've never had an . . . opportunity . . . like this before. Do you figure toads like things damp and cool?"

Adam nodded.

"But maybe he should have a sunny, breezy screened area, too," Nick mused.

"Yeah, that'd be cool."

"And maybe a tunnel that he can crawl into when he's not feeling social."

"A toad tunnel! Excellent. And how about a lookout tower?" Adam was pushing it now.

"I suppose it could be arranged." Nick pulled a kitchen pad toward him and sat next to her at the bar. He began sketching rapidly while Adam came and looked over his shoulder.

"I'm thinking about Sheetrock, Plexiglass, screening, and stones so far as materials. Oh, and we can sink a shallow bowl in the floor for his pool. What do you think, Adam?"

"How much is this going to cost?" Vinnie asked, wearing a worried frown.

"Nothing. I can pull scraps of all this stuff off a

job site, so don't worry about it." Nick smiled at her, and reached a finger over to smooth the wrinkle from her forehead. "Erase that. I see it too often, and I don't know why."

She felt color bloom on her face, but said nothing, simply gathering the pages of her letter together and tapping the bottom edges on the countertop to straighten them.

She watched the beginnings of hero worship dawn in Adam's eyes, and her stomach clutched nervously. Neither one of them could afford to get too close to Nick. He was a bachelor who came and went and did as he pleased—not a family man.

He'd asked her to stay on a whim, and for convenience's sake. He'd accepted Adam for a week. But just because it suited him at present to be kind didn't mean that next month he wouldn't be sick of them.

Things—and people, too, she imagined—came easily to Nicholas Wright. Things and people did not come easily to Adam. How would he handle it if he became attached to Nick, and the man simply disappeared from his life? She didn't even know how *she* would handle it when he disappeared from their lives, and she wasn't an awkward, sensitive, twelve-year-old boy.

She watched them work together to design Prince Charming's dream house, and her stomach clutched again.

Nick was so handsome, a lock of hair falling over his forehead as he leaned over the drawing and explained to Adam that they'd start with a "foundation" of plywood and build up from there.

The two planned their design until it was time for

Adam to go to bed. Vinnie shooed him off, then turned to Nick.

"Thank you," she said, her eyes unexpectedly filling with tears. "He hasn't been this excited about anything since we came to New York. It's good to see him happy for a change."

"Don't thank me, Vinnie—I enjoy him. I enjoy designing, even if the client is a toad." He grinned and touched her cheek. "Adam'll be okay, you know."

She sniffed. "I really appreciate you teaching him those self-defense moves, too. Not that I approve of violence."

"They're just useful tips. And you're welcome. He's a nice kid."

"Yeah," she agreed softly. "Well, I'm going to take Daffodil on her last outing for the night."

He frowned. "Not by yourself, you're not. I'll come too."

"Nick, nobody's going to bother me with a Doberman on the other end of the leash."

"So call me paranoid. Call me old-fashioned. Call me—"

"A gentleman," she broke in, her expression serious. "A gentleman and a . . . scholar." Her voice was somehow small and hollow, and she said the second word as if it cost her.

"Believe me, if you knew some of the thoughts that enter my mind when I look at you, Vinnie, you wouldn't call me a gentleman." He waggled his brows at her and leered. "See, the truth is that I'm not following you two out for security reasons; I'm following for the view."

"Nick, if you're finding a dog's tush seductive, you need help."

He'd reached for the leash, but now turned to face her. "You know damned well I wasn't talking about the *dog's* butt."

She flapped a hand at him dismissively.

He opened the door and gestured for her to go through it, but she waved him on instead. "Oh, no. After you."

He mock-pouted. "Treating me to my own medicine, eh? God, I feel like such a piece of meat."

Vinnie laughed, and they all trooped down the hall and got into the service elevator.

Nick hit the button for the ground floor and tried not to notice the way Vinnie's hair gleamed under the harsh fluorescent lighting of the car. Most women, illuminated by such unflattering bulbs, would look sallow and gaunt. But her face was sunny, wheat-kissed, fresh. She had lovely skin, skin that needed no cosmetic enhancement—and even if it did, he suspected that Vinnie would ignore such vanities. It was part of her charm, like her unpolished nails and her worn denim. She still wore her habitual running shoes—come to think of it, Nick had never seen her wear anything else—but her feet were small and she wore the sneakers with unconscious grace.

The car bumped slightly as it reached the ground floor, and the door slid open. As they walked down the narrow hall to the service door, Nick wanted to reach out to Vinnie, say something, he didn't know what. He opened his mouth as he opened the door to the street, willing a sentence to spring forth to connect them somehow. But the sentence came from another, unexpected source.

"Help!" it began, in a plea. And then it ended in a demand. "Stop! Thief!"

Chapter 26

Nick ran toward the front of the building. "Stay here," he shouted at Vinnie.

Daffodil, her fur standing up, barked ferociously as a dark figure came hurtling around the corner at them. A dark figure with a purse.

The figure and Nick plowed into each other, and both went down in a tangle of grunts and curses. The purse went flying, and Daffodil ran to it, straining against the leash and dragging Vinnie along.

As she watched in horror, the burly thief punched Nick hard in the mouth. The force of the blow knocked his head back and stunned him momentarily.

The mugger scrambled up and went for the purse, but Daffodil's ordinarily goofy grin had gone missing. She bared every razor-sharp crocodile fang, and sent a hideous bone-chilling growl through them.

The mugger froze.

Vinnie thanked God they hadn't dressed her in her little lamb pajamas yet.

"Make one move," she warned him, "and Killer, here, will rip out your throat."

Daffodil punctuated the sentence with another fearsome growl and a nasty bark.

Nick had rolled to his feet, and the man's momentary hesitation was all he needed to take the mugger down again, flat on his stomach.

He wrenched the guy's arms behind him and sat on him.

"Don't let that dog hurt me, man!" the guy pleaded.

"Then don't move, asshole. She hasn't been fed yet, and she's got the appetite of a wild boar."

Vinnie carefully avoided making eye contact with Nick, afraid that one or both of them might laugh. After all, they'd recently seen the dog-eared kitten best Daffodil in a spat, and she always ran away from the toad.

Daff barked again, and the guy whimpered. "My cousin lost his hand to a Rottweiler. Keep her away from me!"

"Dobie's are a hundred times more vicious, so you'd better keep still. I know you've seen the movies where they track innocent people down and tear 'em apart."

The mugger moaned.

"And Daff—"

"*Killer,*" Vinnie broke in, with a meaningful glance.

"Right. Killer was trained in a Special Forces canine school in Langley, Virginia. Her specialties are rip and tear."

The guy moaned again.

Nick had just been getting warmed up, and had plans to embellish Killer's background even further, but two NYPD officers appeared at that point, followed by the victim of the mugging.

Nick's elation at having done something for social justice popped and shriveled immediately.

Mrs. Blount's iron gray curls were askew, instead of being riveted to her head like the panels of a battleship. She was breathing heavily from shock and fear, which caused her enormous bosom actually to rattle her pearls as it rose and fell.

Nick reluctantly got off the mugger and dusted off his hands.

Vinnie picked up Mrs. Blount's purse and brought it over, Daffodil trotting next to her. Before she could even say anything, the dog, who sensed Mrs. Blount was upset, began to lick her hand.

While Agnes Blount was not one to enjoy dog spit, and pulled away immediately, she didn't shriek or carry on.

"I believe this belongs to you," said Vinnie, shortening Daff's leash and handing over the pocketbook.

The older lady's lips were trembling, as were her hands as she took the purse and slid it over her arm. "Thank you."

"And no, I'm not Talley's cousin. I'm sorry I lied to you. Maybe we should all go upstairs and talk, after the police report is filed."

Mrs. Blount nodded. "Nickel Ass," she said reluctantly, "I owe you a debt of gratitude."

Nick shrugged uncomfortably. "No you don't. But what I want to know is, where was Pete? We have a doorman partly to prevent things like this from happening."

"Pete had gone inside to get my umbrella. I was standing next to the taxi waiting for him when the young hoodlum took advantage of me."

"I see."

"Nickel Ass, let's put an end to prevarication. I want to know: Is that your dog?"

Vinnie gulped.

Nick set his jaw. "Yes, Mrs. Blount, it is."

Once they'd filed the police report, Vinnie, Nick, and Daffodil escorted Mrs. Blount up to her apartment, where the older woman sat heavily in an armchair. She was uncharacteristically silent and subdued, and her skin was pale rather than ruddy.

"Is there someone we can call for you, Mrs. Blount?" asked Vinnie. "A friend or a relative?"

"No, no. I'll be fine."

"Can I make you some tea?"

Mrs. Blount looked at her blankly. "I suppose. That would be very nice."

Vinnie went into the kitchen, found a kettle, filled it, and set it on a burner of the stove.

Then she went back to the formal living room. "Where do you keep your tea, ma'am?"

"The cabinet over the stove. Thank you, dear. Did you say your name was Lavender?"

Vinnie nodded.

"Lovely. Unusual. Old-fashioned." She sat for a moment in silence before remembering her manners. "Make yourself a cup, too, Lavender." She turned to Nick. "And what would you like? Something stronger, I'd wager. Scotch in the left decanter, there"—she pointed to a drinks cart—"bourbon in the middle. Port on the right. I'll let you help yourself, Nickel Ass."

Once Vinnie had brought the tea, and Nick had helped himself to two fingers of scotch, they all sat in an awkward half circle on Mrs. Blount's antique furniture.

Vinnie was sure Nick could name the style and period of each piece, but it was beyond her. All she knew was that it creaked when you sat upon it, and smelled faintly musty.

While Mrs. Blount could never look frail, she did look disarmed and vulnerable. Vinnie fought the urge to go over and smooth her hair and tug her skirt an inch lower, where the edges of her hosiery knee-highs peeked out.

Vinnie knew that trick from her grandmother— when the joints got too old and achy to bother struggling with panty hose, she and her friends had settled for knee-highs and longer skirts.

The fact that Mrs. Blount wore knee-highs made her seem more human.

Daffodil, after sniffing a couple of circles around the room, had sat without moving since they entered the apartment.

Mrs. Blount sipped her tea and gazed at her without comment.

Uh-oh, thought Vinnie. *Here it comes. She's the board president. She's going to ban the dog, and I'll be out of a job again.* Her knees began to shake, and she squeezed them together, hard, to make them stop.

"She's very well behaved," said Mrs. Blount at last.

"Lavender gets all the credit for that," Nick told her. "She's an excellent dog-sitter."

Their hostess sipped her tea. "You lied to me, Nickel Ass."

He took a deep breath. "Yes, I did. I apologize for that. Daffodil belonged to Aunt Edna, you know. I didn't expect to inherit her. But I also didn't feel that I could take her to the pound, or give her away. Aunt Edna was dear to me, and the dog was her special pet. So I figured I'd . . . keep her under wraps until I could get the building's bylaws changed. We own these units—it's not as if we rent them. And it seems out of line to dictate what people can and cannot do in their own homes, short of criminal behavior."

"Still, you lied when I asked you a direct question."

"Yes, I did. Partly it was in response to the manner in which you asked me—"

Mrs. Blount set her cup down. "I'm often abrasive."

Nick looked uncomfortable. "Well, yes."

"Howard used to tell me that." Mrs. Blount smoothed her skirt, and then looked daggers at Nick. "Before he ran off with Edna St. Villiers."

Vinnie gasped.

"*What?*" croaked Nick.

"He was an architect, you know," Agnes Blount murmured into her tea. "Very handsome. Too handsome."

Gigoloesque? Nick closed his eyes.

"Your bloody righteous Aunt Edna refused to have an adulterous affair. If she had, I could have turned a blind eye to it, and Howard and I would still be married. But no. She'd have nothing to do with him as long as he was married, and he found it so noble. The torch he carried for her became a bloody burning redwood tree, and he filed for divorce. Then it didn't work out between them."

Nick's face was ashen. "I'm—I—I don't know what to say."

"You don't have to say anything, Nickel Ass. You've had too much information, and not enough scotch to help process it. Speaking of which, you may now get me a bourbon. Rocks, double."

She looked at Vinnie. "So the canine defended my purse?"

Vinnie nodded, her eyes still wide.

"Then you may go back into the kitchen, where you'll find a small roast in the refrigerator. Cut two slices for—"

"Daffodil."

"—Daffodil, ridiculous name, and heat them in the microwave for her."

"Yes, ma'am."

Nick brought Mrs. Blount her double bourbon.

"Thank you."

He nodded.

"Now I've got to decide what to do, Nickel Ass, and I hate ethical dilemmas."

He folded his arms.

"You lied to me, and you've broken the rules. For that alone I can force you to sell your penthouse unit."

He just stared stonily at her.

"However, you did turn the proposal to review the rules in on time."

She took a gulp of the bourbon. "You're related to the woman I hated most in the world."

"And I can't help that, Mrs. Blount."

"But you stopped my mugger and have ensured that he'll pay for what he did."

Vinnie returned with a plate of cut-up beef for Daffodil, who ate it all with unbecoming and far-from-dainty speed.

They all watched her, having run out of things to say to one another.

Finally, Mrs. Blount said, "I haven't made up my mind. Thank you for what you've done. I'll let you know my decision at a later date."

Without a word, Vinnie picked up the plate and took it back to the kitchen. Daffodil licked her chops and wagged her stumpy tail at Mrs. Blount. They all departed, leaving their hostess in her wing chair, unmoving.

Chapter 27

Upstairs, Vinnie made Nick sit at the bar while she cleaned his face with a kitchen towel soaked in hot water. The mugger had worn a heavy ring, which had scraped an angry red weal into the side of his mouth. Inside, his cheek was bleeding from where his own teeth had cut the tissue during the blow.

"Nick!" she exclaimed. "Your mouth is all bloody."

"Is it? I thought the scotch had stopped that."

"Of course it didn't, you big stupid lug. Hold that there, while I get some salt water. That's the only thing that'll stop it."

He was silent while she mixed the nasty stuff, and grimaced when she set it in front of him. "Awwww. Do I have to?"

"Yes."

"But it tastes disgusting."

"Take a big gulp and hold it in your mouth for sixty seconds. Then do it again."

"I know the drill," he grumbled.

"Oh, you've been in fights before?"

He nodded sheepishly. "Long time ago. When I was Adam's age. A couple of kids used to pound on me, too."

"So that's why you taught him—"

Nick shrugged and tipped back some of the gargle, effectively cutting off conversation. He got up and walked to the sink.

"So who taught you?"

"Gaaaarrrrgggghhhhhh."

She put her hands on her hips. "You can wait before you answer the question, you know." With his cheeks puffed out like a blowfish, Nick looked a lot less handsome, but she wanted to put her arms around him and hold him close.

"You were a real hero out there," she said softly.

He rolled his eyes at her.

"Oh, yeah, I know what you're going to say— you're embarrassed that the guy got away at first. But you would have run him down, even if Daff and I hadn't distracted him. It's just part of who you are."

"Arraggghhhggggrrrrrooouuu."

"Oh, shut up. And what's more, you'd have done it even if you'd known in advance that Mrs. Blount was the victim."

Nick shook his head violently.

"Yes, you would have. Because even though you don't like her, you're still a gentleman, and that's what I lo—like about you."

Nick spit the salt water into the sink.

"Now, do that again," she ordered.

"No. You're going to take horrible advantage of

me and start again with compliments I don't deserve." He rinsed his mouth with tap water and dried his face with a paper towel.

"Come here, Vinnie." He pointed at his injured mouth. "I need you to kiss it and make it better."

She stared warily at him.

"Just a kiss. One teeny, weeny, tiny kiss. It doesn't have to be any more than that."

She might never have a chance to kiss Nick again if Mrs. Blount made him get rid of Daffodil, or worse, made him sell the penthouse. And unfortunately the woman had made her motives for loathing Nick all too clear. What horrid twist of fate had made her husband fall for Aunt Edna?

Vinnie moved toward him and stood on tiptoe in front of him. He bent his head, and she touched her lips to his.

They were warm and firm and hungry—not to mention salty. He smelled of soap and fine wool and adrenaline and man.

As he opened his mouth to her and the tip of his tongue sought hers, he let the hand holding the ice pack fall to the counter, where he ditched it. Then he wrapped both arms around her as if he'd never let her go.

She tasted scotch, and salt, and the faintly metallic traces of blood in his mouth. Her hands cupped his face and caressed it, carefully bypassing the wounded area. She tried not to notice the powerful combination of hot skin and tough bristle and firm jaw . . .

Nick groaned and pulled her firmly against him,

her hips against his hard thighs, her belly against his arousal.

His clever fingers stroked and massaged the muscles of her back, and then moved up, under her hair, to the back of her neck.

She shivered as he touched her there, an unexpectedly sensual spot. He broke the kiss, turned her, and lifted her hair. Gently his lips whispered over her skin, sending delicious chills coursing through her whole body. His mouth moved from nape to shoulders and back into her hairline, and Vinnie's whole body trembled, her nipples hardening helplessly under the tender assault.

Nick tucked her hair over her shoulder and continued to explore her neck and the backs of her ears as his hands moved down her shoulders, massaging her arms, and finally reached her waist, where they crept under her sweater and took her aching breasts into custody.

Nick lifted her breasts and ran his thumbs over the nipples, causing her to gasp and strain against him.

His erection now pressed into her backside, and he made circles with his tongue at her ear, echoing them perfectly on her nipples. She whimpered, unable to stop herself or the rising tide of longing in her body. If she could have stuffed herself whole into his hot, wet, teasing mouth, she would have.

He toyed with one breast, squeezing and stroking, lifting and caressing, while his other hand reached down to her waist, splayed for a hot moment across her belly, and then undid the top button of her jeans. The zipper yielded easily, and Nick's hand went marauding into forbidden zones.

His long, sure fingers teased at her hidden curls, dipping into the top ridges of the V between her legs. She met him with heat and desire, shifting anxiously, yet still shy.

He pushed her jeans down over her hips, and they made a denim puddle on the floor. She stepped out of them, and he kicked them aside. Then he drew off her sweater and unhooked her bra, dispensing with those.

She felt briefly embarrassed that she didn't wear sexier underwear, but he didn't seem to mind the plain Jane cotton, and drew the panties off slowly, as if he were unwrapping a delicate cake.

He turned her to face him, and his breath caught. "My God, you're beautiful," he whispered.

The praise soaked into her like warm rum, and by the time his mouth was on her breasts again it had ignited. It ran from there through her belly and pooled, burning, between her legs, while cool shivers fanned vapors over the rest of her body.

His hands moved down her back again to her bare bottom, which he cupped and stroked, squeezed and caressed. Then his fingers moved between her buttocks and down to hidden folds. Softly they played her there until she thought she'd die, only plunging inside her slickness later.

Then Nick lifted her bodily, and before she knew it he'd set her, stark naked, on top of Mrs. Hegel's stand-alone butcher block. She started to protest, but he laid a finger across her lips and winked at her.

She chalked it up to the devil that she simply unzipped his pants then, and handled him while he let a moan escape and threw off his shirt. Then he spread her knees and drew her to the very edge of the chopping block, where he plunged into her.

Her body stretched and thrilled to accommodate him, while her breasts rubbed against the curly golden hair of his chest.

As he stroked and plunged, the heat within her built and built, in contrast to the cool wood under her bottom. Nick's hands gripped her, by turns tender and fierce, and her thighs encapsulated him.

While he'd started at a quick tempo, it was his careful slowing and measured withdrawals that flung her over the edge. The other men she'd been with had seen to her pleasure only after their own. Nick was holding back, giving her everything he had to please her. No matter how much he might protest the term, he was a gentleman in the truest sense of the word. It made her sigh. It touched her in ways that even his magic fingers couldn't. And she came in a thousand rainbows.

Nick returned to situational awareness slowly and reluctantly. He was still sheathed in Vinnie, their heads turned into one another's damp necks. He felt like staying there all night.

But suddenly she tensed, her head came up violently, knocking into his jaw, and she pushed her hands against his chest. She said one predictable word.

"Adam!"

Nick rubbed at his jaw and battled the sudden

flare of resentment at the specter of her little brother. Every time he got close to the core of this woman, began experiencing some sort of intimacy with her, her concern for someone or something else derailed him. It made him crazy.

While he knew it was entirely reasonable for her not to want Adam to see her naked with him on Mrs. Hegel's chopping block, he wished that, just once, he could have Vinnie's attention all to himself.

Immediately he felt ashamed. Of course she cared about her brother. Of course she set herself up as a role model for him. He was her family, her responsibility.

But not having any responsibilities quite that intense and gut-wrenching, Nick could sympathize but not empathize. Was he selfish? Yes. Could he help it? He wasn't sure.

All he knew was the nameless longing to give to Vinnie, on many different planes. He'd given to her sexually tonight something that he'd never given any other woman. He didn't even know what to call it. All he knew was that her pleasure had been far more important to him than his own, and it irritated the hell out of him now that her pleasure had been abridged by thoughts of her younger brother.

If Adam hadn't been in the house to initiate her fear of discovery, they could have made pancakes, naked. He could have spread her with butter and syrup and taken her again and again.

But because of Adam she'd slid off the butcher block and was hurriedly dressing, putting an end to their intimacy as well as his viewing pleasure.

Nick liked to look at naked women. He found it

an entirely natural urge. But he'd never until now wanted quite so badly to see a woman's—what, soul?—naked. He blinked in disgust at the cliché. Vinnie's eyes weren't windows to her soul, or any such nonsense. But her actions were. And her actions indicated that her soul got squeezed like a sardine into the can of all her obligations.

She was fully dressed now, and twisting her hair into a ramshackle knot at her neck. Her face was flushed as she said, "Nick—that was amazing, but—"

"Amazing," he repeated, and folded his arms in disgust. *Yeah, as in, Gee, Nick, that was a great ride, but put Mr. Happy back in your pants now and run along so that I can save the world and be a good role model.*

His tone was grating and sarcastic even to his own ears. Damn. Why couldn't he just remain neutral around this woman? If she were Dana, he'd be grateful for her to just zip up and scram.

Vinnie's flush darkened, and she said, "Well, pardon me."

Huh?

"Pardon me, Nick. Do I not have your highly aesthetic and worldly vocabulary? Should I use Shakespearean verse to describe what just happened between us? Sorry, I can't. I don't know any crummy sonnets, okay? I barely know song lyrics. I didn't go to one of your fancy prep schools or your highfalutin Yale University, so give me a break."

"Where in the hell is this coming from?" Nick growled. "I didn't criticize your choice of adjective. All I did was repeat it."

Vinnie turned on the kitchen tap and splashed water over her rosy face. "Yeah, you repeated it in a nasty sort of way. Like I'm good enough to . . . to screw, but not good enough to paint a poetic picture of it afterward, because I use such lowbrow words!"

"Vinnie—"

"And I use lowbrow words since I come from a lowbrow background, you know? That's what that snotty foreign woman meant when she told me I 'luke wrongk,' I 'act wrongk,' I 'yam wrongk.' She fired me because I don't look or talk RICH. I don't look smooth and shiny and manicured, like that upscale whore who bounced in here in the multi-thousand-dollar coat and five-hundred-dollar heels!"

"Vinnie, I have no idea where this is coming from, okay? This is out of left field."

"No, it's not! And I have one more thing to say. I may never be rich, like you, but I'm going to be educated one day. One day, after Adam's through college, I'm going myself, for my social work degree. And no one will ever be able to look down on me again."

Nick threw up his hands. "Vinnie, listen to me. I don't look down on you. I repeated the word 'amazing' not because I thought it was lowbrow, but because of the word that came after it. The word 'but'."

She was drying her face on a paper towel, and she blew her nose into it for good measure.

"I got angry because all I can have with you is a brief interlude, before you start worrying about something or somebody else. We make love, and instead of spending time in my arms afterward, all you can think about is Adam! He's a great kid, but you have to have your own life, too."

"I do have my own life!"

"Oh, sure you do. You take care of someone else's dog, you pick up strays, and you worry about your mother and brother all the time. That's some life, Vinnie."

She drew back her hand as if to slap him, and he waited for the crack and the sting of it on his right cheek.

Slowly, she lowered her hand, and he was almost disappointed. *Saint Vinnie takes over again.*

"You have quite a nerve, Nicholas Wright, and I guess I misjudged you earlier when I called you a gentleman. What you really are is competitive to the point of nausea. Did you make love to me like that so you'd win first place? Take the championship trophy as best lay of my life?"

He drew in his breath in a hiss.

"Is that why you'd have brought the mugger down without us? Because you refuse to lose? Is that why you'll get your partnership in the firm?" She nodded sagely.

"Nick, it's true. You're the best. You've got it all—great job, fabulous penthouse, supermodel-look-alike girlfriends. But you keep going, don't you? None of it's enough for you. You've got to win every challenge that comes along, including me. And worse, you've got to have more of me than Adam does."

Her voice lowered so that he had to strain to hear

it, even though he didn't want to, not in the least. "Well, you know what, Nick? I'm not a marathon to be run, I'm not a trophy to be had. You can't put me on your personal shelf and shine a spotlight on me so that I glow and sparkle *only for you*. Adam and my mother were with me long before you came into my life. And I'll never stop thinking about them, no matter how great a lover you are."

Her words made him so angry he saw white, not red. Consumed with a frozen fury, he said very little, afraid of what else might come pouring forth. He was afraid of losing control completely. Jaw clenched, he bit out his last words to her that night, his last words to her for days. "You know nothing about me, Vinnie. And now you never will."

Chapter 28

Vinnie knew her defensiveness about her education had made her go haywire. Perhaps fear had triggered her outburst: fear that she was becoming far too vulnerable to Nick, who *could* make her forget everything but him. How could she have gotten naked with Nick again while Adam was in the house? The thought shocked and horrified her, made her furious with herself. She'd obviously lost her mind, and she couldn't afford to lose her heart.

Not to someone with a whole different background and set of expectations than hers. Nick would raise the bar for her so that she'd never be happy with any *average* man, and then he'd soon tire of her, like William had. How could she hold the interest of someone like him?

Nick was a dream man, not a man she could have and hold from any day forward. If she hadn't come into contact with him through a fluke—Daffodil—their social circles would never have crossed.

Even the *thought* of Nick's social circles scared her. If she were to go to a mere cocktail party with him, what would she say to anyone there?

Hi, my name's Vinnie, and I specialize in poop-scooping?

Hi, my name's Vinnie, and I could tell you your dog's chest size at a glance. Do you know how much it costs to dry-clean a canine sweater?

She'd be the laughingstock of the party, while they continued their discussions of architecture and the latest foreign films, and how outrageous it had gotten to stay at the Paris Ritz.

Vinnie would never, ever fit into Nick's world. And she couldn't imagine taking him home to Mama, either. What would Nick think if they took him for a burger at DeFever-Osborn Drugstore? She and Adam loved to sit at the lunch counter there, but Nick wasn't just plain folks.

Vinnie pushed all these troubling thoughts out of her mind—they didn't make sense, given the fact that she was *furious* at Nick.

She couldn't remember a time when she'd been so angry. Well, perhaps, when her father died, but being mad at God and circumstance wasn't the same as being mad at a person.

How *dare* Nicholas Wright tell her to get a life? How dare he? A man who lived only for himself and the next rung up the ladder of success—how could he be so insensitive as to criticize her for helping others?

Didn't the Good Book say that one should place others ahead of oneself? Hadn't she felt the glow of giving and enjoyed it? And what would Adam and Mama do without her?

Vinnie filled the bathtub with gallons of Nick's endless hot water and sat in it to think.

She was still stunned that she'd raised her hand to Nick, almost slapped him. Where had that amount of rage come from? She didn't *do* rage. She did thoughtfulness, and caring, and troubleshooting.

Rage doesn't come from nowhere, Vinnie. The truth hurts most of all.

Was her father talking to her, after all these years?

She closed her eyes. Her father had occasionally gone into rages. Her mother hadn't. Mama had just gone silent, and rocked back and forth in her chair.

Daddy's rage had been frightening, but never dangerous. He'd just let off steam when the need arose. Mama's reaction to frustration was really the scarier of the two. For she had simply tuned them all out—just as she'd done when the news came that Daddy was dead. She'd tuned out grief and life and Vinnie and Adam. She'd become a scary rocking robot, and hadn't left her room for that whole year.

Suddenly Vinnie felt grateful for the rage. It reassured her that she wasn't another Mama—except, *was* she?

Mama had focused entirely on them. She hadn't had any outside interests that Vinnie could think of, certainly no career aspirations or even silly dreams. Had the narrowness of her life caused her to fold inward and crumple when Daddy died?

Vinnie shivered. *My God*, she thought. *What*

*would I do, who would I be, if anything ever hap-
pened to Adam?*

She pushed the thought away as morbid. But it
came back and nudged her in another form: *What
will I do and who will I be when Adam doesn't
need me anymore? When he's all grown-up and has
his own life to live?*

Vinnie stood up and let the water sluice off of her
body. Then she opened the drain and let Nick's no-
longer-hot water flow away. *Perhaps he's a complete jerk for saying it, but darn it, he's right. I may
hate him, but I do need to get a life.*

Nick simply disappeared for the next three days,
knowing that if he didn't, Vinnie would move out.
And despite his anger with her, despite her total
misunderstanding of his motives, he didn't want
her to do that.

He threw himself into the job, working until after midnight on revised plans and specs for the
Southwick Soda Dome. He was trying hard to im-
bue it with a modicum of dignity, but this was extremely difficult to do when the client had all the
aesthetic vision of Mickey Mouse. Nick had come
to hate the projected building more than anything
he'd ever designed. Per Southwick's insistence, it
looked like a soda bottle and a Crackerjack box
had screwed the Taj Mahal—and really, he
thought, that was putting it charitably. So it wasn't
a box—it was an architectural perversion.

But he'd fought long and hard to win the project
for the firm, and he'd come out, as usual, on top. It
was a blessing and a curse that the media was so in-

terested in the building. They'd get a lot of press, but he'd undoubtedly be mocked by architectural purists all over the world.

So much for his dreams of doing something fabulous and unprecedented—like Frank Gehry. Gehry, of any modern architect save perhaps Philip Johnson, was Nick's hero. And the bottom line was that if ever Gehry should see the designs for the Soda Dome, he'd turn away in disgust.

So, why, in fact why the *hell*, was he still working on them?

Vinnie's words came back to haunt him. *You've got to win every challenge that comes along.*

Nick pinched the bridge of his nose between thumb and forefinger and admitted silently that she was right. She just didn't understand *why* he had to win. That losing wasn't acceptable; losing might prove that his parents were right to be uninterested in him.

Southwick and his hideous building were a challenge, and he instinctively refused to back down, even if the result wouldn't be good for his career.

But what, exactly, was he trying to prove? All the clients and all the prestige and all the money in the world wouldn't make the past right. Even if his name were the only one on the door, in giant gold letters, his parents wouldn't show up at the reception desk to say, "Son, the day you were born was the happiest in our lives. We are so proud of you. We love you more than life itself."

The goddamned newspapers could write an obsequious article on him each day, and Larry King could kiss his feet on the air nightly, and Barbara

Walters could proclaim him the man of the whole freakin' century, and he'd still feel he had to prove himself. He would still ache for the tens of thousands of hugs he'd never gotten as a child.

Nick threw his mouse at his computer screen.

Vinnie didn't understand. All his life he'd competed, and grasped and taken any kudos he could. He'd stocked up on them.

The fact that he wanted to *give* to her was momentous. He could actually feel the impulse inside him, twisting and turning and not knowing which way to go. It was an alien impulse, one he wasn't sure how to process.

Dana—and Emily, and Lorelei before that—he'd treated well, but he always took something from them. He took their beauty and appreciated it; or their bodies; he took the way they coveted him, a bachelor treasure; he took their poise and their charm, and he walked them in the moonlight. They reflected well upon him. He took the envy of other men when they drooled over his dates.

And he wasn't without a sense of fair play. In return, he gave them lovely dinners and entertaining conversation and dates to select events. He just didn't give them much thought.

And he certainly didn't give them his attention at work, dammit.

But Elly May the dog-sitter had gotten under his skin. He adored her for her generosity and selflessness just as much as the same qualities irritated him.

Nick sighed. Well, at least he knew now that Vinnie was human, and not an angel. Who could have known she'd be so sensitive on the education issue?

She'd always been vocal about Adam's education, not her own.

Nick wanted to show her that he didn't look down upon her. He wanted to show her that he wasn't selfish. He wanted to show her . . . that he could be a better person. So where the hell did a guy start?

Nick began by going full force ahead on Adam's Villa de Toad. Since the thing was going to be huge, at least the size of an executive desk, he decided to construct it in four parts so that it could be moved if necessary. He took Adam on Saturday to one of his job sites, where he first told him some dire cautionary tales.

Then he gave him a hard hat and goggles and taught him how to use a table saw (for the straight cuts) and a jigsaw (for the curved ones).

They constructed a shallow wooden box for the toad's pool room, then purchased a four-inch-deep ceramic bowl with a fourteen-inch diameter on the way back to the apartment.

Adam helped Nick spread some plastic sheeting on the floor of his room, then they set the box on it. Vinnie still wasn't speaking to Nick, but she came and stood in the doorway while Adam excitedly mixed plaster in a bucket with water from the bathroom.

"Be careful not to add *too* much water," Nick told him.

" 'Kay."

"Now, stir it really well, and keep stirring until it gets warm."

"How do I tell?"

"You stick your finger in it." Nick grinned at him.

Adam cautiously stuck his index finger in. "Wow! I can feel heat."

"Keep stirring."

"It's getting really hot, now."

"Okay, good. Now, let's set the bowl in the middle of the box. You hold it in place while I pour the plaster in."

"Awww. Can I pour?"

"I don't know if you're strong enough. That bucket's really heavy."

"I can lift it! I promise."

Nick looked at Vinnie, who shrugged. "Tell you what, Adam. Why don't we both lift it with one hand, and both hold the bowl with the other. Then, once we've poured it in, you get the box of stuff."

The "box of stuff" contained interesting rocks, found objects, coins, and glass pebbles that they would sink into the plaster so that Prince Charming would have a nice terrazzo around his pool.

"Now, while we're letting that set and dry for a while, we'll work on the screen room."

"Can we put a little bonsai tree in there for him?"

"Sure," said Nick. He looked up to find Vinnie had gone, and was disappointed. But he was actually having a great time with Adam, which frankly surprised him.

What had begun as a kindness was turning into a friendship with the kid. Nick had just never had a twelve-year-old friend before.

They used window screening, a staple gun and some plywood to create the toad's breezy porch, then covered the ugly areas with decorative molding, which they attached using tiny finishing nails.

By that time it was dark, and both were starving. "We'll finish it up next Saturday, okay?"

Adam looked relaxed and happy—an entirely different kid than the one he'd met initially. "That's cool," he responded. "Hey, Nick? Thanks."

Nick restrained himself from ruffling the boy's hair, something he probably wouldn't appreciate. He put a hand on his shoulder instead and patted him a little awkwardly. "You're welcome, buddy."

Vinnie was a nervous wreck. A nervous wreck who didn't wish to speak to her host, but felt obligated to do so since she and Adam were living there for free.

If Mrs. Blount forced Nick to get rid of Daffodil, then she'd be out of a job *and* out of a place to live. Adam would have to go back and live at his school, and she'd have to start washing dishes or something immediately until she found a job that was better paid.

It occurred to her suddenly that Adam had been at Nick's for longer than a week. It had been around three weeks, actually, and Nick hadn't said a word about his leaving.

If anything, he seemed happy to have him stay. He had taught Adam how to use his computer for games, and they now had nightly battles of Rogue Six, Tony Hawk's Pro-Skater, or Grand Theft Auto: Vice City, a game Vinnie really didn't approve of.

While he didn't seem to care for Darla, the girl with black lipstick—and Vinnie couldn't say she did, either—he'd never forbidden Adam to have her over.

It was probably time she spoke to Nick again. And she should apologize for flying off the handle like that, letting her defensiveness take over. She just didn't know exactly what to say . . . and then the idea hit her. Maybe she should start with actions, not words.

Chapter 29

Nick didn't come home that evening until past eleven, and the whole place was dark except for a small lamp on the hall table that Vinnie had left on for him. He was exhausted, his neck muscles had gone beyond stiff to screaming, and all he wanted in the world was a good, stiff scotch. Beer wasn't going to do the trick.

He made his way into the kitchen, tossed some ice into a double old-fashioned glass, and retrieved his bottle of Macallan from the liquor cabinet. Nick tipped a healthy dose into the glass, then held up the bottle. It looked . . . off. Cloudy, and darker than it should be. He sniffed the bottle, and it smelled odd as well.

He took a tiny taste from his glass and spit it out. Someone had watered down his good, aged scotch with tea. Furious, he threw the contents of the glass down the sink and grabbed the bottle of VSOP brandy instead. If his brandy had been messed with, he'd—a sip reassured him that it was fine.

But who the hell had tampered with his scotch? Mrs. Hegel didn't drink. Vinnie hardly drank at all. By process of elimination he came to Adam, who was after all twelve, and probably starting to experiment with things. Maybe he thought drinking some of Nick's scotch would make him more a man. And then, fearing discovery, he'd filled up the bottle with tea.

Nick was not pleased. But he remembered getting his hands on some of his father's beer at that age. He'd been punished for it. Nick didn't want to punish Adam, but all the same . . . stealing his liquor wasn't acceptable.

He thought some more about it, rubbing his hand over his jaw. Should he tell Vinnie? Or would it just upset her? After all, it wasn't as if Adam were old enough to get behind the wheel of a car and hurt either himself or others. Maybe Nick should just let it slide, and buy another bottle of scotch.

He closed his eyes to savor the brandy, then went into the living room, intending to sit in his favorite leather chair, but it was occupied by the one-and-a-half-eared kitten Vinnie had foisted upon him.

"Hey," he complained.

It opened its eyes, blinked at him, yawned, and went back to sleep. Nick didn't have the heart to boot it to the floor, so he sat in his chair instead. That's when he noticed the candy wrappers everywhere and the crumbs in his keyboard.

Damn it! Bad enough that his space was being invaded—but did it have to be defiled, too? He didn't mind if the kid played games on his unit, but leaving crumbs and garbage there was disgusting.

Nick swept the wrappers into his hand and tossed them in the wastebasket. Then he picked up the keyboard and shook it out upside down. Yuck. Cookie crumbs, a couple of potato chip fragments, and a . . . black fake fingernail? Jesus. He wanted to spray the whole thing with Lysol.

Still, he vaguely remembered that at the age of twelve, he'd had banana peels, dirty clothes, empty soda cans, and wrappers of all kinds scattered across the room he shared with another kid at school. A maid service had terrorized them once a week, but the other six days had been pretty barbaric.

Again, Nick decided not to say anything. He leaned back in his chair to flex his back, and that's when he saw it.

On its usual shelf sat the model Vinnie had accidentally crushed—now fully restored to its original condition.

Nick's heart stopped, and he'd have sworn it turned upside down before it started beating again. He blinked and stared at the model, finally getting up and taking it down to look closely at it. She must have taken the old one apart piece by tiny piece, cut new ones, and put it all together again—a painstaking and almost impossible task for someone who wasn't used to building architectural models. It must have taken her hours and hours with a box cutter and glue.

Ridiculous, but a lump formed in his throat. He turned it in his hands, impressed and stunned at the job she'd done.

The kitten hopped up on him and stabbed him with ten tiny claws just as Vinnie appeared in the doorway, dressed in baggy flannel pajamas, her mangy robe, and the Eeyore slippers.

"Hi," she said, her voice tentative.

"Hi." Nick cleared his throat and set the model on his desk. "I can't believe you did this. Thank you."

"It's probably not done right—I don't know if the angles are completely accurate."

"It's perfect."

"Yeah?" Her lovely face flushed with pleasure at the compliment. "I—I just felt bad. For ruining it. And . . ." Her voice trailed off. She took a couple of steps toward him. "Can we—can we talk?"

He nodded. How a woman could look desirable in what she was wearing he really didn't know. He'd certainly never found furry slippers with ears sexy. At least not before now.

She came in and sat in the adjacent chair with her legs tucked under her. Daffodil, in a ridiculous Tweety Bird jammy set, followed, yawned, and lay down at her feet.

"I just wanted to say I'm sorry for the other night. I got really defensive and flew off the handle."

He nodded and took a sip of brandy. "At least I know where you're coming from now."

She shifted position so that she was hugging her knees. She looked like a little kid that way—young, vulnerable, innocent.

"Yeah," she said softly. "I feel like such an ignoramus sometimes. Especially when I come in here and see all of these books . . ." She made a sweeping gesture at the shelves.

"You shouldn't feel that way. You've taken on

some heavy burdens, and every time I turn around, I see you taking on more."

"There are just so many people out there who need help," Vinnie said in a low voice. "So many who are hopeless and depressed and just need a little looking after."

"And you're determined to help all of them." Nick's mouth twisted. "You can't, you know. People have to help themselves, for the most part. Though I'm willing to take a gamble on your homeless man."

"What do you mean?"

"I looked into a few programs on the Internet. Rehab programs."

She stared at him.

"And if you can talk him into going, and checking himself in, I'll foot the bill."

Vinnie put a trembling hand over her mouth. "Why?"

Nick tossed back the rest of his brandy and shrugged.

"Why, Nick?"

"You were so passionate about him. So vehement that nobody is a lost cause. I kept seeing you with that damned paper plate, heading out my door."

She said nothing.

"You make me feel so selfish, Vinnie. I guess I want to do something that's . . . not."

"So you're going to do this to relieve feelings of guilt? Or to somehow impress me?"

God, she made him feel like a worm. "No . . . yes. No, that's not it, exactly. It's more than that. Oh, hell. I don't know!"

The kitten rose and stretched, and he felt ten needle pricks in his left thigh, like an attack of conscience. This time, he picked it up and deposited it on the floor. It flounced its tail at him and approached Vinnie instead.

"How did you fixate on this particular old man, anyway? Why him?"

Vinnie pulled the ears of her Eeyore slippers. "He was wearing a coat like one my dad used to have. Military-issue."

"How old were you, Vinnie? The year your dad didn't come home?"

"Fourteen."

Nick sighed. "A hell of an age to become an instant adult."

"He made me promise before he left that I'd look after Adam and Mama. So." She shrugged. "I have."

"At the expense of your own life."

The comment brought her chin up high. "What does your own life mean without family?"

She might as well have shot him in the stomach. Nick sucked in his breath. "Sometimes," he said tightly, "family isn't what you expect it to be. Sometimes family just entails a sense of obligation. Sometimes it's up to you, yourself, to find the sense of worth that your family doesn't bestow upon you."

"Oh, Nick, I'm sorry—"

"You might look for it in *books*," he said sardonically. "Or in trophies, awards, career achievements. Other people's praise. You might seek comfort in material things. Or in the beauty of proportion, the integrity of engineering. You might be a little self-centered, since nobody else focuses on you. You might feel a constant need to win."

"Nick, you had it even worse than Adam, didn't you? Boarding school at six?"

"Worse? I don't know about that. I came from the 'right' background, so on some levels I probably didn't feel as much an alien as he does. But he has known your love, and your mother's love, all his life."

"What are your parents like?"

Nick said the first word that came into his mind. "Rigid. And neutral. And by the book. They're sedate dinner-party people. They play a lot of golf. They laugh in controlled voices. They drink controlled amounts. They take two vacations a year. And they never meant to have me.

"But once they did, they always did their duty by me. They weren't cruel. They didn't abuse me. But I was a huge inconvenience, and as soon as they could, they got me out of the way. I went to Choate at age six and stayed there twelve years. Then I went to Yale, and stayed there for six." Nick set his snifter down with a snap. "Oh, shit, Vinnie. Don't look at me that way—I'm not scarred for life, or anything. It is what it is."

She got off her chair and came over to him. "Scarred? Maybe, maybe not. But you do need a hug." She bent down, kissed his cheek, and gathered him in her arms. She smelled of sunshine, clean flannel, and herbal shampoo. She smelled of goodness. She smelled like a lifetime of love.

He felt pathetic and unmasculine, accepting this particular hug.

His balls would undoubtedly drop off in a moment, roll out of the chair, and bounce across the floor into the fireplace.

Awkwardly, he patted Vinnie's back and set her away from him.

She looked at him with a depth of understanding in her eyes that made him uncomfortable. "The hug was a thank-you, actually. For what you're doing for my homeless man."

Nick nodded, but he knew that her hug had been no such thing. He swallowed the lump in his throat. Did it consist of male pride, or simple need?

Vinnie found it endearing and sweet that Nick was obviously struggling with his own self-absorption. He surprised her at every turn. Just when she thought she had him pegged, he went and did something incredible. She looked down at the check in her hand and shook her head.

Time to go find her homeless man. She made a couple of tuna sandwiches and grabbed a banana and an apple for him, plus some napkins. She began spinning words in her head. How would she explain to him? How would she get him to come with her, to the rehab center she'd chosen for him? Would it work? If it did, would he help her to help others like himself?

"Terence," she'd say. "We don't know each other so well, but I want to help you." But what if he didn't want her help? What if he laughed at her? Vinnie swallowed and set her jaw. She'd find a way.

She trudged the long blocks to where she knew she'd find him, huddled behind some plastic sheeting that adorned "his" scaffolding. Nick's check sat snugly in her pocket, a good deed waiting to be done.

And Terence wasn't there.

Nor was he around the corner, or on any other block around. He was simply gone. Gone before she could help him.

Vinnie returned to the spot where he usually was and fingered the useless check. She felt numb. She put the sandwiches and fruit down, and turned to go home. Maybe Terence would be there tomorrow.

As she walked back toward Fifth, something niggled at her, some uneasy thought turning backflips in the recesses of her cortex, but she couldn't get it to come forward and identify itself. She tried to shrug it off.

She went home to controlled chaos: Adam and Nick were finishing up the crenellated lookout tower for Prince Charming, but the toad had escaped from his newly manufactured mud room, creating a brown, slimy trail wherever he hopped— and he'd hopped pretty much all over Nick's apartment.

They'd eventually caught him and stuck him in his pool, but hadn't taken the time to clean up yet.

Since they were absorbed in some technical difficulties and still had to paint the exterior, Vinnie sighed and followed P.C.'s happy trail with damp towels and household cleaners. Mrs. Hegel would have a heart attack if she found the dried mud on Monday.

It was while she crouched on her hands and knees, de-sliming the place, that the phantom thought stopped niggling and burst out at her with all the subtlety of a locomotive.

She was in love with Nick.

She sat on her haunches for a moment, jaw slack, while she listened to Adam and Nick debate where Prince Charming's insect depository should go.

No, she thought. *I can't afford to be in love with Nick. We're just temporary entertainment for him, a passing challenge.*

With the towel she was holding, she tried to scrub away the realization along with Prince Charming's mud.

No, no, no, Vinnie. Bad move. Strategically idiotic. Take it back. Change emotional course.

But she couldn't.

Vinnie stood up and trudged to the washing machine with the dirty towels. She cast them in along with some detergent, and watched them crumple and slosh, like her thoughts. Finally, she closed the lid on them. She needed to get out of the apartment and into the cold December air.

Vinnie whistled for Daffodil and stuffed her into an old sweatshirt of her own, rolling up the sleeves so they wouldn't drag. "Daff," she said, "I am the stupidest woman alive." How could she have fallen for *Nick?*

Nick, who never wanted to marry. Nick, who didn't want children. Nick, who thought family values were supersize portions at the grocery store.

Was this God's idea of a joke? How had she fallen in love with someone like him?

Chapter 30

Nick sat back and stretched as Adam painted the last two inches of Prince Charming's front door. They'd painted the body of the toad's house lemon yellow with white trim, then Adam had chosen cobalt blue for the door.

Nick grinned with satisfaction, and Adam beamed with pride and excitement. They'd even added a "lawn" to the place, stapling green outdoor carpeting to a piece of plywood.

Adam laid the last stroke of paint on the little door and went into the bathroom to wash the brush out and wipe the smudges off the can of latex. He sported lots of smudges himself—yellow on his arms and hands, white on his nose, a little blue over his mouth and on his left cheek. The kid looked like the Bosnian flag.

Nick's grin faded as Adam turned on the water and began to wash out the brush, then his face. "That's an awfully big, fancy house for Prince Charming to live in by himself, don't you think?"

Adam emerged, wiping his face on a towel. He stuck his glasses back onto his nose and looked critically at the structure. "Yeah," he agreed. "Prince Charming needs a beautiful green princess and a bunch of tadpoles for it to be a real home."

Nick swallowed. Then he nodded.

"Hey, can we trim it with colored Christmas lights for your office party next week?"

"Sure we can. We'll even get him a little tree and decorate that."

"Cool. Vinnie can help. She's good at that stuff. Maybe she'll even make a bunch of gingerbread men . . . hey, they could attack the toad castle! And Charming can jump from the tower and flatten 'em all."

"No pun intended," Nick said solemnly.

Adam smirked.

Nick felt a rush of affection for the kid. Adam was bright and energetic and creative. He wanted to do something special for him.

On the following Tuesday, as he checked lists with the interns helping on the party and confirmed final numbers for Mrs. Hegel, he decided what the "something special" would be, and ordered it.

Vinnie returned the next day to Terence's scaffolding, and the next and the next. But he was gone. He'd moved on. He was beyond her help.

She tried not to feel desolate and dark. She tried not to let a little piece of herself wither and die inside. *You've only got one heart. You can only share it with so many people.* Nick's words reverberated in her head and lit an unexpected fury inside of her.

Yes, she only had one heart, and she'd lost it to Nicholas Wright, who couldn't care and couldn't share.

He hadn't really given a damn about Terence. He'd just written a check. He'd done it to impress her, not because he was struggling with his selfishness. He was most likely trying to manipulate her back into his bed, where he could make her forget about the rest of the world and focus only on *him*.

Open your eyes, Vin. His actions over the past weeks have been completely out of character. He's got to have an agenda. He's got to win.

She'd taken the money for Terence, and it had become tainted somehow, and the old man had fled. Vinnie pulled the check from her pocket and tore it into small bits, letting them float to the street.

Though somehow in the back of her mind she knew she was being irrational, Vinnie felt stronger coming to this conclusion. Less defenseless against the tide of her unwanted feelings for Nick.

The boxes Nick had ordered arrived four days later, on the morning of the party.

He went to answer the buzzer when it rang. "Yes?"

"Yah, delivery for Mr. Adam Hart," Pete's voice said.

Excellent. "Send it on up."

The delivery came in big white boxes with cow spots on them, and Adam looked at them wide-eyed.

"Well, go ahead, open them. Looks like Santa sent you an early Christmas present."

Adam ran to his room and got his scissors with

the orange handles. He used these to cut through the tape on the biggest box. He opened the flaps and removed a big piece of styrofoam to see a computer monitor underneath. "Holy cow!" he said. "Holy, holy, holy cow!"

The expression on Adam's face undid Nick. The kid was wide-eyed with astonishment and disbelief, peppered with an excitement that Nick wished he could still achieve—about anything.

He helped him lift the monitor out of its box, and watched as Adam next opened the computer, the keyboard, and the mouse. Adam's small, freckled hands, so steady as they'd painted, now shook. He wiped his palms on his jeans and looked up at Nick. "You're Santa, aren't you."

He phrased it as a statement, not a question.

Nick was perfecting the art of the shrug these days. He did it again.

Adam swallowed, stood up, and threw his arms around him. "Thank you! This is the coolest present I've ever, ever gotten. You're the best."

Nick could accept *this* hug without feeling emasculated, and he returned it, looking a little mistily down at the red curls and the snub nose buried in his chest. But he still felt a twinge of guilt.

"You know, Adam, that your sister constantly gives you something a lot better than any machine, right?"

Adam pulled away and looked at him. "Huh?"

"I mean that she struggles every single day to make money for your school and for your college."

Adam stuck his hands in his pockets. "Yeah, I

know. She's always worried about money. It's a drag."

"You know why, though, right? It's because she loves you, very much."

"Yeah."

"Well, don't ever take that for granted, okay? My friends and I didn't have computers growing up, because they weren't invented. But I sure would have liked to have had a Vinnie in my life."

"You can borrow her sometimes, if you want. As long as you don't do the kissy stuff."

Nick laughed. "I'd love to borrow her sometimes."

"You know when the best time would be?"

"No, when?"

"Right around bedtime, so she forgets to make me floss my teeth."

Vinnie's feelings about the computer were violently mixed. On the one hand, Adam's excitement was infectious, and she was thrilled for him. On the other hand, she was angry that Nick hadn't consulted her before giving him the gift, and it was far too expensive to accept. She wouldn't have let him buy it, had she known.

More troubling was the way the whole incident made her feel, and once again it all boiled down to Nick's money. On some level it enraged her that he could, on a whim, supply Adam with something for which it would take her two years to save.

While she got to be the bad guy, denying Adam all sorts of small things that she'd *love* to get him, if only she didn't have to save for his education, Nick had in a single gesture established himself as more than a good guy—he'd achieved superhero status in one fell swoop.

It infuriated her . . . and at the same time, she couldn't help but love him for it. Darn it.

The way Adam looked at him, with hero worship in his eyes, also scared her. What happened when Nick got bored with playing superhero?

All her protective instincts surfaced, and it was hard to force out a gruff thank-you. Adam was too enthralled with the new toy to notice her misgivings, but Nick picked up on them right away.

He followed her out to the living room, where she'd gone to warm her hands by the fire.

"I screwed up, didn't I?" He stood with his hands shoved into his pockets, jingling some change.

She sighed and turned her backside to the fire, warming it, too. She met his eyes, which reflected concern. "He loves the computer, Nick. And you've supplied him with a tool that will help him learn and endlessly pique his curiosity."

"But?"

"But I guess I'm . . . jealous, in a way. You've given him something it would have taken me a couple of years to save up for. And you did it easily, I'm sure—just by reading off some numbers and an expiration date into the phone."

His face fell. "I don't know what to say."

"I know I sound ungrateful, and I don't mean to be."

"I realize that. Look, if it makes you feel any better, that was just a machine from work that wasn't being used."

"I doubt that. It wouldn't have arrived here in all the original boxes, addressed to Adam Hart."

Nick's face was completely deadpan and gave nothing away, but she knew he was lying. Lying to soothe her.

"I'm also feeling way beyond indebted to you. You're not charging us rent, you're paying me a wild amount of money to baby-sit your dog, you're doing all these things for people dear to me. And I have to ask myself—*why*? What's the catch, here?"

"Why do you assume that there's a catch?"

"Just a long-standing theory that nobody gets a free lunch, Nick."

"Maybe you've taught me a different way of thinking, of being. Maybe you've shown me how to"—he broke off, a peculiar expression on his face—"how to give."

She laughed a dubious laugh. "And what, you're teaching me how to receive?"

Nick reached out and brushed her cheek with the back of a knuckle. He pushed a strand of hair out of her eyes. "Something like that," he said. He looked as if he were going to kiss her, and she sucked in her breath nervously. Vinnie swallowed hard, and reminded herself again not to be an idiot.

"Giving's a pretty simple thing, Nick," she said. "But it needs to come from your heart, not your wallet. You gave Adam something far more valuable when you spent the time with him to build Prince Charming's house."

She brushed past Nick, murmuring something about getting her laundry done.

Nick stood in the middle of his living room, feeling bruised, and like a fool.

He'd experienced a moment there with Vinnie, a moment he'd wanted to seal with a kiss, and she'd walked away.

It wasn't that he expected her to reward him for his gift to Adam. And he certainly didn't expect her to pay him back sexually. Was that what she'd been hinting at? Was that the "catch" to which she'd referred?

If so, she was way out of line. He found it insulting that she suspected his motives. In fact, the more he thought about it, the angrier he got.

His own actions enraged him as well. Was he guilty of her previous accusation? Had he been competing somehow for her affections, as he'd competed for everything else in his life?

The idea of it made him sick. Was he trying to impress Vinnie, win her love, the same way he'd always tried to win that of his parents? Or was it more complicated than that?

Nick kicked at the logs in the fireplace, succeeding in scorching his shoe. Damn it all to hell. Damn this situation. Damn these feelings he had for Vinnie. Damn her as well—and the cloud of self-sacrifice she'd ridden in on.

Nick ran a hand through his hair and glanced at his reflection in the contemporary mirror over the mantel. Funny, he looked the same. How was that possible when he'd changed so much inside?

Seething, he went after Vinnie, followed her right into her bedroom. "Why is it that you're the only person who can give? Is that some kind of rule you have?"

She swung around and stared at him. "What are you talking about?"

"I'm saying that when you give, it makes you pure, or noble or something, but when I give, my motives are suspect! That seems a little unfair to me."

"Unfair? No. I suspect your motives because"—she groped for defenses—"your actions are out of character." That was it. She wasn't in love with the man, because these sweet gestures weren't really him. They were suspect.

"Think about it, Nick. All of a sudden you're told 'no'—that you can't have me in your bed. And then you start doing all kinds of nice things. I'm not stupid, Nick. I have to wonder whether it's all manipulation, whether this is just your way of winning. Soften me up so I'll break down and sleep with you again."

Nick's jaw worked, and he saw red. Win? No. He'd been trying to change. *For her.* He was so angry he couldn't even respond.

Vinnie went on. "I refuse to fall for you, Nicholas Wright! You're not the right man for me, so *back off*. You're trying to win again. Trying to win me back into your bed, even win my love. And then what do you plan to do with it? Huh?" She had tears in her eyes. "Are you going to put it on a shelf with all your other trophies? You've said you don't want marriage or children, and that's the only place bed leads me." She dashed at her eyes furiously with the back of her hand. "Quit trying to manipulate me into loving you, because you're only going to hurt me, and I don't need to be hurt by another rich jerk."

Somehow, through the fog of anger, Nick registered her last words and remained semicalm. "Another rich jerk? Would you care to explain that to me?"

"Oh, sure. What the hey, right? My last boyfriend, the last guy I trusted and loved, was Grade-A-Country-Club material, just like you. And it turned out I was good enough to *screw*, but not to marry. I'm from the wrong side of the tracks, and we all know it. I don't even have a full college degree. He used me for his own purposes, and then dropped me. And I'm not falling for that ever again."

"So you figure I'm the same. Oh, that's fair. That's great, Vinnie." His fist hit the wall of its own accord, and he was vaguely surprised when a starburst of cracks appeared in the plaster.

"I'm just a rich jerk, a master of manipulation. I couldn't possibly have developed feelings for you. Thanks a lot." Nick turned on his heel and left, slamming the door on Vinnie's stunned expression.

Nick stalked back out to the living room and kicked the logs in the fireplace again, scorching his other shoe. He slammed his fist down on the mantel.

He noticed then that the Louis Sullivan candlesticks, one of which Adam had threatened him with on the first day he'd come here—weren't in their spots on either side of the mirror. He frowned. Perhaps Mrs. Hegel had taken them down to polish them in preparation for the party tonight.

Party. Right. He was in a helluva festive mood. He glared around at the garlands, the brightly colored tree, the platoon of crystal stemware and stacks of china waiting to be used that night by a bunch of people from work. Bah frigging humbug. He needed to get out of there for a while.

Vinnie stared at her bedroom door, not knowing what to think. Nick had developed feelings for her? What did that mean?

They obviously weren't pleasant feelings, judging by the cracks he'd left in the plaster of the wall. And she didn't think they were feelings that would lead to much. This was, after all, Nick. Captain of Emotional Distance. Dater of Psychotic Mannequins. Builder of Boxes.

No, Nick was just furious that she'd called his bluff. Because people who had feelings for one another invited each other to their parties, for God's sake.

But had Nick bothered to invite her to his party? No, he had not. No matter that they had been intimate, she was still the hired help, not good enough to attend his social functions.

He was kinder than William. She'd give him that. William had never bothered to look in Adam's direction, much less spend time with him or give him expensive gifts. But they both wanted the same thing in the end: sex with her, no strings attached. Vinnie threw a pillow at the door. *Right. Feelings. All men are pigs.*

Chapter 31

When Nick later questioned Mrs. Hegel, who'd arrived to set up the food, she announced that she had not touched the candlesticks. Her Teutonic bosom heaved in offense at the very suggestion. After all her years of faithful service to Nick, after she had prepared his dinner *sousands* of times, it was a disgrace that he should accuse her of stealing.

"No, no, no!" Nick said. "I never meant to suggest—"

She was appalled, outraged, cut to the core. She was devastated! She could not find words to express the chaos of her emotions . . . how could he?

"Mrs. Hegel!" shouted Nick. "Of course I don't think you stole them."

She wiped at her eyes. "*Nein?*"

"*Nein!*"

Well, why hadn't he said so to begin with?

Nick gritted his teeth.

And where could they be? Had that *Schlampe* taken off with them?

"Mrs. Hegel, don't you *ever* call her that again. Understand?"

The housekeeper sniffed, but nodded.

Nick knew Vinnie hadn't stolen them. She didn't have it in her to take something that didn't belong to her.

The kitten certainly hadn't, nor had Daffodil.

The only other person with access to his apartment was Adam. But surely the boy wouldn't steal from him? It was impossible.

All the same, Nick began to look over the penthouse to see if anything else was missing.

He checked his dresser drawer, and discovered a pair of gold cuff links gone. A special edition Mont Blanc pen set had vanished from his phone table. And about twenty of his CDs were missing.

Shock coursed through his system. *Adam?* No. Ridiculous.

It must have been a deliveryman, or a repair person. He'd ask Vinnie about it.

But just in case, to prepare himself for an answer he didn't want, he went down the hallway to Adam's room, opened the door, and looked around. Was there anything in the room that the kid hadn't had a few days ago?

Nick didn't honestly believe he'd find anything. He did a quick scan, then sighed in relief when he saw nothing unusual.

It was as he closed the door again that he saw the video games on Adam's desk chair, video games that cost around forty dollars apiece. And there were three of them.

He didn't want to believe it. He couldn't have

been more shocked if he'd found Pamela Anderson and an erect midget in the kid's bed.

But the video games were there, and Adam certainly hadn't had them a few days earlier. He was equally sure that Vinnie hadn't purchased them, since she was always watching money, something Adam thought was a "drag."

He'd thought he had a friendship with the kid—but maybe he was fooling himself. He thought about the tea in his scotch. He remembered that us-against-them feeling kids developed about adults at Adam's age.

Nick went into the kitchen and slumped on a barstool. He supposed he'd wait there until Vinnie, Adam, and Daffodil returned from their walk, then talk to them.

Both Nick and Vinnie chose to ignore their most recent conversation, for which she was profoundly thankful. They sat with Adam and the dog in front of the fire.

She knit her brows as she tried to think of any delivery or repair person who had come to the penthouse in her presence. "No, I can't recall anybody coming here," she told Nick.

"What about anyone else who's been here—the old lady with the social security problem? Darla, Adam's friend with the black lipstick?"

"Nobody's been alone to wander through the house."

Nick was behaving oddly, as if he were uncomfortable. Almost as if he suspected *her*.

Oh, my God. What if—Vinnie felt the blood

drain from her face. *He did.* The son of a bitch actually suspected her of stealing from him! How could he?

Though the sense of hurt and betrayal was almost physical, she decided to clear it up right away.

"Nick, you're obviously pussyfooting around— is there something you'd like to say to me?"

He looked at the floor, but remained silent.

"Nick! All right, I'll save you the trouble," Vinnie exclaimed. "Are you actually wondering if I stole from you? Can you possibly think that of me?"

"*No!*" he said, his face exhibiting horror. "Of course I don't think that."

His shock was so genuine that she relaxed, and the anger drained out of her with a whoosh. But when he still looked agonized, and when he wouldn't look at Adam, her heart flash-froze.

"No," she whispered. She stared at Nick incredulously and put her arm protectively around her brother.

Nick turned his gaze to the fireplace and stared without seeming to see it.

"Don't even say it!" Vinnie heard her own voice crack in the middle of the sentence.

The timbre of Nick's voice was curiously metallic and neutral. "Adam, I couldn't help but notice that you have some brand-new computer games in your room."

Adam sucked in his breath and looked at Nick as if he'd just guillotined a puppy. "*I didn't do it!*"

He said the words at the same time as Vinnie's expression changed, and she repeated, "Computer games?"

"I didn't do it!" Adam shouted. "How can you think I would do that?"

Vinnie felt as if an elephant were sitting on her chest. But she told herself to calm down, to breathe. She'd never known Adam to lie. Oh, maybe once or twice about having flossed his teeth, but never on a level like this.

Breathe, Vinnie. *Breathe*. But where was the air? She couldn't seem to find any to force into her lungs.

"I thought you were my *friend*!" shouted Adam to Nick, jumping up and away from her. He trembled with outrage and hurt. "I thought you liked me. I thought—" He broke off on an anguished sob and ran from the room.

Nick sat motionless on the sofa, looking like a stricken Madame Tussaud version of himself, and Vinnie wanted to melt him into a puddle right there.

She ignored him to go after Adam, who had run to his room and slammed the door. Hearing heartbreaking sobs behind it, she knocked and went in, stepping over three computer game boxes that Adam had hurled against the wooden panels.

She sat next to him on the bed, where he'd thrown himself face down. "Oh, honey, I'm sorry. I'm so sorry."

Brokenly, Adam cried, "I wanna go home."

"Shhhh, honey. Shhhhh."

"I hate New York, and I hate school, and most of all, I hate Nick . . . he can take his computer and stuff it!"

She stroked his hot, wet, trembling cheek and then his hair, letting him cry it out.

"I thought he was my friend," he sobbed again. "But he thinks I stole from him. I didn't, I didn't, I didn't!"

"I know you didn't, honey. I know."

Long minutes went by before Adam had shed all his tears of hurt and betrayal.

It was only then that Vinnie asked him quietly where he'd gotten the games. "Darla," he muttered. "She loaned them to me."

"Did Darla's parents give them to her?"

He shrugged.

"Adam, has Darla ever been here when I've been gone?"

He hesitated, and finally nodded.

"Then I need to talk to that young lady right away."

When Adam didn't say anything, she knew she was on the right track. He would have stuck up for his friend if he'd had no doubts about her innocence.

Nick hadn't moved a muscle when Vinnie left Adam's room and charged him, rather like a beautiful, dainty bull. On one level, he wished someone would just shoot him. On another, he felt like howling himself—after all, Adam had betrayed his trust and friendship.

That is, if he had stolen the items in question. Nick was no longer sure he had. The boy's face had been too shocked, too earnest, too hurt.

Vinnie had invaded his space, now, and stood over him with sparks in her eyes. "I have two things to say to you," she said in a shaking voice. "One, Adam did not take a thing out of your apartment. And two, you should have talked to me privately before bringing it up with him. You had no right."

"Vinnie, it involved him directly."

"Actually, it didn't, since—"

"Vinnie, you know what I'm saying. Why should I have talked to you first, when my issue was with him?"

"Because I'm his—"

"His *what*? You're not his mother. You're not even his guardian. You're his sister, and you can't protect him from life forever."

She stuck her finger in his face. "I *can* protect him from . . . from . . . *assholes*."

His jaw dropped, and he pushed her finger out of his face. He stood up, towering over her, but she didn't back up an inch.

He'd never heard her swear before, not once. And after all the things he'd done for her, to call him an asshole!

"That's not fair," he shouted. "What am I supposed to think, huh? The stuff is gone. I know neither you nor Mrs. Hegel took it. He has new, expensive computer games. Why am I an asshole for being logical?"

"For your information, the games belong to Darla. And mostly likely the blame lies with her, too."

Oh, shit. Nick closed his eyes. "How do you know?"

"Because when I questioned Adam, he admitted

that she's been here when I wasn't around to supervise. And he didn't stick up for her when I told him I wanted to talk with her. So let's go."

"I've got to apologize to Adam."

She looked at him scornfully. "I really don't think he wants to see you right now. And I'd just as soon get to the bottom of it so you have the right person to blame, instead of an innocent kid who is *sick* that you think he did it. Why should you have talked to me first? Because you know *nothing* about how to handle kids, *nothing* about parenting. I could have gotten to the bottom of this without you hurting him this way."

"I'm sorry."

"Save it. Tell that to Adam later."

"I'm not finished, okay? I'm sorry that he's been hurt by this, but as I told you before, you can't protect him for the rest of his life. Why, Vinnie, isn't he telling me his side of the story himself? Why is he in there crying and letting you tell me? You're babying him."

This time when her hand drew back, it followed through. The crack and the sting of her slap shocked both of them. It shocked Vinnie so much that she backed away from him with her hands over her mouth.

Worst of all, they had witnesses. "*Stop it!*" shouted Adam, and Daffodil let out a long, shrill, mournful whine.

"Oh, my God," Vinnie said, tears springing to her eyes. "Oh, my God. I shouldn't have done that. Oh, my God."

Chapter 32

Nick stood frozen in place, a hundred different emotions raging through him. And they all seemed to meet and throb at the spot on his cheek where Vinnie had planted her hand so violently.

He tried to absorb the terrible irony of the situation: Saint Vinnie had fallen off her pedestal and splintered, right in front of the very boy she'd been trying to shield from all ugliness.

Her expression stricken, she seemed for once at a total loss in the parenting department, and he was angry enough to feel that she deserved it.

Adam whirled and ran back to his room. Nick wondered why the hell he'd come out, especially at that colossally inappropriate moment.

What a cheerful mood they were all in before the party. Nick laughed an unamused, sardonic laugh.

"I'm sorry, Nick." Vinnie said it in an ashamed whisper.

Her eyes had gone from stormy to flat. That wild

hair of hers even seemed to droop a bit around her face, and her mouth trembled.

"Are you? You wanted to hit me. You've been wanting to do it for days—you wanted to hit me out there on the terrace that night."

"That doesn't make it okay."

Nick's mouth twisted. "But you wanted to—and you finally did. You were finally true to yourself and your own needs. It's about time."

"Excuse me? Don't go there again—and especially not with *this*. You're the person I hit. You're not supposed to congratulate me for hitting you!"

Nick just gazed at her somberly.

"I said I'm sorry. It was unforgivable."

"The problem," Nick began, "is that I'm not sorry for what I said. So you may want to hit me again. Adam doesn't behave like a normal twelve-year-old. He's way too needy for his age—"

"Oh," said Vinnie, stamping her foot, "and you're *not*?"

"Me?" Nick let out a strangled laugh. "I'm not needy."

"Bullshit!" So much for Vinnie never swearing. "You've got denial down to a science, Nick. You don't need anyone? Let's take a look at your need to win. Your need to be a 'success,' to show the world how great you are. You've bricked yourself into an emotional box and a professional box. You don't need anyone?" She laughed. "Oh, that's rich. You need money, awards, media attention, a partnership—you need all of that to fill up the giant hole inside of you. And you know why that hole is there?

"It's there because you NEED to be true to your

344 • Karen Kendall

own artistic vision, and to yourself as a human being. Need isn't weakness, Nick! It's strength and
life and development. And it's love."

Nick opened his mouth to speak, but she rode
right over him.

"Partnership and box manufacturing aren't going to make you happy, no matter how practical
they are. I want to see you break out of all your
boxes. I want to see you design what you really
want to design. Buildings like your crazy models.

"Nick, we're all needy! Daffodil's needy, Adam's
needy, I'm needy. It's part of the human condition.
And guess what? If you 'develop feelings' for someone, Nick, you *need* them. You give, but you also
accept that you need. And there's no shame in it."

Vinnie took a deep breath. "I hit you partly because I was angry for Adam. But I hit you also because I'm angry for *me*—I've been stupid enough to
fall in love with you—a guy who can't give me love
in return."

Nick's jaw fell open, but the breath he'd drawn
stayed trapped in his chest. He couldn't get any
oxygen out of it, but nor could he release it. He
simply stared at her, not knowing what to say.

Her face shuttered, and though he wanted to
reach out to her, wanted to say something, he
couldn't seem to manage it.

Vinnie turned her head to the living room clock,
dismissing him. "It's six."

"Yeah," he said.

They stood staring at each other for another long
moment before Nick did the only thing he could do
at that moment. He retreated from the battlefield.

He couldn't win. "I've got to go get dressed. People will be arriving momentarily."

He turned his back to Vinnie and moved toward his bedroom. Then he stopped. Without turning his head, he said mechanically, "D'Orsay will be announcing my partnership tonight. Please keep the dog out of the way."

Vinnie slumped on her bed, remembering all the times when she'd told Adam over and over that violence was never acceptable. What on earth was she going to say to him that would excuse her own behavior? There *was* no excuse.

How could she have raised her hand to Nick? She knew her anger went back to previous conversations they'd had, and it had just mounted until he'd stepped over some line with her this evening.

"I have a life!" she remembered shouting at him only days before.

Oh, sure you do. You take care of someone else's dog, you pick up strays, and you worry about your mother and brother all the time. That's some life, Vinnie . . .

He'd cut into her as if she were a stale sandwich, and found her lacking. And she'd still been furious about it when today's fiasco had commenced.

It had simply infuriated her that he should criticize her life choices, find fault with her self-sacrifice, point to it as some kind of excuse to avoid her own life. And *then*, on top of that, to find fault with the way she parented Adam! It had simply been too much.

She'd have felt violent toward anyone who did

that, much less a person with whom she'd been stupid enough to fall in love.

Still, that didn't excuse the fact that she'd slapped him. She'd done it without thinking, simply reacted. She'd wanted to smack those dimples right off his face, wipe them off so they no longer had the power to disturb her.

She'd wanted to punish him—not only for his criticism of her, but for making her fall in love with him.

So much for love being a many-splendored thing. Love was a virulent scourge that inspired her to commit violence.

Now here she was, sitting on the other side of a wall from her little brother, with no idea at all how to talk to him. No idea how to make things right. And she was awash in embarrassment and shame that he'd seen her lose control like that.

Vinnie heard Mrs. Hegel bustle through the door, the various rustling noises and thumps indicating that she was loaded down with supplies for the party.

She thanked God that at least the housekeeper hadn't been a witness to the debacle.

Nick's deep voice carried to her as well, murmuring instructions and questions to his housekeeper.

He hadn't even invited her to his stupid party, and that hurt like hell. Because she was the dogsitter. A paid servant, not good enough to attend. Tears sprang to her eyes.

She should get dressed nicely and at least try to make herself helpful in the kitchen, or pass hors d'oeuvres or something.

But her fears about fitting in with Nick's social circle reared their ugly heads. *Loser!* They hissed. These people will love your cheap shoes and dress from Sears.

Wallflower! They taunted. Exactly what do you have to say to the socialite wife of the head of a top architectural firm?

Doofus! You'll probably spill wine on the furniture and food down your dress. And you don't walk gracefully in heels, either . . . you'll probably catch one in the carpet and fly headlong into a cheese-and-olive tray.

You should stay back here with the dog, where you belong . . .

Vinnie vaulted off the bed and stared into the mirror. No, darn it! She did *not* belong with the dog. Nick had told her to get a life, hadn't he? Fine. Then she was going to start getting one tonight. She was going to make herself look fabulous, and she was going to go out there into his showplace of an apartment and drink wine and maybe even flirt a little. She would simply pretend she was somebody else, somebody more glamorous, more mysterious, more elegant than her.

But her heart rolled over and played dead when she opened her closet. Vinnie owned nothing suitable to wear to the party, not a thing. She certainly wasn't going to wear any of the three dresses she had for church in Independence. She'd stick out like a sore thumb—a thumb with a particularly ugly splint on it.

There was only one thing to do with an hour before the party: go shopping. She remembered seeing an advertisement for a designer resale shop, somewhere around Fifty-fourth, right off Madison. Surely she could afford something in a consignment shop? She'd check with Richie to see if he knew the exact address.

Vinnie shoved her feet into her sneakers and grabbed her backpack. She swallowed briefly as she remembered she'd have to tell Adam she was going out.

She knocked on his door, but got no answer. So she opened it slightly, to find that he was hunched under his covers. "Adam, honey? We have to talk later, okay?"

"Whatever," he mumbled.

"I'm going to go out for a little while. Will you keep Daffodil with you so she doesn't get in Mrs. Hegel's way or interfere with the guests?"

"Whatever," he said again.

"Okay. Thanks." She shut the door with a sigh. She was going to have to think of what to say to him, but she'd do that on the way to the shop.

The woman in Play It Again, Sam looked worldly and intimidating, but Vinnie forced herself to explain to her what she needed, and she got into the spirit of the enterprise.

"Oh, honey," she said, in a thick Brooklyn accent, "I know just the thing for you. Or foah or five! But fuhst, what's your shoe soyze?"

"Eight and a half."

"Okay. We'll staht theya, since our shoe selection is limited. Then we'll find the outfit."

The prettiest pair of evening shoes she had in

Vinnie's size were a strappy pale gold satin, studded with tiny rhinestones at the side buckles.

They were beautiful, and had barely been worn, but Vinnie eyed them dubiously, wondering what they could find to go with them.

"Don'tcha worry, doll. It just so happens that I have a little evening bag that'll look divine with those. And gold—we can work almost anything with that."

"Almost anything" turned out to be a deep emerald silk sheath that was made to showcase Vinnie's generous bosom. Mama and Pastor Brownlow would have covered her with the entire congregations's raincoats if they could have seen it.

Vinnie stood in the tiny closet of a dressing room and tried self-consciously to hitch it up.

The shop owner actually smacked her hand. "Stop that, honey! Throw back your shoulders and shimmy those puppies instead. If you're gonna wear this dress, you've got an obligation to the designer to show it off. Know what I mean?"

Vinnie had never heard of the designer—some Italian guy—but she allowed herself to be bullied.

"Now whatuhya doin' with your hayah?"

"My hair?" She shrugged. "I don't have a clue."

"When didja say this pahty was?"

"Oh, pretty much right now. I'm going straight there."

The woman shook her head. "Talk about puttin' things off to the last minute!"

"Yeah, I know."

The woman sighed and cocked her head, inspecting Vinnie. Then she popped a piece of gum into her mouth and chewed reflectively. "Come 'eah, hon. Sit down. I'll fix it for you. Then I want you to go down the street to that pharmacy and buy you some deep ruby lip gloss and a liner, okay? Take your wallet, put it in the tiny pocketbook, and leave your pack here with me. You can pick it up on Monday. You wanna make an entrance, right?"

Vinnie nodded. She felt like kissing the woman. "Will you tell me your name?"

"Maxine, honey. The name's Maxine. Now sit still."

"I can't thank you enough, Maxine."

"Yeah, yeah, yeah. Bring me a picture."

Vinnie promised that she would. On her way out, a thought struck her. "Hey, Maxine? Would you want a bunch of designer dog clothes for the shop?"

Chapter 33

Nick made sure that old D'Orsay and his wife had their drinks, then turned with a graceful "excuse me" to see who Mrs. Hegel was letting in. Instead of taking the person's coat, his housekeeper stood stock-still, her broad, black backside unmoving.

Nick moved through the throng of guests with a smile here, a touch on the arm there, until he could get a glimpse of the new arrival.

When he saw her, he had much the same reaction as Mrs. Hegel.

The newcomer was an absolute stunner in emerald green silk, with her hair twisted up in an elegant chignon. Simple Austrian crystals winked from her ears like stars over a heartbreaking expanse of creamy bosom.

She held her shoulders back proudly and stood tall in the entryway. The only other jewelry she wore was at her ankles, where tiny rhinestones flashed from the sexy buckles of strappy sandals.

Nick studied her face again, thinking that she

looked somehow familiar. And when her long, dark lashes swept up and her gaze met his, he almost staggered.

Lavender Hart was a knockout. Her normally clear, bright eyes were dusky, smoky pools of temptation, her lips, full and wet, pouted provocatively, and her long, soft neck would lure a vampire straight into the sun.

She dangled a tiny, pale gold bag from her wrist like a naughty sexual favor. Needless to say, all traces of sainthood had vanished.

Nick became gradually aware that he'd been staring at her, and reeled in his tongue before he left a puddle on the toe of his left dress shoe.

He forced himself to move forward and gently nudged Mrs. Hegel in the direction of the kitchen.

Vinnie held out her hand, as if they were meeting for the first time that day. He took it and brushed the back of it with his lips.

"If I were speaking to you," Nick said to her, "I'd have to tell you that you look beyond sensational. Incredibly lovely."

Vinnie colored faintly, then pulled her hand away. "Thank you. My invitation must have gotten lost in the mail."

Nick sucked in his breath. He couldn't miss the hurt in her voice. "Vinnie, I didn't think you'd—"

Her chin went up, and her eyes got chilly. "You didn't think I'd fit in? You didn't think I was good enough to mingle with your highbrow associates?"

Shock left him speechless for a moment. "No! I honest-to-God didn't think you'd want to come—I thought you'd be bored out of your skull. Listen to me: I've never thought of you as inferior, and you *know* it."

She trembled visibly but then seemed to steady herself through sheer force of will. "Then you'll get me a glass of wine."

"I'll be happy to do that."

"White, please."

He nodded. As she walked with him, he brushed her bare shoulders with his hand and felt her shiver. Vinnie was terrified, but she was holding her own and giving him orders. What wasn't to love about her?

Nick froze at the thought. Then he reached for the bottle that lay gracefully in a silver ice bucket on his dining room table. As he poured her wine, he glanced over the top of the glass at her three-and-a-half-inch heels. He allowed himself the glimmer of a smile. "How did you learn to walk in those, Vinnie?"

She accepted the glass of wine from him. "Carefully. They merited a splurge on a cab from the shop."

He laughed. "Let me introduce you to some people."

She hesitated, and he read the discomfort in her eyes. "They don't bite, sweetheart. I promise."

She met Mr. and Mrs. D'Orsay, and Mr. and Mrs. McDonough, and two other junior partners with their wives. She met dozens of draftspeople, and several engineers, and numerous interior designers. She met city officials, and interns, and a couple of columnists for well-known magazines and newspapers. Most of them looked at her admiringly and were very pleasant, to her relief.

Vinnie had another glass of wine and actually began to enjoy herself. Of course, she immediately felt guilty, since poor Adam was still holed up in his room, miserable and depressed. She needed to go talk to him. And he'd probably enjoy seeing her all decked out.

Yet as she turned to set down her glass of wine, a man to whom she hadn't been introduced touched her arm. "I'm Doug," he said with a smile. "I work on a couple of projects with Nick."

She was forced to exchange pleasantries with him for a while, then he introduced her to another couple, and so forth. Vinnie had drained her second glass of wine and a nice gentleman had offered to fetch her a third when an outraged female squawk caused her to whirl and teeter on her slim gold heels.

The squawk had come from Mrs. McDonough, one of the senior partners' wives, and it was followed by an angry, "How *dare* you?!"

The man standing beside her looked flabbergasted. "B-beg pardon?"

"How DARE you?" she said to him again. And then to her husband, "Ted, this horrid man just goosed me!"

"I did nothing of the sort, madam."

A feeling of foreboding stole over Vinnie, and behind the arguing trio a shadow moved.

She caught Nick's narrowed gaze across the room and moved toward the scene of the crime, but saw nothing suspicious.

Mrs. Hegel had set up a long buffet table in a

corner of the room, covered it with a floor-length cloth, and loaded it with tasty dishes. Two of the junior partners stood on the opposite side of it, filling their plates with such items as succulent roast beef, slices of spiral-cut honey-roasted ham, Yorkshire pudding, and yams.

As one of them—Vinnie thought his name was Tanaka—helped himself to a serving of parsleyed new potatoes, his eyes rolled violently, and the tubers flew off the serving spoon to land behind the table.

Vinnie knew exactly what had happened, even if he didn't, yet. Tanaka looked wildly behind him, and she could see the table rattle as the poor guy, mortified, dropped behind it to retrieve his airborne potatoes. And she heard his terrified yelp as he came nose to nose with a grinning Daffodil.

Had Adam decided this was a good way to get his revenge? She was going to kill him—right after she got the dog out of Nick's important party. Vinnie cursed herself for not talking to Adam earlier. She had chickened out, and now Nick was going to pay the consequences. Vinnie arrived at the buffet table and looked down at the quaking Tanaka. "It's okay," she said to him. "The dog won't bite you. I'm so sorry she scared you." To Daffodil she said, "Get over here, bad girl!"

Daffodil backed away from Tanaka and crawled again under the buffet table. She had obvious forebodings about the consequences she could hear in Vinnie's tone of voice.

"Excuse me," Vinnie said to Tanaka, and, trying to be as calm and elegant as possible, she squatted in her heels and silk and swiped under the table for the escaped dog.

Daffodil was too fast for her, though, and pushed out, under the cloth, on the other side. She emerged precisely where D'Orsay and a very important client sat, their plates on a low coffee table between them.

As they stopped talking and froze, Daff grinned, ran her tongue over the fruit and cheese on D'Orsay's plate, and completely heisted the Very Important Client's roast beef. Then she ran, a wise move, as Mrs. Hegel had spied her and tried to wallop her with a guest's umbrella.

Nick had excused himself from a knot of horrified guests and threw himself into the chase as well. Despite the three of them, Daffodil managed another lap of the room, stopping once to have a large bite of pâté and a salmon croquette off another plate.

"My apologies to you all!" panted Nick as he dived around an armchair to grab the errant dog. "She's harmless, really."

But Daffodil was a Doberman, and despite her ridiculous patchwork velvet vest and red-ruffled scarf, she looked a little diabolical under the current circumstances. Nobody in attendance seemed to want a rabid, festering dog bite for the holidays—even a designer one.

Daff made a final lap of the room and snatched the remainder of the spiral-cut ham clean off the buffet table. Nick would have had her there, too, if it weren't so impossible to maneuver with the hundred or so people in his apartment.

She looked left, and saw Vinnie. To the right was Mrs. Hegel, wielding the umbrella. Behind her, almost on top of her, was Nick. Daffodil made a quick canine tactical decision: She had to go over the modern settee directly in front of her, no matter that there were people sitting on it.

She galloped forward.

"No," gasped Vinnie.

"*Nein!*" shouted Mrs. Hegel.

"Oh, *shit*," said Nick.

Mrs. D'Orsay and Mrs. McDonough sat on the doomed piece of furniture. Daffodil hurtled toward them, picking up speed. Their twin glasses of red wine flew as she leaped at them, ham and all, and scrambled over.

It all happened in slow motion for Nick. His career flashed in front of his eyes, much as Daffodil's red toenails (not to mention her teeth or the remnants of the spiral-cut ham) had flashed in front of the eyes of Mrs. D'Orsay and Mrs. McDonough.

Daffodil ran down the long hallway to Adam's room, and Vinnie ran after her, wobbling dangerously in her high heels. Ordinarily, Nick would have admired the view. But, needless to say, this was not the time.

He cleared his throat, somehow excavated his dimples, and raised his voice in apology. "I deeply regret the inconvenience and indeed chaos caused by my runaway dog . . ."

Mrs. Hegel had flown to the kitchen and back to the settee with linen napkins and club soda for the bedraggled wives.

Tanaka did two shots of bourbon in rapid succession.

McDonough, looking as if he had a mouthful of nails, soothed his wife.

D'Orsay either choked or laughed into his handkerchief.

Nick finished his apology, urged the guests to have another drink, and personally cleared any and all dishes that had been molested by Daffodil.

To his astonishment, old D'Orsay got up again, and said, "Now where were we, before the canine interruption? I believe Ted and I were about to make an announcement of great consequence to this firm. We'd like to end this almost old year with a flourish, and start the new one with a bang, you see." He turned towards McDonough. "Ted? Won't you join me?"

McDonough glared at him. He glared at Nick. His kissed his wife's forehead. Finally, he stood up and buttoned his jacket. "Yes, all right," he said reluctantly. "Where were we?"

"Ted and I," said D'Orsay, "would like to welcome a new partner to the firm. He's someone who has worked long, hard hours and provided us with creative solutions to every sort of problem imaginable. He's someone who troubleshoots well, has an excellent record of bringing new clients in to the firm, and has won numerous design awards. Will you please join me in congratulating—"

"*Nick!*" Vinnie screamed, running down the hall with no shoes on. "Nick, oh God!"

He whirled as Vinnie sobbed, "Adam's *gone*! He's run away!"

Chapter 34

Nick neither knew nor cared that D'Orsay had stopped speaking, because his entire focus was on Vinnie and Adam.

"Run away?" he repeated. He drew her to him, encircling her with his arms and stroking her hair. She shook violently against him for a moment, maybe two, then pulled away, her face streaked with tears. "There's no time for this, Nick. I have to find him—I have to go."

"Shoes," he said pointedly to her. "Get some shoes on. And a coat. We're going together."

"But—"

"Shoes, Vinnie," Nick repeated. "Go get them."

He turned to all the guests gathered in his apartment. "I'm very sorry about this, but I've got to leave. Please stay and enjoy yourselves. My housekeeper, Mrs. Hegel, will supply you with anything you need and, er, keep the dog away from you."

Nick brushed past the sputtering D'Orsay and the livid McDonough and grabbed two coats out of the hall closet. Both were his, but he knew Vinnie only owned a short jacket, that wouldn't do much to keep her lower body warm.

D'Orsay laid a hand on his arm. "*Who* has run away? I must tell you that I have strong feelings against your leaving, Nicholas."

"A twelve-year-old friend of mine. And I apologize, but don't try to stop me from going, Mr. D'Orsay. It won't work."

The founding partner stood rigid and exchanged a glance with McDonough. "Let me make this clear to you: Leave now, and you're jeopardizing everything you've worked for at the firm. I don't know what's come over you, boy. You've already embarrassed yourself tonight with the dog. Don't add insult to injury."

Nick clenched his jaw. "Are you issuing an ultimatum, D'Orsay?"

McDonough replied for him. "Yes."

Nick registered their smug faces, the smiles that advertised their certainty that he would back down and not completely ruin their occasion. He'd worked hard to be the Golden Boy, and if he had any sense, he'd bow down and enjoy being gilded in public.

Vinnie sprinted down the back hallway and past everyone in her running shoes and the emerald green sheath.

Nick stepped in front of her quite deliberately before she could get out the door, and wrapped her in his London Fog. Then he put his arm around her.

Before they exited, he turned his head toward

D'Orsay and McDonough. "Gentlemen," he said, "you can go to hell."

Outside on the pavement, Nick's voice reached Vinnie from what seemed like miles away. "Did Adam leave any kind of note?"

Pete was trying to hail them a cab, but was having difficulties since traffic was so heavy. Finally, he got one to pull over, and they scrambled inside.

"Just that he was going home," Vinnie finally answered.

"Address?" The cab driver asked, in an accent she couldn't identify.

"Just a moment. Let me think."

"Take a deep breath, honey. It's going to be okay." Nick put his arms around her again and kissed her temple.

"Going home involves either a plane, a train, or a bus," she said into his neck. He smelled of comfort and aftershave and rain.

"He wouldn't try to hitchhike, would he?"

Vinnie shook her head. "I have drummed into him since he was old enough to walk *never* to hitchhike or go anywhere with a stranger. He's upset right now, but he's not stupid." She closed her eyes, her mouth quivering.

"I should have apologized, right there and then," Nick said. "God, I'm such an idiot."

"No you're not. And you were angry—you had to change—I'm the one who should have gone and talked to him right away. I was just so embarrassed, so horrified, that I had slapped you and that he'd *seen* me. If you knew the number of times I've lectured him about violence . . ."

"Address?" the cab driver repeated, impatiently this time.

"Just a minute!" Nick snapped.

"He doesn't have enough money for a plane," Vinnie concluded quickly. "He's never taken a train, but I suppose he could . . . my best guess, though, is Port Authority, where he and I came in on the bus."

"Port Authority, then," Nick ordered the driver.

Though the Port Authority bus station had been spruced up inside quite a bit in recent years, it was surrounded by such fine establishments as The Playground Adult Entertainment, and was not in the best neighborhood. Vinnie refused to think about the things that could happen to Adam around there and focused instead on the practical.

Adam would have a number of choices as far as venues. She prayed that he hadn't already gotten on a bus. However, he hated the subways with a passion, and he wouldn't have spent the money on a cab. So chances were that he'd made his way on foot to the station, and that would have taken him a long time.

They checked the departures, found four possibilities for Adam, and questioned the clerks. One of them clearly remembered selling a ticket to a young boy traveling alone, a one-way ticket to Kansas.

No, it hadn't yet departed and wouldn't for another forty minutes. Vinnie felt herself go limp with relief. That meant that logically Adam was somewhere there in the Port Authority terminal.

She still wouldn't even let herself think about scarier alternatives.

They checked McCann's Pub and the Fairmont Lanes bowling alley with no luck. Just to be safe, they looked for him in the New York lottery place, even though he was too young to purchase a ticket. No dice.

Nick checked all the men's rooms, and irrationally, Vinnie checked the ladies' rooms, frantically calling her little brother's name.

They finally found Adam hunched over an X-Men comic book, in a bank of plastic chairs behind an information billboard. On the chair next to him was a vile-looking vending machine sandwich out of which he'd pulled the lettuce and tomato. They gleamed anemically under the fluorescent lighting, spackled with yellow mustard.

Vinnie gave an audible sob of relief and flew at her little brother. He squeaked in protest as she smothered him in a tangle of arms, emotion, and London Fog.

"We've been worried *sick* about you, Adam!" she exclaimed.

Nick slumped against the information sign as if his legs were made of rubber.

Adam looked at him over Vinnie's shoulder. "What're *you* doing here?"

"Adam!" said Vinnie.

Nick held up a hand to quiet her. "I came because I was worried out of my mind, Adam. I came because you're my good friend, and because I owe you a serious apology."

"Yeah, you do," Adam muttered. "A big fat one."

"A big fat one," Nick agreed. "And probably some Mets tickets. That's how sorry I am."

Adam considered the offer, as Vinnie finally stood up and let him breathe.

Nick continued, "I never wanted to think you'd stolen the things. I just couldn't come up with anyone else. I was so wrong. I hope that you'll be able to forgive me."

Adam folded his arms and pursed his lips.

Nick looked miserable. He said again, "I'm sorry."

Finally, Adam relented, but cagily. "I dunno. Summer's a long ways off. What if you threw in some Knicks tickets in the meantime?"

"Adam Jackson Hart!" said his sister. "You will be lucky if we don't skin you alive after the scare you just gave us. I imagined you were dead in a ditch, or worse! Now if you think—"

Nick nodded. "Okay, kid, you got it."

Adam brightened for a moment, then frowned and began to kick at the underside of the plastic chair. "Nah. Thanks, but it doesn't matter. I'm gonna go home."

"But Adam—" Vinnie began.

"Look, I've been nothing but trouble. And Nick's right, you're *not* my mom. You should do some stuff YOU wanna do. Like go to school yourself and get kissy-kissy with Nick. You can't really do that when I'm around. I just make you guys fight, and you'll never get married if you keep doing that."

"*What?*" Vinnie croaked, so stunned that any other words failed her.

Nick stepped forward. "Adam, your sister and I

don't fight because of you. You shouldn't feel at all as if you're to blame for that."

Vinnie finally found her voice, after clearing her throat a few times. "Adam, you need to understand something." Why did her whole face have to throb in embarrassment?

"In order for two people to get married," she continued, "they have to, um, *love* each other. Nick and I are not going to get married, because we don't love each other."

"Then why do you do the kissy thing?"

"Well, uh, sometimes friends exchange kisses. But Nick and I aren't going to be more than friends, because we're too . . . different. Nick—if he ever gets married—will end up with somebody who's a little more—oh, I don't know—perfect than me. Somebody who's probably very thin, and elegant, and educated. Somebody who speaks a few different languages and has a whole closetful of dresses like this one, and does something a lot more important than taking care of a dog. Do you know what I mean?"

As Nick listened to her speech, his internal organs all seemed to flip around and take each other's places. His pulse throbbed in protest against Vinnie's words, and his heart clearly read all the white space between her carefully chosen lines. The message jumped from his heart to his head: Vinnie didn't think she was good enough for him. She felt inferior, lowborn, stupid in comparison to him.

She couldn't be more wrong. She'd somehow, in just a few short months, become the best and brightest aspect of his life.

Nick gazed down at her sweet face, her cheeks flushed with mortification and self-consciousness. Her hair was hanging half-out of the elegant knot with which she'd started the evening, and she had two different runs in her stockings. Her ancient running shoes looked incongruous with the cocktail dress and his London Fog. His Bud Babe was a certified mess—but God, he loved her. He adored this woman, cross as she was right now between Jessica Rabbit, Dick Tracy, and Florence Griffith Joyner.

Lavender Hart was a woman with whom any man would be lucky to spend the rest of his life. Formal education be damned—she had the wisdom of the ages and the heart of a lion. She had enough love for the entire world, not just two guys and a few pets.

Vinnie had taught him how to give, but most importantly, she'd taught him how to share.

"Adam," said Nick, "while I'd normally argue that your sister is one of the smartest women we know, please disregard everything she's just told you."

"*Excuse* me?" Vinnie asked.

"I can't speak for *her* feelings of course, but I can lay mine right out on the table. You see, I love your sister beyond the point of foolishness. I love her more than anyone, and in fact I do love her more than enough to marry her."

Adam's mouth formed an "O," and he blinked.

Vinnie wobbled to the left, and then wobbled to the right, and finally wobbled backward until she sat down right on top of the disgusting sandwich next to her brother.

So much for my London Fog, Nick thought. He went down on one knee in front of her. "Vinnie, sweetheart? I probably could choose a more romantic spot for a proposal than the Port Authority bus station, but will you marry me?"

His light and his love burst into tears and shook her head. Then she blubbered something incomprehensible, the tail end of which was "not good enough."

Nick frowned. This was not at all the way he wanted the fairy tale to end. This was a real bummer of an answer, in fact, and it made him feel like the sandwich underneath her: squashed and limp.

"Vinnie, honey, did you just babble something at me to the effect that you're not good enough?"

She nodded and gave an inelegant, woeful sniff.

"Because that's the craziest thing I've ever heard anyone say, and I'm sorry, but I demand that you take it back."

He took her hands and held them in his own. "Vinnie, you beautiful nut job, you're a better person than I am in a hundred thousand ways: you just may not have had the opportunities I've had. You've had different priorities in your life, honey, ones that you didn't even choose. And you never walked away from them—you took them to heart as your own. You've got to be the bravest, truest, most loving person I've ever met, and I adore you for it. So please, won't you marry me so I can have a chance to spoil and corrupt you?" He looked over at Adam. "Both of you. I think I'd go into a deep depression and hurl myself off the Brooklyn Bridge if Adam or Prince Charming left. I *need*"—

he gave her a significant glance—"all of you guys."

He brought Vinnie's hands to his lips and kissed them. "So what do you say, Lavender Hart?"

She nodded, which gave him an excuse to move his mouth from her hands to her lips. "Oh, Vinnie. I'll try to deserve you. I really will."

She threw her arms around him.

"I love you, too, Nick. I've . . . I've always dreamed of someone like you." She stood up, her nose pink and her cheeks sparkling with tears.

Nick, who was almost a good foot taller, began to laugh.

"What?" She looked down at the chair she'd been sitting in, only to discover a very flat sandwich and a destroyed slice of tomato. The limp lettuce leaf was nowhere to be seen. Which could only mean . . . *oh, no.*

Through the coat she felt Nick's hands on her rear end, and he said to Adam, "Would you go and get a couple of napkins for your sister? I think she'd be very grateful . . ."

Chapter 35

Nick reluctantly answered the telephone on the fifth ring, since it involved having to stop kissing Vinnie, and even after six months it hadn't gotten old.

"Yeah," he barked. Caller ID told him it was Hutchins, G., so he should have been more polite, but Kissus Interruptus was a serious offense.

"Mr. Wright? George Hutchins, here."

"Esquire," said Nick. He forced himself to be nicer to the man, since he'd never have met Vinnie if Hutchins hadn't saddled him with Daffodil. "So how can I help you, sir?"

"I'm calling to tell you that the mystery is solved at last."

"And which mystery would that be?"

"The one involving your aunt Edna St. Villiers and her money. As you know, I put an investigator on the case. And after an intensive search, he's at last uncovered a cash transaction Mrs. St. Villiers made on the day before she . . . ahem . . . passed on."

370   🐾   Karen Kendall

"Yes?"

"Mrs. St. Villiers purchased a three-million-dollar diamond dog collar, Mr. Wright."

"She *what*?" Nick, who'd made his way back to the sofa, sat down on Vinnie, who squeaked in protest. "Sorry, sweetheart." He got up again.

"Your aunt paid cash for a dog collar. A lot of cash. She'd had it custom-made, at Van Cleef and Arpels."

"But—but—"

"I can only suppose her intention was for the bauble to go to whoever gave her dog a good home. She obviously meant to give you the first shot, but if you failed, someone else would be rewarded."

"Right. Well, thank you for calling, Mr. Hutchins. I, um . . . appreciate the information."

Nick pressed the phone's OFF button and turned to Vinnie, dread climbing. After all, he hadn't seen the damned dog collar for months.

"Sweetheart? Tell me we still have Daffodil's unspeakably vulgar rhinestone collar."

Vinnie yawned. "Um, yeah. But not for long. It's in that trunk over there, full of her clothes to take to Maxine at Play It Again, Sam. I've been procrastinating about taking it to her."

"Let's not give the collar away. Hutchins just called to tell me it's not made of rhinestones."

Vinnie blinked. "You mean it's—"

"Real."

"Nick, are you serious?!" She stared at him.

He nodded. "Yeah."

"Nick, this means you can start your own firm!"

"And you can go to NYU to get your social work degree."

They discussed the future some more, and then Vinnie clapped her hands and laughed. "I forgot to tell you: Mrs. Blount got an English bulldog."

"No!"

"Yes, she did. His name is Biscuit, and he has the hots for Daffodil. You should see him, grunting and snorting and sort of jumping up and down around her."

"Does Daffodil return his affections?"

"I think so. But she's playing hard to get. They've only met a couple of times, anyway."

"She's gotta be tall for him."

"Well, yeah, but he's very determined."

They both looked down at Daffodil, snoozing by the fireplace in a cropped Harley Davidson T-shirt.

"Vinnie, are her nails *blue*?"

"Yep. It's very hip."

"Hip," Nick repeated.

"Don't complain—Adam wants her to have a nose ring. But don't worry, I said no."

"Adam's getting a little big for his britches since he dropped Joey Balthus to his knees, don't you think?"

"Hey, you taught him how. You created a monster, there, sweetie."

Nick pulled her into his arms and kissed her thoroughly. "*I* created a monster? I still can't get used to seeing Darla in little flowered dresses, scrubbed clean of tattoos. What did you *do* to that girl? She's getting downright sweet, and it's unnerving."

Vinnie shrugged. "I gave her a little love, after the lecture of her life."

He kissed her again. "Where do you get all that love? You seem to have an endless supply."

She looked up at him, and he tumbled helplessly into the goodness of her big brown eyes. "It's not endless," she murmured, stroking his jaw. "But when I start running low, you regenerate it."

"Kind of like this?" Nick asked, rolling her on top of him and hugging her close.

"Mmmm hmmm."

And they got on with the business of making more love.

Romance is always better with Avon Books . . . look for these crowd pleasers in November

THE PLEASURE OF HER KISS by Linda Needham
An Avon Romantic Treasure

The Earl of Hawkesly exchanged wedding vows with a woman he barely knew, then left her to play the spy for his country. Now two years later, he's ready to perform his much neglected husbandly duties . . . except Kate doesn't recognize him! He may have met his match in this spirited woman, and it will take a special seduction to win her heart.

A THOROUGHLY MODERN PRINCESS by Wendy Corsi Staub
An Avon Contemporary Romance

Her Highness, Emmaline of Verdunia, would have wed her suitable prince and be done with it—if she hadn't been swept off her feet by Granger Lockwood IV, "America's Sexiest Single Man." Now she's hurtling across the Atlantic in the private jet of the surprised playboy . . . and falling in love with the last man she could ever marry!

TO TEMPT A BRIDE by Edith Layton
An Avon Romance

From the moment she first saw tall, dashing Eric Ford, Camille's heart was lost. But Eric seems content to be no more than her unofficial protector, watching over the younger sister of his dear friend. When danger and betrayal threaten, will it destroy a secret love . . . or bind two hearts for all eternity?

WICKEDLY YOURS by Brenda Hiatt
An Avon Romance

The *ton* is abuzz over the arrival of Sarah Killian, a stunning stranger who shrouds her past in mystery. And no one is more intrigued than Lord Peter Northrup. The handsome rake wants to know *everything* about this beauty who has so enflamed his desire. But the enchantress guards her secrets well, even as she pulls him into a world of danger any self-respecting gentleman would be well advised to avoid.

Avon Romantic Treasures

*Unforgettable, enthralling love stories,
sparkling with passion and adventure
from Romance's bestselling authors*